P

Short story Index   c.1

SC

Lamb, Hugh, comp.
   Victorian tales of terror. N.Y.,
Taplinger Publishing Co. [c1974]

   Contents:-Shiel,M.P. Xélucha.-Dickens,C.
Black veil.-Braddon,E. Mystery at Fernwood.-
Boothby,G. Black lady of Brin Tor.-De
Maupassant,G. Mother of monsters.-Erckmann-
Chatrian. Murderer's violin.-Marsh,R. Mask.-
Anon. Dead man of Varley Grange.-Bierce,A.
My favourite murder.-Mrs.Molesworth. Shadow in
the moonlight.-Riddell,J.H.(Mrs.) Last of
Squire Ennismore.-Barry,J.A. Red warder of the
Reef.-Allen,G. Wolverden Tower.-Le Fanu,J.S.
Madam Crowl's ghost.-Donovan,D. Cave of blood.

   1.Horror tales   2. Short stories I.
Title
4/75   74-20217

stained 1/89

Victorian Tales of Terror

Other books by the same editor

A TIDE OF TERROR
A WAVE OF FEAR

Victorian Tales of Terror

edited by
HUGH LAMB

Taplinger Publishing Company / New York

First published in the United States in 1975 by
TAPLINGER PUBLISHING CO., INC.
New York, New York

Library of Congress Catalog Card Number: 74-20217

ISBN 0-8008-7986-4

ACKNOWLEDGEMENT

Grateful acknowledgement is made for permission to include the
following copyright material:

"Xelucha" by M. P. Shiel. From *Shapes in the Fire* by M. P. Shiel.
Copyright 1896. Reprinted with the permission of the Estate of the
late T. I. F. Armstrong.

For Andrew

Contents

Foreword

It is understandable that, at a time when Britain and the British least resemble their Victorian counterparts, they should be looking back fondly to the days of empire and power.

For the Victorian era was truly momentous. It saw the consolidation of the British Empire and the establishment of Britain as the most influential country in the world. It was a time when a British subject could go almost anywhere with impunity and the phrase 'to send a gunboat' had real meaning.

Victorians lived in a world that was their oyster. It was, however, an oyster with a rotten pearl. Together with the pomp and circumstance of empire, there was an appalling rate of poverty and hardship, where a working man in Britain was sometimes materially worse off than his colonized compatriots that he often looked down on. As wealth grew, so did poverty. As science flourished, so too did disease. As knowledge increased, ignorance and hypocrisy deepened.

This dichotomy was crystallized in Victorian literature, not least in the macabre tales of the period. As you will see in this anthology, while authors like Elizabeth Braddon and Mrs Molesworth wrote of terrors in rich families with big houses, others like Dick Donovan and Charles Dickens described appalling crimes in squalid surroundings.

As a distinct period in the unique history of the macabre tale, the Victorian era has been rather neglected by anthologists. Not in terms of single stories included in general anthologies—and many of those have been repeated far too many times for inclusion here—but in the number of anthologies dealing solely with that period.

Montague Summers researched and edited two classic anthologies from the period, *Victorian Ghost Stories* (1933) and *The Grimoire* (1936), but these apart, I have seen few others. Mr Summers's research for these books was impeccable, many of his stories being reprinted from contemporary journals. I have not tried to emulate his efforts at bibliography but have instead concentrated solely on stories that have been previously published in book form. I hasten to reassure the connoisseur that of the fifteen tales in this book, more than half have been out of print since their original publication over 70 years ago, and the rest have been unobtainable for too many years to make them familiar.

So, in order to redress the neglect of this spectral era, here is *Victorian Tales of Terror*. These fifteen tales, which include representatives from contemporary America, France and Germany, form an excellent cross-section of the Victorian world of the macabre. I have endeavoured to make it as varied as possible, with known and unknown authors.

Among those authors who will probably be unfamiliar to the reader are Grant Allen, Richard Marsh, John Arthur Barry, Guy Boothby, Emile Erckmann and Pierre Chatrian, and Dick Donovan. All their tales included here have been unobtainable and forgotten for over 70 years.

America's Ambrose Bierce is represented with a tale that, as far as I can ascertain, has not been published in Britain before. It appeared in his collected works, a twelve-volume set issued in America at the turn of the century and never published in Britain. Only one or two sets found their way here; I was fortunate in being able to consult one and am proud to present 'My Favourite Murder' in what is probably its British debut.

Those Victorian gentlewomen who specialized in ghost stories are represented by three of their leading names, Mrs J. H. Riddell, Mrs Mary Molesworth and Elizabeth Braddon.

I have also included a tale each from four writers who either enriched, or were enriched by, Victorian macabre literature —Charles Dickens, J. Sheridan le Fanu, Guy de Maupassant and M. P. Shiel.

I am indebted to the Estate of the late T. I. F. Armstrong for permission to use 'Xélucha' by M. P. Shiel.

So, now step back into the days of gaslight and gore and sample the delights of Victorian terror. But be warned—they liked their thrills neat in those days, so tread carefully...

HUGH LAMB
Sutton, Surrey.

Xélucha

by

M. P. SHIEL

With a background as bizarre as he had, it is hardly sur-
prising that Matthew Phipps Shiel (1865–1947) turned
out to be one of England's most unconventional writers.
Born in the West Indies, the son of an Irish preacher, he
was crowned King of Redonda at the age of 15. This was
at his father's behest, Redonda being a small island then
unclaimed by any government, and the coronation was
performed by the Bishop of Antigua. King Matthew
then came to England where he attended King's College,
London, and became a medical student at St Bartholo-
mew's. However, he preferred writing to medicine and
left after a short time.

Some of Shiel's best books were written during the
1890s, including Prince Zaleski *(1895) and* Shapes in the
Fire *(1896) from which this story is taken. At the time it*
was written, Shiel was part of the literary circle domina-
ted by Oscar Wilde, in the days of the Yellow Book *and*
Aubrey Beardsley. Though rewritten before his death,
'Xélucha' in style and content reflects perfectly the atmo-
sphere that was to influence Shiel all his life. It is a fitting
start to this anthology of Victorian stories, for it repre-
sents a part of English literature that was swept away by
the First World War.

Three days ago! By heaven! it seems an age. But I am shaken
—my reason is debauched. A while since I fell into a coma
precisely resembling an attack of *petit mal*. 'Tombs, and

worms, and epitaphs'—that is the fantasy of my dream. At my age, with my physique, to walk staggery, like a man stricken! But all that will pass: I must collect myself—my reason is debauched. Three days ago! It seems an age! Sitting on the floor before an old cista full of letters, I lighted upon a packet of Cosmo's. Why, I had forgotten them! They are turning sere! Truly, I can no more call myself a young man. I sat reading, listlessly, rapt back by memory. But to muse is to be lost! Of *that* evil habit I must wring the neck, or look to perish. Once more I threaded the mazy sphere-harmony of the minuet, reeled in the waltz, long pomps of candelabra, the noon-day of the bacchanal, about me. Cosmo was the very tsar and maharajah of the Sybarites! The Priap of the *détraqués*! In every unexpected alcove of his Roman Villa was a couch, raised high, with necessary foot-stool, flanked and canopied with mirrors of clarified gold. Consumption fastened upon him; reclining at last at table, he could, till warmed, scarce lift the wine! his eyes were like glow-worms coiled together! haloed with vaporous emanations of phosphorus! Desperate, one could see, was his struggle with the Devourer. But to the end the princely smile persisted; to the end—to the last day—he continued among that comic crew unchallenged choragus of all the rites, I will not say of Paphos, but of Chemos! and Baal-Peor: warmed, he did not refuse the revel, the dance, the darkened chamber. It was black, that chamber, rayless; approached by a secret passage; in shape circular; the air hot, haunted by odours of balms, bdellium, hints of dulcimer, flute, and all round it ottomans of Morocco. Here Lucy Hill stabbed to the heart Caccofogo, mistaking the scar on his back for the scar of Soriac. In a bath of malachite the Princess Egla, waking late one morning, found Cosmo lying stiffly dead, the bath-water covering him wholly.

'But in God's name, Mérimée!' (so he wrote), 'to think of Xélucha dead! Xélucha! Can a moon-beam, then, perish of suppurations? Can the rainbow be eaten by worms? Ha! ha! ha! laugh with me, my friend: *"elle dérangera l'Enfer!"* She will introduce the *pas de tarantule* into Tophet!

Xélucha, the feminine! Xélucha recalling the splendid harlots of history! Weep with me—*manat rara meas lacrima per genas!* expert as Thargelia; cultured as Aspatia; purple as Semiramis. She comprehended the human tabernacle, my friend, its secret springs and tempers, more intimately than any *savant* of Salamanca who breathes. Tarare—but Xélucha is not dead! Vitality is not mortal; you cannot wrap flame in a shroud. Xélucha! where, then, is she? Translated, perhaps—rapt to a constellation like the daughter of Leda. She journeyed to Hindostan, accompanied by the train and appurtenance of a Begum, threatening descent upon the Emperor of Tartary. I spoke of the desolation of the West; she kissed me, and promised return. Mentioned you too, Mérimée—"her Conqueror"—"Mérimée. Destroyer of Woman". Breaths from the conservatory rioted among her blowing hair, threads of it astray over the thulite tint you know. Costumed cap-à-pie, she had, my friend, the dainty completeness of a daisy mirrored bright in the eye of the browsing brute. A simile of Milton had for years, she said, inflamed the lust of her eye: "The barren plains of Sericana, where Chinese drive with sails and wind their cany wagons light". I, and the Sabæans, she assured me, wrongly considered Flame the whole of being; the other half of things being Aristotle's quintessential Light. In the Ourania Hierrarchia and the Faust-book you meet a completeness; burning Seraph, Cherûb full of eyes. Xélucha combined them. She would reconquer the Orient for Dionysius, and return. I heard of her blazing at Delhi; drawn in a chariot by lions. Then this rumour—probably false. Like Odin, Arthur, and the rest, Xélucha—will reappear.'

Soon subsequently Cosmo lay down in his balneum of malachite, and slept, having drawn over him the water as a coverlet. I, in England, heard little of Xélucha; first that she was alive, then dead, then had alighted at old Tadmor in the Wilderness, Palmyra now. Nor did I greatly care, Xélucha having long since turned to apples of Sodom in my mouth. Till I sat by the cista of letters and re-read Cosmo, she had for some years passed from my active memories.

The habit is now confirmed in me of spending the greater

part of the day in sleep, while by night I wander far and wide through the city under the sedative influence of a tincture which has become necessary to my life. Such an existence of shadow is not without charm; nor, I think, could many minds be subjected to its conditions without elevation, deepened awe. To travel alone with the Primordial cannot but be solemn. The moon is of the hue of the glow-worm; and Night of the sepulchre. Nux bore not less Thanatos than Hypnos, and the bitter tears of Isis redundulate to a flood. At three, if a cab rolls by, the sound has the augustness of thunder. Once, at two, near a corner, I came upon a priest, seated, dead, leering, his legs bent. One arm, supported on a knee, pointed with accusing forefinger upward. By exact observation, I found that he indicated Betelgeuse, the star 'α' of rainy Orion. He was hideously swollen, having perished of dropsy. Thus in all Supremes is a *grotesquerie*; and one of the sons of Night is—Buffo.

In a London square deserted, I imagine, even in the day, I was aware of the metallic, silvery-clinking approach of little shoes. It was three in a morning of winter, a day after my rediscovery of Cosmo. I had stood by a railing, looking at clouds sailing as under the steering of a moon wrapped in cloaks of inclemency. Turning, I saw a little lady, very gloriously dressed. She had walked straight to me. Her head was bare, and crisped with ripples which rolled to a globe, rich with jewels, at her nape. In the redundance of her *décolleté* development, she resembled Parvati, love-goddess of the luscious fancy of the Brahmin.

She addressed to me the question:

'What are you doing there, darling?'

Her loveliness stirred me, and Night is *bon camarade*. I replied:

'Sunning myself by means of the moon.'

'All that is borrowed lustre,' she returned, 'you have got it from old Drummond's *Flowers of Sion*.'

Looking back, I cannot remember that this reply astonished me, though it should—of course—have done so. I said:

'On my soul, no; but you?'

'You might guess whence *I* come!'

'You are dazzling: you come from Paz.'

'Oh, farther than that, my son! Say a subscription ball in Soho.'

'Yes? ... and alone? in the cold? on foot ... ?'

'Why, I am old, and a philosopher. I can pick you out riding Andromeda yonder from the ridden Ram. They are in error, M'sieur, who suppose an atmosphere on the broad side of the moon. I have reason to believe that on Mars dwells a race whose lids are transparent like glass; so that the eyes are visible during sleep; and every dream moves imaged forth to the beholder in tiny panorama on the iris. You cannot imagine me a mere *fille*! To be escorted is to admit yourself a woman, and that is improper in Nowhere. Young Eos drives an *equipage à quatre*, but Artemis "walks" alone. Get out of my borrowed light in the name of Diogenes! I am going home.'

'Far?'

'Near Piccadilly.'

'But a cab?'

'No cabs for *me*, thank you. The distance is a mere nothing. Come.'

We set off. My companion at once put an interval between us, quoting from the *Spanish Curate* that the open is an enemy to love. The Talmudists, she twice insisted, rightly held the hand the sacredest part of the person, and at that point also contact was for the moment interdict. Her walk was extremely rapid. I followed. Not a cat was anywhere visible. We reached at length the door of a mansion in St James's: no light, it seemed tenantless, windows uncurtained, pasted across, some of them, with the words, To Let. My companion, however, flitted up the steps, and, beckoning, passed inward. I, following, slammed the door, and was in darkness. I heard her ascend, and presently a region of glimmer above revealed a stairway, curving broadly up. On that lowest floor where I stood was no carpet, nor furniture; the dust thick. I had begun to mount when, to my surprise, she stood by my side, returned; and whispered:

'To the very top, darling.'

She soared nimbly up, anticipating me. Higher, I could no longer doubt that the house was empty but for us. All was a vacuum full of dust and echoes. But at the top, light streamed from a door, and I entered a good-sized saloon. I was dazzled by the sudden resplendence of the apartment, at the middle of which was a spread table, square, opulent with gold plate, fruit, dishes; three ponderous chandeliers of electric light above; and I noticed also (what was very *bizarre*) one little candlestick of tin containing an old curve of tallow, on the table. But the impression of the whole was one of gorgeousness not less than Assyrian: an ivory couch at one end of the table had a head-piece of chalcedony forming a sea for the sport of emerald ichthyosauri; copper-coloured hangings, panelled with mirrors, corresponded with a dome of copper; yet this latter, I now remember, produced upon my glance an impression of actual grime. My companion reclined on a sigma couch, raised to the table-level in the Semitic manner, visible to her saffron slippers of satin. She pointed me a seat opposite, the incongruity of whose presence in the midst of this pomp so tickled me, that no power could have kept me from a smile: it was a mean chair, all wood, nor was I long in discovering one leg shorter than its fellows.

She indicated wine in a black bottle, and a tumbler, but herself made no pretence of drinking or eating, lay on hip and elbow, *petite*, resplendent, and gazed gravely upward. I, however, drank.

'You are tired,' I said, 'one sees that.'

'It is precious little that *you* see!' she returned, dreamy, hardly glancing.

'How! your mood is changed, then? You are morose.'

'You never, I think, saw a Norse passage-grave?'

'And abrupt.'

'Never?'

'A passage-grave? No.'

'It is worth a journey! They are circular chambers of stone, covered by earth-mounds, with a "passage" of slabs connecting them with the outer air. All round the chamber the dead sit, head resting on bent knees, and consult together in silence.'

'Drink wine with me, and be less Tartarean.'

'You certainly seem to be a fool,' she replied with a sardonic iciness. 'Is it not, then, highly romantic? They belong, you know, to the Neolithic Age. As the teeth fall, one by one, from the lipless mouths—they are caught by the lap. When the lap thins—they roll to the floor. Thereafter, every tooth that drops all round the chamber sharply breaks the silence.'

'Ha! ha! ha!'

'Yes. It is like a century-slow dripping in some cavern of the far *subterrène*.'

'Ha! ha! This wine seems heady! They express themselves in a dialect largely dental.'

'The Ape, on the other hand, in a language wholly guttural.'

A town-clock tolled four. Our talk was holed with silences, and heavy-paced. The wine's exhalation reached my brain: I saw her through mist, dilating large, uncertain, shrinking again to dainty compactness. But amorousness had died within me.

'Do you know,' she asked, 'what has been discovered in one of the Danish *Kjökkenmöddings* by a little boy? It was ghastly. The skeleton of a huge fish with human—'

'You are most unhappy.'

'Be silent.'

'You are full of care.'

'I think you a great fool.'

'You are racked with misery.'

'You are a child. You have not an instinct of the meaning of the words.'

'How! Am I not a man? I, too, miserable, careful?'

'You are not, really, *anything*—until you can create.'

'Create what?'

'Matter.'

'That is foppish. Matter cannot be created, nor destroyed.'

'Truly, then, you must be a creature of unusually weak

intellect. I see that now. Matter does not exist, then, there is no such thing, really—it is an appearance, a spectrum—every writer not imbecile from Plato to Fichte has, voluntary or involuntary, proved that for your good. To create it is to produce an impression of its reality upon the senses; to destroy it is to wipe a wet rag across a scribbled slate.'

'Perhaps. I do not care. Since no one can do it.'

'No one? You are mere embryo—'

'Who, then?'

'*Anyone*, whose power of Will is equivalent to the gravitating force of a star of the First Magnitude.'

'Ha! ha! ha! By heaven, you choose to be facetious. Are there, then, wills of such equivalence?'

'There have been three, the founders of religions. There was a fourth: a cobbler of Herculaneum, whose volition induced the cataclysm of Vesuvius in '79, in direct opposition to the gravity of Sirius. There are more fames than *you* have ever sung, you know. The greater number of disembodied spirits, too, I feel certain—'

'By heaven, I cannot but think you full of sorrow! Poor wight! come, drink with me. The wine is thick and boon. Is it not Setian? It makes you sway and swell before me, I swear, like a purple cloud of evening—'

'But you are mere ponderance!—I did not know that!—you are no companion! Your little interest revolves round the lowest centres.'

'Come—forget your agonies—'

'What, think you, is the portion of the buried body first sought by the worm?'

'The eyes! the eyes!'

'You are *hideously* wrong—you are so *utterly* at sea—'

'My God!'

She had bent forward with such rage of contradiction as to approach me closely. A loose gown of amber silk, wide-sleeved, had replaced her ball attire, though at what opportunity I could not guess; wondering, I noticed it as she now placed her palms far forth upon the table. A sudden wafture as of orange-flowers, mingled with the faint odour of mortality over-ready for the tomb, greeted my sense. A chill crept upon my flesh.

'You are so *hopelessly* at fault—'

'For God's sake—'

'You are so *miserably* deluded! Not the eyes *at all*!'

'Then, in Heaven's name, what?'

Five tolled from a clock.

'The *Uvula*! that drop of mucous flesh, you know, suspended from the palate above the glottis: they eat through the face-cloth and cheek, or crawl by the lips between defective teeth, filling the mouth. They make straight for it: it is the *deliciæ of the vault*.'

At her horror of interest I grew sick, at her odour, and her words. Some unspeakable sense of insignificance, of debility, held me dumb.

'You say I am full of sorrows. You say I am racked with woe; that I gnash with anguish. Well, you are a child in intellect. You use words without realization of meaning like those minds in what Leibnitz calls "symbolical consciousness". But suppose it were so—'

'It *is* so.'

'You know nothing.'

'I see you twist and grind. Your eyes are very pale. I thought they were hazel: they are of the bluishness of phosphorus shimmerings seen in darkness.'

'That proves nothing.'

'But the "white" of the sclerotic is dyed to yellow. And you look inward. Why do you look so paley inward, so woeworn, upon your soul? Why can you speak of nothing but of the sepulchre, and its rottenness? Your eyes seem to me wan with centuries of vigil, with mysteries and millenniums of pain.'

'Pain! but you know so *little* of it! you are wind and words! of its philosophy and *rationale* nothing!'

'Who knows?'

'I will give you a hint. Pain is the sub-consciousness in conscious creatures of Eternity, and of eternal loss. The least prick of a pin not Pæan and Æsculapius and the powers of

heaven and hell can utterly heal. Of an everlasting loss of
wholeness the conscious body is sub-conscious, and "pain" is
its sigh at the tragedy. So with all pain—greater, the greater
the loss. The hugest of losses is, of course, the loss of Time.
If you lose that, any of it, you plunge at once into the trans-
cendentalisms, the infinitudes, of Loss; if you lose *all of it*—'

'But you so wildly exaggerate! You rant, I tell you, of
commonplaces with the woe—'

'Hell is where a clear, untrammelled Spirit is sub-
conscious of lost Time; where it writhes with envy of the
living world; *hating* it for ever, and all the sons of Life!'

'But curb yourself! Drink—I implore—I *implore*—for
God's sake—but *once*—'

'To *hasten* to the snare—*that* is woe! to drive your ship
upon the *lighthouse* rock—that is Marah! To wake, and feel
it irrevocably true that you went after her—*and the dead
were there*—and her guests were in the depths of hell—*and
you did not know it!*—though you *might* have. Look out
upon the houses of the city this dawning day: not one, I tell
you, but in its haunts some soul—walking up and down the
old theatre of its little Day—goading imagination by a thousand childish tricks, vraisemblances—elaborately duping
itself into the fantasy *that it still lives*, that the chance of life
is not for ever and for ever lost—yet riving all the time with
under-memories of the wasted Summer, the lapsed brief light
between the two eternal glooms—riving I say and shriek to
you!—riving, *Mérimée, you destroying fiend*—'

She had sprung—*tall* now, she seemed to me—between
couch and table.

'Mérimée!' I screamed,—'*my* name, harlot, in your maniac
mouth? By God, woman, you terrify me to death!'

I too sprang, the hairs of my head catching stiff horror
from my fancies.

'Your name? Can you imagine me ignorant of your name,
or anything concerning you? Mérimée! Why, did you not
sit yesterday and read of me in a letter of Cosmo's?'

'Ah-h...,' hysteria bursting in sob and laughter from my
arid lips—'Ah! ha! ha! Xélucha! My memory grows palsied

and grey, Xélucha! pity me—my walk is in the very valley
of shadow!—senile and sere!—observe my hair, Xélucha, its
grizzled growth—trepidant Xélucha, clouded—I am not the
man you knew, Xélucha, in the palaces—of Cosmo! You are
Xélucha!'

'You rave, poor worm!' she cried, her face contorted by a
species of malicious contempt. 'Xélucha died of cholera ten
years ago at Antioch. I wiped the froth from her lips. Her
nose underwent a green decay before burial. So far sunken
into the brain was the left eye—'

'You are—*you are Xélucha!*' I shrieked; 'voices now of
thunder howl it within my consciousness—and by the holy
God, Xélucha, though you blight me with the breath of the
hell you are, I shall clasp you,—living or damned—'

I rushed towards her. The word 'Madman!' hissed as by
the tongues of ten thousand serpents through the chamber,
I heard; for a moment to my wild eyes there seemed to rear
itself, swelling to the roof, a tower of ragged cloud, and, as
my arms closed upon emptiness, I was tossed by the operation
of some Behemoth potency backward to a wall of the
chamber, where I fell, shocked into insensibility.

When the sun was low towards night, I lay awake, and listlessly observed the grimy roof, and the sordid chair, and the
candlestick of tin, and the bottle of which I had drunk. The
table was filthy, of deal, uncovered. All bore the appearance
of having stood there for years. But for them, the room was
void, the vision of luxury thinned to air. Sudden memory
flashed upon me. I scrambled to my feet, and ran tottering,
bawling, through the evening into the streets.

The Black Veil

by

CHARLES DICKENS

*England's greatest novelist was born in 1812 at Lands-
port, near Portsmouth, where his father was a poorly-
paid clerk in the Navy pay office. Dickens was brought
up in poverty and hardship, circumstances which not
only made him determined to improve his own condition, but made him constantly aware of the appalling
quality of life of the majority of the population around
him. Despite the fact that some of his greatest works were
those that depicted the misery and squalor of nineteenth-
century urban life, his first major success was The Pick-
wick Papers (1838). This humorous work appeared in
monthly parts and, in the words of one critic, 'took the
country by storm'. Two years before this, Dickens had
published Sketches by Boz, which was a collected edition
of a series of papers he had written as a parliamentary
reporter. 'The Black Veil' comes from this first book of
Charles Dickens, and despite the grim theme of the tale,
shows definite signs of the crusading spirit that the
author had on behalf of the poor.*

One winter's evening, towards the close of the year 1800, or
within a year or two of that time, a young medical prac-
titioner, recently established in business, was seated by a
cheerful fire, in his little parlour, listening to the wind which
was beating the rain in pattering drops against the window,
and rumbling dismally in the chimney. The night was wet
and cold; he had been walking through mud and water the

whole day, and was now comfortably reposing in his dressing-gown and slippers, more than half asleep and less than half awake, revolving a thousand matters in his wandering imagination. First, he thought how hard the wind was blowing, and how the cold sharp rain would be at that moment beating in his face, if he were not comfortably housed at home. Then his mind reverted to his annual Christmas visit to his native place and dearest friends; he thought how glad they would all be to see him, and how happy it would make Rose if he could only tell her that he had found a patient at last, and hoped to have more, and to come down again, in a few months' time, and marry her, and take her home to gladden his lonely fireside, and stimulate him to fresh exertions. Then he began to wonder when his first patient would appear, or whether he was destined by a special dispensation of Providence, never to have any patients at all; and then he thought about Rose again, and dropped to sleep and dreamed about her, till the tones of her sweet merry voice sounded in his ears, and her soft tiny hand rested on his shoulder.

There *was* a hand upon his shoulder, but it was neither soft nor tiny; its owner being a corpulent, round-headed boy, who, in consideration of the sum of one shilling per week and his food, was let out by the parish to carry medicine and messages. As there was no demand for the medicine, however, and no necessity for the messages, he usually occupied his unemployed hours—averaging fourteen a day—in abstracting peppermint drops, taking animal nourishment, and going to sleep.

'A lady, sir—a lady!' whispered the boy, rousing his master with a shake.

'What lady?' cried our friend, starting up, not quite certain that his dream was an illusion, and half-expecting that it might be Rose herself. 'What lady? Where?'

'*There*, sir!' replied the boy, pointing to the glass door leading into the surgery, with an expression of alarm which the very unusual apparition of a customer might have tended to excite.

The surgeon looked towards the door, and started himself, for an instant, on beholding the appearance of his un-looked-for visitor.

It was a singularly tall woman, dressed in deep mourning, and standing so close to the door that her face almost touched the glass. The upper part of her figure was carefully muffled in a black shawl, as if for the purpose of concealment; and her face was shrouded by a thick black veil. She stood perfectly erect; her figure was drawn up to its full height, and though the surgeon *felt* that the eyes beneath the veil were fixed on him, she stood perfectly motionless, and evinced, by no gesture whatever, the slightest consciousness of his having turned towards her.

'Do you wish to consult me?' he inquired, with some hesitation, holding open the door. It opened inwards, and therefore the action did not alter the position of the figure, which still remained motionless on the same spot.

She slightly inclined her head in token of acquiescence.

'Pray walk in,' said the surgeon.

The figure moved a step forward; and then, turning its head in the direction of the boy—to his infinite horror—appeared to hesitate.

'Leave the room, Tom,' said the young man, addressing the boy, whose large round eyes had been extended to their utmost width during this brief interview. 'Draw the curtain, and shut the door.'

The boy drew a green curtain across the glass part of the door, retired into the surgery, closed the door after him, and immediately applied one of his large eyes to the keyhole on the other side.

The surgeon drew a chair to the fire, and motioned the visitor to a seat. The mysterious figure slowly moved towards it. As the blaze shone upon the black dress, the surgeon observed that the bottom of it was saturated with mud and rain.

'You are very wet,' he said.

'I am,' said the stranger, in a low, deep voice.

'And you are ill?' added the surgeon compassionately, for the tone was that of a person in pain.

'I am,' was the reply—'very ill: not bodily, but mentally.

It is not for myself, or on my own behalf,' continued the stranger, 'that I come to you. If I laboured under bodily disease, I should not be out alone at such an hour, or on such a night as this; and, if I were afflicted with it twenty-four hours hence, God knows how gladly I would lie down and pray to die. It is for another that I beseech your aid, sir. I may be mad to ask it for him—I think I am; but, night after night, through the long dreary hours of watching and weeping, the thought has been ever present to my mind; and though even *I* see the hopelessness of human assistance availing him, the bare thought of laying him in his grave without it makes my blood run cold!' And the shudder, such as the surgeon well knew art could not produce, trembled through the speaker's frame.

There was a desperate earnestness in this woman's manner that went to the young man's heart. He was young in his profession, and had not yet witnessed enough of the miseries which are daily presented before the eyes of its members, to have grown comparatively callous to human suffering.

'If,' he said, rising hastily, 'the person of whom you speak be in so hopeless a condition as you describe, not a moment is to be lost. I will go with you instantly. Why did you not obtain medical advice before?'

'Because it would have been useless before—because it is useless even now,' replied the woman, clasping her hands passionately.

The surgeon gazed for a moment on the black veil, as if to ascertain the expression of the features beneath it; its thickness, however, rendered such a result impossible.

'You *are* ill,' he said gently, 'although you do not know it. The fever which has enabled you to bear, without feeling it, the fatigue you have evidently undergone, is burning within you now. Put that to your lips,' he continued, pouring out a glass of water—'compose yourself for a few moments, and then tell me, as calmly as you can, what the disease of the patient is, and how long he has been ill. When I know what it is necessary I should know, to render my visit serviceable to him, I am ready to accompany you.'

The stranger lifted the glass of water to her mouth without raising the veil; put it down again untasted; and burst into tears.

'I know,' she said, sobbing aloud, 'that what I say to you now seems like the ravings of a fever. I have been told so before, less kindly than by you. I am not a young woman; and they do say that, as life steals on towards its final close, the last short remnant, worthless as it may seem to all beside, is dearer to its possessor than all the years that have gone before, connected though they be with the recollection of old friends long since dead, and young ones—children, perhaps —who have fallen off from and forgotten one as completely as if they had died too. My natural term of life cannot be many years longer, and should be dear on that account; but I would lay it down without a sigh—with cheerfulness—with joy—if what I tell you now were only false or imaginary. Tomorrow morning, he of whom I speak will be, I *know*, though I would fain think otherwise, beyond the reach of human aid; and yet tonight, though he is in deadly peril, you must not see, and could not serve him.'

'I am unwilling to increase your distress,' said the surgeon, after a short pause, 'by making any comment on what you have just said, or appearing desirous to investigate a subject you are so anxious to conceal; but there is an inconsistency in your statement which I cannot reconcile with probability. This person is dying tonight, and I cannot see him when my assistance might possibly avail; you apprehend it will be useless tomorrow, and yet you would have me see him then! If he be indeed as dear to you as your words and manner would imply, why not try to save his life before delay and the progress of his disease render it impracticable?'

'God help me!' exclaimed the woman, weeping bitterly, 'how can I hope strangers will believe what appears incredible even to myself? You will *not* see him, then, sir?' she added, rising suddenly.

'I did not say that I declined to see him,' replied the surgeon; 'but I warn you, that if you persist in this extraordinary procrastination, and the individual dies, a fearful responsibility rests with you.'

'The responsibility will rest heavily somewhere,' replied the stranger bitterly. 'Whatever responsibility rests with me, I am content to bear, and ready to answer.'

'As I incur none,' continued the surgeon, 'by acceding to your request, I will see him in the morning, if you leave me the address. At what hour can he be seen?'

'Nine,' replied the stranger.

'You must excuse my pressing these inquiries,' said the surgeon, 'but is he in your charge now?'

'He is not,' was her rejoinder.

'Then, if I gave you instructions for his treatment through the night you could not assist him?'

The woman wept bitterly as she replied, 'I could not.'

Finding that there was but little prospect of obtaining more information by prolonging the interview, and anxious to spare the woman's feelings, which, subdued at first by a violent effort, were now irrepressible and most painful to witness, the surgeon repeated his promise of calling in the morning at the appointed hour. His visitor, after giving him a direction to an obscure part of Walworth, left the house in the same mysterious manner in which she had entered it.

It will be readily believed that so extraordinary a visit produced a considerable impression on the mind of the young surgeon; and that he speculated a great deal, and to very little purpose, on the possible circumstances of the case. In common with the generality of people, he had often heard and read of singular instances, in which a presentiment of death, at a particular day, or even minute, had been entertained and realized. At one moment, he was inclined to think that the present might be such a case; but then it occurred to him that all the anecdotes of the kind he had ever heard were of persons who had been troubled with a foreboding of their own death. This woman, however, spoke of another person—a man; and it was impossible to suppose that a mere dream or delusion of fancy would induce her to speak of his approaching dissolution with such terrible certainty as she had spoken. It could not be that the man was to be murdered in the morning, and that the woman, originally a consenting party, and bound to secrecy by an oath, had relented, and though unable to prevent the commission of some outrage on the victim, had determined to prevent his death, if possible, by the timely interposition of medical aid? The idea of such things happening within two miles of the metropolis appeared too wild and preposterous to be entertained beyond the instant. Then his original impression, that the woman's intellects were disordered, recurred; and, as it was the only mode of solving the difficulty with any degree of satisfaction, he obstinately made up his mind to believe that she was mad. Certain misgivings upon this point, however, stole upon his thoughts at the time, and presented themselves again and again through the long, dull course of a sleepless night; during which, in spite of all his efforts to the contrary, he was unable to banish the black veil from his disturbed imagination.

The back part of Walworth, at its greatest distance from town, is a straggling, miserable place enough, even in these days; but, five-and-thirty years ago the greater portion of it was little better than a dreary waste, inhabited by a few scattered people of questionable character, whose poverty prevented their living in any better neighbourhood, or whose pursuits and mode of life rendered its solitude desirable. Very many of the houses which have since sprung up on all sides were not built until some years afterwards; and the great majority even of those which were sprinkled about, at irregular intervals, were of the rudest and most miserable description.

The appearance of the place through which he walked in the morning was not calculated to raise the spirits of the young surgeon, or to dispel any feeling of anxiety or depression which the singular kind of visit he was about to make had awakened. Striking off from the high-road, his way lay across a marshy common, through irregular lanes, with here and there a ruinous and dismantled cottage fast falling to pieces with decay and neglect. A stunted tree, or pool of stagnant water, roused into a sluggish action by the heavy rain of the preceding night, skirted the path occasionally; and now and then a miserable patch of garden ground, with a few old boards knocked together for a summer-house, and old palings imperfectly mended with stakes pilfered from the neighbouring hedges, bore testimony at once to the poverty of the inhabitants and the little scruple they entertained in appropriating the property of other people to their own use. Occasionally a filthy-looking woman would make her appearance from the door of a dirty house, to empty the contents of some cooking utensil into the gutter in front, or to scream after a little slipshod girl who had contrived to stagger a few yards from the door under the weight of a sallow infant almost as big as herself; but scarcely anything was stirring around; and so much of the prospect as could be faintly traced through the cold damp mist which hung heavily over it, presented a lonely and dreary appearance, perfectly in keeping with the objects we have described.

After plodding wearily through the mud and mire; making many inquiries for the place to which he had been directed; and receiving as many contradictory and unsatisfactory replies in return; the young man at length arrived before the house which had been pointed out to him as the object of his destination. It was a small, low building, one storey above the ground, with even a more desolate and unpromising exterior than any he had yet passed. An old yellow curtain was closely drawn across the window upstairs, and the parlour shutters were closed, but not fastened. The house was detached from any other, and, as it stood at an angle of a narrow lane, there was no other habitation in sight.

When we say that the surgeon hesitated, and walked a few paces beyond the house, before he could prevail upon himself to lift the knocker, we say nothing that need raise a smile upon the face of the boldest reader. The police of London were a very different body in that day; the isolated position of the suburbs, when the rage for building and the progress of improvement had not yet begun to connect them with the main body of the city and its environs, rendered many of them (and this in particular) a place of resort for the worst and most depraved characters. Even the streets in the gayest parts of London were imperfectly lighted at that time; and such places as these were left entirely to the mercy of the moon and stars. The chances of detecting desperate characters, or of tracing them to their haunts, were thus rendered very few, and their offences naturally increased in boldness, as the consciousness of comparative security became the more impressed upon them by daily experience. Added to these considerations, it must be remembered that the young man had spent some time in the public hospitals of the metropolis; and, although neither Burke nor Bishop had then gained a horrible notoriety, his own observation might have suggested to him how easily the atrocities to which the former has since given his name might be committed. Be this as it may, whatever reflection made him hesitate, he *did* hesitate; but, being a young man of strong mind and great personal courage, it was only for an instant. He stepped briskly back and knocked gently at the door.

A low whispering was audible immediately afterwards, as if some person at the end of the passage were conversing stealthily with another on the landing above. It was succeeded by the noise of a pair of heavy boots upon the bare floor. The door-chain was softly unfastened; the door opened; and a tall, ill-favoured man, with black hair and a face, as the surgeon often declared afterwards, as pale and haggard as the countenance of any dead man he ever saw, presented himself.

'Walk in, sir,' he said, in a low tone.

The surgeon did so, and the man, having secured the door again by the chain, led the way to a small back-parlour at the extremity of the passage.

'Am I in time?'

'Too soon!' replied the man. The surgeon turned hastily round, with a gesture of astonishment not unmixed with alarm, which he found it impossible to repress.

'If you'll step in here, sir,' said the man, who had evidently noticed the action—'if you'll step in here, sir, you won't be detained five minutes, I assure you.'

The surgeon at once walked into the room. The man closed the door, and left him alone.

It was a little cold room, with no other furniture than two deal chairs, and a table of the same material. A handful of fire, unguarded by any fender, was burning in the grate, which brought out the damp, if it served no more comfortable purpose, for the unwholesome moisture was stealing down the walls in long, slug-like tracks. The window, which was broken and patched in many places, looked into a small enclosed piece of ground, almost covered with water. Not a sound was to be heard, either within the house or without. The young surgeon sat down by the fire-place, to await the result of his first professional visit.

He had not remained in this position many minutes when the noise of some approaching vehicle struck his ear. It stopped; the street-door was opened; a low talking succeeded, accompanied with a shuffling noise of footsteps along the passage and on the stairs, as if two or three men were engaged in carrying some heavy body to the room above. The creaking of the stairs, a few seconds afterwards, announced that the newcomers, having completed their task, whatever it was, were leaving the house. The door was again closed, and the former silence was restored.

Another five minutes elapsed; and the surgeon had resolved to explore the house, in search of someone to whom he might make his errand known, when the room door opened, and his last night's visitor, dressed in exactly the same manner, with the veil lowered as before, motioned him to advance. The singular height of her form, coupled with the circumstances of her not speaking, caused the idea to pass across his brain, for an instant, that it might be a man disguised in woman's attire. The hysteric sobs which issued from beneath the veil, and the convulsive attitude of grief of the whole figure, however, at once exposed the absurdity of the suspicion; and he hastily followed.

The woman led the way upstairs to the front room, and

paused at the door, to let him enter first. It was scantily furnished with an old deal box, a few chairs, and a tent bedstead, without hangings or cross-rails, which was covered with
a patchwork counterpane. The dim light admitted through
the curtain which he had noticed from the outside, rendered
the objects in the room so indistinct, and communicated to
all of them so uniform a hue, that he did not at first perceive the object on which his eye at once rested when the
woman rushed frantically past him, and flung herself on her
knees by the bedside.

Stretched upon the bed, closely enveloped in a linen wrap-
per, and covered with blankets, lay a human form, stiff and
motionless. The head and face, which were those of a man,
were uncovered, save by a bandage which passed over the
head and under the chin. The eyes were closed. The left arm
lay heavily across the bed, and the woman held the passive
hand.

The surgeon gently pushed the woman aside, and took the
hand in his.

'My God!' he exclaimed, letting it fall involuntarily—
'the man is dead!'

The woman started to her feet, and beat her hands together. 'Oh, don't say so, sir!' she exclaimed, with a burst of
passion amounting almost to frenzy. 'Oh, don't say so, sir! I
can't bear it! Men have been brought to life before, when
unskilful people have given them up for lost; and men have
died, who might have been restored if proper means had
been resorted to. Don't let him lie here, sir, without one
effort to save him! This very moment life may be passing
away. Do try, sir—do, for Heaven's sake!' And, while speaking, she hurriedly chafed, first the forehead, and then the
breast of the senseless form before her; and then wildly beat
the cold hands, which, when she ceased to hold them, fell
listlessly and heavily back on the coverlet.

'It is of no use, my good woman,' said the surgeon sooth-
ingly, as he withdrew his hand from the man's breast. 'Stay
—undraw that curtain!'

'Why?' said the woman, starting up.

'Undraw that curtain!' repeated the surgeon, in an agitated tone.

'*I* darkened the room on purpose,' said the woman, throwing herself before him as he rose to withdraw it. 'Oh, sir, have pity on me! If it can be of no use, and he is really dead, do not expose that form to other eyes than mine!'

'This man died no natural or easy death,' said the surgeon. 'I *must* see the body!' With a motion so sudden that the woman hardly knew that he had slipped from beside her, he tore open the curtain, admitted the full light of day, and returned to the bedside.

'There has been violence here,' he said, pointing towards the body, and gazing intently at her face, from which the black veil was now, for the first time, removed. In the excitement of a minute before, the female had thrown off the bonnet and veil, and now stood with her eyes fixed upon him. Her features were those of a woman of about fifty, who had once been handsome. Sorrow and weeping had left traces upon them which not time itself would ever have produced without their aid; her face was deadly pale; and there was a nervous contortion of the lip, and an unnatural fire in her eye, which showed too plainly that her bodily and mental powers had nearly sunk beneath an accumulation of misery.

'There has been violence here,' said the surgeon, preserving his searching glance.

'There has!' replied the woman.

'This man has been murdered.'

'That I call God to witness he has,' said the woman passionately; 'pitilessly, inhumanly murdered!'

'By whom?' said the surgeon, seizing the woman by the arm.

'Look at the butchers' marks, and then ask me!' she replied.

The surgeon turned his face towards the bed, and bent over the body which now lay full in the light of the window. The throat was swollen, and a livid mark encircled it. The truth flashed suddenly upon him.

'That is one of the men who were hanged this morning!'

he exclaimed, turning away with a shudder.

'It is,' replied the woman, with a cold, unmeaning stare.

'Who was he?' inquired the surgeon.

'*My son*,' rejoined the woman; and fell senseless at his feet.

It was true. A companion, equally guilty with himself, had been acquitted for want of evidence; and this man had been left for death, and executed. To recount the circumstances of the case, at this distant period, must be unnecessary, and might give pain to some persons still alive. The history was an everyday one. The mother was a widow without friends or money, and had denied herself necessities to bestow them on her orphan boy. That boy, unmindful of her prayers, and forgetful of the sufferings she had endured for him—incessant anxiety of mind, and voluntary starvation of body—had plunged into a career of dissipation and crime. And this was the result; his own death by the hangman's hands, and his mother's shame and incurable insanity.

For many years after this occurrence, and when profitable and arduous avocations would have led many men to forget that such a miserable being existed, the young surgeon was a daily visitor at the side of the harmless mad-woman; not only soothing her by his presence and kindness, but alleviating the rigour of her condition by pecuniary donations for her comfort and support, bestowed with no sparing hand. In the transient gleam of recollection and consciousness which preceded her death, a prayer for his welfare and protection, as fervent as mortal ever breathed, rose from the lips of this poor, friendless creature. That prayer flew to heaven, and was heard. The blessings he was instrumental in conferring have been repaid to him a thousand-fold: but, amid all the honours of rank and station which have since been heaped upon him, and which he has so well earned, he can have no reminiscence more gratifying to his heart than that connected with The Black Veil.

The Mystery at Fernwood

by

ELIZABETH BRADDON

Elizabeth Braddon (1837–1915) achieved an overwhelming success with her first novel Lady Audley's Secret *(1862) which made both her and her publisher's fortune. From then on, she produced a continuous stream of plays, poems, novels and short stories, publishing her 80th novel when she was 74. In 1874 she married the publisher John Maxwell and their son was the famous novelist W. B. Maxwell. As well as writing, she also edited various magazines, including* Temple Bar *and* Belgravia. *Like so many Victorian ladies, she was attracted by the macabre and supernatural and wrote several excellent ghost stories. 'The Mystery at Fernwood', while not a real ghost story, is probably the first to utilize a chilling plot device which has become very popular with horror film makers.*

'No, Isabel, I do *not* consider that Lady Adela seconded her son's invitation at all warmly.'

This was the third time within the last hour that my aunt had made the above remark. We were seated opposite to each other in a first-class carriage of the York express, and the flat fields of ripening wheat were flitting by us like yellow shadows under the afternoon sunshine. We were going on a visit to Fernwood, a country mansion twenty miles from York, in order that I might become acquainted with the family of Mr Lewis Wendale, to whose only son Laurence I was engaged to be married.

Laurence Wendale and I had only been acquainted during the brief May and June of my first London season, which I—the orphan heiress of a wealthy Calcutta merchant—had passed under the roof of my aunt, Mrs Maddison Trevor, the dashing widow of a major in the Life Guards, and the only sister of my dead father. Mrs Trevor had made many objections to this brief six weeks' engagement between Laurence and I; but the impetuous young Yorkshireman had over-ruled everything. What objection could there be? he asked. He was to have two thousand a year and Fernwood at his father's death; forty thousand pounds from a maiden aunt the day he came of age—for he was not yet one-and-twenty, my impetuous young lover. As for his family, let Mrs Trevor look into Burke's *County Families* for the Wendales of Fern-wood. His mother was Lady Adela, youngest daughter of Lord Kingwood, of Castle Kingwood, County Kildare. What objection could my aunt have, then? His family did not know me, and might not approve of the match, urged my aunt. Laurence laughed aloud; a long ringing peal of that merry, musical laughter I loved so well to hear.

'Not approve!' he cried—'not love my little Bella! That is too good a joke!' On which immediately followed an invitation to Fernwood, seconded by a note from Lady Adela Wendale.

It was to this very note that my aunt was never tired of taking objection. It was cold, it was stiff, constrained; it had been only written to please Laurence. How little I thought of the letter! and yet it was the first faint and shadowy indication of that terrible rock ahead upon which my life was to be wrecked; the first feeble link in the chain of the one great mystery in which the fate of so many was involved.

The letter was cold, certainly. Lady Adela started by de-claring she should be most happy to see us; she was all anxiety to be introduced to her charming daughter-in-law. And then my lady ran off to tell us how dull Fernwood was, and how she feared we should regret our long journey into the heart of Yorkshire to a lonely country-house, where we should find no one but a captious invalid, a couple of nervous women, and a young man devoted to farming and field-sports.

But I was not afraid of being dull where my light-hearted Laurence was; and I overruled all my aunt's objections, ordered half a dozen new dresses, and carried Mrs Maddison Trevor off to the Great Northern Station before she had time to remonstrate.

Laurence had gone on before to see that all was prepared for us; and had promised to meet us at York, and drive us over to Fernwood in his mail-phaeton. He was standing on the platform as the train entered the station, with the sunshine glittering about his chestnut curls, and his clear blue eyes radiant with life and happiness.

Laurence Wendale was very handsome; but perhaps his greatest charm consisted in that wonderful vitality, that untiring energy and indomitable spirit, which made him so different to all other young men whom I had met. So great was this vitality, that, by some magnetic influence, it seemed to communicate itself to others. I was never tired when Laurence was with me. I could waltz longer with him for my partner; ride longer in the Row with him for my cavalier; sit out an opera or examine an exhibition of pictures with less fatigue when he was near. His presence pervaded a whole house; his joyous laugh rang through every room. It seemed as if where he was sorrow could not come. I felt this more than ever as we drew nearer Fernwood. The country was bleak and bare; wide wastes of moorland stretched away on either side of the by-road down which we drove. The afternoon sunshine had faded out, leaving a cold grey sky, with low masses of leaden clouds brooding close over the landscape, and shutting in the dim horizon. But no influence of scenery or atmosphere could affect Laurence Wendale. His spirits were even higher than usual this afternoon.

'They have fitted up the oak-rooms for you, ladies,' he said. 'Such solemn and stately chambers, with high canopied beds crowned with funeral plumes; black oak panelling; portraits of dead-and-gone Wendales: Mistress Aurora, with pannier-hoops and a shepherdess's crook; Mistress Lydia with ringlets à la Sévigné and a pearl necklace; Mortimer Wendale, in a Ramillies wig; Theodore, with love-locks, velvet doublet, and Spanish-leather boots. Such a collection of them! You may expect to see them all descend from their frames in the witching time of night to warm their icy fingers at your sea-coal fires. Your expected arrival has made quite a sensation in our dull old abode. My mother has looked up from the last new novel she had from Mudie half a dozen times this day, I verily believe, to ask if all due preparations were being made; while my dear active, patient, indefatigable sister Lucy has been running about superintending the arrangements ever since breakfast.'

'Your sister Lucy,' I said, catching at his last words; 'I shall so love her, Laurence.'

'I hope you will, darling,' he answered, almost gravely, 'for she has been the best and dearest sister to me. And yet I'm half afraid; Lucy is ten years older than you—grave, re-served, sometimes almost melancholy; but if ever there was a banished angel treading this earth in human form, my sister Lucy surely is that guardian spirit.'

'Is she like you, Laurence?'

'Like me? Oh, no, not in the least. She is only my half-sister, you know. She resembles her mother, who died young.'

We were at the gates of Fernwood when he said this—high wooden gates with stone pillars moss-grown and dilapi-dated; a tumble-down looking lodge, kept by a slatternly woman, whose children were at play in a square patch of ground planted with cabbages and currant-bushes, fenced in with a rotten paling, and ambitiously called a garden. From this lodge-entrance a long avenue stretched away for about half a mile, at the end of which a great red-brick mansion, built in the Tudor style, frowned at us, rather as if in defi-ance than in welcome. The park was entirely uncultivated: the trunks of the trees were choked with the tangled under-wood; the fern grew deep in the long vistas, broken here and there by solitary pools of black water, on whose quiet borders we heard the flap of the heron's wing, and the dull croaking of an army of frogs.

Lady Adela was right. Fernwood *was* a dull place. I could scarcely repress a shudder as we drove under the dark avenue; while, as for my poor aunt, her teeth chattered audibly. Accustomed to spend three parts of the year in Onslow Square, and the autumn months at Brighton or Ryde, this dreary Yorkshire mansion was a terrible trial to her rather over-sensitive nerves.

Laurence seemed to divine the reason of our silence. 'The place is frightfully neglected, Mrs Trevor,' he said apologetically: 'but I do not mean this sort of thing to last, I assure you. Before ever I bring my delicate little Bella to Fernwood, I will have landscape-gardeners and upholsterers down by the score, and try to convert this dreary wilderness into a terrestrial paradise. I cannot tell you why the place has been suffered to fall into decay; certainly not for want of money, still less for want of opportunity, for my father is an idle man, to whom one would imagine restoring and rebuilding would afford a delightful hobby. No, there is no reason why the place should have been so neglected.'

He said this more to himself than to us, as if the words were spoken in answer to some long train of thought of his own, and then, growing silent, he seemed to relapse into this old reverie. I watched his face earnestly, for I had seldom seen him look so thoughtful. Presently he said, with more his old manner:

'As you are close upon the threshold of Fernwood now, ladies, I ought perhaps to tell you that you will find ours a most low-spirited family. With everything in life to make us happy, we seem for ever under a cloud. Ever since I can remember my poor father, he has been dropping slowly into decay, almost in the same way as this neglected place, till now he is a confirmed invalid, without any positive illness. My mother reads novels all day, and half lives upon salvolatile and spirits of lavender. My sister, the only active person in the house, is always thoughtful, and very often melancholy. Mind, I merely tell you this to prepare you for anything you may see; not to depress you, for you may depend upon my exertions towards reforming this dreary household, which has sunk into habitual despondency from sheer easy fortune and want of vexation.'

The phaeton drew up before a broad flight of stone steps as Laurence ceased speaking, and in five minutes more he had assisted my aunt and myself to alight, and had ushered us into the presence of Lady Adela and Miss Lucy Wendale.

We found Lady Adela, as her son's description had given us reason to expect, absorbed in a novel. She threw down her book as we entered, and advanced to meet us with considerable cordiality; rather, indeed, as if she really were grateful to us for breaking in upon her solitary life.

'It is so good of you to come,' she said, folding me in her slender arms with an almost motherly embrace, 'and so kind of you, too, my dear Mrs Trevor, to abandon all your town pleasures for the sake of bringing this dear girl to me. Believe me, we will do all in our power to make you comfortable, if you can put up with very limited society; for we have received no company whatever since my son's childhood, and I do not think my visiting-list could muster half a dozen names.'

Lady Adela was an elegant-looking woman, in the very prime of life; but her handsome face was thin and careworn, and premature wrinkles gathered about her melancholy blue eyes and thoughtful mouth. While she was talking to my aunt, Lucy Wendale and I drew nearer to each other.

Laurence's half-sister was by no means handsome; pale and sallow, with dark hair and rather dull grey eyes, she looked as if some hidden sorrow had quenched out the light of her life long ago, in her earliest youth; some sorrow that had neither been forgotten nor decreased by time, but that had rather grown with her growth, and strengthened with her strength, until it had become a part of her very self— some disappointed attachment, I thought, some cruel blow that had shattered a girl's first dream, and left a broken-hearted woman to mourn the fatal delusion. In my utter ignorance of life, I thought these were the only griefs which ever left a woman's life desolate.

'You will try and be happy at Fernwood, Isabel,' Lucy

Wendale said gently, as she drew me into a seat by her side, while Laurence bent fondly over us both. I do not believe, dear as we were to each other, that my Laurence ever loved me as he loved this pale-faced half-sister. 'You will try and be happy, will you not, dear Isabel? Laurence has been breaking-in the prettiest chestnut mare in all Yorkshire, I think, that you may explore the country with us. I have heard what a daring horsewoman you are. The pianos have been put in tune for you, and the billiard-table re-covered that you may have exercise on rainy days; and if we cannot give you much society, we will do all else to prevent your feeling dull.'

'I shall be very happy here with you, dear Lucy,' I said; 'but you tell me so much of the dullness of Fernwood, while, I dare say, you yourself have a hundred associations that make the old place very dear to you.'

She looked down as I spoke, and a very faint flush broke through the sallow paleness of her complexion.

'I am not very fond of Fernwood,' she said gravely.

It was at Fernwood, then, that the great sorrow of her life came upon her, I thought.

'No, Lucy,' said Laurence almost impatiently, 'everybody knows this dull place is killing you by inches, and yet nothing on earth can induce you to quit it. When we all go to Scarborough or Burlington, when Mamma goes to Harrogate, when I run up to Town to rub off my provincial rust, and see what the world is made of outside these dreary gates— you obstinately persist in staying at home; and the only reason you can urge for doing so is, that you must remain here to take care of that unfortunate invalid of yours, Mr Thomas.'

I was holding Lucy's hand in mine, and I felt the poor wasted little fingers tremble as her brother spoke. My curiosity was strongly aroused.

'Mr Thomas!' I exclaimed, half involuntarily.

'Ah, to be sure, Bella, I forgot to tell you of that member of our household, but as I have never seen him, I may be forgiven the omission. This Mr Thomas is a poor relative of my father's: a hopeless invalid, bedridden, I believe, is he not, Lucy?—who requires a strong man and an experienced nurse to look after him, and who occupies the entire upper storey of one wing of the house. Poor Mr Thomas, invalid as he is, must certainly be a most fascinating person. My mother goes to see him every day, but as stealthily as if she were paying a secret visit to some condemned criminal. I have often met my father coming away from his rooms, pale and melancholy; and, as for my sister Lucy, she is so attached to this sick dependant of ours, that, as I have just said, nothing will induce her to leave the house, for fear his nurse or his valet should fail in their care of him.'

I still held Lucy's hand, but it was perfectly steady now. Could this poor relative, this invalid dependant, have any part in the sorrowful mystery that had overshadowed her life? And yet, no; I thought that could scarcely be, for she looked up with such perfect self-possession as she answered her brother.

'My whole life has gradually fallen into the duty of attendance upon this poor young man, Laurence; and I will never leave Fernwood while he lives.'

A young man! Mr Thomas was a young man, then.

Lucy herself led my aunt and I to the handsome suite of apartments prepared for us. Mrs Trevor's room was separated from mine by a corridor, out of which opened two dressing-rooms and a pretty little boudoir, all looking on to the park. My room was at the extreme angle of the building; it had two doors, one leading to the corridor communicating with my aunt's apartments, the other opening into a gallery running the entire length of the house. Looking out into this gallery, I saw that the opposite wing was shut in by a baize door. It was most likely the barrier which closed the outer world upon Laurence Wendale's invalid relation.

Lucy left us as soon as she had installed my aunt and I in our apartments. While I was dressing for dinner, the housekeeper, a stout, elderly woman, came to ask me if I found everything I required.

'As you haven't brought your own servant with you, miss,'

she said, 'Miss Lucy told me to place her maid Sarah entirely at your service. Miss Lucy gives very little work to a maid herself, so Sarah has plenty of leisure time on her hands, and you'll find her a very respectable young woman.'

I told her I could do all I wanted for myself; but before she left me I could not resist asking her one question about the mysterious invalid.

'Are Mr Thomas's rooms at this end of the house?' I asked.

The woman looked at me with an almost scared expression, and was silent for a moment.

'Has Mr Laurence been saying anything to you about Mr Thomas?' she asked; rather anxiously, as I thought.

'Mr Laurence and his sister Miss Lucy were both talking of him just now.'

'Oh, indeed, miss,' answered the woman, with an air of relief; 'the poor gentleman's rooms are at the other end of the gallery, miss.'

'Has he lived here long?' I asked.

'Nigh upon twenty years, miss—above twenty years, I'm thinking.'

'I suppose he is distantly related to the family.'

'Yes, miss.'

'And quite dependent on Mr Wendale?'

'Yes, miss.'

'It is very good of your master to have supported him for so many years, and to keep him in such comfort.'

'My master is a very good man, miss.'

The woman seemed determined to give me as little information as possible; but I could not resist one more question.

'How is it that in all these years Mr Laurence has never seen this invalid relation?' I asked.

It seemed that this question, of all others, was the most embarrassing to the housekeeper. She turned first red and then pale, and said, in a very confused manner, 'The poor gentleman, never leaves his rooms, miss; and Mr Laurence has such high spirits, bless his dear heart, and has such a noisy, rackety way with him, that he's no fit company for an invalid.'

It was evidently useless trying for further information, so I abandoned the attempt, and bidding the housekeeper good afternoon, began to dress my hair before the massive oak-framed looking-glass.

'The truth of the matter is,' I said to myself, 'that after all there is nothing more to be said about it. I have tried to create a mystery out of the simplest possible family arrangement. Mr Wendale has a bedridden relative, too poor and too helpless to support himself. What more natural than that he should give him house-room in this dreary old mansion, where there seems space enough to lodge a regiment?'

I found the family assembled in the drawing-room. Mr Wendale was the wreck of a very handsome man. He must in early life have resembled Laurence; but, as my lover had said, it seemed indeed as if he and the house and grounds of Fernwood had fallen into decay together. But notwithstanding his weak state of health, he gave us a warm welcome, and did the honours of his hospitable dinner-table with the easy grace of a finished gentleman.

After dinner, my aunt and Lady Adela sat at one of the windows talking; while Laurence, Lucy, and I gathered together upon a long stone terrace outside the drawing-room, watching the last low crimson streak of the August sunset fade out behind the black trunks of the trees, and melt away into faint red splashes upon the water-pools amongst the brushwood. We were very happy together: Laurence and I talking of a hundred different subjects, telling Lucy our London adventures, describing our fashionable friends, our drives and rides, *fêtes*, balls, and dinners; she, with a grave smile upon her lips, listening to us with almost maternal patience.

'I must take you over the old house tomorrow, Isabel,' Laurence said, in the course of the evening. 'I suppose Lucy did not tell you that she had put you into the haunted room?'

'No, indeed!'

'You must not listen to this silly boy, my dear Isabel,' said Miss Wendale. 'Of course, like all other old houses, Fernwood can boast its ghost-story; but since no one in my father's lifetime has ever seen the phantom, you may imagine that it is not a very formidable one.'

'But you own there *is* a ghost?' I exclaimed eagerly. 'Pray tell me the story.'

'I'll tell you, Bella,' answered Laurence, 'and then you'll know what sort of visitor to expect when the bells of Fernwood church, hidden away behind the elms yonder, tremble on the stroke of midnight. A certain Sir Humphrey Wendale, who lived in the time of Henry the Eighth, was wronged by his wife, a very beautiful woman. Had he acted according to the ordinary fashion of the time, he would have murdered the lady and his rival; but our ancestor was of a more original turn of mind, and he hit upon an original plan of vengeance. He turned every servant out of Fernwood House; and one morning, when the unhappy lady was sleeping, he locked every door of the mansion, secured every outlet and inlet, and rode away merrily in the summer sunshine, leaving his wife to die the slow and hideous death of starvation. Fernwood is lonely enough even now, Heaven knows! but it was lonelier in those distant days. A passing traveller may now and then have glanced upward at the smokeless chimneys, dimly visible across the trees, as he rode under the park-palings; but none ever dreamed that the deserted mansion had one luckless tenant. Fifteen months afterwards, when Sir Humphrey rode home from foreign travel, he had some difficulty in forcing the door of the chamber in which you are to sleep: the withered and skeleton form of his dead wife had fallen across the threshold.'

'What a horrible story!' I exclaimed, with a shiver.

'It is only a legend, dear Isabel,' said Lucy; 'like all tradition, exaggerated and distorted into due proportions of poetic horror. Pray, do not suffer your mind to dwell upon such a fable.'

'Indeed I hope it is not true,' I answered. 'How fond people are of linking mysteries and horrors such as this with the history of an old family! And yet we never fall across any such family mystery in our own days.'

I slept soundly that night at Fernwood, undisturbed by

the attenuated shadow of Sybil Wendale, Sir Humphrey's unhappy wife. The bright sunshine was reflected in the oak-panels of my room, and the larks were singing high up in a cloudless blue sky, when I awoke. I found my aunt quite reconciled to her visit.

'Lady Adela is a very agreeable woman,' she said; 'quiet, perhaps, to a fault, but with that high tone of manner which is always charming. Lucy Wendale seems a dear good girl, though evidently a confirmed old maid. You will find her of inestimable use when you are married, that is to say, if you ever have to manage this great rambling place, which will of course fall to your lot in the event of poor Mr Wendale's death.'

As for myself, I was as happy at Fernwood as the August days were long. Lucy Wendale rode remarkably well. It was the only amusement for which she cared; and she and her horses were on terms of the most devoted attachment. Laurence, his sister, and I were therefore constantly out together, riding amongst the hills about Fernwood, and exploring the country for twenty miles round.

Indoors, Lucy left us very much to ourselves. She was the ruling spirit of the house, and but for her everything must have fallen utterly to decay. Lady Adela read novels, or made a feeble attempt at amusing my aunt with her conversation. Mr Wendale kept to his room during the fore part of the day; while Laurence and I played, sang, sketched, and rattled the billiard-balls over the green cloth whenever bad weather drove us to indoor amusements.

It was one day that I was sketching the castellated façade of the old mansion, that I noticed one peculiar circumstance, connected with the suite of rooms occupied by the invalid, Mr Thomas. These rooms were at the extreme left angle of the building, and were lighted by a range of six windows. I was surprised by observing that every one of these windows was of ground glass. I asked Laurence the reason of this.

'Why, I believe the glare of light was too much for Mr Thomas,' he answered; 'so my father, who is the kindest creature in Christendom, had the windows made opaque, as you see them now.'

'Has the alteration been long made?'

'It was made when I was about six years old; I have rather a vague recollection of the event, and I should not perhaps remember it but for one circumstance. I was riding about down here one morning on my Shetland pony, when my attention was attracted by a child who was looking through one of those windows. I was not near enough to see his face, but I fancy he must have been about my own age. He beckoned to me, and I was riding across the grass to respond to his invitation, when my sister Lucy appeared at the window and snatched the child away. I suppose he was someone belonging to the female attendant upon Mr Thomas, and had strayed unnoticed into the invalid's rooms. I never saw him again; and the next day a glazier came over from York, and made the alteration in the windows.'

'But Mr Thomas must have air; I suppose the windows are sometimes opened,' I said.

'Never; they are each ventilated by a single pane, which, if you observe, is open now.'

'I cannot help pitying this poor man,' I said, after a pause, 'shut out almost from the light of heaven by his infirmities, deprived of all society.'

'Not entirely so,' answered Laurence. 'No one knows how many stolen hours my sister Lucy devotes to her poor invalid.'

'Perhaps he is a very studious man, and finds his consolation in literary or scientific pursuits,' I said; 'does he read very much?'

'I think not. I never heard of his having any books got for him.'

'But one thing has puzzled me, Laurence,' I continued. 'Lucy spoke of him the other day as a young man, and yet Mrs Porson, your housekeeper, told me he had lived at Fernwood for upwards of twenty years.'

'As for that,' answered Laurence carelessly, 'Lucy no doubt remembers him as a young man upon his first arrival here, and continues to call him so from mere force of habit. But, pray, my little inquisitive Bella, do not rack your brains about this poor relation of ours. To tell the truth, I have become so used to his unseen presence in the house, that I have ceased to think of him at all. I meet a grim woman, dressed in black merino, coming out of the green-baize door, and I know that she is Mr Thomas's nurse; or I see a solemn-faced man, and I am equally assured that he is Mr Thomas's servant, James Beck, who has grown grey in his office; I encounter the doctor riding away from Fernwood on his brown cob, and I feel convinced that he has just looked in to see how Mr Thomas is going on; if I miss my sister for an hour in the twilight, I know that she is in the west wing talking to Mr Thomas; but as nobody ever calls upon me to do anything for the poor man, I think no more of the matter.'

I felt these words almost a reproof to what might have appeared idle, or even impertinent, curiosity on my part. And yet the careless indifference of Laurence's manner seemed to jar upon my senses. Could it be that this glad and high-hearted being, whom I so tenderly loved, was selfish— heedless of the sufferings of others? No, it was surely not this that prompted his thoughtless words. It is a positive impossibility for one whose whole nature is life and motion, animation and vigour, to comprehend for one brief moment the terrors of the invalid's darkened rooms and solitary days.

I had been nearly a month at Fernwood, when, for the first time during our visit, Laurence left us. One of his old school-fellows, a lieutenant in the army, was quartered with his regiment at York, and Laurence had promised to dine at the mess. Though I had been most earnest in requesting him to accept this invitation, I could not help feeling dull and dispirited as I watched him drive away down the avenue, and felt that for the first time we were to spend the long autumn evening without him. Do what I would, the time hung heavily on my hands. The September sunset was beautiful, and Lucy and I walked up and down the terrace after dinner, while Mr Wendale slept in his easy chair, and my aunt and

Lady Adela exchanged drowsy monosyllabic sentences on a couch near the fire, which was always lighted in the evening.

It was in vain that I tried to listen to Lucy's conversation. My thoughts wandered in spite of myself—sometimes to Laurence in the brilliantly-lighted mess-room, enlivening a cluster of *blasé* officers with his boisterous gaiety; sometimes, as if in contrast to this, to the dark west rooms in which the invalid counted the long hours; sometimes to that dim future in whose shadowy years death was to claim our weary host, and Laurence and I were to be master and mistress at Fernwood. I had often tried to picture the place as it would be when it fell into Laurence's hands, and architects and landscape-gardeners came to work, their wondrous transformations; but do what I would, I could never imagine it otherwise than as it was—with straggling ivy hanging forlornly about the moss-stained walls, and solitary pools of stagnant water hiding amongst the tangled brushwood.

Laurence and I were to be married in the following spring. He would come of age in February, and I should be twenty in March—scarcely a year between our ages, and both a great deal too young to marry, my aunt said. After tea Lucy and I sang and played. Dreary music it seemed to me that night. I thought my voice and the piano were both out of tune, and I left Lucy very rudely in the middle of our favourite duet. I took up twenty books from the crowded drawing-room table, only to throw them wearily down again. Never had Lady Adela's novels seemed so stupid as when I looked into them that night; never had my aunt's conversation sounded so tiresome. I looked from my watch to the old-fashioned timepiece upon the chimney half a dozen times, to find at last that it was scarcely ten o'clock. Laurence had promised to be home by eleven, and had begged Lucy and I to sit up for him.

Eleven struck at last; but Laurence had not kept his promise. My aunt and Lady Adela rose to light their candles. Mr Wendale always retired a little after nine. I pleaded for half an hour longer, and Lucy was too kind not to comply readily.

'Isabel is right,' she said; 'Laurence is a spoilt boy, you know, Mamma, and will feel himself very much ill-used if he finds no one up to hear his description of the mess-dinner.'

'Only half an hour, then, mind, young ladies,' said my aunt. 'I cannot allow you to spoil your complexions on account of dissipated people who drive twenty miles to a military dinner. One half-hour; not a moment more, or I shall come down again to scold you both.'

We promised obedience, and my aunt left us. Lucy and I seated ourselves on each side of the low fire, which had burned dull and hollow. I was much too dispirited to talk, and I sat listening to the ticking of the clock, and the occasional falling of a cinder in the bright steel fender. Then that thought came to me which comes to all watchers. What if anything had happened to Laurence? I went to one of the windows, and pulled back the heavy wooden shutters. It was a lovely night; clear, though not moonlight, and a myriad stars gleamed in the cloudless sky. I stood at the window for some time, listening for the wheels, and watching for the lights of the phaeton.

I too was a spoilt child; life had for me been bright and smooth, and the least thought of grief or danger to those I loved filled me with a wild panic. I turned suddenly to Lucy, and cried out, 'Lucy! Lucy, I am getting frightened. Suppose anything should have happened to Laurence. Those horses are wild and unmanageable sometimes. If he had taken a few glasses of wine—if he trusted the groom to drive—if—'

She came over to me, and took me in her arms as if I had been indeed a little child.

'My darling,' she said, 'my darling Isabel, you must not distress yourself by such fancies as these. He is only half an hour later than he said, and as for danger, dearest, he is beneath the shelter of Providence, without whose safeguard those we love are never secure even for a moment.'

Her quiet manner calmed my agitation. I left the window, and returned shivering to the expiring fire.

'It is nearly three-quarters of an hour now, Bella, dear,' she said presently; 'we must keep our promise, and as for

Laurence, you will hear the phaeton drive in before you go to sleep, I dare say.'

'I shall not go to sleep until I do hear it,' I answered as I bade her good night.

I could not help listening for the welcome sound of the carriage-wheels as I crossed the hall and went upstairs. I stopped in the corridor to look into my aunt's room; but she was fast asleep, and I closed the door as softly as I had opened it. It was as I left this room that, glancing down the corridor, I was surprised to see that there was a light in my own bed-chamber. I was prepared to find a fire there, but the light shining through the half-open door was something brighter than the red glow of a fire. I had joined Laurence in laughing at the ghost-story, but my first thought on seeing this light was of the shadow of the wretched Lady Sybil. What if I found her crouching over my hearth?

I had half a mind to go back to my aunt's room, awake her, and tell her my fears; but one moment's reflection made me ashamed of my cowardice. I went on, and pushed open the door of my room. There was no pale phantom shivering over the open hearth. There was an old-fashioned silver candlestick upon the table, and Laurence, my lover, was seated by the blazing fire; not dressed in the evening costume he had worn for the dinner-party, but wrapped in a loose grey woollen dressing-gown, and wearing a black-velvet smoking-cap upon his chestnut hair.

Without stopping to think of the strangeness of his appearance in my room; without wondering at the fact of his having entered the house unknown to either Lucy or myself; without one thought but joy and relief of mind in seeing him once more—I ran forward to him, crying out, 'Laurence, Laurence, I am so glad you have come back!'

He—Laurence, my lover, as I thought, the man, the horrible shadow, the dreadful being—rose from his chair, and snatching up some papers that lay loosely on the table by his side, crumpled them into a ball with one fierce gesture of his strong hand, and flung them at my feet; then, with a harsh dissonant laugh that seemed a mocking echo of the

joyous music I loved so well, he stalked out of the door opening on the gallery. I tried to scream, but my dry lips and throat
could form no sound. The oak panelling of the room spun
round, the walls and ceiling contracted, as if they had been
crushing in upon me to destroy me. I fell heavily to the floor;
but as I fell I heard the phaeton-wheels upon the carriage-
drive below, and Laurence Wendale's voice calling to the
servants.

I can remember little more that happened upon that
horrible night. I have a vague recollection of opening my eyes
upon a million dazzling lights, which slowly resolved themselves into the one candle held in Lucy Wendale's hand, as
she stood beside the bed upon which I was lying. My aunt,
wrapped in her dressing-gown, sat by my pillow. My face and
hair were dripping with the vinegar-and-water they had
thrown over me, and I could hear Laurence, in the corridor
outside my bedroom door, asking again and again, 'Is she
better? Has she quite come to?'

But of all this I was only dimly conscious; a load of iron
seemed pressing upon my forehead, and icy hands seemed
riveted upon the back of my head, holding it tightly to the
pillow on which it lay. I could no more have lifted it than I
could have lifted a ton-weight. I could only lie staring with
stupid dull eyes at Lucy's pale face, silently wishing that she
and my aunt would go, and leave me to myself.

I suppose I was feverish and a little light-headed all that
night—acting over and over again the brief scene of my meeting with the weird shadow of my lover. All the stories I had
laughed at might be true, then. I had seen the phantom of
the man I loved! The horrible double, shaped perhaps out of
impalpable air, but as terribly distinct to the eye as if it had
been a form of flesh and blood.

Lucy was sitting by my bedside when I woke from a short
sleep which had succeeded the long night of fever. How in-
tensely refreshing that brief but deep slumber was to me!
How delicious the gradual fading-out of the sense of horror
and bewilderment, with all the hideous confusions of delirium, into the blank tranquillity of dreamless sleep! When

I awoke my head was still painful, and my frame as feeble as if I had lain for a week on a sick bed; but my brain was cleared, and I was able to think quietly of what had happened.

'Lucy,' I said, 'you do not know what frightened me, or why I fainted.'

'No, dearest, not exactly.'

'But you can know nothing of it, Lucy. You were not with me when I came into this room last night. You did not see—'

I paused, unable to finish my sentence.

'Did not see whom—or what, dear Isabel?'

'The shadow of your brother Laurence.'

My whole frame trembled with the recollection of my terror of the night before, as I said this; yet I was able to observe Lucy's face, and I saw that its natural hue had faded to an ashen pallor.

'The shadow, Isabel!' she faltered, not as if in any surprise at my words, but rather as if she merely spoke because she felt obliged to make some reply to me.

'Yes, Lucy,' I said, raising myself upon the pillow, and grasping her wrist, 'the shadow of your brother Laurence. The living, breathing, moving image of your brother, with every lineament and every shade of colouring reflected in the phantom face as they would be reflected in a mirror. Not shadowy, transparent, or vanishing, but as palpable as you are to me at this very moment. Good heavens! Lucy, I give you my solemn word that I heard the phantom footsteps along that gallery as distinctly as I have ever heard the steps of Laurence himself; the firm heavy tread of a strong man.'

Lucy Wendale sat for some time perfectly silent, looking straight before her— not at me, but out at the half-open window, round which the ivy leaves were fluttering, to the dim moorland melting into purple distance across the tree-tops in the park. Her profile was turned towards me; but I could see by her firmly compressed lips and fixed eyes that she was thinking deeply.

Presently she said, slowly and deliberately, without once looking at me as she spoke, 'You must be fully aware, my dearest Isabel, that these delusions are of common occurrence with people of an extremely sensitive temperament. You may be one of these delicately organized persons; you had thrown yourself last night into a very nervous and hysterical state in your anxiety about Laurence. With your whole mind full of his image, with all kinds of shadowy terrors about danger to him, what more likely than that you should conjure up an object such as that which you fancy you saw last night?'

'But so palpable, Lucy, so distinct!'

'It would be as easy for the brain to shape a distinct as an indistinct form. Grant the possibility of optical delusion—a fact established by a host of witnesses—and you cannot limit the character of the delusion. But I must get our doctor, Mr Arden, to talk to you about this. He is something of a metaphysician as well as a medical man, and will be able to cure your mental ills, and regulate this feverish pulse of yours at the same time. Laurence has ridden over to York to fetch him, and I dare say they will both be here directly.'

'Lucy, remember, you must never tell Laurence the cause of my last night's fainting-fit.'

'Never, Isabel. I was about to make the very same request to you. It is much better that he should never know it.'

'Much better; for, oh, Lucy, do you remember that in all ghost-stories the appearance of the shadow, or double, of a living person is a presage of death to that person? The thought of this brings back all my terror. My Laurence, my darling, if anything should happen to him!'

'Come, Bella, Mr Arden must talk to you. In the meantime, here comes Mrs Porson with your breakfast. While you are taking it, I will go to the library, and look for Sir Walter Scott's *Demonology*. You will find several instances in that book of the optical delusions I have spoken of.'

The housekeeper came bustling into the room with a breakfast-tray, which she placed on a table by the bed. When she had arranged everything for my comfort, and propped me up with a luxuriant pile of pillows, she turned round to speak to Lucy Wendale.

'Oh, Miss Lucy,' she said, 'poor James Beck is so awfully

cut up. If you'd only just see him, and tell him—'

Lucy silenced her with one look; a brief but all-expressive glance of warning and reproval. I could not help wondering what possible reason there could be for making a mystery of some little trouble of James Beck's.

Mr Arden, the York surgeon, was the most delightful of men. He came with Lucy into my room, and laughed and chatted me out of my low spirits before he had been with me a quarter of an hour. He talked so much of hysteria, optical delusions, false impressions of outward objects, disordered and abnormal states of the organ of sight, and other semi-mental, semi-physical infirmities, that he fairly bewildered me into agreeing with and believing all he said.

'I hear you are a most accomplished horsewoman, Miss Morley,' he said, as he rose to leave us; 'and as the day promises to be fine, I most strongly recommend a canter across the moors, with Mr Wendale as your cavalier. Go to sleep between this and luncheon; rise in time to eat a mutton-chop and drink a glass of bitter ale; ride for two hours in the sunniest part of the afternoon, take a light dinner, and go to bed early; and I will answer for your seeing no more of the ghost. You have no idea how much indigestion has to do with these things. I dare say if I were to see your bill of fare for yesterday, I should discover that the phantom made his first appearance among the *entrées*. Who can wonder that the Germans are a ghost-seeing people, when it is remembered that they eat raspberry-jam with roast veal?'

I followed the doctor's advice to the letter; and at three o'clock in the afternoon Laurence and I were galloping across the moorland, tinged with a yellow hazy light in the September sunshine. Like most impressionable people, I soon recovered from my nervous shock; and by the time I sprang from the saddle before the wide stone portico at Fernwood I had almost forgotten my terrors of the night before.

A fortnight after this my aunt and I left Yorkshire for Brighton, whither Laurence speedily followed us. Before leaving I did all in my power to induce Lucy to accompany us, but in vain. She thanked my aunt and I for our invitation, but declared that she could not leave Fernwood. We departed, therefore, without having won her, as I had hoped to have done, from the monotony of her solitary life, and without having seen Mr Wendale's invalid dependant, the mysterious occupant of the west wing.

Early in November Laurence was summoned from Brighton by the arrival of a black-bordered letter, written by Lucy, and telling him of his father's death. Mr Wendale had been found by his servant, seated in an easy chair in his study, with his head lying back upon the cushions, and an open book on the carpet at his feet, dead. He had long suffered from disease of the heart.

My lover wrote me long letters from Yorkshire, telling me how his mother and sister bore the blow which had fallen upon them so suddenly. It was a quiet and subdued sorrow, rather than any tempestuous grief, which reigned in the narrow circle at Fernwood. Mr Wendale had been an invalid for many years, giving very little of his society to his wife and daughter. His death, therefore, though sudden, had not been unexpected, nor did his loss leave any great blank in that quiet home. Laurence spent Christmas at Fernwood, but returned to us for the new year; and it was then settled that we should go down to Yorkshire early in February, in order to superintend the restoration and alteration of the old place.

All was arranged for our journey, when, on the very day on which we were to start, Laurence came to Onslow Square with a letter from his mother, which he had only just received. Lady Adela wrote a few hurried lines to beg us to delay our visit for some days, as they had decided on removing Mr Thomas, before the alterations were commenced, to a cottage which was being prepared for him near York. The invalid had not been left a pauper by the death of his patron, as by Mr Wendale's will an annuity of two hundred a year was left to Thomas Wendale.

'I will not hear of the visit being delayed an hour,' Laurence said impatiently, as he thrust Lady Adela's crumpled letter into his pocket. 'My poor foolish mother and sister are really too absurd about this first or fifth cousin of ours, Thomas Wendale. Let him leave Fernwood or let him stay at Fernwood, just as he, or his nurse, or his medical man, may please; but I certainly shall not allow his arrangements to interfere with ours. So, ladies, I shall be perfectly ready to escort you by the eleven o'clock express.'

Mrs Trevor remonstrated, declaring that she would rather delay our visit according to Lady Adela's wish; but my impetuous Laurence would not hear a word, and under a black and moonless February sky we drove up the avenue at Fernwood.

We met Mr Arden in the hall as we entered: there seemed something ominous in receiving our first greeting from the family doctor, and Laurence was for a moment alarmed by his presence.

'My mother? Lucy?' he said anxiously; 'they are well, I hope?'

'Perfectly well; I have not been attending them. I have just come from Mr Thomas.'

'Is he worse?'

'I fear he is rather worse than usual.'

Our welcome was scarcely a cordial one, for both Lucy and Lady Adela were evidently embarrassed by our unexpected arrival. Their black dresses, half covered with crape, the mourning liveries of the servants, the vacant seat of the master, the dismal winter weather and ceaseless beating of the rain upon the window-panes without, gave a more than usually dreary aspect to the place, and seemed to chill us to the very soul.

Those who at any period of their lives have suffered some terrible and crushing affliction, some never-to-be-forgotten trouble, for which even the hand of Time has no lessening influence, which increases rather than diminishes as the slow course of a hopeless life carries us further from it, so that as we look back we do not ask ourselves why the trail seemed so bitter, but wonder rather how we endured even as we did —only those who have sunk under such a grief as this can know how difficult it is to dissociate the period preceding the anguish from the hour in which it came. I say this lest I should be influenced by after-feelings when I describe the dismal shadows that seemed to brood over the hearth round which Lady Adela, my aunt, Laurence, and myself, gathered upon the night of our return to Fernwood.

Lucy had left us; and when her brother inquired about her, Lady Adela said that she was with Mr Thomas.

As usual, Laurence chafed at the answer. It was hard, he said, that his sister should have to act as sick-nurse to this man.

'James Beck has gone to York to prepare for Mr Thomas,' answered Lady Adela, 'and the poor boy has no one with him but his nurse.'

The poor boy! I wondered why it was that Lady Adela and her step-daughter always alluded to Mr Thomas as a young man.

Early the next morning, Laurence insisted upon my aunt and I accompanying him on a circuit of the house, to discuss the intended alterations. I have already described the gallery, running the whole length of the building, at one end of which was situated the suite of rooms occupied by Mr Thomas, and at the other extremity those devoted to Mrs Trevor and myself. Lady Adela's apartments were nearest to those of the invalid, Lucy's next, then the billiard-room, and opening out of that the bed and dressing-room occupied by Laurence. On the other side of the gallery were servants' and visitors' rooms, and a pretty boudoir sacred to Lady Adela.

Laurence was in very high spirits, planning alterations here and renovations there—bay-windows to be thrown out in one direction, and folding doors knocked through in another— till we laughed heartily at him on finding that the pencil memorandum he was preparing for the architect resolved itself into an order for knocking down the old house and building a new one. We had explored every nook and corner in the place, with the one exception of those mysterious apartments in the left wing. Laurence paused before the green-baize door, but after a moment's hesitation tapped for admittance.

'I have never seen Mr Thomas, and it is rather awkward to

have to ask to look at his rooms while he is in them; but the necessity of the case will be my excuse for intruding on him. The architect will be here tomorrow, and I want to have all my plans ready to submit to him.'

The baize door was opened by Lucy Wendale; she started at seeing us.

'What do you want, Laurence?' she said.

'To see Mr Thomas's rooms. I shall not disturb him, if he will kindly allow me to glance round the apartments.'

I could see that there was an inner half-glass door behind that at which Lucy was standing.

'You cannot possibly see the rooms today, Laurence,' she said hurriedly. 'Mr Thomas leaves early tomorrow morning.'

She came out into the gallery, closing the baize door behind her; but as the shutting of the door reverberated through the gallery, I heard another sound that turned my blood to ice, and made me cling convulsively to Laurence's arm.

The laugh, the same dissonant laugh that I had heard from the spectral lips of my lover's shadow!

'Lucy,' I said, 'did you hear that?'

'What?'

'The laugh, the laugh I heard the night that—'

Laurence had thrown his arm round me, alarmed at my terror. His sister was standing a little way behind him; she put her finger to her lips, looking at me significantly.

'You must be mistaken, Isabel,' she said quietly.

There was some mystery, then, connected with this Mr Thomas—a mystery which for some especial reason was to be concealed from Laurence.

Half an hour after this, Lucy Wendale came to me as I was searching for a book in the library.

'Isabel,' she said, 'I wish to say a few words to you.'

'Yes, dear Lucy.'

'You are to be my sister, and I have perhaps done wrong in concealing from you the one unhappy secret which has clouded the lives of my poor father, my step-mother, and myself. But long ago, when Laurence was a child, it was deemed expedient that the grief which was so heavy a load for us should, if possible, be spared to him. My father was so passionately devoted to his handsome light-hearted boy, that he shrank day by day from the thought of revealing to him the afflicting secret which was such a source of grief to himself. We found that, by constant care and watchfulness, it was possible to conceal all from Laurence, and up to this hour we have done so. But it is perhaps better that you should know all; for you will be able to aid us in keeping the knowledge from Laurence, or, if absolutely necessary, you may by and by break it to him gently, and reconcile him to an irremediable affliction.'

'But this secret—this affliction—it concerns your invalid relation, Mr Thomas?'

'It does, Isabel.'

I know that the words which were to reveal all were trembling upon her lips—that in one brief moment she would have spoken, and I should have known all. I should have known in time—but before she could utter a syllable, the door was opened by one of the women servants.

'Oh, miss, if you please,' she said, 'Mrs Peters says would you step upstairs this minute?'

Mrs Peters was the nurse who attended on Mr Thomas.

Lucy pressed my hand. 'Tomorrow, dearest, tomorrow I will tell you all.'

She hurried from the room, and I sank into a chair by the fire, with my book lying open in my lap, unable to read a line, unable to think, except upon one subject—the secret which I was so soon to learn. If she had but spoken then! A few words more, and what unutterable misery might have been averted!

I was aroused from my reverie by Laurence, who came to challenge me to a game at billiards. On my pleading fatigue as an excuse for refusing, he seated himself on a low stool at my feet, offering to read aloud to me.

'What shall it be, Bella? *Paradise Lost*, *Martin Chuzzlewit*, Byron, Shelley, Tennyson—?'

'Tennyson by all means! The dreary rain-blotted sky outside those windows, and the bleak moorland distances, are perfectly Tennysonian. Read *Locksley Hall.*'

His deep melodious voice rolled out the ponderous and swelling verse; but I heard the sound without its meaning. I could only think of the mystery which had been kept so long a secret from my unconscious lover. When he had finished the poem, he threw aside his book, and sat looking earnestly at me.

'My solemn Bella,' he said, 'what on earth are you thinking of?'

The broad glare of the blaze from a tremendous sea-coal fire was full upon his handsome face. I tried to rouse myself, and, laying my hands upon his forehead, pushed back his curling chesnut hair. As I did so, I for the first time perceived a cicatrice across his left temple. A deep gash, as if from the cut of a knife; but a wound of far-distant date.

'Why, Laurence,' I said, 'you tell me you were never thrown, and yet you have a scar here that looks like the evidence of some desperate fall. Did you get it in hunting?'

'No, my inquisitive Bella! No horse is to blame for that personal embellishment. I believe it was done when I was a child of two or three years old; but I have no positive recollection of it, though I have a vague remembrance of wearing a sticking-plaster bandage across my forehead.'

'But it looks like a scar from a cut—from the cut of a knife.'

'I must have fallen upon some sharp instrument—the edge of one of the stone steps, perhaps, or a metal scraper.'

'My poor Laurence, the blow might have killed you!'

He looked grave.

'Do you know, Bella,' he said, 'how difficult it is to dissociate the vague recollections of the actual events of our childhood from childish dreams that are scarcely more vague? Sometimes I have a strange fancy that I can remember getting this cut, and that it was caused by a knife thrown at me by another child.'

'Another child! What child?'

'A boy of my own age and size.'

'Was he your playfellow?'

'I can't tell; I can remember nothing but the circumstance of his throwing the knife at me, and the sensation of the hot blood streaming into my eyes and blinding me.'

'Can you remember where it occurred?'

'Yes; in the gallery upstairs.'

We lunched at two. After luncheon, Laurence went to his own room to write some letters; Lady Adela and my aunt read and worked in the drawing-room, while I sat at the piano, rambling through some sonatas of Beethoven.

We were occupied in this manner when Lucy came into the room, dressed for walking. 'I have ordered the carriage, Mamma,' she said. 'I am going over to York to see that Beck has everything prepared. I shall be back to dinner.'

Lady Adela seemed to grow more helpless every day; every day to rely more and more on her step-daughter.

'You are sure to do all for the best, Lucy,' she said. 'Take plenty of wraps, for it is bitterly cold.'

'Shall I go with you, Lucy?' I asked.

'You! Oh, on no account, dear Isabel. What would Laurence say to me if I carried you off for a whole afternoon?'

She hurried from the room, and in two minutes the lumbering close carriage drove away from the portico. My motive in asking to accompany her was a selfish one. I thought it possible she might resume the morning's interrupted conversation during our drive. If I had but gone with her!

It is so difficult to reconcile oneself to the irrevocable decrees of Providence; it is so difficult to bow the head in meek submission to the awful fiat; so difficult to look back to the careless hours which preceded the falling of the blow, and calculate how it might have been averted.

The black February twilight was closing in. My aunt and Lady Adela had fallen asleep by the fire. I stole softly out of the room to fetch a book which I had left upstairs. There was more light in the hall and on the staircase than in the drawing-room; but the long gallery was growing dark, the dusky shadows gathering about the faded portraits of my lover's ancestry. I stopped at the top of the staircase, and looked for a moment towards the billiard-room. The door was open, and I could see a light streaming from Laurence's little study. I went to my own room, contrived to find the book I wanted, and returned to the gallery. As I left my room, I saw that the green-baize door at the extreme end of the gallery was wide open.

An irresistible curiosity attracted me towards those mysterious apartments. As I drew nearer to the staircase, I could plainly perceive the figure of a man standing at the half-glass door within. The light of a fire shining in the room behind him threw the outline of his head and figure into sharp relief. There was no possibility of mistaking that well-known form—the broad shoulders, the massive head, and clusters of curling hair. It was Laurence Wendale looking through the glass door of the invalid's apartment. He had penetrated those forbidden chambers, then. I thought immediately of the mystery connected with the invalid, and of Lucy's anxiety that it should be kept from her brother, and I hurried forward towards the baize door. As I advanced he saw me, and rattled impatiently at the lock of the inner door. It was locked; but the key was on the outside. He did not speak, but rattled the lock incessantly, signifying by a gesture of his head that I was to open the door. I turned the key, the door opened outwards, and I was nearly knocked down by the force with which he flung it back and dashed past me.

'Laurence!' I said, 'Laurence! what have you been doing here, and who locked you in?'

He did not answer me, but strode along the gallery, looking at each of the doors, till he came to the only open one, that of the billiard-room, which he entered.

I was wounded by his rude manner; but I scarcely thought of that, for I was on the threshold of the apartments occupied by the mysterious invalid, and I could not resist one hurried peep into the room behind the half-glass door.

It was a roomy apartment, very plainly furnished; a large fire burned in the grate, which was closely guarded by a very high brass fender, the highest I had ever seen. There was an easy chair close to this fender, and on the floor beside it a heap of old childish books, with glaring coloured prints, some of them torn to shreds. On the mantelpiece there was a painted wooden figure held together by strings, such as children play with. Exactly opposite to where I stood there was another door, which was half-open, and through which I saw a bedroom, furnished with two iron bedsteads placed side by side. There were no hangings either to these bedsteads or to the windows in the sitting-room; and the latter were protected by iron bars. A horrible fear came over me. Mr Thomas was perhaps a madman. The seclusion, the locked doors, the guarded fire-place and windows, the dreary curtainless beds, the watchfulness of Lucy, James Beck, and the nurse—all pointed to this conclusion.

Tenantless as the rooms looked, the maniac might be lurking in the shadow. I turned to hurry back to the gallery, and found myself face to face with Mrs Peters, the nurse, with a small tea-tray in her hands.

'My word, miss,' she said, 'how you did startle me to be sure! What are you doing here? and why have you unlocked this door?'

'To let out Mr Laurence.'

'Mr Laurence!' she exclaimed in a terrified voice.

'Yes; he was inside this door. Someone had locked him in, I suppose, and he told me to open it for him.'

'Oh, miss, what have you done! what have you done! Today, above all things, when we've had such an awful time with him! What have you done!'

What had I done? I thought the woman must be mad herself by the agitation of her manner.

Oh, merciful Heaven, the laugh!—the harsh, mocking, exulting, idiotic laugh! This time it rang in loud and discordant peals to the very rafters of the old house.

'Oh, for pity's sake,' I cried, clinging to the nurse, 'what is it, what is it?'

She threw me off, and rushing to the balustrades at the head of the staircase, called loudly, 'Andrew, Henry! bring lights.'

They came, the two men-servants—old men, who had

served in that house for thirty to forty years—they came with candles, and followed the nurse to the billiard-room.

The door of communication between that and Laurence Wendale's study was wide open, and on the threshold, with the light shining upon him from within the room, stood the double of my lover; the living, breathing, image of my Laurence, the creature I had seen at the half-glass door, and had mistaken for Laurence himself. His face was distorted by a ghastly grin, and he was uttering some strange unintelligible sounds as we approached him—guttural and unearthly murmurs horrible to hear. Even in that moment of bewilderment and terror I could see that the cambric about his right wrist was splashed with blood. The nurse looked at him severely; he slunk away like a frightened child; and crept into a corner of the billiard-room, where he stood grinning and mouthing at the blood-stains upon his wrist.

We rushed into the little study. Oh, horror of horrors! The writing-table was overturned; ink, papers, pens, all scattered and trampled on the floor; and in the midst of the confusion lay Laurence Wendale, the blood slowly ebbing away, with a dull gurgling sound, from a hideous gash in his throat.

A pen-knife, with which he had been, it is imagined, mending pens when disturbed by his horrible visitor, lay amongst the trampled papers, crimsoned to the hilt.

Laurence Wendale had been murdered by his idiot twin-brother.

There was an inquest. I can recall at any hour, or at any moment, the whole agony of the scene. The dreary room, adjoining that in which the body lay; the dull February sky; the monotonous voice of the coroner, and the medical men; and myself, or some wretched, shuddering, white-lipped creature that I could scarcely believe to be myself, giving evidence. Lady Adela was reproved for having kept her idiot son at Fernwood without the knowledge of the murdered man; but every effort was made to hush up the terrible story. Thomas Wendale was tried at York, and transferred to the county lunatic asylum, there to be detained during Her Majesty's pleasure. His unhappy brother was quietly buried in the Wendale vault, the chief mausoleum in a damp moss-grown church close to the gates of Fernwood.

It is upwards of ten years since all this happened; but the horror of that February twilight is as fresh in my mind today as it was when I lay stricken—not senseless, but stupefied with anguish—on a sofa in the drawing-room at Fernwood, listening to the wailing of the wretched mother and sister.

The misery of that time changed me at once from a young woman to an old one; not by any sudden blanching of my dark hair, but by the blotting-out of every girlish feeling in the dull monotony of resignation. This change in my own nature has drawn Lucy Wendale and I together with a link far stronger than any common sisterhood. Lady Adela died two years after the murder of her son. The Fernwood property (forfeited by the idiot's crime, but afterwards restored by the clemency of the Crown) has passed into the hands of the heir-at-law.

Lucy lives with me at the Isle of Wight. She is my protectress, my elder sister, without whom I should be lost, for I am but a poor helpless creature.

It was months after the quiet funeral in Fernwood Church before Lucy spoke to me of the wretched being who had been the author of so much misery.

'The idiocy of my unhappy brother,' she said, 'was caused by a fall from his nurse's arms, which resulted in a fatal injury to the brain. The two children were infants at the time of the accident, and so much alike that we could only distinguish Laurence from Thomas by the different colour of the ribbons with which the nurse tied the sleeves of the children's little white frocks. My poor father suffered bitterly from his son's affliction; sometimes cherishing hope even in the face of the verdict which medical science pronounced upon the poor child's case, sometimes succumbing to utter despair. It was the intense misery which he himself endured that made him resolve on the course which ultimately led to so fatal a catastrophe. He determined on concealing Thomas's affliction from his twin-brother. At a very early age the idiot child was removed to the apartments in which he lived until the day of his brother's murder. James Beck and the nurse, both experienced in the treatment of mental affliction, were engaged to attend him; and, indeed, the strictest precaution seemed necessary, as, on the only occasion of the two children meeting, Thomas evinced a determined animosity to his brother, and inflicted a blow with a knife, the traces of which Laurence carried to his grave. The doctors attributed this violent hatred to some morbid feeling respecting the likeness between the two boys. Thomas flew at his brother as some wild animal springs upon its reflection in a glass. With me, in his most violent moments, he was comparatively tractable; but the strictest surveillance was always necessary, and the fatal deed which the wretched, but irresponsible, creature at last committed might never have been done but for the imprudent absence of James Beck and myself.'

The Black Lady of Brin Tor

by

GUY BOOTHBY

Born in Australia, where he was at one time private secretary to the mayor of Adelaide, Guy Boothby (1867–1905) moved to England, where he died at the early age of 38. Among his earlier books were those set in his native Australia, including Billy Binks, Hero *(1898) and* Bushigrams *(1897). He found his greatest success with his series of books about Dr Nikola, his equivocal hero constantly on the trail of immortality. There were five Nikola books in all—*A Bid for Fortune *(1895),* Dr Nikola *(1896),* The Lust of Hate *(1898),* Dr Nikola's Experiment *(1899), and* Farewell Nikola *(1901)—and they are a remarkable series about a remarkable person. Boothby also wrote many books of short stories, and occasionally turned out some excellent ghost stories. 'The Black Lady of Brin Tor' has been out of print for 70 years and is a very authentic tale of a Dartmoor ghost.*

I have seen some curious sights, and have taken part in some equally curious affairs, in the course of my career, but I can safely assert that the story I am going to tell you now equals, if it does not excel, anything I have ever known. I had just returned from South America, where I had been ranching for a good number of years, and, having been more successful than the majority of men who go in for that occupation, had returned to the Old Country with the intention of making it my home for the remainder of my existence.

If you are prepared to spend the money it would not seem

difficult to find a house of the description you require. Yet only those who have tried it know what a serious business it can be. One will be too large, and without sufficient land, another too small, and with more land than you care to be bothered with. My wife and I visited innumerable places, and at last were beginning to despair of ever finding what we wanted. Then, quite by chance, I happened to hear of the property with which this story is connected. It was necessary for me to visit Plymouth in order to meet a friend who was returning from Australia. The beauty of Devon is proverbial, and never better than in the autumn. After my long absence abroad it had a charm for me that I find it difficult to express in words. The dark red soil, the luxuriant hedgerows, the babbling brooks, and the vast solitude of Dartmoor appeal to me with overwhelming force. This was the county for me, if only I could find the description of place for which I had been so long and wearily searching. While I was awaiting the arrival of my friend's vessel I made it my business to call on one of the leading house agents in order to make inquiries. Alas for my hopes. He had nothing on his books that I cared even to consider. I tried another, and yet a third, but with the same result. There were houses in plenty in the town, but they were useless; there were others in the immediate neighbourhood, but each had some drawback. I bade the last agent 'good-afternoon' and returned to my hotel, very disappointed at my ill-success. That evening my friend arrived, and, in the pleasure of welcoming him, I forgot, for the time being, my quest of a residence. I was nearer success, however, than I imagined.

On descending to the coffee-room next morning, I found a letter upon my plate. It was from the first agent upon whom I had called on the previous day. Quite by chance, he said, he had happened to hear of an estate situated in a charming little village on the edge of the moor. The house was an old and picturesque one, and the property consisted of some seventy acres. Some slight repairs would have to be effected, for the reason that the house had not been inhabited for some considerable time—the owner being abroad and unable to keep it up. In conclusion, it was stated that the estate would either be let on lease or sold outright. I carefully studied the particulars enclosed, and, as I did so, began to feel that it really looked as if I had at last discovered what I wanted. When my friend descended I told him the news and invited him to remain a day longer in order to come out with me and inspect it. He consented to do so, and that afternoon we chartered a carriage and drove out.

There are reasons why I suppress the name of the village. They will, I expect, be obvious to you. Give a dog a bad name and hang him may apply as well to a property as to the canine race.

The Hall, as the place was called, was on the further side of the village, and was on the very edge of the moor. The agent had described it exactly when he declared it to be a picturesque old building. It stood on high ground, and immediately behind it rose the steep side of Brin Tor, crowned with enormous boulders that gave it a strangely wild appearance. The house itself was approached by a lengthy carriage drive, and, as I learned later, had been built in the days of the early Georges. From the first moment that I saw it I liked it. We drew up at the steps and alighted. Upon my ringing the bell the door was opened to us by an elderly party of the housekeeper persuasion, who soon revealed the fact that she was as deaf as a post, and not only deaf but as stupid as a mule—if a mule can be said to be stupider than anything else. I presented her with the order to view, whereupon she examined it as if it were a bank note for a thousand pounds, and she was not quite certain as to whether it was genuine. At last, however, she condescended to admit us, and we entered the large, square hall. It was paved, and I must confess did not present a very inviting appearance. The oak panelling, however, was handsome, while the grand staircase was massive and finely carved. With no very good grace the old woman threw open the door of the room which I judged to be the dining room; thence we proceeded on our tour of investigation. The house, with the exception of the kitchen and bedroom, was quite unfurnished, and certainly stood in need of repair. It possessed, however, great possibilities, and I felt sure that, when furnished and put in proper order, it would make a charming dwelling. The old woman's husband, who was as decrepit as his wife, took charge of us when we left the house and conducted us to the stables, thence through the garden to the glasshouses. These had evidently been allowed to go to rack and ruin for a very long time past. By the time our inspection was finished the afternoon was well advanced, and, if we desired to get back to Plymouth in time for dinner, it behoved us to start at once.

That evening I wrote a long description of what I had seen to my wife, inviting her to join me in order that I might have her opinion. Next day she arrived. She proved to be as charmed with it as I was, and by the end of the week following, matters were in excellent trim for my becoming its owner. As soon as necessary legal formalities had been complied with, my wife set off for London on furniture-buying thoughts intent, while I remained behind to hurry on the work that had to be completed before we could come into residence. At last—it was the second week in November, if my memory serves me—the furniture began to arrive. A makeshift bedroom was prepared for me, and I exchanged the hotel in Plymouth for my own abode.

For the next few days my life was not altogether a bed of roses. Everything had to be arranged, the servants were new, while the furnisher's men required strict supervision to prevent them from spending the greater part of their time at the village inn. However, it was all done at last, and I felt that, when my wife gave it the few finishing touches which only a woman can do, it would be as nearly perfect as a man could wish to have his home.

It was on the day that my wife arrived that the first serious circumstance occurred, which it is the purpose of this story to relate. We had finished dinner and were sitting in our drawing-room discussing affairs in general, and wondering when the butler was going to bring in the coffee.

'I told him we would have it immediately after dinner,' said my wife.

I rang the bell, and almost immediately he appeared to answer it.

He looked round the room in surprise, as if he expected to find a third person present.

'We will have coffee, Simpson,' said my wife. 'Always let us have it as soon after dinner as possible.'

'You will excuse me, madam, but I thought you were engaged with a lady.'

'I have seen no lady.'

He looked at her in bewilderment. 'A lady came up the hall,' he said, 'just as you left the dining hall, and I thought she came in here.'

I looked at the man sharply; apparently he was sober.

'You must have dreamt it,' I continued.

'No, sir, I did not. I saw her quite distinctly, and would know her again anywhere. She seemed in great trouble, so that is why I did not disturb you. I am very sorry, sir.'

He departed to bring in the coffee. When he returned I asked him to describe the person in question more minutely. I gathered that she was tall, and had a beautiful face, but with a very sad expression. She was dressed entirely in black, and had what he called 'a black lace shawl' upon her head. The man was deeply in earnest, but I could make neither head nor tail of it.

'Let us look round,' I said. 'I am quite certain that the hall door has not been opened since dinner, and if she is in the house now we shall doubtless find her.'

Accompanied by my wife we set off, visited all the rooms on the ground floor, not omitting the servants' hall. My wife questioned the maids, but one and all asserted that they had not been into the hall since dinner. We next tried all the rooms upstairs with the same result. Simpson's mysterious black lady, if she had existed, was certainly not in the house. I felt more than ever convinced that the man must have fallen asleep in his pantry and have dreamt it. But we were not done with her yet. A week or so afterwards, and when we were quite settled in, one of the maids who had been down to the village declared that, on a path that led through the shrubbery to a side gate, she had met a lady who seemed in great distress. According to the girl's story she was wringing her hands. It was too dark for the maid to see her face.

'You are quite sure of what you are saying?' I asked, when Simpson brought the girl into my presence.

'I am quite sure, sir,' was her reply. 'I held the gate open for her to pass through.'

'Did she speak to you?'

'Not a word, sir! She just went by me as if she did not see me.'

'This is really one of the strangest things I have ever heard,' I said to my wife, when we were alone together. 'I wonder who the woman is, and by what right she trespasses on my grounds? If I meet her I shall put the question to her.'

Christmas was now drawing near, and we had invited a large house party to spend the festive season with us. Among the number was a young fellow named Desborough, who had just got his troop in a Lancer regiment. We had placed him in a room in the bachelors' wing, which was the oldest portion of the house. He and I were the first two to reach the drawing-room before dinner.

'I say, old man,' he began, 'how many people have you got in the house?'

I told him.

'Yes, but who is the other one? The lady with the sorrowful countenance, and a jolly pretty one at that!'

'There is no one else,' I replied. 'I have given you the names of all of them.'

'Well, that's funny! For I'll swear she was no housemaid, and I've seen your wife's maid. Are you sure you are not rotting me?'

'Perfectly sure! Describe this mysterious individual to me.'

'Well, I'm not much of a hand at that sort of work, but I know that she was jolly good-looking, with what looked like a lace mantilla on her head, and she seemed to be in rare trouble. She was wringing her hands, and looked so sorrowfully at me that for a moment I was almost tempted to ask her what was the matter.'

'Wait here a moment,' I said. 'I'll run upstairs and see if I can discover who this person can be.'

I did so, muttering as I went that I was getting a little tired of the lady's visits to my house. But though I searched the bachelors' wing, and such other rooms as I could enter, no trace of her could I discover. I returned to the drawing-room and informed Desborough of my ill-success.

'Well, you can say what you like,' he answered. 'I saw her as plainly as I can see you now.'

Thus the matter dropped for the time being.

My wife was the next to be favoured with a glimpse of her. It was Christmas Eve, and the ladies had been down to the church to decorate the edifice for next day. It was almost dark when they started to return. My wife remained behind the party for about ten minutes to discuss certain matters with the Vicar. It was snowing heavily when she left the church, and the country looked indescribably beautiful in the light of the full moon. Her version of the story is that she had just left the shrubbery and was passing along the path that ran at the foot of the terrace, when she looked up and saw a woman, dressed in black, leaning with her hands upon it, looking down upon her. She declares to this day that she was too surprised to be frightened, or to say or do anything. Then the woman walked away from her, wringing her hands as if she were in great grief. Three minutes could not have elapsed before I had been told, and was out on the terrace in pursuit. I looked about, but there was no sign of her, and, stranger still, there was not a footmark other than my own upon the snow. The matter was getting beyond me. I could not make head nor tail of it.

Next day, after morning service, I took the Vicar aside and asked him if he could give me any clue to the mystery. I told him the matter was getting serious. The servants declared that it was a ghost, and, in consequence, were threatening to leave me.

'Well, I will not deny,' he said, 'that something of this sort of thing has been village gossip for a great many years, and more than one person has laid claim to having seen it.

Personally, I have never done so. The story goes that it is the spirit of a Spanish woman who was once the mistress of the house. If you will come into the church again I will show you a tablet to her memory.'

I followed him and discovered the inscription in question. It described her (for reasons already stated I will not give her name) as being the wife of the owner of the house, and also set forth the fact that she had died in the year 1782.

'There's not much to be gained from that,' I said, 'but the coincidence is, to say the least of it, singular.'

I thanked him and rejoined my party.

That evening was devoted to the usual amusements associated with the occasion. I am afraid we were all very juvenile, and must have shocked the grave Simpson. We played dumb crambo, acted charades, and at last came to thought-reading. In my turn I went out of the room while an experiment was preparing. The hall was brilliantly lighted, and I give you my word that I had no thought of the mysterious lady at that moment. Suddenly I looked up, to see her passing along the corridor at the top of the great staircase in the direction of the bachelors' quarter. Seizing a hat and coat, I ran up the stairs just in time to see her turning the corner of the corridor. I set off in pursuit. She was evidently making her way to a little door that led by a flight of steps to the garden below. By the time I reached it she had disappeared; but, throwing open the door, I saw her passing swiftly along the garden path towards the shrubbery. Donning my hat and drawing on my coat, I continued my chase. She passed out of the wicket gate and turned into the narrow lane that led towards the Tor. It was the night of full moon, and was almost as light as day. Without leaving any track upon the snow, she sped on at such a rate that I had great difficulty in keeping her in sight. At last she reached the foot of the Tor and began the ascent. This was more than I had bargained for, for it must be remembered that my feet were in evening dress shoes, and that the snow was lying inches deep upon the ground. However, having come so far, I was determined to see what the end of it would be. Staggering, falling, I began the climb, the black figure speeding on ahead of me, never pausing for a moment. At last it reached the summit and stood, while perhaps I could have counted twenty, upon the topmost boulder. It made a weird picture, I can assure you. Then she raised her arms above her head and fell through the air to the rocks, nearly two hundred feet below. On my honour it was so real that I gave a great cry as I saw it. I scrambled down to see if there was any sign of her, but there was none. The tragedy ended with her death. I went home scarcely able to believe the evidence of my senses.

Next day I took Desborough up the Tor with me and described the scene to him. I believe he thought I had dreamt it all. We stood at the foot and looked up at it.

'By Jove, it would be a ghastly place to take a leap from,' he said. 'Is that a cave up there?'

He pointed half-way up the face of the cliff. There certainly *was* a cave there.

'Perhaps that is the clue of the mystery,' I cried. 'A man could be lowered to it from the top. As soon as the snow goes, I'll have a look at it.'

A week later I took several of my men and a strong rope, and visited the Tor once more. After taking every precaution, they lowered me over the cliff till I reached the narrow entrance to the cave. I managed to squeeze myself in, and then lit a candle which I had brought with me. Three steps took me into a fair-sized cavern, and showed me as strange and terrible a sight as man ever looked upon. Stretched out upon the floor was the skeleton of a man; scattered around him were remains of books and what may once have been a blanket. I took up one of the books, and inside the cover found the name of the man whose wife's tablet I had seen in the village church on Christmas Day. Later on I examined it carefully. Inside was written, 'I am dying of starvation. They will not let my wife bring me food. I have destroyed the papers. Farewell, my own beloved wife.' Thus the mystery was solved. The poor remains were brought down from their long resting-place and decently interred. Since then the Black Lady, as the village folk call her, has not been seen. I do not pretend to account for it. I simply give you the story.

The Mother of Monsters

by

GUY DE MAUPASSANT

It is ironic that the greatest exponent of the art of the short story in Victorian times should have been a Frenchman, for Guy de Maupassant (1850–1893) raised the short story to heights that had only been reached by English and American authors. The author's unhappy life, which was plagued by nervous disorder and finally led to madness and poverty, made him preoccupied with human misery and tragedy and he reflected his morbid view of life in his stories. In his short life he wrote many horrible tales, including 'The Horla' and 'The Tomb', but few more horrible than this brief piece. It was intended as a sarcastic comment on female underwear but goes far beyond that.

I was reminded of this horrible story and this horrible woman on the sea-front the other day, as I stood watching—at a watering-place much frequented by the wealthy—a lady well known in Paris, a young, elegant, and charming girl, universally loved and respected.

My story is now many years old, but such things are not forgotten.

I had been invited by a friend to stay with him in a small country town. In order to do the honours of the district, he took me about all over the place; made me see the most celebrated views, the manor-houses and castles, the local industries, the ruins; he showed me the monuments, the churches, the old carved doors, the trees of specially large size or uncommon shape, the oak of St Andrew and the Roqueboise yew.

When, with exclamations of gratified enthusiasm, I had inspected all the curiosities in the district, my friend confessed, with every sign of acute distress, that there was nothing more to visit. I breathed again. I should be able, at last, to enjoy a little rest under the shade of the trees. But suddenly he exclaimed:

'Why, no, there *is* one more. There's the Mother of Monsters.'

'And who,' I asked, 'is the Mother of Monsters?'

He answered: 'She is a horrible woman, a perfect demon, a creature who every year deliberately produces deformed, hideous, frightful children. monsters, in a word, and sells them to peep-show men.

'The men who follow this ghastly trade come from time to time to discover whether she has brought forth any fresh abortion, and if they like the look of the object, they pay the mother and take it away with them.

'She has dropped eleven of these creatures. She is rich.

'You think I'm joking, making it up, exaggerating. No, my friend, I'm only telling you the truth, the literal truth.

'Come and see this woman. I'll tell you afterwards how she became a monster-factory.'

He took me off to the outskirts of the town.

She lived in a nice little house by the side of the road. It was pretty and well kept. The garden was full of flowers, and smelt delicious. Anyone would have taken it for the home of a retired lawyer.

A servant showed us into a little parlour, and the wretched creature appeared.

She was about forty, tall, hard-featured, but well built, vigorous, and wealthy, the true type of robust peasantry, half animal and half woman.

She was aware of the disapproval in which she was held, and seemed to receive us with malignant humility.

'What do the gentlemen want?' she inquired.

My friend replied: 'We have been told that your last child is just like any other child, and not in the least like his brothers. I wanted to verify this. Is it true?'

She gave us a sly glance of anger and answered:

'Oh, no, sir, oh dear no! He's even uglier, mebbe, than the others. I've no luck, no luck at all, they're all that way, sir, all like that, it's something cruel; how can the good Lord be so hard on a poor woman left all alone in the world!'

She spoke rapidly, keeping her eyes lowered, with a hypocritical air, like a scared wild beast. She softened the harsh tone of her voice, and it was amazing to hear these tearful high-pitched words issuing from that great bony body, with its coarse, angular strength, made for violent gesture and wolfish howling.

'We should like to see your child,' my friend said.

She appeared to blush. Had I perhaps been mistaken? After some moments of silence she said, in a louder voice: 'What would be the use of that to you?'

She had raised her head, and gave us a swift, burning glance.

'Why don't you wish to show him to us?' answered my friend. 'There are many people to whom you show him. You know whom I mean.'

She started up, letting loose the full fury of her voice.

'So that's what you've come for, is it? Just to insult me? Because my bairns are like animals, eh? Well, you'll not see them, no, no, no, you shan't. Get out of here. I know you all, the whole pack of you, bullying me about like this!'

She advanced towards us, her hands on her hips. At the brutal sound of her voice, a sort of moan, or rather a mew, a wretched lunatic screech, issued from the next room. I shivered to the marrow. We drew back before her.

In a severe tone my friend warned her:

'Have a care, She-devil'—the people all called her She-devil—'have a care, one of these days this will bring you bad luck.'

She trembled with rage, waving her arms, mad with fury, and yelling:

'Get out of here, you! What'll bring me bad luck? Get out of here, you pack of beasts, you!'

She almost flew at our throats; we fled, our hearts contracted with horror.

When we were outside the door, my friend asked:

'Well, you've seen her; what do you say to her?'

I answered: 'Tell me the brute's history.'

And this is what he told me, as we walked slowly back along the white high road, bordered on either side by the ripe corn that rippled like a quiet sea under the caress of a small, gentle wind.

The girl had once been a servant on a farm, a splendid worker, well-behaved and careful. She was not known to have a lover, and was not suspected of any weakness.

She fell, as they all do, one harvest night among the heaps of corn, under a stormy sky, when the still, heavy air is hot like a furnace, and the brown bodies of the lads and girls are drenched with sweat.

Feeling soon after that she was pregnant, she was tormented with shame and fear. Desirous at all costs of hiding her misfortune, she forcibly compressed her belly by a method she invented, a horrible corset made of wood and ropes. The more the growing child swelled her body, the more she tightened the instrument of torture, suffering agony, but bearing her pain with courage, always smiling and active, letting no one see or suspect anything.

She crippled the little creature inside her, held tightly in that terrible machine; she crushed him, deformed him, made a monster of him. The skull was squeezed almost flat and ran to a point, with the two great eyes jutting right out from the forehead. The limbs, crushed against the body, were twisted like the stem of a vine, and grew to an inordinate length, with the fingers and toes like spiders' legs.

The trunk remained quite small and round like a nut.

She gave birth to it in the open fields one spring morning.

When the women weeders, who had run to her help, saw

the beast which was appearing, they fled shrieking. And the story ran round the neighbourhood that she had brought a demon into the world. It was then that she got the name 'She-devil'.

She lost her place. She lived on charity, and perhaps on secret love, for she was a fine-looking girl, and not all men are afraid of hell.

She brought up her monster, which, by the way, she hated with a savage hatred, and which she would perhaps have strangled had not the *curé*, foreseeing the likelihood of such a crime, terrified her with threats of the law.

At last one day some passing showmen heard tell of the frightful abortion, and asked to see it, intending to take it away if they liked it. They did like it, and paid the mother five hundred francs down for it. Ashamed at first, she did not want to let them see a beast of this sort; but when she discovered that it was worth money, that these people wanted it, she began to bargain, to dispute it penny by penny, inflaming them with the tale of her child's deformities, raising her prices with peasant tenacity.

In order not to be cheated, she made a contract with them, And they agreed to pay her four hundred francs a year as well, as though they had taken this beast into their service.

The unhoped-for good fortune crazed the mother, and after that she never lost the desire to give birth to another phenomenon, so that she would have a fixed income like the upper classes.

As she was very fertile, she succeeded in her ambition, and apparently became expert at varying the shapes of her monsters according to the pressure they were made to undergo during the period of her pregnancy.

She had them long and short, some like crabs and others like lizards. Several died, whereat she was deeply distressed.

The law attempted to intervene, but nothing could be proved. So she was left to manufacture her marvels in peace.

She now has eleven of them alive, which bring her in from five to six thousand francs, year in and year out. One only is not yet placed, the one she would not show us. But she will not keep it long, for she is known now to all the circus proprietors in the world, and they come from time to time to see whether she has anything new.

She even arranges auctions between them, when the creature in question is worth it.

My friend was silent. A profound disgust surged in my heart, a furious anger, and regret that I had not strangled the brute when I had her in my hands.

'Then who is the father?' I asked.

'Nobody knows,' he replied. 'He or they have a certain modesty. He, or they, remain concealed. Perhaps they share in the spoils.'

I had thought no more of that far-off adventure until the other day, at a fashionable watering-place, when I saw a charming and elegant lady, the most skilful of coquettes, surrounded by several men who have the highest regard for her.

I walked along the front, arm-in-arm with my friend, the local doctor. Ten minutes later I noticed a nurse looking after three children who were rolling about on the sand.

A pathetic little pair of crutches lay on the ground. Then I saw that the three children were deformed, hunch-backed and lame; hideous little creatures.

The doctor said to me: 'Those are the offspring of the charming lady you met just now.'

I felt a profound pity for her and for them.

'The poor mother!' I cried. 'How does she still manage to laugh?'

'Don't pity her, my dear fellow,' replied my friend. 'It's the poor children who are to be pitied. That's the result of keeping the figure graceful right up to the last day. Those monsters are manufactured by corsets. She knows perfectly well that she's risking her life at that game. What does she care, so long as she remains pretty and seductive?'

And I remembered the other, the peasant woman, the She-devil, who sold hers.

The Murderer's Violin

by

ERCKMANN–CHATRIAN

The work of Emile Erckmann (1822–1899) and Pierre Chatrian (1826–1890), two Alsatian writers who collaborated on a long succession of books, has now largely been forgotten. It is a pity, for they produced not only some of the best historical novels in Europe but also some of the finest supernatural tales ever to come from the continent. A quarrel and finally litigation ended their long collaboration. M. R. James described their tale 'Waters of Death' (L'Araignee Crabé) as 'admirable'. Some of their best supernatural tales were to be found in their rare books The Man-Wolf *(1876) and* The Wild Huntsman *(1877). 'The Murderer's Violin' comes from the latter book and one can only regret that the work of two authors with such a talent for the macabre is so unobtainable.*

Karl Hâfitz had spent six years in mastering counterpoint. He had studied Haydn, Glück, Mozart, Beethoven, and Rossini; he enjoyed capital health, and was possessed of ample means which permitted him to indulge his artistic tastes—in a word, he possessed all that goes to make up the grand and beautiful in music, except that insignificant but very necessary thing—inspiration!

Every day, fired with a noble ardour, he carried to his worthy instructor, Albertus Kilian, long pieces harmonious enough, but of which every phrase was 'cribbed'. His master, Albertus, seated in his armchair, his feet on the fender, his elbow on a corner of the table, smoking his pipe all the time, set himself to erase, one after the other, the singular discoveries of his pupil. Karl cried with rage, he got very angry, and disputed the point; but the old master quietly opened one of his numerous music-books, and putting his finger on the passage, said:

'Look there, my boy.'

Then Karl bowed his head and despaired of the future.

But one fine morning, when he had presented to his master as his own composition a fantasia of Boccherini, varied with Viotti, the good man could no longer remain silent.

'Karl,' he exclaimed, 'do you take me for a fool? Do you think that I cannot detect your larcenies? This is really too bad!'

And then perceiving the consternation of his pupil, he added—'Listen. I am willing to believe that your memory is to blame, and that you mistake recollection for originality, but you are growing too fat decidedly; you drink too generous a wine, and, above all, too much beer. That is what is shutting up the avenues of your intellect. You must get thinner!'

'Get thinner!'

'Yes, or give up music. You do not lack science, but ideas, and it is very simple; if you pass your whole life covering the strings of your violin with a coat of grease how can they vibrate?'

These words penetrated the depths of Hâfitz's soul.

'If it is necessary for me to get thin,' exclaimed he, 'I will not shrink from any sacrifice. Since matter oppresses the mind I will starve myself.'

His countenance wore such an expression of heroism at that moment that Albertus was touched; he embraced his pupil and wished him every success.

The very next day Karl Hâfitz, knapsack on his back and bâton in hand, left the hotel of the Three Pigeons and the brewery sacred to King Gambrinus, and set out upon his travels.

He proceeded towards Switzerland.

Unfortunately at the end of six weeks he was much thinner, but inspiration did not come any the more readily for that.

'Can any one be more unhappy than I am?' he said. 'Neither fasting nor good cheer, nor water, wine, or beer can bring me up to the necessary pitch; what have I done to deserve this? While a crowd of ignorant people produce remarkable works, I, with all my science, all my application, all my courage, cannot accomplish anything. Ah! Heaven is not good to me; it is unjust.'

Communing thus with himself, he took the road from Brück to Freibourg; night was coming on; he felt weary and footsore. Just then he perceived by the light of the moon an old ruined inn half-hidden in trees on the opposite side of the way; the door was off its hinges, the small window-panes were broken, the chimney was in ruins. Nettles and briars grew around it in wild luxuriance, and the garret window scarcely topped the heather, in which the wind blew hard enough to take the horns off a cow.

Karl could also perceive through the mist that a branch of a fir-tree waved above the door.

'Well,' he muttered, 'the inn is not prepossessing, it is rather ill-looking indeed, but we must not judge by appearances.'

So, without hesitation, he knocked at the door with his stick.

'Who is there? what do you want?' called out a rough voice within.

'Shelter and food,' replied the traveller.

'Ah ha! very good.'

The door opened suddenly, and Karl found himself confronted by a stout personage with square visage, grey eyes, his shoulders covered with a great-coat loosely thrown over them, and carrying an axe in his hand.

Behind this individual a fire was burning on the hearth, which lighted up the entrance to a small room and the wooden staircase, and close to the flame was crouched a pale young girl clad in a miserable brown dress with little white spots on it. She looked towards the door with an affrighted air; her black eyes had something sad and an indescribably wandering expression in them.

Karl took all this in at a glance, and instinctively grasped his stick tighter.

'Well, come in,' said the man; 'this is no time to keep people out of doors.'

Then Karl, thinking it bad form to appear alarmed, came into the room and sat down by the hearth.

'Give me your knapsack and stick,' said the man.

For the moment the pupil of Albertus trembled to his very marrow; but the knapsack was unbuckled and the stick placed in the corner, and the host was seated quietly before the fire ere he had recovered himself.

This circumstance gave him confidence.

'Landlord,' said he, smiling, 'I am greatly in want of my supper.'

'What would you like for supper, sir?' asked the landlord.

'An omelette, some wine and cheese.'

'Ha, ha! you have got an excellent appetite, but our provisions are exhausted.'

'You have no cheese, then?'

'No.'

'No butter, nor bread, nor milk?'

'No.'

'Well, good heavens! what *have* you got?'

'We can roast some potatoes in the embers.'

Just then Karl caught sight of a whole regiment of hens perched on the staircase in the gloom of all sorts, in all attitudes, some pluming themselves in the most nonchalant manner.

'But,' said Hâfitz, pointing at this troop of fowls, 'you must have some eggs surely?'

'We took them all to market this morning.'

'Well, if the worst comes to the worst you can roast a fowl for me.'

Scarcely had he spoken when the pale girl, with dishevelled hair, darted to the staircase, crying:

'No one shall touch the fowls! no one shall touch my fowls! Ho, ho, ho! God's creatures must be respected.'

Her appearance was so terrible that Hâfitz hastened to say:

'No, no, the fowls shall not be touched. Let us have the potatoes. I devote myself to eating potatoes henceforth. From this moment my object in life is determined. I shall remain here three months—six months—any time that may be necessary to make me as thin as a fakir.'

He expressed himself with such animation that the host cried out to the girl:

'Genovéva, Genovéva, look! The Spirit has taken possession of him; just as the other was—'

The north wind blew more fiercely outside; the fire blazed up on the hearth, and puffed great masses of grey smoke up to the ceiling. The hens appeared to dance in the reflection of the flame while the demented girl sang in a shrill voice a wild air, and the log of green wood, hissing in the midst of the fire, accompanied her with its plaintive sibilations.

Hâfitz began to fancy that he had fallen upon the den of the sorcerer Hecker; he devoured a dozen potatoes, and drank a great draught of cold water. Then he felt somewhat calmer; he noticed that the girl had left the chamber, and that only the man sat opposite to him by the hearth.

'Landlord,' he said, 'show me where I am to sleep.'

The host lit a lamp and slowly ascended the worm-eaten staircase; he opened a heavy trap-door with his grey head, and led Karl to a loft beneath the thatch.

'There is your bed,' he said, as he deposited the lamp on the floor; 'sleep well, and above all things beware of fire.'

He then descended, and Hâfitz was left alone, stooping beneath the low roof in front of a great mattress covered with a sack of feathers.

He considered for a few seconds whether it would be prudent to sleep in such a place, for the man's countenance did not appear very prepossessing, particularly as, recalling his cold grey eyes, his blue lips, his wide bony forehead, his yellow hue, he suddenly recalled to mind that on the Golzenberg he had encountered three men hanging in chains, and that one of them bore a striking resemblance to the landlord; that he had also those grave eyes, the bony elbows, and that the great toe of his left foot protruded from his shoe, cracked by the rain.

He also recollected that that unhappy man named Melchior had been a musician formerly, and that he had been hanged for having murdered the landlord of the Golden Sheep with his pitcher, because he had asked him to pay his scanty reckoning.

This poor fellow's music had affected him powerfully in former days. It was fantastic, and the pupil of Albertus had envied the Bohemian; but just now when he recalled the figure on the gibbet, his tatters agitated by the night wind, and the ravens wheeling around him with discordant screams, he trembled violently, and his fears augmented when he discovered, at the farther end of the loft against the wall, a violin decorated with two faded palm-leaves.

Then indeed he was anxious to escape, but at that moment he heard the rough voice of the landlord.

'Put out that light, will you?' he cried; 'go to bed. I told you particularly to be cautious about fire.'

These words froze Karl; he threw himself upon the mattress and extinguished the light. Silence fell on all the house.

Now, notwithstanding his determination not to close his eyes, Hâfitz, in consequence of hearing the sighing of the wind, the cries of the night-birds, the sound of the mice pattering over the floor, towards one o'clock fell asleep; but he was awakened by a bitter, deep, and most distressing sob. He started up, a cold perspiration standing on his forehead.

He looked up, and saw crouched up beneath the angle of the roof a man. It was Melchior, the executed criminal. His hair fell down to his emaciated ribs; his chest and neck were naked. One might compare him to a skeleton of an immense grasshopper, so thin was he; a ray of moonlight entering through the narrow window gave him a ghastly blue tint, and all around him hung the long webs of spiders.

Hâfitz, speechless, with staring eyes and gaping mouth,

kept gazing at this weird object, as one might be expected to gaze at Death standing at one's bedside when the last hour has come!

Suddenly the skeleton extended its long bony hand and took the violin from the wall, placed it in position against its shoulder, and began to play.

There was in this ghostly music something of the cadence with which the earth falls upon the coffin of a dearly-loved friend—something solemn as the thunder of the waterfall echoed afar by the surrounding rocks, majestic as the wild blasts of the autumn tempest in the midst of the sonorous forest trees; sometimes it was sad—sad as never-ending despair. Then, in the midst of all this, he would strike into a lively measure, persuasive, silvery as the notes of a flock of goldfinches fluttering from twig to twig. These pleasing trills soared up with an ineffable tremolo of careless happiness, only to take flight all at once, frightened away by the waltz, foolish, palpitating, bewildering—love, joy, despair—all together singing, weeping, hurrying pell-mell over the quivering strings!

And Karl, notwithstanding his extreme terror, extended his arms and exclaimed:

'Oh, great, great artist! oh, sublime genius! oh, how I lament your sad fate, to be hanged for having murdered that brute of an innkeeper who did not know a note of music!— to wander through the forest by moonlight!—never to live in the world again—and with such talents! O Heaven!'

But as he thus cried out he was interrupted by the rough tones of his host.

'Hullo up there! will you be quiet? Are you ill, or is the house on fire?'

Heavy steps ascended the staircase, a bright light shone through the chinks of the door, which was opened by a thrust of the shoulder, and the landlord appeared.

'Oh!' exclaimed Hâfitz, 'what things happen here! First I am awakened by celestial music and entranced by heavenly strains; and then it all vanishes as if it were but a dream.'

The innkeeper's face assumed a thoughtful expression.

'Yes, yes,' he muttered, 'I might have thought as much. Melchior has come to disturb your rest. He will always come. Now we have lost our night's sleep; it is no use to think of rest any more. Come along, friend; get up and smoke a pipe with me.'

Karl waited no second bidding; he hastily left the room. But when he got downstairs, seeing that it was still dark night, he buried his head in his hands and remained for a long time plunged in melancholy meditation. The host relighted the fire, and taking up his position in the opposite corner of the hearth, smoked in silence.

At length the grey dawn appeared through the little diamond-shaped panes; then the cock crew, and the hens began to hop down from step to step of the staircase.

'How much do I owe you?' asked Karl, as he buckled on his knapsack and resumed his walking-staff.

'You owe us a prayer at the chapel of St Blaise,' said the man, with a curious emphasis—'one prayer for the soul of Melchior, who was hanged, and another for his *fiancée*, Genovéva, the poor idiot.'

'Is that all?'

'That is all.'

'Well, then, good-bye—I shall not forget.'

And, indeed, the first thing that Karl did on his arrival at Freibourg was to offer up a prayer for the poor man and for the girl he had loved, and then he went to the Grape Hotel, spread his sheet of paper upon the table, and, fortified by a bottle of 'rikevir', he wrote at the top of the page *The Murderer's Violin*, and then on the spot he traced the score of his first original composition.

The Mask

by

RICHARD MARSH

Richard Marsh (1857–1915) is now mainly remembered for his macabre novel The Beetle *(1897), despite being one of the Victorian era's most prolific thriller writers. He only occasionally branched out into the realms of the supernatural but usually with telling effect, in such books as* The Seen and the Unseen *(1900),* Tom Ossington's Ghost *(1898) and* Marvels and Mysteries *(1900). 'The Mask' comes from the latter book and is a quite unique tale of madness and mystery. The distinguished ghost-story writer and anthologist, Robert Aickman, is carrying on the Marsh family tradition, for he is Richard Marsh's grandson.*

I. WHAT HAPPENED IN THE TRAIN

'Wigmakers have brought their art to such perfection that it is difficult to detect false hair from real. Why should not the same skill be shown in the manufacture of a mask? Our faces, in one sense, are nothing but masks. Why should not the imitation be as good as the reality? Why, for instance, should not this face of mine, as you see it, be nothing but a mask—a something which I can take off and on?'

She laid her two hands softly against her cheeks. There was a ring of laughter in her voice.

'Such a mask would not only be, in the highest sense, a work of art, but it would also be a thing of beauty—a joy for ever.'

'You think that I am beautiful?'

I could not doubt it—with her velvet skin just tinted with the bloom of health, her little dimpled chin, her ripe red lips, her flashing teeth, her great, inscrutable dark eyes, her wealth of hair which gleamed in the sunlight. I told her so.

'So you think that I am beautiful? How odd—how very odd!'

I could not tell if she was in jest or earnest. Her lips were parted by a smile. But it did not seem to me that it was laughter which was in her eyes.

'And you have only seen me, for the first time, a few hours ago?'

'Such has been my ill-fortune.'

She rose. She stood for a moment looking down at me.

'And you think there is nothing in my theory about—a mask?'

'On the contrary, I think there is a great deal in any theory you may advance.'

A waiter brought me a card on a salver.

'Gentleman wishes to see you, sir.'

I glanced at the card. On it was printed, 'George Davis, Scotland Yard.' As I was looking at the piece of pasteboard she passed behind me.

'Perhaps I shall see you again, when we will continue our discussion about—a mask.'

I rose and bowed. She went from the verandah down the steps into the garden. I turned to the waiter. 'Who is that lady?'

'I don't know her name, sir. She came in last night. She has a private sitting-room at No. 22.' He hesitated. Then he added, 'I'm not sure, sir, but I think the lady's name is Jaynes —Mrs Jaynes.'

'Where is Mr Davis? Show him into my room.'

I went to my room and awaited him. Mr Davis proved to be a short, spare man, with iron-grey whiskers and a quiet, unassuming manner.

'You had my telegram, Mr Davis?'

'We had, sir.'

'I believe you are not unacquainted with my name?'

'Know it very well, sir.'

'The circumstances of my case are so peculiar, Mr Davis, that, instead of going to the local police, I thought it better to at once place myself in communication with headquarters.' Mr Davis bowed. 'I came down yesterday afternoon by the express from Paddington. I was alone in a first-class carriage. At Swindon a young gentleman got in. He seemed to me to be about twenty-three or four years of age, and unmistakably a gentleman. We had some conversation together. At Bath he offered me a drink out of his flask. It was getting evening then. I have been hard at it for the last few weeks. I was tired. I suppose I fell asleep. In my sleep I dreamed.'

'You dreamed?'

'I dreamed that I was being robbed.' The detective smiled. 'As you surmise, I woke up to find that my dream was real. But the curious part of the matter is that I am unable to tell you where my dream ended, and where my wakefulness began. I dreamed that something was leaning over me, rifling my person—some hideous, gasping thing which, in its eagerness, kept emitting short cries which were of the nature of barks. Although I say I dreamed this, I am not at all sure I did not actually see it taking place. The purse was drawn from my trousers pocket; something was taken out of it. I distinctly heard the chink of money, and then the purse was returned to where it was before. My watch and chain were taken, the studs out of my shirt, the links out of my wristbands. My pocket-book was treated as my purse had been—something was taken out of it and the book returned. My keys were taken. My dressing bag was taken from the rack, opened, and articles were taken out of it, though I could not see what articles they were. The bag was replaced on the rack, the keys in my pocket.'

'Didn't you see the face of the person who did all this?'

'That was the curious part of it. I tried to, but I failed. It seemed to me that the face was hidden by a veil.'

'The thing was simple enough. We shall have to look for your young gentleman friend.'

'Wait till I have finished. The thing—I say the thing because, in my dream, I was strongly, nay, horribly under the impression that I was at the mercy of some sort of animal, some creature of the ape or monkey tribe.'

'There, certainly, you dreamed.'

'You think so? Still, wait a moment. The thing, whatever it was, when it had robbed me, opened my shirt at the breast, and, deliberately tearing my skin with what seemed to me to be talons, put its mouth to the wound, and, gathering my flesh between its teeth, bit me to the bone. Here is sufficient evidence to prove that then, at least, I did not dream.'

Unbuttoning my shirt I showed Mr Davis the open cicatrice.

'The pain was so intense that it awoke me. I sprang to my feet. I saw the thing.'

'You saw it?'

'I saw it. It was crouching at the other end of the carriage. The door was open. I saw it for an instant as it leaped into the night.'

'At what rate do you suppose the train was travelling?'

'The carriage blinds were drawn. The train had just left Newton Abbot. The creature must have been biting me when the train was actually drawn up at the platform. It leaped out of the carriage as the train was restarting.'

'And did you see the face?'

'I did. It was the face of a devil.'

'Excuse me, Mr Fountain, but you're not trying on me the plot of your next novel—just to see how it goes?'

'I wish I were, my lad, but I am not. It was the face of a devil—so hideous a face that the only detail I was able to grasp was that it had a pair of eyes which gleamed at me like burning coals.'

'Where was the young gentleman?'

'He had disappeared.'

'Precisely. And I suppose you did not only dream you had been robbed?'

'I had been robbed of everything which was of the slightest value, except eighteen shillings. Exactly that sum had been left in my purse.'

'Now perhaps you will give me a description of the young gentleman and his flask.'

'I swear it was not he who robbed me.'

'The possibility is that he was disguised. To my eye it seems unreasonable to suppose that he should have removed his disguise while engaged in the very act of robbing you. Anyhow, you give me his description, and I shouldn't be surprised if I was able to lay my finger on him on the spot.'

I described him—the well-knit young man, with his merry eyes, his slight moustache, his graceful manners.

'If he was a thief, then I am no judge of character. There was something about him which, to my eyes, marked him as emphatically a gentleman.'

The detective only smiled.

'The first thing I shall have to do will be to telegraph all over the country a list of the stolen property. Then I may possibly treat myself to a little private think. Your story is rather a curious one, Mr Fountain. And then later in the day I may want to say a word or two with you again. I shall find you here?'

I said that he would. When he had gone I sat down and wrote a letter. When I had finished the letter I went along the corridor towards the front door of the hotel. As I was going I saw in front of me a figure—the figure of a man. He was standing still, and his back was turned my way. But something about him struck me with such a sudden force of recognition that, stopping short, I stared. I suppose I must, unconsciously, have uttered some sort of exclamation, because the instant I stopped short, with a quick movement, he wheeled right round. We faced each other.

'You!' I exclaimed.

I hurried forward with a cry of recognition. He advanced, as though, to greet me. But he had only taken a step or two in my direction when he turned into a room upon his right, and, shutting the door behind him, disappeared.

'The man in the train!' I told myself.

If I had had any doubt upon the subject his sudden disappearance would have cleared my doubt away. If he was anxious to avoid a meeting with me, all the more reason why I should seek an interview with him. I went to the door of the room which he had entered and, without the slightest hesitation, I turned the handle. The room was empty—there could be no doubt of that. It was an ordinary hotel sitting-room, own brother to the one which I occupied myself, and, as I saw at a glance, contained no article of furniture behind which a person could be concealed. But at the other side of the room was another door.

'My gentleman,' I said, 'has gone through that.'

Crossing the room again I turned the handle. This time without result—the door was locked. I rapped against the panels. Instantly someone addressed me from within.

'Who's that?'

The voice, to my surprise, and also somewhat to my discomfiture, was a woman's.

'Excuse me, but might I say one word to the gentleman who has just entered the room?'

'What's that? Who are you?'

'I'm the gentleman who came down with him in the train.'

'What?'

The door opened. A woman appeared—the lady whom the waiter had said he believed was a Mrs Jaynes, and who had advanced that curious story about a mask being made to imitate the human face. She had a dressing jacket on, and her glorious hair was flowing loose over her shoulders. I was so surprised to see her that for a moment I was tongue-tied. The surprise seemed to be mutual, for, with a pretty air of bewilderment, stepping back into the room she partially closed the door.

'I thought it was the waiter. May I ask, sir, what it is you want?'

'I beg ten thousand pardons; but might I just have one word with your husband?'

'With whom, sir?'

'Your husband.'

'My husband?'

Again throwing the door wide open she stood and stared at me.

'I refer, madam, to the gentleman whom I just saw enter the room.'

'I don't know if you intend an impertinence, sir, or merely a jest.'

Her lip curled, her eyes flashed—it was plain she was offended.

'I just saw, madam, in the corridor a gentleman with whom I travelled yesterday from London. I advanced to meet him. As I did so he turned into your sitting-room. When I followed him I found it empty, so I took it for granted he had come in here.'

'You are mistaken, sir. I know no gentleman in the hotel. As for my husband, my husband has been dead three years.'

I could not contradict her, yet it was certain I had seen the stranger turn into the outer room. I told her so.

'If any man entered my sitting-room—which was an unwarrantable liberty to take—he must be in it now. Except yourself, no one has come near my bedroom. I have had the door locked, and, as you see, I have been dressing. Are you sure you have not been dreaming?'

If I had been dreaming I had been dreaming with my eyes open; and yet, if I had seen the man enter the room—and I could have sworn I had—where was he now? She offered, with scathing irony, to let me examine her own apartment. Indeed, she opened the door so wide that I could see all over it from where I stood. It was plain enough that, with the exception of herself, it had no occupant.

And yet, I asked myself, as I retreated with my tail a little between my legs, how could I have been mistaken? The only hypothesis I could hit upon was, that my thoughts had been so deeply engaged upon the matter that they had made me the victim of hallucination. Perhaps my nervous system had temporarily been disorganized by my misadventures of the day before. And yet—and this was the final conclusion to which I came upon the matter—if I had not seen my fellow-passenger standing in front of me, a creature of flesh and blood, I would never trust the evidence of my eyes again. The most ardent ghost-seer never saw a ghost in the middle of the day.

I went for a walk towards Babbicombe. My nerves might be a little out of order—though not to the extent of seeing things which were non-existent, and it was quite possible that fresh air and exercise might do them good. I lunched at Babbicombe, spending the afternoon, as the weather was so fine, upon the seashore, in company with my thoughts, my pipe, and a book. But as the day wore on a sea mist stole over the land, and as I returned Torquay-wards it was already growing dusk. I went back by way of the sea-front. As I was passing Hesketh Crescent I stood for a moment looking out into the gloom which was gathering over the sea. As I looked I heard, or I thought that I heard, a sound just behind me. As I heard it the blood seemed to run cold in my veins, and I had to clutch at the coping of the sea-wall to prevent my knees from giving way under me. It was the sound which I had heard in my dream in the train, and which had seemed to come from the creature which was robbing me : the cry or bark of some wild beast. It came once, one short, quick, gasping bark, then all was still. I looked round, fearing to see I know not what. Nothing was in sight. Yet, although nothing could be seen, I felt that there was something there. But, as the silence continued, I began to laugh at myself beneath my breath. I had not supposed that I was such a coward as to be frightened at less than a shadow! Moving away from the wall, I was about to resume my walk, when it came again—the choking, breathless bark—so close to me that I seemed to feel the warm breath upon my cheek. Looking swiftly round, I saw, almost touching mine, the face of the creature which I had seen, but only for an instant, in the train.

II. MARY BROOKER

'Are you ill?'
'I am a little tired.'

'You look as though you had seen a ghost. I am sure you are not well.'

I did not feel well. I felt as though I had seen a ghost, and something worse than a ghost! I had found my way back to the hotel—how, I scarcely knew. The first person I met was Mrs Jaynes. She was in the garden, which ran all round the building. My appearance seemed to occasion her anxiety.

'I am sure you are not well! Do sit down! Let me get you something to drink.'

'Thanks; I will go to my own room. I have not been very well lately. A little upsets me.'

She seemed reluctant to let me go. Her solicitude was flattering; though if there had been a little less of it I should have been equally content. She even offered me her arm. That I laughingly declined. I was not quite in such a piteous plight as to be in need of that. At last I escaped her. As I entered my sitting-room someone rose to greet me. It was Mr Davis.

'Mr Fountain, are you not well?'

My appearance seemed to strike him as it had struck the lady.

'I have had a shock. Will you ring the bell and order me some brandy?'

'A shock?' He looked at me curiously. 'What sort of a shock?'

'I will tell you when you have ordered the brandy. I really am in need of something to revive me. I fancy my nervous system must be altogether out of order.'

He rang the bell. I sank into an easy-chair, really grateful for the support which it afforded me. Although he sat still I was conscious that his eyes were on me all the time. When the waiter had brought the brandy Mr Davis gave rein to his curiosity.

'I hope that nothing serious has happened.'

'It depends upon what you call serious.' I paused to allow the spirit to take effect. It did me good. 'You remember what I told you about the strange sound which was uttered by the creature which robbed me in the train? I have heard that sound again.'

'Indeed!' He observed me attentively. I had thought he would be sceptical; he was not. 'Can you describe the sound?'

'It is difficult to describe, though when it is once heard it is impossible not to recognize it when it is heard again.' I shuddered as I thought of it. 'It is like the cry of some wild beast when in a state of frenzy—just a short, jerky, half-strangled yelp.'

'May I ask what were the circumstances under which you heard it?'

'I was looking at the sea in front of Hesketh Crescent. I heard it close behind me, not once, but twice; and the second time I—I saw the face which I saw in the train.'

I took another drink of brandy. I fancy that Mr Davis saw how even the mere recollection affected me.

'Do you think that your assailant could by any possibility have been a woman?'

'A woman!'

'Was the face you saw anything like that?'

He produced from his pocket a pocket-book, and from the pocket-book a photograph. He handed it to me. I regarded it intently. It was not a good photograph, but it was a strange one. The more I looked at it the more it grew upon me that there was a likeness—a dim and fugitive likeness, but still a likeness, to the face which had glared at me only half an hour before.

'But surely this is not a woman?'

'Tell me, first of all, if you trace in it any resemblance.'

'I do, and I don't. In the portrait the face, as I know it, is grossly flattered; and yet in the portrait it is sufficiently hideous.'

Mr Davis stood up. He seemed a little excited.

'I believe I have hit it!'

'You have hit it?'

'The portrait which you hold in your hand is the portrait of a criminal lunatic who escaped last week from Broadmoor.'

'A criminal lunatic!'

As I looked at the portrait I perceived that it was the face of a lunatic.

'The woman—for it is a woman—is a perfect devil—as artful as she is wicked. She was there during Her Majesty's pleasure for a murder which was attended with details of horrible cruelty. She was more than suspected of having had a hand in other crimes. Since that portrait was taken she has deliberately burnt her face with a red-hot poker, disfiguring herself almost beyond recognition.'

'There is another circumstance which I should mention, Mr Davis. Do you know that this morning I saw the young gentleman too?'

The detective stared.

'What young gentleman?'

'The young fellow who got into the train at Swindon, and who offered me his flask.'

'You saw him! Where?'

'Here, in the hotel.'

'The devil you did! And you spoke to him?'

'I tried to.'

'And he hooked it?'

'That is the odd part of the thing. You will say there is something odd about everything I tell you; and I must confess there is. When you left me this morning I wrote a letter; when I had written it I left the room. As I was going along the corridor I saw, in front of me, the young man who was with me in the train.'

'You are sure it was he?'

'Certain. When first I saw him he had his back to me. I suppose he heard me coming. Anyhow, he turned, and we were face to face. The recognition, I believe, was mutual, because as I advanced—'

'He ran away?'

'He turned into a room upon his right.'

'Of course you followed him?'

'I did. I made no bones about it. I was not three seconds after him, but when I entered, the room was empty.'

'Empty!'

'It was an ordinary sitting-room like this, but on the other side of it there was a door. I tried that door. It was locked. I rapped with my knuckles. A woman answered.'

'A woman?'

'A woman. She not only answered, she came out.'

'Was she anything like that portrait?'

I laughed. The idea of instituting any comparison between the horror in the portrait and that vision of health and loveliness was too ludicrous.

'She was a lady who is stopping in the hotel, with whom I already had had some conversation, and who is about as unlike that portrait as anything could possibly be—a Mrs Jaynes.'

'Jaynes? A Mrs Jaynes?' The detective bit his finger-nails. He seemed to be turning something over in his mind. 'And did you see the man?'

'That is where the oddness of the thing comes in. She declared that there was no man.'

'What do you mean?'

'She declared that no one had been near her bedroom while she had been in it. That there was no one in it at that particular moment is beyond a doubt, because she opened the door to let me see. I am inclined to think, upon reflection, that, after all, the man may have been concealed in the outer room, that I overlooked him in my haste, and that he made good his escape while I was knocking at the lady's door.'

'But if he had a finger in the pie, that knocks the other theory upon the head.' He nodded towards the portrait which I still was holding in my hand. 'A man like that would scarcely have such a pal as Mary Brooker.'

'I confess, Mr Davis, that the whole affair is a mystery to me. I suppose that your theory is that the flask out of which I drank was drugged?'

'I should say upon the face of it that there can't be two doubts about that.' The detective stood reflecting. 'I should like to have a look at this Mrs Jaynes. I will have a look at her. I'll go down to the office here, and I think it's just possible that I may be treated to a peep at her room.'

When he had gone I was haunted by the thought of that criminal lunatic, who was at least so far sane that she had been able to make good her escape from Broadmoor. It was only when Mr Davis had left me that I discovered that he had left the portrait behind him. I looked at it. What a face it was!

'Think,' I said to myself, 'of being left at the mercy of such a woman as that!'

The words had scarcely left my lips when, without any warning, the door of my room opened, and, just as I was taking it for granted that it was Mr Davis come back for the portrait, in walked the young man with whom I had travelled in the train! He was dressed exactly as he had been yesterday, and wore the same indefinable but unmistakable something which denotes good breeding.

'Excuse me,' he observed, as he stood with the handle of the door in one hand and his hat in the other, 'but I believe you are the gentleman with whom I travelled yesterday from Swindon?' In my surprise I was for a moment tongue-tied. 'I do not think I have made a mistake.'

'No,' I said, or rather stammered, 'you have not made a mistake.'

'It is only by a fortunate accident that I have just learnt that you are staying in the hotel. Pardon my intrusion, but when I changed carriages at Exeter I left behind me a cigar-case.'

'A cigar-case?'

'Did you notice it? I thought it might have caught your eye. It was a present to me, and one I greatly valued. It matched this flask.'

Coming a step or two towards me he held out a flask—the identical flask from which I had drunk! I stared alternately at him and at his flask.

'I was not aware that you changed carriages at Exeter.'

'I wondered if you noticed it. I fancy you were asleep.'

'A singular thing happened to me before I reached my journey's end—a singular and a disagreeable thing.'

'How do you mean?'

'I was robbed.'

'Robbed?'

'Did you notice anybody get into the carriage when you, as you say, got out?'

'Not that I am aware of. You know it was pretty dark. Why, good gracious! is it possible that after all it wasn't my imagination?'

'What wasn't your imagination?'

He came closer to me—so close that he touched my sleeve with his gloved hand.

'Do you know why I left the carriage when I did? I left it because I was bothered by the thought that there was someone in it besides us two.'

'Someone in it besides us two?'

'Someone underneath the seat. I was dozing off as you were doing. More than once I woke up under the impression that someone was twitching my legs beneath the seat; pinching them—even pricking them.'

'Did you not look to see if anyone was there?'

'You will laugh at me, but—I suppose I was silly—something restrained me. I preferred to make a bolt of it, and become the victim of my own imagination.'

'You left me to become the victim of something besides your imagination, if what you say is correct.'

All at once the stranger made a dart at the table. I suppose he had seen the portrait lying there, because, without any sort of ceremony, he picked it up and stared at it. As I observed him, commenting inwardly about the fellow's coolness, I distinctly saw a shudder pass all over him. Possibly it was a shudder of aversion, because, when he had stared his fill, he turned to me and asked:

'Who, may I ask, is this hideous-looking creature?'

'That is a criminal lunatic who has escaped from Broadmoor—one Mary Brooker.'

'Mary Brooker! Mary Brooker! Mary Brooker's face will haunt me for many a day.'

He laid the portrait down hesitatingly, as if it had for him some dreadful fascination which made him reluctant to let it go. Wholly at a loss what to say or do, whether to detain the man or to permit him to depart, I turned away and moved across the room. The instant I did so I heard behind me the sharp, frenzied yelp which I had heard in the train, and which I had heard again when I had been looking at the sea in front of Hesketh Crescent. I turned as on a pivot. The young man was staring at me.

'Did you hear that?' he said.

'Hear it! Of course I heard it.'

'Good God!' He was shuddering so that it seemed to me that he could scarcely stand. 'Do you know that it was that sound, coming from underneath the seat in the carriage, which made me make a bolt of it? I—I'm afraid you must excuse me. There—there's my card. I'm staying at the "Royal". I will perhaps look you up again tomorrow.'

Before I had recovered my presence of mind sufficiently to interfere he had moved to the door and was out of the room. As he went out Mr Davis entered; they must have brushed each other as they passed.

'I forgot the portrait of that Brooker woman,' Mr Davis began.

'Why didn't you stop him?' I exclaimed.

'Stop whom?'

'Didn't you see him—the man who just went out?'

'Why should I stop him? Isn't he a friend of yours?'

'He's the man who travelled in the carriage with me from Swindon.'

Davis was out of the room like a flash of lightning. When he returned he returned alone.

'Where is he?' I demanded.

'That's what I should like to know.' Mr Davis wiped his brow. 'He must have travelled at the rate of about sixty miles an hour—he's nowhere to be seen. Whatever made you let him go?'

'He has left his card.' I took it up. It was inscribed "George Etherege, Coliseum Club". 'He says he is staying at the "Royal Hotel". I don't believe he had anything to do with the robbery. He came to me in the most natural manner possible to inquire for a cigar-case which he left behind him in the carriage. He says that while I was sleeping he changed carriages at Exeter because he suspected that someone was underneath the seat.'

'Did he, indeed?'

'He says that he did not look to see if anybody was actually there because—well, something restrained him.'

'I should like to have a little conversation with that young gentleman.'

'I believe he speaks the truth, for this reason. While he was talking there came the sound which I have described to you before.'

'The sort of bark?'

'The sort of bark. There was nothing to show from whence it came. I declare to you that it seemed to me that it came out of space. I never saw a man so frightened as he was. As he stood trembling, just where you are standing now, he stammered out that it was because he had heard that sound come from underneath the seat in the carriage that he had decided that discretion was the better part of valour, and, instead of gratifying his curiosity, had chosen to retreat.'

III. THE SECRET OF THE MASK

Table d'hôte had commenced when I sat down. My right-hand neighbour was Mrs Jaynes. She asked me if I still suffered any ill effects from my fatigue.

'I suppose,' she said, when I assured her that all ill effects had passed away, 'that you have not thought anything of what I said to you this morning—about my theory of the mask?'

I confessed that I had not.

'You should. It is a subject which is a crotchet of mine, and to which I have devoted many years—many curious years of my life.'

'I own that, personally, I do not see exactly where the interest comes in.'

'No? Do me a favour. Come to my sitting-room after dinner, and I will show you where the interest comes in.'

'How do you mean?'

'Come and see.'

She amused me. I went and saw. Dinner being finished, her proceedings, when together we entered her apartment —that apartment which in the morning I thought I had seen entered by my fellow-passenger—took me a little by surprise.

'Now I am going to make you my confidant—you, an entire stranger—you, whom I never saw in my life before this morning. I am a judge of character, and in you I feel that I may place implicit confidence. I am going to show you all my secrets; I am going to induct you into the hidden mysteries; I am going to lay bare before you the mind of an inventor. But it doesn't follow because I have confidence in you that I have confidence in all the world besides, so, before we begin, if you please, I will lock the door.'

As she was suiting the action to the word I ventured to remonstrate.

'But, my dear madam, don't you think—'

'I think nothing. I know that I don't wish to be taken unawares, and to have published what I have devoted the better portion of my life to keeping secret.'

'But if these matters are of such a confidential nature I assure you—'

'My good sir, I *will* lock the door.'

She did. I was sorry that I had accepted so hastily her invitation, but I yielded. The door was locked. Going to the fire-place she leaned her arm upon the mantel-shelf.

'Did it ever occur to you,' she asked, 'what possibilities might be open to us if, for instance, Smith could temporarily become Jones?'

'I don't quite follow you,' I said. I did not.

'Suppose that you could at will become another person, and in the character of that other person could move about unrecognized among your friends, what lessons you might learn!'

'I suspect,' I murmured, 'that they would for the most part be lessons of a decidedly unpleasant kind.'

'Carry the idea a step further. Think of the possibilities of

a dual existence. Think of living two distinct and separate
lives. Think of doing as Robinson what you condemn as
Brown. Think of doubling the parts and hiding within your
own breast the secret of the double; think of leading a triple
life; think of leading many lives in one—of being the old
man and the young, the husband and the wife, the father
and the son.'

'Think, in other words, of the unattainable.'

'Not unattainable!' Moving away from the mantel-shelf
she raised her hand above her head with a gesture which was
all at once dramatic. 'I have attained!'

'You have attained? To what?'

'To the multiple existence. It is the secret of the mask. I
told myself some years ago that it ought to be possible to
make a mask which should in every respect so closely resemble the human countenance that it would be difficult, if
not impossible, even under the most trying conditions, to
tell the false face from the real. I made experiments. I succeeded. I learnt the secret of the mask. Look at that.'

She took a leather case from her pocket. Abstracting its
contents, she handed them to me. I was holding in my hand
what seemed to me to be a preparation of some sort of skin
—gold-beater's skin, it might have been. On one side it was
curiously, and even delicately, painted. On the other side
there were fastened to the skin some oddly-shaped bosses or
pads. The whole affair, I suppose, did not weigh half an
ounce. While I was examining it Mrs Jaynes stood looking
down at me.

'You hold in your hand,' she said, 'the secret of the mask.
Give it to me.'

I gave it to her. With it in her hand she disappeared into
the room beyond. Hardly had she vanished than the bedroom
door reopened, and an old lady came out.

'My daughter begs you will excuse her.' She was a quaint
old lady, about sixty years of age, with silver hair, and the
corkscrew ringlets of a bygone day. 'My daughter is not very
ceremonious, and is so wrapt up in what she calls her experiments that I sometimes tell her she is wanting in considera-

tion. While she is making her preparations, perhaps you will allow me to offer you a cup of tea.'

The old lady carried a canister in her hand, which, apparently, contained tea. A tea-service was standing on a little side-table; a kettle was singing on the hob. The old lady began to measure out the tea into the teapot.

'We always carry our tea with us. Neither my daughter nor I care for the tea which they give you in hotels.'

I meekly acquiesced. To tell the truth, I was a trifle bewildered. I had had no idea that Mrs Jaynes was accompanied by her mother. Had not the old lady come out of the room immediately after the young one had gone into it I should have suspected a trick—that I was being made the subject of experiment with the mysterious 'mask'. As it was, I was more than half inclined to ask her if she was really what she seemed to be. But I decided—as it turned out most unfortunately—to keep my own counsel and to watch the sequence of events. Pouring me out a cup of tea, the old lady seated herself on a low chair in front of the fire.

'My daughter thinks a great deal of her experiments. I hope you will not encourage her. She quite frightens me at times; she says such dreadful things.'

I sipped my tea and smiled.

'I don't think there is much cause for fear.'

'No cause for fear when she tells one that she might commit a murder; that a hundred thousand people might see her do it, and that not by any possibility could the crime be brought home to her!'

'Perhaps she exaggerates a little.'

'Do you think that she can hear?'

The old lady glanced round in the direction of the bedroom door.

'You should know better than I. Perhaps it would be as well to say nothing which you would not like her to hear.'

'But I must tell someone. It frightens me. She says it is a dream she had.'

'I don't think, if I were you, I would pay much attention to a dream.'

The old lady rose from her seat. I did not altogether like her manner. She came and stood in front of me, rubbing her hands, nervously, one over the other. She certainly seemed considerably disturbed.

'She came down yesterday from London, and she says she dreamed that she tried one of her experiments—in the train.'

'In the train!'

'And in order that her experiment might be thorough she robbed a man.'

'She robbed a man!'

'And in her pocket I found this.'

The old lady held out my watch and chain! It was unmistakable. The watch was a Hunter. I could see that my crest and monogram were engraved upon the case. I stood up. The strangest part of the affair was that when I gained my feet it seemed as though something had happened to my legs —I could not move them. Probably something in my demeanour struck the old lady as strange. She smiled at me.

'What is the matter with you? Why do you look so funny?' she exclaimed.

'That is my watch and chain.'

'Your watch and chain—yours! Then why don't you take them?'

She held them out to me in her extended palm. She was not six feet from where I stood, yet I could not reach them. My feet seemed glued to the floor.

'I—I cannot move. Something has happened to my legs.'

'Perhaps it is the tea. I will go and tell my daughter.'

Before I could say a word to stop her she was gone. I was fastened like a post to the ground. What had happened to me was more than I could say. It had all come in an instant. I felt as I had felt in the railway carriage the day before—as though I were in a dream. I looked around me. I saw the teacup on the little table at my side, I saw the flickering fire, I saw the shaded lamps; I was conscious of the presence of all these things, but I saw them as if I saw them in a dream. A sense of nausea was stealing over me—a sense of horror. I was afraid of I knew not what. I was unable to ward off or to control my fear.

I cannot say how long I stood there—certainly some minutes—helpless, struggling against the pressure which seemed to weigh upon my brain. Suddenly, without any sort of warning, the bedroom door opened, and there walked into the room the young man who, before dinner, had visited me in my own apartment, and who yesterday had travelled with me in the train. He came straight across the room, and, with the most perfect coolness, stood right in front of me. I could see that in his shirt-front were my studs. When he raised his hands I could see that in his wristbands were my links. I could see that he was wearing my watch and chain. He was actually holding my watch in his hand when he addressed me.

'I have only half a minute to spare, but I wanted to speak to you about—Mary Brooker. I saw her portrait in your room —you remember? She's what is called a criminal lunatic, and she's escaped from Broadmoor. Let me see, I think it was a week today, and just about this time—no, it's now a quarter to nine; it was just after nine.' He slipped my watch into his waistcoat-pocket. 'She's still at large, you know. They're on the look-out for her all over England, but she's still at large. They say she's a lunatic. There are lunatics at Broadmoor, but she's not one. She's no more a lunatic than you or I.'

He touched me lightly on the chest; such was my extreme disgust at being brought into physical contact with him that even before the slight pressure of his fingers my legs gave way under me, and I sank back into my chair.

'You're not asleep?'

'No,' I said, 'I'm not asleep.'

Even in my stupefied condition I was conscious of a desire to leap up and take him by the throat. Nothing of this, however, was portrayed upon my face, or, at any rate, he showed no sign of being struck by it.

'She's a misunderstood genius, that's what Mary Brooker is. She has her tastes and people do not understand them; she likes to kill—to kill! One of these days she means to kill herself, but in the meantime she takes pleasure in killing others.'

Seating himself on a corner of the table at my side, allowing one foot to rest upon the ground, he swung the other in the air.

'She's a bit of an actress too. She wanted to go upon the stage, but they said that she was mad. They were jealous, that's what it was. She's the finest actress in the world. Her acting would deceive the devil himself—they allowed that even at Broadmoor—but she only uses her powers for acting to gratify her taste—for killing. It was only the other day she bought this knife.'

He took, apparently out of the bosom of his vest, a long, glittering, cruel-looking knife.

'It's sharp. Feel the point—and the edge.'

He held it out towards me. I did not attempt to touch it; it is probable that I should not have succeeded even if I had attempted.

'You won't? Well, perhaps you're right. It's not much fun killing people with a knife. A knife's all very well for cutting them up afterwards, but she likes to do the actual killing with her own hands and nails. I shouldn't be surprised if, one of these days, she were to kill you—perhaps tonight. It is a long time since she killed anyone, and she is hungry. Sorry I can't stay; but this day week she escaped from Broadmoor as the clock had finished striking nine, and it only wants ten minutes, you see.'

He looked at my watch, even holding it out for me to see. 'Good night.'

With a careless nod he moved across the room, holding the glittering knife in his hand. When he reached the bedroom door he turned and smiled. Raising the knife he waved it towards me in the air; then he disappeared into the inner room.

I was again alone—possibly for a minute or more; but this time it seemed to me that my solitude continued only for a few fleeting seconds. Perhaps the time went faster because I felt, or thought I felt, that the pressure on my brain was giving way, that I only had to make an effort of sufficient force to be myself again and free. The power of making such an effort was temporarily absent, but something within seemed to tell me that at any moment it might return. The bedroom door—that door which, even as I look back, seems to have been really and truly a door in some unpleasant dream—reopened. Mrs Jaynes came in; with rapid strides she swept across the room; she had something in her right hand, which she threw upon the table.

'Well,' she cried, 'what do you think of the secret of the mask?'

'The secret of the mask?'

Although my limbs were powerless throughout it all I retained, to a certain extent, the control of my own voice.

'See here, it is such a little thing.' She picked up the two objects which she had thrown upon the table. One of them was the preparation of some sort of skin which she had shown to me before. 'These are the masks. You would not think that they were perfect representations of the human face—that masterpiece of creative art—and yet they are. All the world would be deceived by them as you have been. This is an old woman's face, this is the face of a young man.' As she held them up I could see, though still a little dimly, that the objects which she dangled before my eyes were, as she said, veritable masks. 'So perfect are they, they might have been skinned from the faces of living creatures. They are such little things, yet I have made them with what toil! They have been the work of years, these two, and just one other. You see nothing satisfied me but perfection; I have made hundreds to make these two. People could not make out what I was doing; they thought that I was making toys; I told them that I was. They smiled at me; they thought that it was a new phase of madness. If that be so, then in madness there is more cool, enduring, unconquerable resolution than in all your sanity. I meant to conquer, and I did. Failure did not dishearten me; I went straight on. I had a purpose to fulfil;

I would have fulfilled it even though I should have had first to die. Well, it is fulfilled.'

Turning, she flung the masks into the fire; they were immediately in flames. She pointed to them as they burned.

'The labour of years is soon consumed. But I should not have triumphed had I not been endowed with genius—the genius of the actor's art. I told myself that I would play certain parts—parts which would fit the masks—and that I would be the parts I played. Not only across the footlights, not only with a certain amount of space between my audience and me, not only for the passing hour, but, if I chose, for ever and for aye. So all through the years I rehearsed these parts when I was not engaged upon the masks. That, they thought, was madness in another phase. One of the parts'—she came closer to me; her voice became shriller—'one of the parts was that of an old woman. Have you seen her? She is in the fire.' She jerked her thumb in the direction of the fireplace. 'Her part is played—she had to see that the tea was drunk. Another of the parts was that of a young gentleman. Think of my playing the man! Absurd. For there is that about a woman which is not to be disguised. She always reveals her sex when she puts on men's clothes. You noticed it, did you not—when, before dinner, he came to you; when you saw him in the corridor this morning; when yesterday he spent an hour with you in the train? I know you noticed it because of these.'

She drew out of her pocket a handful of things. There were my links, my studs, my watch and chain, and other properties of mine. Although the influence of the drug which had been administered to me in the tea was passing off, I felt, even more than ever, as though I were an actor in a dream.

'The third part which I chose to play was the part of—Mrs Jaynes!'

Clasping her hands behind her back, she posed in front of me in an attitude which was essentially dramatic.

'Look at me well. Scan all my points. Appraise me. You say that I am beautiful. I saw that you admired my hair, which flows loose upon my shoulders'—she unloosed the fastenings of her hair so that it did flow loose upon her shoulders—'the bloom upon my cheeks, the dimple in my chin, my face in its entirety. It is the secret of the mask, my friend, the secret of the mask! You ask me why I have watched, and toiled, and schemed to make the secret mine.' She stretched out her hand with an uncanny gesture. 'Because I wished to gratify my taste for killing. Yesterday I might have killed you; tonight I will.'

She did something to her head and dress. There was a rustle of drapery. It was like a conjurer's change. Mrs Jaynes had gone, and instead there stood before me the creature with, as I had described it to Davis, the face of a devil—the face I had seen in the train. The transformation in its entirety was wonderful. Mrs Jaynes was a fine, stately woman with a swelling bust and in the prime of life. This was a lank, scraggy creature, with short, grey hair—fifty if a day. The change extended even to the voice. Mrs Jaynes had the soft, cultivated accents of a lady. This creature shrieked rather than spoke.

'I,' she screamed, 'am Mary Brooker. It is a week today since I won freedom. The bloodhounds are everywhere upon my track. They are drawing near. But they shall not have me till I have first of all had you.'

She came closer, crouching forward, glaring at me with a maniac's eyes. From her lips there came that hideous cry, half gasp, half yelp, which had haunted me since the day before, when I heard it in my stupor in the train.

'I scratched you yesterday. I bit you. I sucked your blood. Now I will suck it dry, for you are mine.'

She reckoned without her host. I had only sipped the tea. I had not, as I had doubtless been intended to do, emptied the cup. I was again master of myself; I was only awaiting a favourable opportunity to close. I meant to fight for life.

She came nearer to me and nearer, uttering all the time that blood-curdling sound which was so like the frenzied cry of some maddened animal. When her extended hands were all but touching me I rose up and took her by the throat. She had evidently supposed that I was still under the influence of the drug, because when I seized her she gave a shriek of astonished rage. I had taken her unawares. I had her over on her back. But I soon found that I had undertaken more than I could carry through. She had not only the face of a devil, she had the strength of one. She flung me off as easily as though I were a child. In her turn she had me down upon my back. Her fingers closed about my neck. I could not shake her off. She was strangling me!

She would have strangled me—she nearly did. When, attracted by the creature's hideous cries, which were heard from without, they forced their way into the room, they found me lying unconscious, and, as they thought, dead, upon the floor. For days I hung between life and death. When life did come back again Mary Brooker was once more an inmate of Her Majesty's house of detention at Broadmoor.

The Dead Man of Varley Grange

ANONYMOUS

One of the many delights of the Victorian era was the popularity of the ghost story. It is not hard to see why. Victorians lived in an age when all things were possible, or at least would be possible in a year or two. The general scientific attitude of those days was summed up in the reputedly true anecdote of the scientist, who, while discussing the possibility of life on other planets and the chance of such life visiting us, gravely stated that it would be best to ascertain what kind of person they might be dealing with before making up their minds whether they would have anything to do with them or not. It never seemed to cross the satisfied Victorian mind that the choice of whether or not to have anything to do with a creature that could traverse a few million miles of space may not exist at all. However, such things were remotely considered and discussed, and life continued in much the same way. Ghosts were much easier food for thought and it was generally considered that all the answers about the hereafter and spiritualism would very soon be found (they never were or even look likely to be) and it was nice to speculate about gruesome phantoms and haunted castles. Ghost stories were popular but still retained a slight literary stigma which is why many Victorian ghost tales are anonymous. This particular one turned up in an old anthology and I am unable to find out who the real author was. It is a pity, because someone *deserves congratulations for writing such a chilling tale.*

'Hallo, Jack! where are you off to? Going down to the governor's place for Christmas?'

Jack Darent, who was in my old regiment, stood drawing on his dogskin gloves upon the 23rd of December the year before last. He was equipped in a long Ulster and top hat, and a hansom, already loaded with a gun-case and portmanteau, stood awaiting him. He had a tall, strong figure, a fair, fresh-looking face, and the merriest blue eyes in the world. He held a cigarette between his lips, and late as was the season of the year there was a flower in his buttonhole. When did I ever see handsome Jack Darent and he did not look well dressed and well fed and jaunty? As I ran up the steps of the Club he turned round and laughed merrily.

'My dear fellow, do I look the sort of man to be victimized at a family Christmas meeting? Do you know the kind of business they have at home? Three maiden aunts and a bachelor uncle, my eldest brother and his insipid wife, and all my sister's six noisy children at dinner. Church twice a day, and snap-dragon between the services! No, thank you! I have a great affection for my old parents, but you don't catch me going in for that sort of national festival!'

'You irreverent ruffian!' I replied, laughing. 'Ah, if you were a married man—'

'Ah, if I were a married man!' replied Captain Darent with something that was almost a sigh, and then lowering his voice, he said hurriedly, 'How is Miss Lester, Fred?'

'My sister is quite well, thank you,' I answered with becoming gravity; and it was not without a spice of malice that I added, 'She has been going out to a great many balls and enjoying herself very much.'

Captain Darent looked profoundly miserable.

'I don't see how a poor fellow in a marching regiment, a younger son too, with nothing in the future to look to, is ever to marry nowadays,' he said almost savagely; 'when girls, too, are used to so much luxury and extravagance that they can't live without it. Matrimony is at a deadlock in this century, Fred, chiefly owing to the price of butcher's meat and bonnets. In fifty years' time it will become extinct and the country will be depopulated. But I must be off, old man, or I shall miss my train.'

'You have never told me where you are going to, Jack.'

'Oh, I am going to stay with old Henderson, in Westernshire; he has taken a furnished house, with some first-rate pheasant shooting, for a year. There are eight of us going—all bachelors, and all kindred spirits. We shall shoot all day and smoke half the night. Think what you have lost, old fellow, by becoming a Benedick!'

'In Westernshire, is it?' I inquired. 'Whereabouts is this place, and what is the name of it? For I am a Westernshire man by birth myself, and I know every place in the county.'

'Oh, it's a tumbledown sort of old house, I believe,' answered Jack carelessly. 'Gables and twisted chimneys outside, and uncomfortable spindle-legged furniture inside—you know the sort of thing; but the shooting is capital, Henderson says, and we must put up with our quarters. He has taken his French cook down, and plenty of liquor, so I've no doubt we shan't starve.'

'Well, but what is the name of it?' I persisted, with a growing interest in the subject.

'Let me see,' referring to a letter he pulled out of his pocket. 'Oh, here it is—Varley Grange.'

'Varley Grange!' I repeated, aghast. 'Why, it has not been inhabited for years.'

'I believe not,' answered Jack unconcernedly. 'The shooting has been let separately; but Henderson took a fancy to the house too and thought it would do for him, furniture and all, just as it is. My dear Fred, what are you looking so solemnly at me for?'

'Jack, let me entreat of you not to go to this place,' I said, laying my hand on his arm.

'Not go! Why, Lester, you must be mad! Why on earth shouldn't I go there?'

'There are stories—uncomfortable things said of that

house.' I had not the moral courage to say, 'It is haunted,' and I felt myself how weak and childish was my attempt to deter him from his intended visit; only—I knew all about Varley Grange.

I think handsome Jack Darent thought privately that I was slightly out of my senses, for I am sure I looked unaccountably upset and dismayed by the mention of the name of the house that Mr Henderson had taken.

'I daresay it's cold and draughty and infested with rats and mice,' he said laughingly; 'and I have no doubt the creature-comforts will not be equal to Queen's Gate; but I stand pledged to go now, and I must be off this very minute, so have no time, old fellow, to inquire into the meaning of your sensational warning. Good-bye, and—and remember me to the ladies.'

He ran down the steps and jumped into the hansom.

'Write to me if you have time!' I cried out after him; but I don't think he heard me in the rattle of the departing cab. He nodded and smiled at me and was swiftly whirled out of sight.

As for me, I walked slowly back to my comfortable house in Queen's Gate. There was my wife presiding at the little five o'clock tea-table, our two fat, pink and white little children tumbling about upon the hearthrug amongst dolls and bricks, and two utterly spoilt and overfed pugs; and my sister Bella—who, between ourselves, was the prettiest as well as dearest girl in all London—sitting on the floor in her handsome brown velvet gown, resigning herself gracefully to be trampled upon by the dogs, and to have her hair pulled by the babies.

'Why, Fred, you look as if you had heard bad news,' said my wife, looking up anxiously as I entered.

'I don't know that I have heard of anything very bad; I have just seen Jack Darent off for Christmas,' I said, turning instinctively towards my sister. He was a poor man and a younger son, and of course a very bad match for the beautiful Miss Lester; but for all that I had an inkling that Bella was not quite indifferent to her brother's friend.

'Oh!' says that hypocrite. 'Shall I give you a cup of tea, Fred?'

It is wonderful how women can control their faces and pretend not to care a straw when they hear the name of their lover mentioned. I think Bella overdid it, she looked so supremely indifferent.

'Where on earth do you suppose he is going to stay, Bella?'

'Who? Oh, Captain Darent! How should I possibly know where he is going? Archie, pet, please don't poke the doll's head quite down Ponto's throat; I know he will bite it off if you do.'

This last observation was addressed to my son and heir.

'Well, I think you will be surprised when you hear: he is going to Westernshire, to stay at Varley Grange.'

'*What!*' No doubt about her interest in the subject now! Miss Lester turned as white as her collar and sprang to her feet impetuously, scattering dogs, babies and toys in all directions away from her skirts as she rose.

'You cannot mean it, Fred! Varley Grange, why, it has not been inhabited for ten years; and the last time— Oh, do you remember those poor people who took it? What a terrible story it has!' She shuddered.

'Well, it is taken now,' I said, 'by a man I know, called Henderson—a bachelor; he has asked down a party of men for a week's shooting, and Jack Darent is one of them.'

'For Heaven's sake prevent him from going!' cried Bella, clasping her hands.

'My dear, he is gone!'

'Oh, then write to him—telegraph—tell him to come back!' she urged breathlessly.

'I am afraid it is no use,' I said gravely. 'He would not come back; he would not believe me; he would think I was mad.'

'Did you tell him anything?' she asked faintly.

'No, I had not time. I did say a word or two, but he began to laugh.'

'Yes, that is how it always is!' she said distractedly. 'People laugh and pooh-pooh the whole thing, and then they go there and see for themselves, and it is too late!'

She was so thoroughly upset that she left the room. My wife turned to me in astonishment; not being a Westernshire woman, she was not well up in the traditions of that venerable county.

'What on earth does it all mean, Fred?' she asked me in amazement. 'What is the matter with Bella, and why is she so distressed that Captain Darent is going to stay at that particular house?'

'It is said to be haunted, and—'

'You don't mean to say you believe in such rubbish, Fred?' interrupted my wife sternly, with a side-glance of apprehension at our first-born, who, needless to say, stood by, all eyes and ears, drinking in every word of the conversation of his elders.

'I never know what I believe or what I don't believe,' I answered gravely. 'All I can say is that there are very singular traditions about that house, and that a great many credible witnesses have seen a very strange thing there, and that a great many disasters have happened to the persons who have seen it.'

'What has been seen, Fred? Pray tell me the story! Wait, I think I will send the children away.'

My wife rang the bell for the nurse, and as soon as the little ones had been taken from the room she turned to me again.

'I don't believe in ghosts or any such rubbish one bit, but I should like to hear your story.'

'The story is vague enough,' I answered.

'In the old days Varley Grange belonged to the ancient family of Varley, now completely extinct. There was, some hundred years ago, a daughter, famed for her beauty and her fascination. She wanted to marry a poor, penniless squire, who loved her devotedly. Her brother, Dennis Varley, the new owner of Varley Grange, refused his consent and shut his sister up in the nunnery that used to stand outside his park gates—there are a few ruins of it left still. The poor nun broke her vows and ran away in the night with her lover. But her brother pursued her and brought her back with him.

The lover escaped, but the lord of Varley murdered his sister under his own roof, swearing that no scion of his race should live to disgrace and dishonour his ancient name.

'Ever since that day Dennis Varley's spirit cannot rest in its grave—he wanders about the old house at night-time, and those who have seen him are numberless. Now and then the pale, shadowy form of a nun flits across the old hall, or along the gloomy passages, and when both strange shapes are seen thus together misfortune and illness, and even death, are sure to pursue the luckless man who has seen them, with remorseless cruelty.'

'I wonder you believe in such rubbish,' says my wife at the conclusion of my tale.

I shrug my shoulders and answer nothing, for who are so obstinate as those who persist in disbelieving everything that they cannot understand?

It was little more than a week later that, walking by myself along Pall Mall one afternoon, I suddenly came upon Jack Darent walking towards me.

'Hallo, Jack! Back again? Why, man, how odd you look!'

There was a change in the man that I was instantly aware of. His frank, careless face looked clouded and anxious, and the merry smile was missing from his handsome countenance.

'Come into the Club, Fred,' he said, taking me by the arm. 'I have something to say to you.'

He drew me into a corner of the Club smoking-room.

'You were quite right. I wish to Heaven I had never gone to that house.'

'You mean—have you seen anything?' I inquired eagerly.

'I have seen *everything*,' he answered with a shudder. 'They say one dies within a year—'

'My dear fellow, don't be so upset about it,' I interrupted; I was quite distressed to see how thoroughly the man had altered.

'Let me tell you about it, Fred.'

He drew his chair close to mine and told me his story,

pretty nearly in the following words:

'You remember the day I went down you had kept me talking at the Club door; I had a race to catch the train; however, I just did it. I found the other fellows all waiting for me. There was Charlie Wells, the two Harfords, old Colonel Riddell, who is such a crack shot, two fellows in the Guards, both pretty fair, a man called Thompson, a barrister, Henderson and myself—nine of us in all. We had a remarkably lively journey down, as you may imagine, and reached Varley Grange in the highest possible spirits. We all slept like tops that night.

'The next day we were out from eleven till dusk among the coverts, and a better day's shooting I never enjoyed in the whole course of my life, the birds literally swarmed. We bagged a hundred and thirty brace. We were all pretty well tired when we got home, and did full justice to a very good dinner and first-class Perrier-Jouet. After dinner we adjourned to the hall to smoke. This hall is quite the feature of the house. It is large and bright, panelled half-way up with sombre old oak, and vaulted with heavy carved oaken rafters. At the farther end runs a gallery, into which opened the door of my bedroom, and shut off from the rest of the passages by a swing door at either end.

'Well, all we fellows sat up there smoking and drinking brandy and soda, and jawing, you know—as men always do when they are together—about sport of all kinds, hunting and shooting and salmon-fishing; and I assure you not one of us had a thought in our heads beyond relating some wonderful incident of a long shot or big fence by which we could each cap the last speaker's experiences. We were just, I recollect, listening to a long story of the old Colonel's, about his experiences among bisons in Cachemire, when suddenly one of us—I can't remember who it was—gave a sort of shout and started to his feet, pointing up to the gallery behind us. We all turned round, and there—I give you my word of honour, Lester—stood a man leaning over the rail of the gallery, staring down upon us.

'We all saw him. Every one of us. Nine of us, remember.

He stood there full ten seconds, looking down with horrible glittering eyes at us. He had a long tawny beard, and his hands, that were crossed together before him, were nothing but skin and bone. But it was his face that was so unspeakably dreadful. It was livid—the face of a dead man!'

'How was he dressed?'

'I could not see; he wore some kind of a black cloak over his shoulders, I think, but the lower part of his figure was hidden behind the railings. Well, we all stood perfectly speechless for, as I said, about ten seconds; and then the figure moved, backing slowly into the door of the room behind him, which stood open. It was the door of my bedroom! As soon as he had disappeared our senses seemed to return to us. There was a general rush for the staircase, and, as you may imagine, there was not a corner of the house that was left unsearched; my bedroom especially was ransacked in every part of it. But all in vain; there was not the slightest trace to be found of any living being. You may suppose that not one of us slept that night. We lighted every candle and lamp we could lay hands upon and sat up till daylight, but nothing more was seen.

'The next morning, at breakfast, Henderson, who seemed very much annoyed by the whole thing, begged us not to speak of it any more. He said that he had been told, before he had taken the house, that it was supposed to be haunted; but, not being a believer in such childish follies, he had paid but little attention to the rumour. He did not, however, want it talked about, because of the servants, who would be so easily frightened. He was quite certain, he said, that the figure we had seen last night must be somebody dressed up to practise a trick upon us, and he recommended us all to bring our guns down loaded after dinner, but meanwhile to forget the startling apparition as far as we could.

'We, of course, readily agreed to do as he wished, although I do not think that one of us imagined for a moment that any amount of dressing-up would be able to simulate the awful countenance that we had all of us seen too plainly. It would have taken a Hare or an Arthur Cecil, with all the theatrical appliances known only to those two talented actors, to have "made-up" the face, that was literally that of a corpse. Such a person could not be amongst us—actually in the house— without our knowledge.

'We had another good day's shooting, and by degrees the fresh air and exercise and the excitement of the sport obliterated the impression of what we had seen in some measure from the minds of most of us. That evening we all appeared in the hall after dinner with our loaded guns beside us; but, although we sat up till the small hours and looked frequently up at the gallery at the end of the hall, nothing at all disturbed us that night.

'Two nights thus went by and nothing further was seen of the gentleman with the tawny beard. What with the good company, the good cheer and the pheasants, we had pretty well forgotten all about him.

'We were sitting as usual upon the third night, with our pipes and our cigars; a pleasant glow from the bright wood fire in the great chimney lighted up the old hall, and shed a genial warmth about us; when suddenly it seemed to me as if there came a breath of cold, chill air behind me, such as one feels when going down into some damp, cold vault or cellar.

'A strong shiver shook me from head to foot. Before even I saw it I *knew* that It was there.

'It leant over the railing of the gallery and looked down at us all just as it had done before. There was no change in the attitude, no alteration in the fixed, malignant glare in those stony, lifeless eyes; no movement in the white and bloodless features. Below, amongst the nine of us gathered there, there arose a panic of terror. Nine strong, healthy, well-educated nineteenth-century Englishmen, and yet I am not ashamed to say that we were paralysed with fear. Then one, more quickly recovering his senses than the rest, caught at his gun, that leant against the wide chimney-corner, and fired.

'The hall was filled with smoke, but as it cleared away every one of us could see the figure of our supernatural visitant slowly backing, as he had done on the previous occasion, into the chamber behind him, with something like a sardonic smile of scornful derision upon his horrible, death-like face.

'The next morning it is a singular and remarkable fact that five out of the nine of us received by the morning post —so they stated—letters of importance which called them up to town by the very first train! One man's mother was ill, another had to consult his lawyer, whilst pressing engagements, to which they could assign no definite name, called away the other three.

'There were left in the house that day but four of us— Wells, Bob Harford, our host, and myself. A sort of dogged determination not to be worsted by a scare of this kind kept us still there. The morning light brought a return of common sense and of natural courage to us. We could manage to laugh over last night's terrors whilst digesting our bacon and kidneys and hot coffee at the late breakfast in the pleasant morning-room, with the sunshine streaming cheerily in through the diamond-paned windows.

'"It *must* be a delusion of our brains," said one.

'"Our host's champagne," suggested another.

'"A well-organized hoax," opined a third.

'"I will tell you what we will do," said our host. "Now that those other fellows have all gone—and I suppose we don't any of us believe much in those elaborate family reasons which have so unaccountably summoned them away—we four will sit up regularly night after night and watch for this thing, whatever it may be. I do not believe in ghosts. However, this morning I have taken the trouble to go out before breakfast to see the Rector of the parish, an old gentleman who is well up in all the traditions of the neighbourhood, and I have learnt from him the whole of the supposed story of our friend of the tawny beard, which, if you like, I will relate to you."

'Henderson then proceeded to tell us the tradition concerning the Dennis Varley who murdered his sister, the nun —a story which I will not repeat to you, Lester, as I see you know it already.

'The clergyman had furthermore told him that the figure of the murdered nun was also sometimes seen in the same gallery, but that this was a very rare occurrence. When both the murderer and his victim are seen together terrible misfortunes are sure to assail the unfortunate living man who sees them; and if the nun's face is revealed, death within the year is the doom of the ill-fated person who has seen it.

' "Of course," concluded our host, "I consider all these stories to be absolutely childish. At the same time I cannot help thinking that some human agency—probably a gang of thieves or housebreakers—is at work, and that we shall probably be able to unearth an organized system of villainy by which the rogues, presuming on the credulity of the persons who have inhabited the place, have been able to plant themselves securely among some secret passages and hidden rooms in the house, and have carried on their depredations undiscovered and unsuspected. Now, will all of you help me to unravel this mystery?"

'We all promised readily to do so. It is astonishing how brave we felt at eleven o'clock in the morning; what an amount of pluck and courage each man professed himself to be endued with; how lightly we jested about the "old boy with the beard", and what jokes we cracked about the murdered nun!

' "She would show her face oftener if she was good-looking. No fear of her looking at Bob Harford, he was too ugly. It was Jack Darent who was the showman of the party; she'd be sure to make straight for him if she could, he was always run after by the women," and so on, till we were all laughing loudly and heartily over our own witticisms. That was eleven o'clock in the morning.

'At eleven o'clock at night we could have given a very different report of ourselves.

'At eleven o'clock at night each man took up his appointed post in solemn and somewhat depressed silence.

'The plan of our campaign had been carefully organized by our host. Each man was posted separately with about thirty yards between them, so that no optical delusion, such as an effect of firelight upon the oak panelling, nor any reflection from the circular mirror over the chimney-piece, should be able to deceive more than one of us. Our host fixed himself in the very centre of the hall, facing the gallery at the end; Wells took up his position half-way up the short, straight flight of steps; Harford was at the top of the stairs upon the gallery itself; I was opposite to him at the further end. In this manner, whenever the figure—ghost or burglar —should appear, it must necessarily be between two of us, and be seen from both the right and the left side. We were prepared to believe that one amongst us might be deceived by his senses or by his imagination, but it was clear that two persons could not see the same object from a different point of view and be simultaneously deluded by any effect of light or any optical hallucination.

'Each man was provided with a loaded revolver, a brandy and soda and a sufficient stock of pipes or cigars to last him through the night. We took up our positions at eleven o'clock exactly, and waited.

'At first we were all four very silent and, as I have said before, slightly depressed; but as the hour wore away and nothing was seen or heard we began to talk to each other. Talking, however, was rather a difficulty. To begin with, we had to shout—at least we in the gallery had to shout to Henderson, down in the hall; and though Harford and Wells could converse quite comfortably, I, not being able to see the latter at all from my end of the gallery, had to pass my remarks to him second-hand through Harford, who amused himself in misquoting every intelligent remark that I entrusted him with; added to which natural impediments to the "flow of the soul", the elements thought fit to create such a hullabaloo outside that conversation was rendered still further a work of difficulty.

'I never remember such a night in all my life. The rain came down in torrents; the wind howled and shrieked wildly amongst the tall chimneys and the bare elm-trees without. Every now and then there was a lull, and then, again and again, a long sobbing moan came swirling round and round the house, for all the world like the cry of a human being in agony. It was a night to make one shudder, and thank Heaven for a roof over one's head.

'We all sat on at our separate posts hour after hour, listening to the wind and talking at intervals; but as the time wore on insensibly we became less and less talkative, and a sort of depression crept over us.

'At last we relapsed into a profound silence; then suddenly there came upon us all that chill blast of air, like a breath from a charnel-house, that we had experienced before, and almost simultaneously a hoarse cry broke from Henderson in the body of the hall below, and from Wells half-way up the stairs.

'Harford and I sprang to our feet, and we too saw it.

'The dead man was slowly coming up the stairs. He passed silently up with a sort of still, gliding motion, within a few inches of poor Wells, who shrank back, white with terror, against the wall. Henderson rushed wildly up the staircase in pursuit, whilst Harford and I, up on the gallery fell instinctively back at his approach.

'He passed between us.

'We saw the glitter of his sightless eyes—the shrivelled skin upon his withered face—the mouth that fell away, like the mouth of a corpse, beneath his tawny beard. We felt the cold death-like blast that came with him, and the sickening horror of his terrible presence. Ah! can I ever forget it?'

With a strong shudder Jack Darent buried his face in his hands, and seemed too much overcome for some minutes to be able to proceed.

'My dear fellow, are you *sure*?' I said in an awe-struck whisper.

He lifted his head.

'Forgive me, Lester; the whole business has shaken my nerves so thoroughly that I have not yet been able to get over it. But I have not yet told you the worst.'

'Good heavens—is there worse?' I ejaculated.

He nodded.

'No sooner,' he continued, 'had this awful creature passed

us than Harford clutched at my arm and pointed to the further end of the gallery.

'"Look!" he cried hoarsely, "the nun!"'

'There, coming towards us from the opposite direction, was the veiled figure of a nun.

'There were the long, flowing black and white garments —the gleam of the crucifix at her neck—the jangle of her rosary-beads from her waist; but her face was hidden.

'A sort of desperation seized me. With a violent effort over myself, I went towards this fresh apparition.

'"It *must* be a hoax," I said to myself, and there was a half-formed intention in my mind of wrenching aside the flowing draperies and of seeing for myself who and what it was. I strode towards the figure—I stood within half a yard of it. The nun raised her head slowly—and, Lester—*I saw her face!*'

There was a moment's silence.

'What was it like, Jack?' I asked him presently.

He shook his head.

'That I can never tell to any living creature.'

'Was it so horrible?'

He nodded assent, shuddering.

'And what happened next?'

'I believe I fainted. At all events I remembered nothing further. They made me go to the vicarage the next day. I was so knocked over by it all—I was quite ill. I could not have stayed in the house. I stopped there all yesterday, and I got up to town this morning. I wish to Heaven I had taken your advice, old man, and had never gone to that horrible house.'

'I wish you had, Jack,' I answered fervently.

'Do you know that I shall die within the year?' he asked me presently.

I tried to pooh-pooh it.

'My dear fellow, don't take the thing so seriously as all that. Whatever may be the meaning of these horrible apparitions, there can be nothing but an old wife's fable in *that* saying. Why on earth should you die—you of all people, a great strong fellow with a constitution of iron? You don't look much like dying!'

'For all that I shall die. I cannot tell you why I am so certain —but I know that it will be so,' he answered in a low voice. 'And some terrible misfortune will happen to Harford—the other two never saw her—it is he and I who are doomed.'

A year has passed away. Last summer fashionable society rang for a week or more with the tale of poor Bob Harford's misfortune. The girl whom he was engaged to, and to whom he was devotedly attached—young, beautiful and wealthy— ran away on the eve of her wedding-day with a drinking, swindling villain who had been turned out of ever so many clubs and tabooed for ages by every respectable man in town, and who had nothing but a handsome face and a fascinating manner to recommend him, and who by dint of these had succeeded in gaining a complete ascendancy over the fickle heart of poor Bob's lovely fiancée. As to Harford, he sold out and went off to the backwoods of Canada, and has never been heard of since.

And what of Jack Darent? Poor, handsome Jack, with his tall figure and his bright, happy face, and the merry blue eyes that had wiled Bella Lester's heart away! Alas! far away in Southern Africa, poor Jack Darent lies in an unknown grave—slain by a Zulu assegai on the fatal plain of Isandula!

And Bella goes about clad in sable garments, heavy-eyed and stricken with sore grief. A widow in heart, if not in name.

My Favourite Murder

by

AMBROSE BIERCE

It is not surprising that Ambrose Bierce (1842–1913?) should have grown up into a neurotic twisted man, proud of being called 'Bitter' Bierce by newspaper colleagues, and described as 'obnoxious' by his home-town paper when it reported his decoration in the American Civil War. His father, Marcus Aurelius Bierce, was a weak man dominated by his wife and his fierce Calvinism. His strangest feat was in naming all of his thirteen children with names beginning with 'A'. At the age of 19, Bierce enlisted in the Ninth Indiana Volunteers, at the outbreak of the Civil War, and it has been suggested that this was more to get away from home than to fight for his country. Either way, Bierce was a success in the Army and after his discharge, turned his talents to what was then the next best thing to fighting— journalism. In those days, journalists carried guns and often had occasion to use them. Bierce excelled at the type of newspaper work then in vogue and indulged his acid writing talents to the full. In 1913, an old and still bitter man, he crossed into Mexico to cover the civil war then raging, and was never seen again.

'My Favourite Murder' is a unique story by Bierce. I cannot ascertain it having appeared in this country before, so this is probably its debut here. It has certainly been out of print for over 60 years. Apart from being quite shocking at face value, underneath it all lies the dreadful cynicism and callous desire to shock that made

Ambrose Bierce the most unique author of his era.

Having murdered my mother under circumstances of singular atrocity, I was arrested and put upon my trial, which lasted seven years. In charging the jury, the judge of the Court of Acquittal remarked that it was one of the most ghastly crimes that he had ever been called upon to explain away.

At this, my attorney rose and said:

'May it please your Honour, crimes are ghastly or agreeable only by comparison. If you were familiar with the details of my client's previous murder of his uncle you would discern in his later offence (if offence it may be called) something in the nature of tender forbearance and filial consideration for the feelings of the victim. The appalling ferocity of the former assassination was indeed inconsistent with any hypothesis but that of guilt; and had it not been for the fact that the honourable judge before whom he was tried was the president of a life insurance company that took risks on hanging, and in which my client held a policy, it is hard to see how he could decently have been acquitted. If your Honour would like to hear about it for instruction and guidance of your Honour's mind, this unfortunate man, my client, will consent to give himself the pain of relating it under oath.'

The district attorney said: 'Your Honour, I object. Such a statement would be in the nature of evidence, and the testimony in this case is closed. The prisoner's statement should have been introduced three years ago, in the spring of 1881.'

'In a statutory sense,' said the judge, 'you are right, and in the Court of Objections and Technicalities you would get a ruling in your favour. But not in a Court of Acquittal. The objection is overruled.'

'I except,' said the district attorney.

'You cannot do that,' the judge said. 'I must remind you that in order to take an exception you must first get this case transferred for a time to the Court of Exceptions on a formal motion duly supported by affidavits. A motion to that effect by your predecessor in office was denied by me during the first year of this trial. Mr Clerk, swear the prisoner.'

The customary oath having been administered, I made the following statement, which impressed the judge with so strong a sense of the comparative triviality of the offence for which I was on trial that he made no further search for mitigating circumstances, but simply instructed the jury to acquit, and I left the court, without a stain upon my reputation:

'I was born in 1856 in Kalamakee, Mich., of honest and reputable parents, one of whom Heaven has mercifully spared to comfort me in my later years. In 1867 the family came to California and settled near Nigger Head, where my father opened a road agency and prospered beyond the dreams of avarice. He was a reticent, saturnine man then, though his increasing years have now somewhat relaxed the austerity of his disposition, and I believe that nothing but his memory of the sad event for which I am now on trial prevents him from manifesting a genuine hilarity.

'Four years after we had set up the road agency an itinerant preacher came along, and having no other way to pay for the night's lodging that we gave him, favoured us with an exhortation of such power that, praise God, we were all converted to religion. My father at once sent for his brother, the Hon. William Ridley of Stockton, and on his arrival turned over the agency to him, charging him nothing for the franchise nor plant—the latter consisting of a Winchester rifle, a sawed-off shotgun, and an assortment of masks made out of flour sacks. The family then moved to Ghost Rock and opened a dance house. It was called "The Saints' Rest Hurdy-Gurdy", and the proceedings each night began with prayer. It was there that my now sainted mother, by her grace in the dance, acquired the *sobriquet* of "The Bucking Walrus".

'In the fall of '75 I had occasion to visit Coyote, on the road to Mahala, and took the stage at Ghost Rock. There were four other passengers. About three miles beyond Nigger Head, persons whom I identified as my Uncle William and his two sons held up the stage. Finding nothing in the express box, they went through the passengers. I acted a most honourable part in the affair, placing myself in line with the others, holding up my hands and permitting myself to be deprived of forty dollars and a gold watch. From my behaviour no one could have suspected that I knew the gentlemen who gave the entertainment. A few days later, when I went to Nigger Head and asked for the return of my money and watch, my uncle and cousins swore they knew nothing of the matter, and they affected a belief that my father and I had done the job ourselves in dishonest violation of commercial good faith. Uncle William even threatened to retaliate by starting an opposition dance house at Ghost Rock. As "The Saints' Rest" had become rather unpopular, I saw that this would assuredly ruin it and prove a paying enterprise, so I told my uncle that I was willing to overlook the past if he would take me into the scheme and keep the partnership a secret from my father. This fair offer he rejected, and I then perceived that it would be better and more satisfactory if he were dead.

'My plans to that end were soon perfected, and communicating them to my dear parents I had the gratification of receiving their approval. My father said he was proud of me, and my mother promised that although her religion forbade her to assist in taking human life I should have the advantage of her prayers for my success. As a preliminary measure looking to my security in case of detection I made an application for membership in that powerful order, the Knights of Murder, and in due course was received as a member of the Ghost Rock commandery. On the day that my probation ended I was for the first time permitted to inspect the records of the order and learn who belonged to it—all the rites of initation having been conducted in masks. Fancy my delight when, in looking over the roll of membership, I found the third name to be that of my uncle, who indeed was junior vice-chancellor of the order! Here was an opportunity exceeding my wildest dreams—to murder I could add insubordination and treachery. It was what my good mother would have called "a Special Providence".

'At about this time something occurred which caused my

cup of joy, already full, to overflow on all sides, a circular cataract of bliss. Three men, strangers in that locality, were arrested for the stage robbery in which I had lost my money and watch. They were brought to trial and, despite my efforts to clear them and fasten the guilt upon three of the most respectable and worthy citizens of Ghost Rock, convicted on the clearest proof. The murder would now be as wanton and reasonless as I could wish.

'One morning I shouldered my Winchester rifle, and going over to my uncle's house, near Nigger Head, asked my Aunt Mary, his wife, if he were at home, adding that I had come to kill him. My aunt replied with her peculiar smile that so many gentlemen called on that errand and were afterwards carried away without having performed it that I must excuse her for doubting my good faith in the matter. She said I did not look as if I could kill anybody, so, as a proof of good faith I levelled my rifle and wounded a Chinaman who happened to be passing the house. She said she knew whole families that could do a thing of that kind, but Bill Ridley was a horse of another colour. She said, however, that I would find him over on the other side of the creek in the sheep lot; and she added that she hoped the best man would win.

'My Aunt Mary was one of the most fair-minded women that I have ever met.

'I found my uncle down on his knees engaged in skinning a sheep. Seeing that he had neither gun nor pistol handy I had not the heart to shoot him, so I approached him, greeted him pleasantly and struck him a powerful blow on the head with the butt of my rifle. I have a very good delivery and Uncle William lay down on his side, then rolled over on his back, spread out his fingers and shivered. Before he could recover the use of his limbs I seized the knife that he had been using and cut his hamstrings. You know, doubtless, that when you sever the *tendo Achillis* the patient has no further use of his leg; it is just the same as if he had no leg. Well, I parted them both, and when he revived he was at my service. As soon as he comprehended the situation, he said:

'"Samuel, you have got the drop on me and can afford to

be generous. I have only one thing to ask of you, and that is that you carry me to the house and finish me in the bosom of my family."

'I told him I thought that a pretty reasonable request and I would do so if he would let me put him into a wheat sack; he would be easier to carry that way and if we were seen by the neighbours *en route* it would cause less remark. He agreed to that, and going to the barn I got a sack. This, however, did not fit him; it was too short and much wider than he; so I bent his legs, forced his knees up against his breast and got him into it that way, tying the sack above his head. He was a heavy man and I had all that I could do to get him on my back, but I staggered along for some distance until I came to a swing that some of the children had suspended to the branch of an oak. Here I laid him down and sat upon him to rest, and the sight of the rope gave me a happy inspiration. In twenty minutes my uncle, still in the sack, swung free to the sport of the wind.

'I had taken down the rope, tied one end tightly about the mouth of the bag, thrown the other across the limb and hauled him up about five feet from the ground. Fastening the other end of the rope also about the mouth of the sack, I had the satisfaction to see my uncle converted into a large, fine pendulum. I must add that he was not himself entirely aware of the nature of the change that he had undergone in his relation to the exterior world, though in justice to a good man's memory I ought to say that I do not think he would in any case have wasted much of my time in vain remonstrance.

'Uncle William had a ram that was famous in all that region as a fighter. It was in a state of chronic constitutional indignation. Some deep disappointment in early life had soured its disposition and it had declared war upon the whole world. To say that it would butt anything accessible is but faintly to express the nature and scope of its military activity : the universe was its antagonist; its methods that of a projectile. It fought like the angels and devils, in mid-air, cleaving the atmosphere like a bird, describing a parabolic curve and descending upon its victim at just the exact angle of incidence to make the most of its velocity and weight. Its momentum, calculated in foot-tons, was something incredible. It had been seen to destroy a four-year-old bull by a single impact upon that animal's gnarly forehead. No stone wall had ever been known to resist its downward swoop; there were no trees tough enough to stay it; it would splinter them into matchwood and defile their leafy honours in the dust. This irascible and implacable brute—this incarnate thunderbolt—this monster of the upper deep, I had seen reposing in the shade of an adjacent tree, dreaming dreams of conquest and glory. It was with a view to summoning it forth to the field of honour that I suspended its master in the manner described.

'Having completed my preparations, I imparted to the avuncular pendulum a gentle oscillation, and retiring to cover behind a contiguous rock, lifted up my voice in a long rasping cry whose diminishing final note was drowned in a noise like that of a swearing cat, which emanated from the sack. Instantly that formidable sheep was upon its feet and had taken in the military situation at a glance. In a few moments it had approached, stamping, to within fifty yards of the swinging foeman, who, now retreating and anon advancing, seemed to invite the fray. Suddenly I saw the beast's head drop earthward as if depressed by the weight of its enormous horns; then a dim, white, wavy streak of sheep prolonged itself from that spot in a generally horizontal direction to within about four yards of a point immediately beneath the enemy. There it struck sharply upward, and before it had faded from my gaze at the place whence it had set out I heard a horrid thump and a piercing scream, and my poor uncle shot forward, with a slack rope higher than the limb to which he was attached. Here the rope tautened with a jerk, arresting his flight, and back he swung in a breathless curve to the other end of his arc. The ram had fallen, a heap of indistinguishable legs, wool and horns, but pulling itself together and dodging as its antagonist swept downward it retired at random, alternately shaking its head

and stamping its fore-feet. When it had backed about the
same distance as that from which it had delivered the assault
it paused again, bowed its head as if in prayer for victory
and again shot forward, dimly visible as before—a prolonging white streak with monstrous undulations, ending with a
sharp ascension. Its course this time was at a right angle to its
former one, and its impatience so great that it struck the
enemy before he had nearly reached the lowest point of his
arc. In consequence he went flying round and round in a
horizontal circle whose radius was about equal to half the
length of the rope, which I forgot to say was nearly twenty
feet long. His shrieks, *crescendo* in approach and *diminuendo*
in recession, made the rapidity of his revolution more obvious to the ear than to the eye. He had evidently not yet
been struck in a vital spot. His posture in the sack and the
distance from the ground at which he hung compelled the
ram to operate upon his lower extremities and the end of his
back. Like a plant that has struck its root into some poison-
ous mineral, my poor uncle was dying slowly upward.

'After delivering its second blow the ram had not again
retired. The fever of battle burned hot in its heart; its brain
was intoxicated with the wine of strife. Like a pugilist who
in his rage forgets his skill and fights ineffectively at half-
arm's length, the angry beast endeavoured to reach its fleeting foe by awkward vertical leaps as he passed overhead,
sometimes, indeed, succeeding in striking him feebly, but
more frequently overthrown by its own misguided eagerness. But as the impetus was exhausted and the man's circles
narrowed in scope and diminished in speed, bringing him
nearer to the ground, these tactics produced better results,
eliciting a superior quality of screams, which I greatly enjoyed.

'Suddenly, as if the bugles had sung truce, the ram suspended hostilities and walked away, thoughtfully wrinkling
and smoothing its great aquiline nose, and occasionally crop-
ping a bunch of grass and slowly munching it. It seemed to
have tired of war's alarms and resolved to beat the sword into
a plough-share and cultivate the arts of peace. Steadily it

held its course away from the field of fame until it had gained a distance of nearly a quarter of a mile. There it stopped and stood with its rear to the foe, chewing its cud and apparently half asleep. I observed, however, an occasional slight turn of its head, as if its apathy were more affected than real.

'Meantime Uncle William's shrieks had abated with his motion, and nothing was heard from him but long, low moans, and at long intervals my name, uttered in pleading tones exceedingly grateful to my ear. Evidently the man had not the faintest notion of what was being done to him, and was inexpressibly terrified. When Death comes cloaked in mystery he is terrible indeed. Little by little my uncle's oscillations diminished, and finally he hung motionless. I went to him and was about to give him the *coup de grâce*, when I heard and felt a succession of smart shocks which shook the ground like a series of light earthquakes, and turning in the direction of the ram, saw a long cloud of dust approaching me with inconceivable rapidity and alarming effect! At a distance of some thirty yards away it stopped short, and from the near end of it rose into the air what I at first thought a great white bird. Its ascent was so smooth and easy and regular that I could not realize its extraordinary celerity, and was lost in admiration of its grace. To this day the impression remains that it was a slow, deliberate movement, the ram—for it was that animal—being upborne by some power other than its own impetus, and supported through the successive stages of its flight with infinite tenderness and care. My eyes followed its progress through the air with unspeakable pleasure, all the greater by contrast with my former terror of its approach by land. Onward and upward the noble animal sailed, its head bent down almost between its knees, its fore-feet thrown back, its hinder legs trailing to rear like the legs of a soaring heron.

'At a height of forty or fifty feet, as fond recollection presents it to view, it attained its zenith and appeared to remain an instant stationary; then, tilting suddenly forward without altering the relative position of its parts, it shot downward on a steeper and steeper course with augmenting velocity, passed immediately above me with a noise like the rush of a cannon shot and struck my poor uncle almost squarely on the top of the head! So frightful was the impact that not only the man's neck was broken, but the rope too; and the body of the deceased, forced against the earth, was crushed to pulp beneath the awful front of that meteoric sheep! The concussion stopped all the clocks between Lone Hand and Dutch Dan's, and Professor Davidson, a distinguished authority in matters seismic, who happened to be in the vicinity, promptly explained that the vibrations were from north to southwest.

'Altogether, I cannot help thinking that in point of artistic atrocity my murder of Uncle William has seldom been excelled.'

The Shadow in the Moonlight

by

MRS MOLESWORTH

Nearly a hundred years later, the children's stories written by Mrs Mary Molesworth (1839–1921) are being reprinted, a glowing tribute to one of the finest writers of tales for young people this country has produced. In the forty-year period between 1870 and 1911, Mrs Molesworth produced well over 100 books, all mainly for children. However, in common with many of her Victorian female counterparts, she had a fascination for ghost stories and produced two complete volumes, Four Ghost Stories (1888) and Uncanny Tales (1896). 'The Shadow in the Moonlight' is a splendid example of the Victorian ghost story, with its haunted castle by the sea and wandering ghost seeking rest. Hardly surprisingly, the first to perceive Mrs Molesworth's spectral creation are children.

We never thought of Finster St Mabyn's being haunted. We really never did.

This may seem strange, but it is absolutely true. It was such an extremely interesting and curious place in many ways that it required nothing extraneous to add to its attractions. Perhaps this was the reason. Nowadays, immediately that you hear of a house being 'very old', the next remark is sure to be 'I hope it is'—or 'is not'—that depends on the taste of the speaker—'haunted'.

But Finster was more than very old; it was *ancient* and, in a modest way, historical. I will not take up time by relating its history, however, or by referring my readers to the chronicles in which mention of it may be found. Nor shall I yield to the temptation of describing the room in which a certain royalty spent one night, if not two or three nights, four centuries ago, or the tower, now in ruins, where an even more renowned personage was imprisoned, for several months. All these facts—or legends—have nothing to do with what I have to tell. Nor, strictly speaking, has Finster itself, except as a sort of prologue to my narrative.

We heard of the house through friends living in the same county, though some distance farther inland. They—Mr and Miss Miles, it is convenient to give their name at once—knew that we had been ordered to leave our own home for some months, to get over the effects of a very trying visitation of influenza, and that sea-air was specially desirable.

We grumbled at this. Seaside places are often so dull and commonplace. But when we heard of Finster we grumbled no longer.

'Dull' in a sense it might be, but assuredly not 'commonplace'. Janet Miles's description of it, though she was not particularly clever at description, read like a fairy tale, or one of Longfellow's poems.

'A castle by the sea—how perfect!' we all exclaimed. 'Do, oh, do fix for it, Mother!'

The objections were quickly over-ruled. It was rather isolated, said Miss Miles, standing, as was not difficult to trace in its name, on a point of land—a corner rather—with sea on two sides. It had not been lived in, save spasmodically, for some years, for the late owner was one of those happy, or unhappy people, who have more houses than they can use, and the present one was a minor. Eventually it was to be overhauled and some additions and alterations made, but the trustees would be glad to let it at a moderate rent for some months, and had intended putting it into some agents' hands when Mr Miles happened to meet one of them, who mentioned it to him. There was nothing against it; it was absolutely healthy. But the furniture was old and shabby, and there was none too much of it. If we wanted to have visitors we should

certainly require to add to it. This, however, could easily
be done, our informant went on to say. There was a very
good upholsterer and furniture dealer at Raxtrew, the nearest
town, who was in the habit of hiring out things to the officers
at the fort. 'Indeed,' she added, 'we often pick up charming
old pieces of furniture from him for next to nothing, so you
could both hire and buy.'

Of course, we should have visitors—and our own house
would not be the worse for some additional chairs and tables
here and there, in place of some excellent monstrosities Phil
and Nugent and I had persuaded Mother to get rid of.

'If I go down to spy the land with Father,' I said, 'I shall
certainly go to the furniture dealer's and have a good look
about me.'

I did go with Father. I was nineteen—it is four years ago—
and a capable sort of girl. Then I was the only one who had
not been ill, and Mother had been the worst of all, Mother
and Dormy—poor little chap—for *he* nearly died.

He is the youngest of us—we are four boys and two girls.
Sophy was then fifteen. My own name is Leila.

If I attempted to give any idea of the impression Finster
St Mabyn's made upon us, I should go on for hours. It simply
took our breath away. It really felt like going back a few
centuries merely to enter within the walls and gaze round
you. And yet we did not see it to any advantage, so at least
said the two Miles's who were our guides. It was a gloomy
day, with the feeling of rain not far off, early in April. It
might have been November, though it was not cold.

'You can scarcely imagine what it is on a bright day,' said
Janet, eager, as people always are in such circumstances, to
show off her *trouvaille*. 'The lights and shadows are so exquisite.'

'I love it as it is,' I said. 'I don't think I shall ever regret
having seen it first on a grey day. It is just perfect.'

She was pleased at my admiration, and did her utmost to
facilitate matters. Father was taken with the place, too, I
could see, but he hummed and hawed a good deal about the
bareness of the rooms—the bedrooms especially. So Janet and

I went into it at once in a businesslike way, making lists of the actually necessary additions, which did not prove very formidable after all.

'Hunter will manage all that *easily*,' said Miss Miles, upon which Father gave in—I believe he had meant to do so all the time. The rent was really so low that a little furniture-hire could be afforded, I suggested. And Father agreed. 'It is extremely low,' he said, 'for a place possessing so many advantages.'

But even then it did not occur to any of us to suggest 'suspiciously low'.

We had the Miles's guarantee for it all, to begin with. Had there been any objection they must have known it. We spent the night with them and the next morning at the furniture dealer's. He was a quick, obliging little man, and took in the situation at a glance. And *his* terms were so moderate that Father said to me amiably: 'There are some quaint odds and ends here, Leila. You might choose a few things, to use at Finster in the first place, and then to take home with us.'

I was only too ready to profit by the permission, and with Janet's help a few charmingly quaint chairs and tables, a three-cornered wall cabinet, and some other trifles were soon put aside for us. We were just leaving, when at one end of the shop some tempting-looking draperies caught my eye.

'What are these?' I asked the upholsterer. 'Curtains! Why, this is real old tapestry!'

The obliging Hunter drew out the material in question.

'They are not exactly curtains, miss,' he said. 'I thought they would make nice *portières*. You see the tapestry is set into cloth. It was so frail when I got it that it was the only thing to do with it.'

He had managed it very ingeniously. Two panels, so to say, of old tapestry, very charming in tone, had been lined and framed with dull green cloth, making a very good pair of *portières* indeed.

'Oh, Papa!' I cried, 'do let us have these. There are sure

to be draughty doors at Finster, and afterwards they would make perfect *portières* for the two side doors in the hall at home.'

Father eyed the tapestry appreciatively, but first prudently inquired the price. It seemed higher in proportion than Hunter's other charges.

'You see, sir,' he said half apologetically, 'the panels are real antique work, though so much the worse for wear.'

'Where did they come from?' asked Father.

Hunter hesitated.

'To tell you the truth, sir,' he replied, 'I was asked not to name the party that I bought it from. It seems a pity to part with heir-looms, but—it happens sometimes—I bought several things together of a family quite lately. The *portières* have only come out of the workroom this morning. We hurried on with them to stop them fraying more—you see where they were before, they must have been nailed to the wall.'

Janet Miles, who was something of a connoisseur, had been examining the tapestry.

'It is well worth what he asks,' she said, in a low voice. 'You don't often come across such tapestry in England.'

So the bargain was struck, and Hunter promised to see all that we had chosen, both purchased and hired, delivered at Finster the week before we proposed to come.

Nothing interfered with our plans. By the end of the month we found ourselves at our temporary home—all of us except Nat, our third brother, who was at school. Dormer, the small boy, still did lessons with Sophy's governess. The two older 'boys', as we called them, happened to be at home for different reasons—one, Nugent, on leave from India; Phil, forced to miss a term at college through an attack of the same illness which had treated Mother and Dormy so badly.

But now that everybody was well again, and going to be much better, thanks to Finster air, we thought the ill wind had brought us some very distinct good. It would not have been half such fun had we not been a large family party to start with, and before we had been a week at the place we had added to our numbers by the first detachment of the guests we had invited.

It was not a very large house; besides ourselves we had not room for more than three or four others. For some of the rooms—those on the top storey—were really too dilapidated to suit anyone but rats—'rats or ghosts'—said someone laughingly one day, when we had been exploring them. Afterwards the words returned to my memory.

We had made ourselves very comfortable, thanks to the invaluable Hunter. And every day the weather grew milder and more spring-like. The woods on the inland side were full of primroses. It promised to be a lovely season. There was a gallery along one side of the house, which soon became a favourite resort; it made a pleasant lounging-place, in the day-time especially, though less so in the evening, as the fireplace at one end warmed it but imperfectly, and besides this it was difficult to light up. It was draughty, too, as there was a superfluity of doors, two of which, one at each end, we at once condemned. They were not needed, as the one led by a very long spiral staircase to the unused attic rooms, the other to the kitchen and offices. And when we did have afternoon tea in the gallery, it was easy to bring it through the dining- or drawing-rooms, long rooms, lighted at their extreme ends, which ran parallel to the gallery lengthways, both of which had a door opening on to it as well as from the hall on the other side. For all the principal rooms at Finster were on the first floor, not on the ground floor.

The closing of these doors got rid of a great deal of draught, and, as I have said, the weather was really mild and calm.

One afternoon—I am trying to begin at the beginning of our strange experiences; even at the risk of long-windedness it seems better to do so—we were all assembled in the gallery at tea-time. The 'children', as we called Sophy and Dormer, much to Sophy's disgust, and their governess, were with us, for rules were relaxed at Finster, and Miss Larpent was a great favourite with us all.

Suddenly Sophy gave an exclamation of annoyance.

'Mamma,' she said, 'I wish you would speak to Dormer. He has thrown over my tea-cup—only look at my frock! If you cannot sit still,' she added, turning herself to the boy, 'I don't think you should be allowed to come to tea here.'

'What is the matter, Dormy?' said Mother.

Dormer was standing beside Sophy, looking very guilty, and rather white.

'Mamma,' he said, 'I was only drawing a chair out. It got so dreadfully cold where I was sitting, I really could not stay there,' and he shivered slightly.

He had been sitting with his back to one of the locked-up doors. Phil, who was nearest, moved his hand slowly across the spot.

'You are fanciful, Dormy,' he said, 'there is really no draught whatever.'

This did not satisfy Mother.

'He must have got a chill, then,' she said, and she went on to question the child as to what he had been doing all day, for, as I have said, he was still delicate.

But he persisted that he was quite well, and no longer cold.

'It wasn't exactly a draught,' he said, 'it was—oh! just icy, all of a sudden. I've felt it before—sitting in that chair.'

Mother said no more, and Dormer went on with his tea, and when bed-time came he seemed just as usual, so that her anxiety faded. But she made thorough investigation as to the possibility of any draught coming up from the back stairs, with which this door communicated. None was to be discovered—the door fitted fairly well, and beside this, Hunter had tacked felt round the edges—furthermore, one of the thick heavy portières had been hung in front. An evening or two later we were sitting in the drawing-room after dinner, when a cousin who was staying with us suddenly missed her fan.

'Run and fetch Muriel's fan, Dormy,' I said, for Muriel felt sure it had slipped under the dinner table. None of the men had as yet joined us.

'Why, where are you going, child?' as he turned towards the farther door. 'It is much quicker by the gallery.' He said nothing, but went out, walking rather slowly, by the gallery door. And in a few minutes he returned, fan in hand, but by the *other* door.

He was a sensitive child, and though I wondered what he had got into his head against the gallery, I did not say anything before the others. But when, soon after, Dormy said 'Good night,' and went off to bed, I followed him. 'What do you want, Leila?' he said rather crossly. 'Don't be vexed, child,' I said. 'I can see there is something the matter. Why do you not like the gallery?'

He hesitated, but I had laid my hand on his shoulder, and he knew I meant to be kind.

'Leila,' he said, with a glance round, to be sure that no one was within hearing—we were standing, he and I, near the inner dining-room door, which was open—'you'll laugh at me, but—there's something queer there—sometimes!'

'What? And how do you mean "sometimes"?' I asked, with a slight thrill at his tone.

'I mean not always, I've felt it several times—there was the cold the day before yesterday, and besides that, I've felt a—a sort of *breaving*'—Dormy was not perfect in his 'th's'—'like somebody very unhappy.'

'Sighing?' I suggested.

'Like sighing in a whisper,' he replied, 'and that's always near the door. But last week—no, not so long ago, it was on Monday—I went round that way when I was going to bed. I didn't want to be silly. But it was moonlight—and—Leila, a shadow went all along the wall on that side, and stopped at the door. I saw it waggling about—its *hands*' and here he shivered—'on that funny curtain that hangs up, as if it were feeling for a minute or two, and then—'

'Well—what then?'

'It just went out,' he said simply. 'But it's moonlight again tonight, sister, and I daren't see it again. I just *daren't*.'

'But you did go to the dining-room that way,' I reminded him.

'Yes, but I shut my eyes and ran, and even then I felt as if something cold was behind me.'

'Dormy, dear,' I said, a good deal concerned, 'I do think it's your fancy. You are not *quite* well yet, you know.'

'Yes, I am,' he replied sturdily. 'I'm not a bit frightened anywhere else. I sleep in a room alone, you know. It's not *me*, sister, it's somefing in the gallery.'

'Would you be frightened to go there with me now? We can run through the dining-room; there's no one to see us,' and I turned in that direction as I spoke.

Again my little brother hesitated.

'I'll go with you if you'll hold hands,' he said, 'but I'll shut my eyes. And I won't open them till you tell me there's no shadow on the wall. You must tell me truly.'

'But there must be some shadows,' I said, 'in this bright moonlight, trees and branches, or even clouds scudding across —something of that kind is what you must have seen, dear.'

He shook his head.

'No, no, of course I wouldn't mind that. I know the difference. No—you couldn't mistake. It goes along, right along, in a creeping way, and then at the door its hands come farther out, and it *feels*.'

'Is it like a man or a woman?' I said, beginning to feel rather creepy myself.

'I think it's most like a rather little man,' he replied, 'but I'm not sure. Its head has got something fuzzy about it—oh, I know, like a sticking-out wig. But lower down it seems wrapped up, like in a cloak. Oh, it's *horrid*.'

And again he shivered—it was quite time all this nightmare nonsense was put out of his poor little head.

I took his hand and held it firmly; we went through the dining-room. Nothing could have looked more comfortable and less ghostly. For the lights were still burning on the table, and the flowers in their silver bowls, some wine gleaming in the glasses, the fruit and pretty dishes, made a pleasant glow of colour. It certainly seemed a curiously sudden contrast when we found ourselves in the gallery beyond, cold and unillumined, save by the pale moonlight streaming through the unshuttered windows. For the door closed with a bang as we passed through—the gallery *was* a draughty place.

Dormy's hold tightened.

'Sister,' he whispered, 'I've shut my eyes now. You must stand with your back to the windows—between them, or else you'll think it's our own shadows—and watch.'

I did as he said, and I had not long to wait.

It came—from the farther end, the second condemned door, whence the winding stair mounted to the attics—it seemed to begin or at least take form there, creeping along, just as Dormy said—stealthily but steadily—right down to the other extremity of the long room. And then it grew blacker—more concentrated—and out from the vague outline came two bony hands, and, as the child had said, too, you could see that they were *feeling*—all over the upper part of the door.

I stood and watched. I wondered afterwards at my own courage, if courage it was. It was the shadow of a small man, I felt sure. The head seemed large in proportion, and—yes —it—the original of the shadow—was evidently covered by an antique wig. Half mechanically I glanced round—as if in search of the material body that *must* be there. But no; there was nothing, literally *nothing*, that could throw this extraordinary shadow.

Of this I was instantly convinced; and here I may as well say once for all, that never was it maintained by anyone, however previously sceptical, who had fully witnessed the whole, that it could be accounted for by ordinary, or, as people say, 'natural' causes. There was this peculiarity at least about our ghost.

Though I had fast hold of his hand, I had almost forgotten Dormy—I seemed in a trance.

Suddenly he spoke, though in a whisper.

'You see it, sister, I know you do,' he said.

'Wait, wait a minute, dear,' I managed to reply in the same tone, though I could not have explained why I waited. Dormer had said that after a time—after the ghastly and apparently fruitless *feeling* all over the door—'it'—'went out.'

I think it was this that I was waiting for. It was not quite as he had said. The door was in the extreme corner of the wall, the hinges almost in the angle, and as the shadow began to move on again, it *looked* as if it disappeared; but no, it was only fainter. My eyes, preternaturally sharpened by my intense gaze, still saw it, working its way round the corner, as assuredly no *shadow* in the real sense of the word ever did nor could do. I realized this, and the sense of horror grew all but intolerable; yet I stood still, clasping the cold little hand in mine tighter and tighter. And an instinct of protection of the child gave me strength. Besides, it was coming on so quickly—we could not have escaped—it was coming, nay, it *was behind* us.

'Leila!' gasped Dormy, 'the cold—you feel it now?'

Yes, truly—like no icy breath that I had ever felt before was that momentary but horrible thrill of utter cold. If it had lasted another second I think it would have killed us both. But, mercifully, it passed, in far less time than it has taken me to tell it, and then we seemed in some strange way to be released.

'Open your eyes, Dormy,' I said, 'you won't see anything, I promise you. I want to rush across to the dining-room.'

He obeyed me. I felt there was time to escape before that awful presence would again have arrived at the dining-room door, though it was *coming*—ah, yes, it was coming, steadily pursuing its ghastly round. And, alas! the dining-room door was closed. But I kept my nerve to some extent. I turned the handle without over much trembling, and in another moment, the door shut and locked behind us, we stood in safety, looking at each other, in the bright cheerful room we had left so short a time ago.

Was it so short a time? I said to myself. It seemed hours! And through the door open to the hall came at that moment the sound of cheerful laughing voices from the drawing-room. Someone was coming out. It seemed impossible, incredible, that within a few feet of the matter-of-fact pleasant material life, this horrible inexplicable drama should be going on, as doubtless it still was.

Of the two I was now more upset than my little brother. I

was older and 'took in' more. He, boy-like, was in a sense triumphant at having proved himself correct and no coward, and though he was still pale, his eyes shone with excitement and a queer kind of satisfaction.

But before we had done more than look at each other, a figure appeared at the open doorway. It was Sophy.

'Leila,' she said, 'Mamma wants to know what you are doing with Dormy? He is to go to bed at once. We saw you go out of the room after him, and then a door banged. Mamma says if you are playing with him it's very bad for him so late at night.'

Dormy was very quick. He was still holding my hand, and he pinched it to stop my replying.

'Rubbish!' he said. 'I am speaking to Leila quietly, and she is coming up to my room while I undress. Good night, Sophy.'

'Tell Mamma Dormy really wants me,' I added, and then Sophy departed.

'We mustn't tell *her*, Leila,' said the boy. 'She'd have 'sterics.'

'Whom shall we tell?' I said, for I was beginning to feel very helpless and upset.

'Nobody, tonight,' he replied sensibly. 'You *mustn't* go in there,' and he shivered a little as he moved his head towards the gallery; 'you're not fit for it, and they'd be wanting you to. Wait till the morning and then I'd—I think I'd tell Philip first. You needn't be frightened tonight, sister. It won't stop you sleeping. It didn't me the time I saw it before.'

He was right. I slept dreamlessly. It was as if the nervous strain of those few minutes had utterly exhausted me.

Phil is our soldier brother. And there is nothing fanciful about *him*! He is a rock of sturdy common-sense and unfailing good nature. He was the very best person to confide our strange secret to, and my respect for Dormy increased.

We did tell him—the very next morning. He listened very attentively, only putting in a question here and there, and

though, of course, he was incredulous—had I not been so myself?—he was not mocking.

'I am glad you have told no one else,' he said, when we
had related the whole as circumstantially as possible. 'You
see Mother is not very strong yet, and it would be a pity to
bother Father, just when he's taken this place and settled it
all. And for goodness' sake, don't let a breath of it get about
among the servants; there'd be the—something to pay, if you
did.'

'I won't tell anybody,' said Dormy.

'Nor shall I,' I added. 'Sophy is far too excitable, and if she
knew, she would certainly tell Nannie.' Nannie is our old
nurse.

'If we tell anyone,' Philip went on, 'that means,' with a
rather irritating smile of self-confidence, 'if by any possibility
I do not succeed in making an end of your ghost and we
want another opinion about it, the person to tell would be
Miss Larpent.'

'Yes,' I said, 'I think so, too.'

I would not risk irritating him by saying how convinced
I was that conviction awaited *him* as surely it had come to
myself, and I knew that Miss Larpent, though far from credu-
lous, was equally far from stupid scepticism concerning the
mysteries 'not dreamt of' in ordinary 'philosophy'.

'What do you mean to do?' I went on. 'You have a theory,
I see. Won't you tell me what it is?'

'I have two,' said Phil, rolling up a cigarette as he spoke.
'It is either some queer optical illusion, partly the effect of
some odd reflection outside—or it is a clever trick.'

'A trick!' I exclaimed; 'what *possible* motive could there
be for a trick?'

Phil shook his head.

'Ah,' he said, 'that I cannot at present say.'

'And what are you going to do?'

'I shall sit up tonight in the gallery and see for myself.'

'Alone?' I exclaimed, with some misgiving. For big, sturdy
fellow as he was, I scarcely liked to think of him—of *anyone*
—alone with that awful thing.

'I don't suppose you or Dormy would care to keep me company,' he replied, 'and on the whole I would rather not have you.'

'I wouldn't do it,' said the child honestly, 'not for—for nothing.'

'I shall keep Tim with me,' said Philip, 'I would rather have him than anyone.'

Tim is Phil's bull-dog, and certainly, I agreed, much better than nobody.

So it was settled.

Dormy and I went to bed unusually early that night, for as the day wore on we both felt exceedingly tired. I pleaded a headache, which was not altogether a fiction, though I repented having complained at all when I found that poor Mamma immediately began worrying herself with fears that 'after all' I, too, was to fall a victim to the influenza.

'I shall be all right in the morning,' I assured her.

I knew no further details of Phil's arrangements. I fell asleep almost at once. I usually do. And it seemed to me that I had slept a whole night when I was awakened by a glimmering light at my door, and heard Philip's voice speaking softly.

'Are you awake, Lel?' he said, as people always say when they awake you in any untimely way. Of course, *now* I was awake, very much awake indeed.

'What is it?' I exclaimed eagerly, my heart beginning to beat very fast.

'Oh, nothing, nothing at all,' said my brother, advancing a little into the room. 'I just thought I'd look in on my way to bed to reassure you I have seen *nothing*, absolutely nothing.'

I do not know if I was relieved or disappointed.

'Was it moonlight?' I asked abruptly.

'No,' he replied, 'unluckily the moon did not come out at all, though it is nearly at the full. I carried in a small lamp, which made things less eerie. But I should have preferred the moon.'

I glanced up at him. Was it the reflection of the candle he held, or did he look paler than usual?

'And,' I added suddenly, 'did you *feel* nothing?'

He hesitated.

'It—it was chilly, certainly,' he said. 'I fancy I must have dozed a little, for I did feel pretty cold once or twice.'

'Ah, indeed!' thought I to myself. 'And how about Tim?'

Phil smiled, but not very successfully.

'Well,' he said, 'I must confess Tim did not altogether like it. He started snarling, then he growled, and finished up with whining in a decidedly unhappy way. He's rather upset —poor old chap!'

And then I saw that the dog was beside him—rubbing up close to Philip's legs—a very dejected, reproachful Tim—all the starch taken out of him.

'Good night, Phil,' I said, turning round on my pillow. 'I'm glad you are satisfied. Tomorrow morning you must tell me which of your theories holds most water. Good night, and many thanks.'

He was going to say more, but my manner for the moment stopped him, and he went off.

Poor old Phil!

We had it out the next morning. He and I alone. He was *not* satisfied. Far from it. In the bottom of his heart I believe it was a strange yearning for a breath of human companionship, for the sound of a human voice, that had made him look in on me the night before.

For he had felt the cold passing him.

But he was very plucky.

'I'll sit up again tonight, Leila,' he said.

'Not tonight,' I objected. 'This sort of adventure requires one to be at one's best. If you take my advice you will go to bed early and have a good stretch of sleep, so that you will be quite fresh by tomorrow. There will be a moon for some nights still.'

'Why do you keep harping on the moon?' said Phil rather crossly for him.

'Because—I have some idea that it is only in the moonlight that—that anything is to be *seen*.'

'Bosh!' said my brother politely—he was certainly rather

discomposed—'we are talking at cross-purposes. You are satisfied—'

'Far from satisfied,' I interpolated.

'Well, convinced, whatever you like to call it—that the
whole thing is supernatural, whereas I am equally sure it is a
trick; a clever trick, I allow, though I haven't yet got at the
motive of it.'

'You need your nerves to be at their best to discover a
trick of this kind, if a trick it be,' I said quietly.

Philip had left his seat, and walked up and down the room;
his way of doing so gave me a feeling that he wanted to walk
off some unusual consciousness of irritability. I felt half pro-
voked and half sorry for him.

At that moment—we were alone in the drawing-room—
the door opened and Miss Larpent came in.

'I cannot find Sophy,' she said, peering about through her
rather short-sighted eyes, which, nevertheless, see a great deal
sometimes; 'do you know where she is?'

'I saw her setting off somewhere with Nugent,' said Philip,
stopping his quarter-deck exercise for a moment.

'Ah, then it is hopeless. I suppose I must resign myself to
very irregular ways for a little longer,' Miss Larpent replied
with a smile.

She is not young, and not good-looking, but she is gifted
with a delightful way of smiling, and she is—well, the dearest
and almost the wisest of women.

She looked at Philip as she spoke. She had known us nearly
since our babyhood.

'Is there anything the matter?' she said suddenly. 'You
look fagged, Leila, and Philip seems worried.'

I glanced at Philip. He understood me.

'Yes,' he replied, 'I am irritated, and Leila is—' he hesitated.

'What?' asked Miss Larpent.

'Oh, I don't know—obstinate, I suppose. Sit down, Miss
Larpent, and hear our story. Leila, you can tell it.'

I did so—first obtaining a promise of secrecy, and making
Phil relate his own experience.

Our new *confidante* listened attentively, her face very grave. When she had heard all, she said quietly, after a moment's silence: 'It's very strange, very. Philip, if you will wait till tomorrow night, and I quite agree with Leila that you had better do so, I will sit up with you. I have pretty good nerves, and I have always wanted an experience of that kind.'

'Then you don't think it is a trick?' I said eagerly. I was like Dormer, divided between my real underlying longing to explain the thing, and get rid of the horror of it, and a half childish wish to prove that I had not exaggerated its ghastliness.

'I will tell you that the day after tomorrow,' she said. I could not repress a little shiver as she spoke.

She *had* good nerves, and she was extremely sensible.

But I almost blamed myself afterwards for having acquiesced in the plan. For the effect on her was very great. They never told me exactly what happened; 'You know,' said Miss Larpent. I imagine their experience was almost precisely similar to Dormy's and mine, intensified, perhaps, by the feeling of loneliness. For it was not till all the rest of the family was in bed that this second vigil began. It was a bright moonlight night—they had the whole thing complete.

It was impossible to throw off the effect; even in the daytime the four of us who had seen and heard, shrank from the gallery, and made any conceivable excuse for avoiding it.

But Phil, however convinced, behaved consistently. He examined the closed door thoroughly, to detect any possible trickery. He explored the attics, he went up and down the staircase leading to the offices, till the servants must have thought he was going crazy. He found *nothing*—no vaguest hint even as to why the gallery was chosen by the ghostly shadow for its nightly round.

Strange to say, however, as the moon waned, our horror faded, so that we almost began to hope the thing was at an end, and to trust that in time we should forget about it. And we congratulated ourselves that we had kept our own counsel and not disturbed any of the others—even Father, who would, no doubt, have hooted at the idea—by the baleful whisper that our charming castle by the sea was haunted!

And the days passed by, growing into weeks. The second detachment of our guests had left, and a third had just arrived, when one morning as I was waiting at what we called 'the sea-door' for some of the others to join me in a walk along the sands, someone touched me on the shoulder. It was Philip.

'Leila,' he said, 'I am not happy about Dormer. He is looking ill again, and—'

'I thought he seemed so much stronger,' I said, surprised and distressed, 'quite rosy, and so much merrier.'

'So he was till a few days ago,' said Philip. 'But if you notice him well you'll see that he's getting that white look again. And I've got it into my head—he is an extraordinarily sensitive child—that it has something to do with the moon. It's getting on to the full.'

For the moment I stupidly forgot the association.

'Really, Phil,' I said, 'you are too absurd! Do you actually —oh,' as he was beginning to interrupt me, and my face fell, I feel sure—'you don't mean about the gallery.'

'Yes, I do,' he said.

'How? Has Dormy told you anything?' and a sort of sick feeling came over me. 'I had begun to hope,' I went on, 'that somehow it had gone; that, perhaps, it only comes once a year at a certain season, or possibly that newcomers see it at the first and not again. Oh, Phil, we *can't* stay here, however nice it is, if it is really haunted.'

'Dormy hasn't said much,' Philip replied. 'He only told me he had *felt the cold* once or twice, "since the moon came again," he said. But I can see the fear of more is upon him. And this determined me to speak to you. I have to go to London for ten days or so, to see the doctors about my leave, and a few other things. I don't like it for you and Miss Larpent if—if this thing is to return—with no one else in your confidence, especially on Dormy's account. Do you think we must tell Father before I go?'

I hesitated. For many reasons I was reluctant to do so.

Father would be exaggeratedly sceptical at first, and then, if he were convinced, as I *knew* he would be, he would go to the other extreme and insist upon leaving Finster, and there would be a regular upset, trying for Mother and everybody concerned. And Mother liked the place, and was looking so much better!

'After all,' I said, 'it has not hurt any of us. Miss Larpent got a shake, so did I. But it wasn't as great a shock to us as to you, Phil, to have to believe in a ghost. And we can avoid the gallery while you are away. No, except for Dormy, I would rather keep it to ourselves—after all, we are not going to live here always. Yet it is so nice, it seems such a pity.'

It was such an exquisite morning; the air, faintly breathing of the sea, was like elixir; the heights and shadows on the cliffs, thrown out by the darker woods behind, were indeed, as Janet Miles had said, 'wonderful'.

'Yes,' Phil agreed, 'it is an awful nuisance. But as for Dormy,' he went on, 'supposing I get Mother to let me take him with me? He'd be as jolly as a sand-boy in London, and my old landlady would look after him like anything if ever I had to be out late. And I'd let my doctor see him—quietly, you know—he might give him a tonic or something.'

I heartily approved of the idea. So did Mamma when Phil broached it—she, too, had thought her 'baby' looked quite pale lately. A London doctor's opinion would be such a satisfaction. So it was settled, and the very next day the two set off, Dormer, in his 'old-fashioned', reticent way, in the greatest delight, though only by one remark did the brave little fellow hint at what was, no doubt, the principal cause of his satisfaction.

'The moon will be long past the full when we come back,' he said. 'And after that there'll only be one other time before we go, won't there, Leila? We've only got this house for three months?'

'Yes,' I said, 'Father only took it for three,' though in my heart I knew it was with the option of three more—six in all.

And Miss Larpent and I were left alone, not with the ghost, certainly, but with our fateful knowledge of its unwelcome proximity. We did not speak of it to each other, but we tacitly avoided the gallery, even, as much as possible, in the day-time. I felt, and so, she has since confessed, did she, that it would be impossible to endure *that cold* without betraying ourselves.

And I began to breathe more freely, trusting that the dread of the shadow's possible return was really only due to the child's over-wrought nerves.

Till—one morning—my fool's paradise was abruptly destroyed. Father came in late to breakfast—he had been for an early walk, he said, to get rid of a headache. But he did not look altogether as if he had succeeded in doing so.

'Leila,' he said, as I was leaving the room after pouring out his coffee—Mamma was not yet allowed to get up early— 'Leila, don't go. I want to speak to you.'

I stopped short, and turned towards the table. There was something very odd about his manner. He is usually hearty and eager, almost impetuous in his way of speaking.

'Leila,' he began again, 'you are a sensible girl, and your nerves are strong, I fancy. Besides, you have not been ill like the others. Don't speak of what I am going to tell you.'

I nodded in assent; I could scarcely have spoken. My heart was beginning to thump. Father would not have commended my nerves had he known it.

'Something odd and inexplicable happened last night,' he went on. 'Nugent and I were sitting in the gallery. It was a mild night, and the moon magnificent. We thought the gallery would be pleasanter than the smoking-room, now that Phil and his pipes are away. Well—we were sitting quietly. I had lighted my reading-lamp on the little table at one end of the room, and Nugent was half lying in his chair, doing nothing in particular except admiring the night, when all at once he started violently with an exclamation, and, jumping up, came towards me. Leila, his teeth were chattering, and he was *blue* with cold. I was very much alarmed—you know how ill he was at college. But in a moment or two he recovered.

' "What on earth is the matter?" I said to him. He tried

to laugh. ' "I really don't know," he said; "I felt as if I had had an electric shock of *cold*—but I'm all right again now."

'I went into the dining-room, and made him take a little brandy and water, and sent him off to bed. Then I came back, still feeling rather uneasy about him, and sat down with my book, when, Leila—you will scarcely credit it—I myself felt the same shock exactly. A perfectly *hideous* thrill of cold. That was how it began. I started up, and then, Leila, by degrees, in some instinctive way, I seemed to realize what had caused it. My dear child, you will think I have gone crazy when I tell you that there was a shadow—a shadow in the moonlight—*chasing* me, so to say, round the room, and once again it caught me up, and again came that appalling sensation. I would not give in. I dodged it after that, and set myself to watch it, and then—'

I need not quote my father further; suffice to say his experience matched that of the rest of us entirely—no, I think it surpassed them. It was the worst of all.

Poor Father! I shuddered for him. I think a shock of that kind is harder upon a man than upon a woman. Our sex is less sceptical, less entrenched in sturdy matters of fact, more imaginative, or whatever you like to call the readiness to believe what we cannot explain. And it was astounding to me to see how my father at once capitulated—never even *alluding* to a possibility of trickery. Astounding, yet at the same time not without a certain satisfaction in it. It was almost a relief to find others in the same boat with ourselves. I told him at once all *we* had to tell, and how painfully exercised we had been as to the advisability of keeping our secret to ourselves. I never saw Father so impressed; he was awfully kind, too, and so sorry for us. He made me fetch Miss Larpent, and we held a council of—I don't know what to call it!—not 'war', assuredly, for none of us thought of fighting the ghost. How could one fight a shadow? We decided to do nothing beyond endeavouring to keep the affair from going further. During the next few days Father arranged to have some work done in the gallery which would prevent our sitting there, without raising any suspicions on Mamma's or Sophy's part.

'And then,' said Father, 'we must see. Possibly this extraordinary influence only makes itself felt periodically.'

'I am almost certain it is so,' said Miss Larpent.

'And in this case,' he continued, 'we may manage to evade it. But I do not feel disposed to continue my tenancy here after three months are over. If once the servants get hold of the story, and they are sure to do so sooner or later, it would be unendurable—the worry and annoyance would do your mother far more harm than any good effect the air and change have had upon her.'

I was glad to hear this decision. Honestly, I did not feel as if I could stand the strain for long, and it might kill poor little Dormy.

But where should we go? Our own home would be quite uninhabitable till the autumn, for extensive alterations and repairs were going on there. I said this to Father.

'Yes,' he agreed, 'it is not convenient'—and he hesitated. 'I cannot make it out,' he went on, 'Miles would have been *sure* to know if the house had a bad name in any way. I think I will go over and see him today, and tell him all about it—at least I shall inquire about some other house in the neighbourhood—and *perhaps* I will tell him our reason for leaving this.'

He did so—he went over to Raxtrew that very afternoon, and, as I quite anticipated would be the case, he told me on his return that he had taken both our friends into his confidence.

'They are extremely concerned about it,' he said, 'and very sympathising, though, naturally, inclined to think us a parcel of very weak-minded folk indeed. But I am glad of one thing —the Rectory there is to be let from the first of July for three months. Miles took me to see it. I think it will do very well— it is quite out of the village, for you really can't call it a town—and a nice little place in its way. Quite modern, and as unghost-like as you could wish, bright and cheery.'

'And what will Mamma think of our leaving so soon?' I asked.

But as to this Father reassured me. He had already spoken of it to her, and somehow she did not seem disappointed. She had got it into her head that Finster did not suit Dormy, and was quite disposed to think that three months of such strong air were enough at a time.

'Then have you decided upon Raxtrew Rectory?' I asked.

'I have the refusal of it,' said my father. 'But you will be almost amused to hear that Miles begged me not to fix absolutely for a few days. He is coming to us tomorrow, to spend the night.'

'You mean to see for himself?'

Father nodded.

'Poor Mr Miles!' I ejaculated. 'You won't sit up with him, I hope, Father?'

'I offered to do so, but he won't hear of it,' was the reply. 'He is bringing one of his keepers with him—a sturdy, trust-worthy young fellow, and they two with their revolvers are going to nab the ghost, so he says. We shall see. We must manage to prevent our servants suspecting anything.'

This *was* managed. I need not go into particulars. Suffice to say that the sturdy keeper reached his own home before dawn on the night of the vigil, no endeavours of his master having succeeded in persuading him to stay another moment at Finster, and that Mr Miles himself looked so ill the next morning when he joined us at the breakfast-table that we, the initiated, could scarcely repress our exclamations, when Sophy, with the curious instinct of touching a sore place which some people have, told him that he looked exactly, 'as if he had seen a ghost'.

His experience had been precisely similar to ours. After that we heard no more from him—about the pity it was to leave a place that suited us so well, etc., etc. On the contrary, before he left, he told my father and myself that he thought us uncommonly plucky for staying out the three months, though at the same time he confessed to feeling completely nonplussed.

'I have lived near Finster St Mabyn's all my life,' he said, 'and my people before me, and *never*, do I honestly assure you, have I heard one breath of the old place being haunted. And in a shut-up neighbourhood like this, such a thing would have leaked out.'

We shook our heads, but what could we say?

We left Finster St Mabyn's towards the middle of July. Nothing worth recording happened during the last few weeks. If the ghostly drama were still re-enacted night after night, or only during some portion of each month, we took care not to assist at the performance. I believe Phil and Nugent planned another vigil, but he gave it up by my father's expressed wish, and on one pretext or another he managed to keep the gallery locked off without arousing any suspicion in my mother or Sophy, or any of our visitors.

It was a cold summer—those early months of it at least—and that made it easier to avoid the room.

Somehow none of us were sorry to go. This was natural, so far as several were concerned, but rather curious as regards those of the family who knew no drawback to the charms of the place. I suppose it was due to some instinctive consciousness of the influence which so many of the party had felt it impossible to resist or explain.

And the Rectory at Raxtrew was really a dear little place. It was so bright and open and sunny. Dormy's pale face was rosy with pleasure the first afternoon when he came rushing in to tell us that there were tame rabbits and a pair of guinea-pigs in an otherwise empty loose box in the stable-yard.

'Do come and look at them,' he begged, and I went with him, pleased to see him so happy.

I did not care for the rabbits, but I always think guinea-pigs rather fascinating, and we stayed playing with them some little time.

'I'll show you another way back into the house,' said Dormy, and he led me through a conservatory into a large, almost unfurnished room, opening again into a tiled passage leading to the offices.

'This is the Warden boys' play-room,' he said. 'They keep their cricket and football things here, you see, and their tricycle. I wonder if I might use it?'

'We must write and ask them,' I said. 'But what are all these big packages?' I went on. 'Oh, I see, it's our heavy luggage from Finster. There is not room in this house for our odds and ends of furniture, I suppose. It's rather a pity they have put it in here, for we could have had some nice games in this big room on a wet day, and see, Dormy, here are several pairs of roller-skates! Oh, we must have this place cleared.'

We spoke to Father about it—and he came and looked at the room and agreed with us that it would be a pity not to have the full use of it. Roller-skating would be good exercise for Dormy, he said, and even for Nat, who would be joining us before long for his holidays.

So our big cases, and the chairs and tables we had bought from Hunter, in their careful swathings of wisps and matting, were carried out to an empty barn—a perfectly dry and weathertight barn—for everything at the Rectory was in excellent repair. In this, as in all other details, our new quarters were a complete contrast to the picturesque abode we had just quitted.

The weather was charming for the first two or three weeks —much warmer and sunnier than at Finster. We all enjoyed it, and seemed to breathe more freely. Miss Larpent, who was staying through the holidays this year, and I congratulated each other more than once, when sure of not being overheard, on the cheerful, wholesome atmosphere in which we found ourselves.

'I do not think I shall ever wish to live in a very old house again,' she said one day. We were in the play-room, and I had been persuading her to try her hand—or feet—at roller-skating. 'Even now,' she went on, 'I own to you, Leila, though it may sound very weak-minded, I cannot think of that horrible night without a shiver. Indeed, I could fancy I feel that thrill of indescribable cold at the present moment.'

She *was* shivering—and extraordinary to relate, as she spoke, her tremor communicated itself to me. Again, I could swear to it, again I felt that blast of unutterable, unearthly cold.

I started up. We were seated on a bench against the wall—a bench belonging to the play-room, and which we had not thought of removing, as a few seats were a convenience.

Miss Larpent caught sight of my face. Her own, which was very white, grew distressed in expression. She grasped my arm.

'My dearest child,' she exclaimed, 'you look blue, and your teeth are chattering! I do wish I had not alluded to that fright we had. I had no idea you were so nervous.'

'I did not know it myself,' I replied. 'I often think of the Finster ghost quite calmly, even in the middle of the night. But just then, Miss Larpent, do you know, I really *felt* that horrid cold again!'

'So did I—or rather my imagination did,' she replied, trying to talk in a matter-of-fact way. She got up as she spoke, and went to the window. 'It can't be *all* imagination,' she added. 'See, Leila, what a gusty, stormy day it is—not like the beginning of August. It really is cold.'

'And this play-room seems nearly as draughty as the gallery at Finster,' I said. 'Don't let us stay here—come into the drawing-room and play some duets. I wish we could quite forget about Finster.'

'Dormy has done so, I hope,' said Miss Larpent.

That chilly morning was the commencement of the real break-up in the weather. We women would not have minded it so much, as there are always plenty of indoor things we can find to do. And my two grown-up brothers were away. Raxtrew held no particular attractions for them, and Phil wanted to see some of our numerous relations before he returned to India. So he and Nugent started on a round of visits. But, unluckily, it was the beginning of the public-school holidays, and poor Nat—the fifteen-years-old boy—had just joined us. It was very disappointing for him in more ways than one. He had set his heart on seeing Finster, impressed by our enthusiastic description of it when we first went there, and now his anticipations had to come down to a comparatively tame and uninteresting village, and every probability—so said the wise—of a stretch of rainy, unsummerlike weather.

Nat was a good-natured, cheery fellow, however—not nearly as clever or as impressionable as Dormy, but with the same common-sense. So he wisely determined to make the best of things, and as we were really sorry for him, he did not, after all, come off very badly.

His principal amusement was roller-skating in the playroom. Dormy had not taken to it in the same way—the greater part of *his* time was spent with the rabbits and guinea-pigs, where Nat, when he himself had had skating enough, was pretty sure to find him.

I suppose it is with being the eldest sister that it always seems my fate to receive the confidences of the rest of the family, and it was about this time, a fortnight or so after his arrival, that it began to strike me that Nat looked as if he had something on his mind.

'He is sure to tell me what it is, sooner or later,' I said to myself. 'Probably he has left some small debts behind him at school—only he did not look worried or anxious when he first came home.'

The confidence was given. One afternoon Nat followed me into the library, where I was going to write some letters, and said he wanted to speak to me. I put my paper aside and waited.

'Leila,' he began, 'you must promise not to laugh at me.'

This was not what I expected.

'Laugh at you—no, certainly not,' I replied, 'especially if you are in any trouble. And I have thought you were looking worried, Nat.'

'Well, yes,' he said, 'I don't know if there is anything coming over me—I feel quite well, but—Leila,' he broke off, 'do you believe in ghosts?'

I started.

'Has anyone—' I was beginning rashly, but the boy interrupted me.

'No, no,' he said eagerly, 'no one has put anything of the kind into my head—no one. It is my own senses that have seen—felt it—or else, if it is fancy, I must be going out of my mind, Leila—I do believe there is a ghost here *in the play-room*.'

I sat silent, an awful dread creeping over me, which, as he went on, grew worse and worse. Had the thing—the Finster shadow—attached itself to us—I had read of such cases—had it journeyed with us to this peaceful, healthful house? The remembrance of the cold thrill experienced by Miss Larpent and myself flashed back upon me. And Nat went on.

Yes, the cold was the first thing he had been startled by, followed, just as in the gallery of our old castle, by the consciousness of the terrible, shadow-like presence gradually taking form in the moonlight. For there had been moonlight the last night or two, and Nat, in his skating ardour, had amused himself alone in the play-room after Dormy had gone to bed.

'The night before last was the worst,' he said. 'It stopped raining, you remember, Leila, and the moon was very bright —I noticed how it glistened on the wet leaves outside. It was by the moonlight I saw the—the shadow. I wouldn't have thought of skating in the evening but for the light, for we've never had a lamp in there. It came round the walls, Leila, and then it seemed to stop and fumble away in one corner —at the end where there is a bench, you know.'

Indeed I did know; it was where our governess and I had been sitting.

'I got so awfully frightened,' said Nat honestly, 'that I ran off. Then yesterday I was ashamed of myself, and went back there in the evening with a candle. But I saw nothing: the moon did not come out. Only—I felt the cold again. I believe it was there—though I could not see it. Leila, what *can* it be? If only I could make you understand! It is so *much* worse than it sounds to tell.'

I said what I could to soothe him. I spoke of odd shadows thrown by the trees outside swaying in the wind, for the weather was still stormy. I repeated the time-worn argument about optical illusions, etc. etc., and in the end he gave in a little. It *might* have been his fancy. And he promised me most faithfully to breathe no hint—not the very faintest—of the fright he had had, to Sophy or Dormy, or anyone.

Then I had to tell my father. I really shrank from doing so, but there seemed no alternative. At first, of course, he pooh-poohed it at once by saying Dormy must have been talking to Nat about the Finster business, or if not Dormy, *someone*—Miss Larpent even! But when all such explanations were entirely set at nought, I must say poor Father looked rather blank. I was sorry for him, and sorry for myself —the idea of being *followed* by this horrible presence was too sickening.

Father took refuge at last in some brain-wave theory— involuntary impressions had been made on Nat by all of us, whose minds were still full of the strange experience. He said he felt sure, and no doubt he tried to think he did, that this theory explained the whole. I felt glad for him to get any satisfaction out of it, and I did my best to take it up too. But it was no use. I felt that Nat's experience had been an 'objective' one, as Miss Larpent expressed it—or, as Dormy had said at first at Finster: 'No, no, sister—it's something *there* —it's nothing to do with me.'

And earnestly I longed for the time to come for our return to our own familiar home.

'I don't think I shall ever wish to leave it again,' I thought. But after a week or two the feeling began to fade again. And Father very sensibly discovered that it would not do to leave our spare furniture and heavy luggage in the barn—it was getting all dusty and cobwebby. So it was all moved back again to the play-room, and stacked as it had been at first, making it impossible for us to skate or amuse ourselves in any way there, at which Sophy grumbled, but Nat did not.

Father was very good to Nat. He took him about with him as much as he could to get the thought of that horrid thing out of his head. But yet it could not have been half as bad for Nat as for the rest of us, for we took the greatest possible precautions against any whisper of the dreadful and mysterious truth reaching him, that the ghost had *followed us* from Finster.

Father did not tell Mr Miles or Jenny about it. They had been worried enough, poor things, by the trouble at Finster, and it would be too bad for them to think that the strange influence was affecting us in the *second* house we had taken at their recommendation.

'In fact,' said Father with a rather rueful smile, 'if we don't take care, we shall begin to be looked upon askance as a haunted family! Our lives would have been in danger in the good old witchcraft days.'

'It is really a mercy that none of the servants have got hold of the story,' said Miss Larpent, who was one of our council of three. 'We must just hope that no further annoyance will befall us till we are safe at home again.'

Her hopes were fulfilled. Nothing else happened while we remained at the Rectory—it really seemed as if the unhappy shade was limited locally, in one sense. For at Finster, even, it had never been seen or felt save in the one room.

The vividness of the impression of poor Nat's experience had almost died away when the time came for us to leave. I felt now that I should rather enjoy telling Phil and Nugent about it, and hearing what *they* could bring forward in the way of explanation.

We left Raxtrew early in October. Our two big brothers were awaiting us at home, having arrived there a few days before us. Nugent was due at Oxford very shortly.

It was very nice to be in our own house again, after several months' absence, and it was most interesting to see how the alterations, including a good deal of new papering and painting, had been carried out. And as soon as the heavy luggage arrived we had grand consultations as to the disposal about the rooms of the charming pieces of furniture we had picked up at Hunter's. Our rooms are large and nicely shaped, most of them. It was not difficult to make a pretty corner here and there with a quaint old chair or two and a delicate spindle-legged table, and when we had arranged them all—Phil, Nugent and I were the movers—we summoned Mother and Miss Larpent to give their opinion.

They quite approved, Mother even saying that she would be glad of a few more odds and ends.

'We might empower Janet Miles,' she said, 'to let us know if she sees anything very tempting. Is that really all we have? They looked so much more important in their swathings.'

The same idea struck me. I glanced round.

'Yes,' I said, 'that's all, except—oh, yes, there are the tapestry *portières*—the best of all. We can't have them in the drawing-room, I fear. It is too modern for them. Where shall we hang them?'

'You are forgetting, Leila,' said Mother. 'We spoke of having them in the hall. They will do beautifully to hang before the two side doors, which are seldom opened. And in cold weather the hall is draughty, though nothing like the gallery at Finster.'

Why did she say that? It made me shiver, but then, of course, she did not know.

Our hall is a very pleasant one. We sit there a great deal. The side doors Mother spoke of are second entrances to the dining-room and library—quite unnecessary, except when we have a large party, a dance or something of that sort. And the *portières* certainly seemed the very thing, the mellow colouring of the tapestry showing to great advantage. The boys—Phil and Nugent, I mean—set to work at once, and in an hour or two the hangings were placed.

'Of course,' said Philip, 'if ever these doors are to be opened, this precious tapestry must be taken down, or very carefully looped back. It is very worn in some places, and in spite of the thick lining it should be tenderly handled. I am afraid it has suffered a little from being so long rolled up at the Rectory. It should have been hung up!'

Still, it looked very well indeed, and when Father, who was away at some magistrates' meeting, came home that afternoon, I showed him our arrangements with pride.

He was very pleased.

'Very nice—very nice indeed,' he said, though it was almost too dusk for him to judge quite fully of the effect of the tapestry. 'But, dear me, child, this hall is very cold. We must have a larger fire. Only October! What sort of a winter are we going to have?'

He shivered as he spoke. He was standing close to one of the *portières*—smoothing the tapestry half absently with one hand. I looked at him with concern.

'I *hope* you have not got a chill, Papa,' I said.

But he seemed all right again when we went into the library, where tea was waiting—an extra late tea for his benefit.

The next day Nugent went to Oxford. Nat had already returned to school. So our home party was reduced to Father and Mother, Miss Larpent, Phil and I, and the children.

We were very glad to have Phil settled at home for some time. There was little fear of his being tempted away, now that the shooting had begun. We were expecting some of our usual guests at this season; the weather was perfect autumn weather; we had thrown off all remembrance of influenza and other depressing 'influences', and were feeling bright and cheerful, when again—ah, yes, even now it gives me a faint, sick sensation to recall the horror of that *third* visitation!

But I must tell it simply, and not give way to painful remembrances.

It was the very day before our first visitors were expected that the blow fell, the awful fear made itself felt. And, as before, the victim was a new one—the one who, for reasons already mentioned, we had specially guarded from any breath of the gruesome terror—poor little Sophy!

What she was doing alone in the hall late that evening I cannot quite recall—yes, I think I remember her saying she had run downstairs when half-way up to bed, to fetch a book she had left there in the afternoon. She had no light, and the one lamp in the hall—we never sat there after dinner— was burning feebly. *It was bright moonlight.*

I was sitting at the piano, where I had been playing in a rather sleepy way—when a sudden touch on my shoulder made me start, and, looking up, I saw my sister standing beside me, white and trembling.

'Leila,' she whispered, 'come with me quickly. I don't want Mamma to notice.'

For Mother was still nervous and delicate.

The drawing-room is very long, and has two or three doors. No one else was at our end. It was easy to make our way out unperceived. Sophy caught my hand and hurried me upstairs without speaking till we reached my own room, where a bright fire was burning cheerfully.

Then she began.

'Leila,' she said, 'I have had such an awful fright. I did not want to speak until we were safe up here.'

'What was it?' I exclaimed breathlessly. Did I already suspect the truth? I really do not know, but my nerves were not what they had been.

Sophy gasped and began to tremble. I put my arm round her.

'It does not sound so bad,' she said. 'But—oh, Leila, what *could* it be? It was in the hall,' and then I think she explained how she had come to be there. 'I was standing near the side door into the library that we never use—and—all of a sudden a sort of darkness came along the wall, and seemed to settle on the door—where the old tapestry is, you know. I thought it was the shadow of something outside, for it was bright moonlight, and the windows were not shuttered. But in a moment I saw it could not be that—there is nothing to throw such a shadow. It seemed to wriggle about—like—like a monstrous spider, or—' and there she hesitated—'almost like a deformed sort of human being. And all at once, Leila, my breath went and I fell down. I really did. I was *choked* with cold. I think my senses went away, but I am not sure. The next thing I remember was rushing across the hall and then down the south corridor to the drawing-room, and then I was so thankful to see you there by the piano.'

I drew her down on my knee, poor child.

'It was very good of you, dear,' I said, 'to control yourself, and not startle Mamma.'

This pleased her, but her terror was still uppermost.

'Leila,' she said piteously, 'can't you explain it? I did so hope you could.'

What *could* I say?

'I—one would need to go to the hall and look well about to see what could cast such a shadow,' I said vaguely, and I suppose I must involuntarily have moved a little, for Sophy started, and clutched me fast.

'Oh, Leila, don't go—you don't mean you are going now?' she entreated.

Nothing truly was farther from my thoughts, but I took care not to say so.

'I won't leave you if you'd rather not,' I said, 'and I tell you what, Sophy, if you would like very much to sleep here with me tonight, you shall. I will ring and tell Freake to bring your things down and undress you—on one condition.'

'What?' she said eagerly. She was much impressed by my amiability.

'That you won't say *one word* about this, or give the least shadow of a hint to anyone that you have had a fright. You don't know the trouble it will cause.'

'Of course I will promise to let no one know, if you think it better, for you are so kind to me,' said Sophy. But there was a touch of reluctance in her tone. 'You—you mean to do something about it though, Leila,' she went on. 'I shall never be able to forget it if you don't.'

'Yes,' I said, 'I shall speak to Father and Phil about it tomorrow. If anyone has been trying to frighten us,' I added unguardedly, 'by playing tricks, they certainly must be exposed.'

'Not *us*,' she corrected, 'it was only me,' and I did not reply. Why I spoke of the possibility of a trick I scarcely know. I had no hope of any such explanation.

But another strange, almost incredible idea was beginning to take shape in my mind, and with it came a faint, very faint touch of relief. Could it be not the *houses*, nor the *rooms*, nor, worst of all, we ourselves that were haunted, but some thing or things among the old furniture we had bought at Raxtrew?

And lying sleepless that night a sudden flash of illumination struck me—could it—whatever the 'it' was—could it have something to do with the tapestry hangings?

The more I thought it over the more striking grew the coincidences at Finster. It had been on one of the closed doors that the shadow seemed to settle, as again here in our own hall. But in both cases the *portière* had hung in front!

And at the Rectory? The tapestry, as Philip had remarked, had been there rolled up all the time. Was it possible that it had never been taken out to the barn at all? What *more* probable than that it should have been left, forgotten, under the bench where Miss Larpent and I had felt for the second time that hideous cold? And, stay, something else was returning to my mind in connection with that bench. Yes—I had it —Nat had said 'it seemed to stop and fumble away in one corner—at the end where there is a bench, you know.'

And then to my unutterable thankfulness at last I fell asleep.

I told Philip the next morning. There was no need to bespeak his attention. I think he felt nearly as horrified as I had done myself at the idea that our own hitherto bright, cheerful home was to be haunted by this awful thing—influence or presence, call it what you will. And the suggestions which I went on to make struck him, too, with a sense of relief.

He sat in silence for some time after making me recapitulate as precisely as possible every detail of Sophy's story.

'You are sure it was the door into the library?' he said at last.

'Quite sure,' I replied; 'and, oh, Philip,' I went on, 'it has just occurred to me that *Father* felt a chill there the other evening.'

For till that moment the little incident in question had escaped my memory.

'Do you remember which of the *portières* hung in front of the door at Finster?' said Philip.

I shook my head.

'Dormy would,' I said, 'he used to examine the pictures in the tapestry with great interest. I should not know one from the other. There is an old castle in the distance in each, and a lot of trees, and something meant for a lake.'

But in his turn Philip shook his head.

'No,' he said, 'I won't speak to Dormy about it if I can possibly help it. Leave it to me, Leila, and try to put it out of your own mind as much as you possibly can, and don't be surprised at anything you may notice in the next few days. I will tell you, first of anyone, whenever I have anything to tell.'

That was all I could get out of him. So I took his advice. Luckily, as it turned out, Mr Miles, the only outsider, so to say (except the unfortunate keeper), who had witnessed the ghostly drama, was one of the shooting party expected that day. And Philip at once determined to consult him about this new and utterly unexpected manifestation.

He did not tell me this. Indeed, it was not till fully a week later that I heard anything, and then in a letter—a very long letter from my brother, which, I think, will relate the sequel of our strange ghost story better than any narration at second-hand, of my own.

Mr Miles only stayed two nights with us. The very day after he came he announced that, to his great regret, he was obliged—most unexpectedly—to return to Raxtrew on important business. 'And,' he continued, 'I am afraid you will all feel much vexed with me when I tell you I am going to carry off Phil with me.'

Father looked very blank indeed.

'Phil!' he exclaimed, 'and how about our shooting?'

'You can easily replace us,' said my brother, 'I have thought of that,' and he added something in a lower tone to Father. He—Phil—was leaving the room at the time. *I* thought it had reference to the real reason of his accompanying Mr Miles, but I was mistaken. Father, however, said nothing more in opposition to the plan, and the next morning the two went off.

We happened to be standing at the hall door—several of us—for we were a large party now—when Phil and his friend drove away. As we turned to re-enter the house, I felt some-one touch me. It was Sophy. She was going out for a consti-tutional with Miss Larpent, but had stopped a moment to speak to me.

'Leila,' she said in a whisper, 'why have they—did you know that the tapestry had been taken down?'

She glanced at me with a peculiar expression. I had not observed it. Now, looking up, I saw that the two locked doors were visible in the dark polish of their old mahogany as of yore—no longer shrouded by the ancient *portières*. I started in surprise. 'No,' I whispered in return, 'I did not know. Never mind, Sophy. I suspect there is a reason for it which we shall know in good time.'

I felt strongly tempted—the moon being still at the full—to visit the hall that night—in hopes of feeling and seeing—*nothing*. But when the time drew near, my courage failed; besides I had tacitly promised Philip to think as little as I possibly could about the matter, and any vigil of the kind would certainly not have been acting in accordance with the spirit of his advice. I think I will now copy, as it stands, the letter from Philip which I received a week or so later. It was dated from his club in London.

My dear Leila,

I have a long story to tell you and a very extraordinary one. I think it is well that it should be put into writing, so I will devote this evening to the task—especially as I shall not be home for ten days or so.

You may have suspected that I took Miles into my con-fidence as soon as he arrived. If you did you were right. He was the best person to speak to for several reasons. He looked, I must say, rather—well, 'blank' scarcely expresses it—when I told him of the ghost's re-appearance, not only at the Rectory, but in our own house, and on both occasions to persons—Nat, and then Sophy—who had not heard a breath of the story. But when I went on to propound your suggestion, Miles cheered up. He had been, I fancy, a trifle touchy about our calling Finster haunted, and it was evidently a satisfaction to him to start another theory. We talked it well over, and we decided to test the thing again —it took some resolution, I own, to do so. We sat up that night—bright moonlight luckily—and—well, I needn't repeat it all. Sophy was quite correct. It came again—the horrid creeping shadow—poor wretch, I'm rather sorry for it now—just in the old way—quite as much at home in ——shire, apparently, as in the Castle. It stopped at the closed library door, and fumbled away, then started off again—ugh! We watched it closely, but kept well in the middle of the room, so that the cold did not strike us so badly. We both noted the special part of the tapestry where its hands seemed to sprawl, and we meant to stay for another round; but—when it came to the point we funked it, and went to bed.

Next morning, on pretence of examining the date of the tapestry, we had it down—you were all out—and we found —*something.* Just where the hands felt about, there had been a cut—three cuts, three sides of a square, as it were, making a sort of door in the stuff, the fourth side having evidently acted as a hinge, for there was a mark where it had been folded back. And just where—treating the thing as a door—you might expect to find a handle to open it by, we found a distinct dint in the tapestry, as if a button or knob had once been there. We looked at each other. The same idea had struck us. The tapestry had been used to conceal a small door in the wall—the door of a secret cupboard probably. The ghostly fingers had been vainly seeking for the spring which in the days of their flesh and bone they had been accustomed to press.

'The first thing to do,' said Miles, 'is to look up Hunter and make him tell where he got the tapestry from. Then we shall see.'

'Shall we take the *portière* with us?' I said.

But Miles shuddered, though he half laughed too.

'No, thank you,' he said. 'I'm not going to travel with the evil thing.'

'We can't hang it up again, though,' I said, 'after this last experience.'

In the end we rolled up the two *portières*, not to attract attention by only moving one, and—well, I thought it just possible the ghost might make a mistake, and I did not want any more scares while I was away—we rolled them up together, first carefully measuring the cut, and its position in the curtain, and then we hid them away in one of the lofts that no one ever enters, where they are at this moment, and where the ghost may have been disporting himself, for all I know, though I fancy he has given it up by this time, for reasons you shall hear.

Then Miles and I, as you know, set off for Raxtrew. I smoothed my father down about it, by reminding him how good-natured they had been to us, and telling him Miles really needed me. We went straight to Hunter. He hummed and hawed a good deal—he had not distinctly promised not to give the name of the place the tapestry had come from, but he knew the gentleman he had bought it from did not want it known.

'Why?' said Miles. 'Is it some family that has come down in the world, and is forced to part with things to get some ready money?'

'Oh, dear no!' said Hunter. 'It is not that, at all. It was only that—I suppose I must give you the name—Captain Devereux—did not want any gossip to get about, as to—'

'Devereux!' repeated Miles, 'you don't mean the people at Hallinger?'

'The same,' said Hunter. 'If you know them, sir, you will be careful, I hope, to assure the Captain that I did my best to carry out his wishes?'

'Certainly,' said Miles, 'I'll exonerate you.'

And then Hunter told us that Devereux, who only came into the Hallinger property a few years ago, had been much annoyed by stories getting about of the place being haunted, and this had led to his dismantling one wing, and—Hunter thought, but was not quite clear as to this— pulling down some rooms altogether. But he, Devereux, was very touchy on the subject—he did not want to be laughed at.

'And the tapestry came from him—you are certain as to that?' Miles repeated.

'Positive, sir. I took it down with my own hands. It was fitted on to two panels in what they call the round room at Hallinger—there were, oh, I daresay, a dozen of them, with tapestry nailed on, but I only bought these two pieces —the others were sold to a London dealer.'

'The round room,' I said. Leila, the expression struck me. Miles, it appeared, knew Devereux fairly well. Hallinger is only ten miles off. We drove over there, but found he was in London. So our next move was to follow him there. We called twice at his club, and then Miles made an appointment, saying he wanted to see him on private business.

He received us civilly, of course. He is quite a young fellow—in the Guards. But when Miles began to explain to him what we had come about, he stiffened.

'I suppose you belong to the Psychical Society?' he said. 'I can only repeat that I have nothing to tell, and I detest the whole subject.'

'Wait a moment,' said Miles, and as he went on I saw that Devereux had changed. His face grew intent with interest and a queer sort of eagerness, and at last he started to his feet. 'Upon my soul,' he said, 'I believe you've run him to earth for me—the ghost, I mean, and if so, you shall have my endless gratitude. I'll go down to Hallinger with you at once—this afternoon, if you like, and see it out.'

He was so excited that he spoke almost incoherently, but after a bit he calmed down, and told us all he had to tell—and that was a good deal—which would indeed have been nuts for the Psychical Society. What Hunter had said was but a small part of the whole. It appeared that on

succeeding to Hallinger, on the death of an uncle, young
Devereux had made considerable changes in the house.
He had, among others, opened out a small wing—a sort of
round tower—which had been completely dismantled and
bricked up for, I think he said, over a hundred years.
There was some story about it. An ancestor of his—an
awful gambler—had used the principal room in this wing
for his orgies. Very queer things went on there, the finish
up being the finding of old Devereux dead there one night,
when his servants were summoned by the man he had been
playing with—with whom he had had an awful quarrel.
This man, a low fellow, probably a professional card-
sharper, vowed that he had been robbed of a jewel which
his host had staked, and it was said that a ring of great
value had disappeared. But it was all hushed up—Devereux had really died in a fit—though soon after, for reasons
only hinted at, the round tower was shut up, till the present
man rashly opened it again.

Almost at once, he said, the annoyances, to use a mild
term, began. First one, then another of the household were
terrified out of their wits, just as we were, Leila. Devereux
himself had seen it two or three times, the 'it', of course,
being his miserable old ancestor. A small man, with a big
wig, and long, thin, claw-like fingers. It all corresponded.
Mrs Devereux is young and nervous. She could not stand
it. So in the end the round tower was shut up again, all
the furniture and hangings sold, and locally speaking, the
ghost laid. That was all Devereux knew.

We started, the three of us, that very afternoon, as excited as a party of schoolboys. Miles and I kept questioning
Devereux, but he had really no more to tell. He had never
thought of examining the walls of the haunted room—it
was wainscoted, he said—and might be lined all through
with secret cupboards for all he knew. But he could not
get over the extraordinariness of the ghost's sticking to the
tapestry—and indeed it does rather lower one's idea of
ghostly intelligence.

We went at it at once—the tower was not bricked up

again, luckily—we got in without difficulty the next morn-ing—Devereux making some excuse to the servants, a new and full of joins in the wood, any one of which might have ceedings. It was a tiresome business. There were so many panels in the room, as Hunter had said, and it was im-possible to tell in which *the* tapestry had been fixed. But we had our measures, and we carefully marked a line as near as we could guess at the height from the floor that the cut in the *portière* must have been. Then we tapped and pummelled and pressed imaginary springs till we were nearly sick of it—there was nothing to guide us. The wains-coting was dark and much shrunk and marked with age, and full of joins in the wood any one of which might have meant a door.

It was Devereux himself who found it at last. We heard an exclamation from where he was standing by himself at the other side of the room. He was quite white and shaky.

'Look here,' he said, and we looked.

Yes—there was a small deep recess, or cupboard in the thickness of the wall, excellently contrived. Devereux had touched the spring at last, and the door, just matching the cut in the tapestry, flew open.

Inside lay what at first we took for a packet of letters, and I hoped to myself they contained nothing that would bring trouble to poor Devereux. They were not letters, however, but two or three incomplete packs of cards— grey and dust-thick with age—and as Miles spread them out, certain markings on them told their own tale. Dever-eux did not like it, naturally—their supposed owner had been a member of his house.

'The ghost has kept a conscience,' he said, with an at-tempt at a laugh. 'Is there nothing more?'

Yes—a small leather bag—black and grimy, though originally, I fancy, of chamois skin. It drew with strings. Devereux pulled it open, and felt inside.

'By George!' he exclaimed. And he held out the most magnificent diamond ring I have ever seen—sparkling away as if it had only just come from the polisher's. 'This must be *the* ring,' he said.

And we all stared—too astonished to speak.

Devereux closed the cupboard again, after carefully examining it to make sure nothing had been left behind. He marked the exact spot where he had pressed the spring so as to find it at any time. Then we all left the round room, locking the door securely after us.

Miles and I spent that night at Hallinger. We sat up late, talking it all over. There are some queer inconsistencies about the thing which will probably never be explained. First and foremost—why has the ghost stuck to the tapestry instead of to the actual spot he seemed to have wished to reveal? Secondly, what was the connection between his visits and the full moon—or is it that only by the moonlight the shade becomes perceptible to human sense? Who can say?

As to the story itself—what was old Devereux's motive in concealing his own ring? Were the marked cards his, or his opponent's, of which he had managed to possess himself, and had secreted as testimony against the other fellow?

I incline, and so does Miles, to this last theory, and when we suggested it to Devereux, I could see it was a relief to him. After all, one likes to think one's ancestors were gentlemen!

'But what, then, has he been worrying about all this century or more?' he said. 'If it were that he wanted the ring returned to its real owner—supposing the fellow *had* won it—I could understand it, though such a thing would be impossible. There is no record of the man at all—his name was never mentioned in the story.'

'He may want the ring restored to its proper owner all the same,' said Miles. 'You are its owner, as the head of the family, and it has been your ancestor's fault that it has been hidden all these years. Besides, we cannot take upon ourselves to explain motives in such a case. Perhaps—who knows?—the poor shade could not help himself. His peregrinations may have been of the nature of punishment.'

'I hope they are over now,' said Devereux, 'for his sake and everybody else's. I should be glad to think he wanted the ring restored to us, but besides that, I should like to do something—something *good* you know—if it would make him easier, poor old chap. I must consult Lilias.' Lilias is Mrs Devereux.

This is all I have to tell you at present, Leila. When I come home we'll have the *portières* up again and see what happens. I want you now to read all this to my father, and if he has no objections—he and my mother, of course—I should like to invite Captain and Mrs Devereux to stay a few days with us—as well as Miles, as soon as I come back.

Philip's wish was acceded to. It was with no little anxiety and interest that we awaited his return.

The tapestry *portières* were restored to their place—and on the first moonlight night, my father, Philip, Captain Devereux and Mr Miles held their vigil.

What happened?

Nothing—the peaceful rays lighted up the quaint landscape of the tapestry, undisturbed by the poor groping fingers—no gruesome unearthly chill as of worse than death made itself felt to the midnight watchers—the weary, may we not hope repentant, spirit was at rest at last!

And never since has anyone been troubled by the shadow in the moonlight.

'I cannot help hoping,' said Mrs Devereux, when talking it over, 'that what Michael has done may have helped to calm the poor ghost.'

And she told us what it was. Captain Devereux is rich, though not immensely so. He had the ring valued—it represented a very large sum, but Philip says I had better not name the figures—and then he, so to say, bought it from himself. And with this money he—no, again Phil says I must not enter into particulars beyond saying that with it he did something very good, and very useful, which had long been a pet scheme of his wife's.

Sophy is grown up now and she knows the whole story. So does our mother. And Dormy too has heard it all. The horror of it has quite gone. We feel rather proud of having been the actual witnesses of a ghostly drama.

The Last of Squire Ennismore

by

MRS J. H. RIDDELL

Victorian Ireland produced two great writers of ghost stories, Sheridan le Fanu and the lesser known, but equally worthy, Mrs J. H. Riddell (1832–1906). Mrs Riddell left Ireland to settle in London and took quite a time to establish her literary reputation, in the meanwhile living in what was termed 'genteel poverty'. From 1861 she was co-proprietor and editor of St James's Magazine, to which she herself contributed many short stories. Her more notable collections of macabre tales were The Uninhabited House *(1883),* Weird Stories *(1884) and* The Banshee's Warning *(1894). However, there were a few little gems of the supernatural scattered amongst her other books of short stories which were not solely devoted to ghostly tales. This particular story comes from* Idle Tales *(1888) and in it Mrs Riddell returns to her native Ireland to tell a neat little yarn about the Devil collecting his dues.*

'Did I see it myself? No, sir; I did not see it: and my father before me did not see it; or his father before him, and he was Phil Regan, just the same as myself. But it is true, for all that; just as true as that you are looking at the very place where the whole thing happened. My great-grandfather (and he did not die till he was ninety-eight) used to tell, many and many's the time, how he met the stranger, night after night, walking lonesome-like about the sands where most of the wreckage came ashore.'

'And the old house, then, stood behind that belt of Scotch firs?'

'Yes; a fine house it was, too. Hearing so much talk about it when a boy, my father said, made him often feel as if he knew every room in the building, though it had all fallen to ruin before he was born. None of the family ever lived in it after the Squire went away. Nobody else could be got to stop in the place. There used to be awful noises, as if something was being pitched from the top of the great staircase down into the hall; and then there would be a sound as if a hundred people were clinking glasses and talking all together at once. And then it seemed as if barrels were rolling in the cellars; and there would be screeches, and howls, and laughing, fit to make your blood run cold. They say there is gold hid away in those cellars; but not one has ever ventured to find it. The very children won't come here to play; and when the men are ploughing the field behind, nothing will make them stay in it, once the day begins to change. When the night is coming on, and the tide creeps in on the sand, more than one thinks he has seen mighty queer things on the shore there.'

'But what is it really they think they see? When I asked my landlord to tell me the story from beginning to end, he said he could not remember it; and, at any rate, the whole rigmarole was nonsense, put together to please strangers.'

'And what is he but a stranger himself? And how should he know about the doings of real quality like the Ennismores? For they were gentry, every one of them—good old stock; and as for wickedness, you might have searched Ireland through and not found their match. It is a sure thing, though, that if Riley can't tell you the story, I can; for, as I said, my own people were in it, of a manner of speaking. So, if your honour will rest yourself off your feet, on that bit of a bank, I'll set down my creel and give you the whole pedigree of how Squire Ennismore went away from Ardwinsagh.'

It was a lovely day, in the early part of June; and, as the Englishman cast himself on a low ridge of sand, he looked over Ardwinsagh Bay with a feeling of ineffable content. To his left lay the Purple Headland; to his right, a long range of breakers, that went straight out into the Atlantic till they were lost from sight; in front lay the Bay of Ardwinsagh, with its bluish-green water sparkling in the summer sunlight, and here and there breaking over some sunken rock, against which the waves spent themselves in foam.

'You see how the currents set, sir? That is what makes it dangerous, for them as doesn't know the coast, to bathe here at any time, or walk when the tide is flowing. Look how the sea is creeping in now, like a race-horse at the finish. It leaves that tongue of sand bare to the last, and then, before you could look round, it has you up to the middle. That is why I made bold to speak to you; for it is not alone on the account of Squire Ennismore the bay has a bad name. But it is about him and the old house you want to hear. The last mortal being that tried to live in it, my great-grandfather said, was a creature, by name Molly Leary; and she had neither kith nor kin, and begged for her bite and sup, sheltering herself at night in a turf cabin she had built at the back of a ditch. You may be sure she thought herself a made woman when the agent said, 'Yes: she might try if she could stop in the house; there was peat and bog-wood,' he told her, 'and half-a-crown a week for the winter, and a golden guinea once Easter came,' when the house was to be put in order for the family; and his wife gave Molly some warm clothes and a blanket or two; and she was well set up.

'You may be sure she didn't choose the worst room to sleep in; and for a while all went quiet, till one night she was wakened by feeling the bedstead lifted by the four corners, and shaken like a carpet. It was a heavy four-post bedstead, with a solid top: and her life seemed to go out of her with the fear. If it had been a ship in a storm off the Headland, it couldn't have pitched worse; and then, all of a sudden, it was dropped with such a bang as nearly drove the heart into her mouth.

'But that, she said, was nothing to the screaming and laughing, and hustling and rushing that filled the house. If a hundred people had been running hard along the passages and tumbling downstairs, they could not have made a greater noise.

'Molly never was able to tell how she got clear of the place; but a man coming late home from Ballycloyne Fair found the creature crouched under the old thorn there, with very little on her—saving your honour's presence. She had a bad fever, and talked about strange things, and never was the same woman after.'

'But what was the beginning of all this? When did the house first get the name of being haunted?'

'After the old Squire went away: that was what I purposed telling you. He did not come here to live regularly till he had got well on in years. He was near seventy at the time I am talking about; but he held himself as upright as ever, and rode as hard as the youngest; and could have drunk a whole roomful under the table, and walked up to bed as unconcerned as you please at the end of the night.

'He was a terrible man. You couldn't lay your tongue to a wickedness he had not been in the fore-front of—drinking, duelling, gambling—all manner of sins had been meat and drink to him since he was a boy almost. But at last he did something in London so bad, so beyond the beyonds, that he thought he had best come home and live among people who did not know so much about his goings on as the English. It was said he wanted to try and stay in this world for ever; and that he had got some secret drops that kept him well and hearty. There was something wonderful queer about him, anyhow.

'He could hold foot with the youngest; and he was strong, and had a fine fresh colour in his face; and his eyes were like a hawk's; and there was not a break in his voice—and him near upon threescore and ten!

'At long and at last it came to be the March before he was seventy—the worst March ever known in all these parts— such blowing, sleeting, snowing, had not been experienced in the memory of man; when one blusterous night some foreign vessel went to bits on the Purple Headland. They say it was an awful sound to hear the death-cry that went up high above the noise of the wind; and it was as bad a sight to see the shore there strewed with corpses of all sorts and sizes, from the little cabin-boy to the grizzled seaman.

'They never knew who they were or where they came from, but some of the men had crosses, and beads, and such like, so the priest said they belonged to him, and they were all buried decently in the chapel graveyard.

'There was not much wreckage of value drifted on shore. Most of what is lost about the Head stays there; but one thing did come into the bay—a queer thing—a puncheon of brandy.

'The Squire claimed it; it was his right to have all that came on his land, and he owned this sea-shore from the Head to the breakers—every foot—so, in course, he had the brandy; and there was sore ill-will because he gave his men nothing —not even a glass of whiskey.

'Well, to make a long story short, that was the most wonderful liquor anybody ever tasted. The gentry came from far and near to take share, and it was cards and dice, and drinking and story-telling night after night—week in, week out. Even on Sundays, God forgive them! the officers would drive over from Ballyclone, and sit emptying tumbler after tumbler till Monday morning came, for it made beautiful punch.

'But all at once people quit coming—a word went round that the liquor was not all it ought to be. Nobody could say what ailed it, but it got about that in some way men found it did not suit them.

'For one thing, they were losing money very fast.

'They could not make head against the Squire's luck, and a hint was dropped the puncheon ought to have been towed out to sea, and sunk in fifty fathoms of water.

'It was getting to the end of April, and fine, warm weather for the time of year, when first one, and then another, and then another still, began to take notice of a stranger who walked the shore alone at night. He was a dark man, the same colour as the drowned crew lying in the chapel grave-yard, and had rings in his ears, and wore a strange kind of hat, and cut wonderful antics as he walked, and had an ambling sort of gait, curious to look at. Many tried to talk to him, but he only shook his head; so, as nobody could make out where he came from or what he wanted, they felt sure he was the spirit of some poor wretch who was tossing about the Head, longing for a snug corner in holy ground.

'The priest went and tried to get some sense out of him.

'"Is it Christian burial you're wanting?" asked his reverence; but the creature only shook his head.

'"Is it word sent to the wives and daughters you've left orphans and widows, you'd like?" but no; it wasn't that.

'"Is it for sin committed you're doomed to walk this way? Would masses comfort ye? There's a heathen," said his reverence; "did you ever hear tell of a Christian that shook his head when masses were mentioned?"

'"Perhaps he doesn't understand English, Father," says one of the officers who was there; "try him with Latin."

'No sooner said than done. The priest started off with such a string of aves and paters that the stranger fairly took to his heels and ran.

'"He is an evil spirit," explained the priest, when he had stopped, tired out, "and I have exorcised him."

'But the next night my gentleman was back again, as unconcerned as ever.

'"And he'll just have to stay," said his reverence, "for I've got lumbago in the small of my back, and pains in all my joints—never to speak of a hoarseness with standing there shouting; and I don't believe he understood a sentence I said."

'Well, this went on for a while, and people got that frightened of the man, or appearance of a man, they would not go near the sands; till in the end Squire Ennismore, who had always scoffed at the talk, took it into his head he would go down one night, and see into the rights of the matter himself. He, maybe, was feeling lonesome, because, as I told your honour before, people had left off coming to the house, and there was nobody for him to drink with.

'Out he goes, then, as bold as brass; and there were a few followed him. The man came forward at sight of the Squire and took off his hat with a foreign flourish. Not to be behind in civility, the Squire lifted his.

'"I have come, sir," he said, speaking very loud, to try to make him understand, "to know if you are looking for anything, and whether I can assist you to find it."

'The man looked at the Squire as if he had taken the greatest liking to him, and took off his hat again.

'"Is it the vessel that was wrecked you are distressed about?"

'There came no answer, only a forbye mournful shake of the head.

'"Well, *I* haven't your ship, you know; it went all to bits months ago; and as for the sailors, they are snug and sound enough in consecrated ground."

'The man stood and looked at the Squire with a queer sort of smile on his face.

'"What *do* you want?' asked Mr Ennismore, in a bit of a passion. "If anything belonging to you went down with the vessel it's about the Head you ought to be looking for it, not here—unless, indeed, it's after the brandy you're fretting."

'Now, the Squire had tried him in English and French, and was now speaking a language you'd have thought nobody could understand; but, faith, it seemed natural as kissing to the stranger.

'"Oh! that's where you are from, is it?" said the Squire. "Why couldn't you have told me so at once? I can't give you the brandy, because it's mostly drunk; but come along, and you shall have as stiff a glass of punch as ever crossed your lips." And without more to-do off they went, as sociable as you please, jabbering together in some outlandish tongue that made moderate folks' jaws ache to hear.

'That, was the first night they conversed together, but it wasn't the last. The stranger must have been the height of good company, for the Squire never tired of him. Every evening, regularly, he came up to the house, always dressed the same, always smiling and polite, and then the Squire called for brandy and hot water, and they drank and played cards till cock-crow, talking and laughing into the small hours.

'This went on for weeks and weeks, nobody knowing where the man came from, or where he went; only two things the old housekeeper did know—that the puncheon was nearly empty, and that the Squire's flesh was wasting off him; and she felt so uneasy she went to the priest, but he could give her no manner of comfort.

'She got so concerned at last that she felt bound to listen at the dining-room door; but they always talked in that foreign gibberish, and whether it was blessing or cursing they were at she couldn't tell.

'Well, the upshot of it came one night in July—on the eve of the Squire's birthday—there wasn't a drop of spirit left in the puncheon—no, not as much as would drown a fly. They had drunk the whole lot clean up—and the old woman stood trembling, expecting every minute to hear the bell ring for more brandy, for where was she to get more if they wanted any?

'All at once the Squire and the stranger came out into the hall. It was a full moon, and light as day.

' "I'll go home with you tonight by way of a change," says the Squire.

' "Will you so?" asked the other.

' "That I will," answered the Squire.

' "It is your own choice, you know."

' "Yes; it is my own choice: let us go."

'So they went. And the housekeeper ran up to the window on the great staircase and watched the way they took. Her niece lived there as housemaid, and she came and watched too; and, after a while, the butler as well. They all turned their faces this way, and looked after their master walking beside the strange man along these very sands. Well, they saw them walk out and out to the very ebb-line—but they didn't stop there—they went on, and on, and on, and on, till the water took them to their knees, and then to their waists, and then to their arm-pits, and then to their heads; but long before that the women and the butler were running out on the shore as fast as they could, shouting for help.'

'Well?' said the Englishman.

'Living or dead, Squire Ennismore never came back again. Next morning, when the tide ebbed again, one walking over the sand saw the print of a cloven foot—that he tracked to the water's edge. Then everybody knew where the Squire had gone, and with whom.'

'And no more search was made?'

'Where would have been the use searching?'

'Not much, I suppose. It's a strange story, anyhow.'

'But true, your honour—every word of it.'

'Oh! I have no doubt of that,' was the satisfactory reply.

The Red Warder of the Reef

by

J. A. BARRY

One of the most popular themes of Victorian novels and short stories was the sea. The greatest sea stories were written in this time, by authors like Herman Melville, Frederick Marryat, William Clark Russell and the forgotten writer of this tale, John Arthur Barry. Barry wrote several books of short stories about the sea, including In The Great Deep *(1896) and* Sea Yarns *(1910). He also wrote two books of stories set in Australia and the South Pacific,* Steve Brown's Bunyip *(1893) and* Red Lion and Blue Star *(1902), from which 'The Red Warder of the Reef' is taken. While it is mainly set ashore, there is a satisfying nautical twist to the macabre end of Barry's villain.*

CHAPTER I

THE BUILDING OF THE 'WARDER'

The Marine Board of Port Endeavour, the capital and chief harbour of Cooksland, had for long turned a deaf ear to petitions presented by many ship-masters, coasting and foreign, that the Cat and Kittens Reef should be either bell-buoyed or lit from a stationary vessel. The Board's contention was that, as the Point Mangrove Light, in addition to its chief duty, also threw a green ray between the bearings of S. ¾ W. and S.S.E., four cables east of the reef, that was ample warning to enable vessels to clear the dangerous Cat and her family.

Two brigs and a coasting schooner had already come to grief on the just awash rocks. Skippers and mates had lost their certificates, and some their lives; and all the survivors swore to the absence of 'the green ray'. But, as the Board knew it must have been there, the excuse availed nothing.

One night, however, the President of the Board himself, coming up from the south in dirty weather on the *Palmetto*, all at once was awakened from sleep by a nasty thumping and bumping that nearly shook him out of his bunk.

Rushing up on to the bridge in his pyjamas, he shouted to the skipper—old Jack Haynes—'What's the matter now? Where the deuce have you got the ship?'

'Hard and fast on the Cat and Kittens,' replied old Jack calmly. 'And now where's your cussed green ray, eh?'

As a matter of fact, nothing at all was visible except a smother of white foam leaping with joyful crashings on the fore-part of the little steamer, and Point Mangrove Light bearing exactly as it should have done to enable the *Palmetto* to clear the reef.

'But I've seen the green light myself many a time!' exclaimed the President, as he hung on and shivered to windward, whilst the engines rattled and clattered full-speed astern for all they were worth in a vain attempt to get out of the Cat's claws.

'So've I,' replied Haynes placidly, 'in clear weather. But not in a southerly smother like this. Just such another night it was that my brother Jim ran on to 'em in the *Star of Judah*. And you broke him for it; and told him he was no sailor because he couldn't see your cussed green ray. Now, when you get to kingdom-come and meet those other poor chaps there, you'll have to admit that even Marine Boards don't know everything.' And with a short laugh the old captain turned away.

But eventually, the lifeboat coming out to them, they all escaped just by the skin of their teeth, leaving the old *Palmetto* to be crushed to pieces by rocky fangs and claws.

And the President being, when convinced, as he was that night, on the whole a just man, not only caused the captain's certificate to be returned to him, but saw, too, that he got another ship. Still, to the end of his life he swore that old Jack Haynes had shoved his vessel on to the reef simply because the President of the Marine Board happened to be a passenger.

However, this was the little incident that quickly caused tenders to be called for the construction, locally, of a bell-buoy. And inasmuch as all young countries like big things, this buoy was to be very big—a record buoy, in fact, carrying a bell as big as a drum.

Sam Johnson, of the Vulcan Foundry, was the man who got the contract, not because he was the lowest tenderer, but because he was the only one.

Other artificers fought shy of the business. Doubtless they could construct the buoy, but the bell bothered them. And by the terms of the contract everything was to be made within the colony. However, nothing daunted, Sam and his men and his one apprentice went to work, with the result that, in a few weeks, a huge double cone of riveted sheet-iron lay in his yard. Each apex of the cone was flat. To the bottom one was bolted a great staple for the mooring-chain; on the top one, hung from a cross-head supported by two uprights, an oblong-shaped fabric of Muntz-metal with, inside it, a tongue as big as a very big water-bottle. This was the bell. And it swung any way to the lightest touch, giving forth a dull boom, that Johnson swore could be heard at Flat Island Light, twenty miles down the coast.

Take one of those Australian bullock-bells their owners set such store by, and which resemble in shape nothing so much as an oval-sided jug, long and narrow, and whose hollow knock, knock can be heard a tremendous distance; then multiply it indefinitely, and you will have a faint conception of what this great bell was like. As for the buoy, it was bigger than any of its family to be seen in Portsmouth Dockyard. And there are some very big ones there.

And as it lay on its side, with its third coat of bright red paint just dry, and its gaping man-hole waiting to be hermetically sealed, the Marine Board and the harbour-master, and all the seafarers of the port, came and inspected it, and pronounced it 'a good job', and congratulated its builder, and prophesied that now the Cat and Kittens should claim no more victims.

Of course, there was a lightship clique who growled. But they were in a minority, and unpopular because the magic word 'retrenchment' was just at that time in the air. And a lightship would be a very expensive matter. Besides, the buoy was a local article manufactured neither in Great Britain nor Germany, but in Cooksland, and probably the first, as it certainly was the biggest, in all the Colonies to be thus made. Therefore, prior to placing it in position, there assuredly must be the usual Greater-British feeding and drinking to mark the event, and show those jealous Southern States what Cooksland could do at a pinch when called upon. And the pretty daughter of the Governor of the great, grim, stone gaol, up there on the hill, was presently asked to give the buoy a name, and break a bottle of wine over its steep sides, up and down and across which rows of round-headed rivets ran like buttons on a coster's Sunday coat.

Perhaps a touch of her own peculiar environment lent itself to the suggestion, as, after a moment's thought, the Governor's blushing daughter pulled the string, and in clear tones said, as the bottle smashed: 'I name you the "Red Warder". And may you ever keep faithful watch and ward; warning with loud voice through storm and darkness the ships to avoid the cruel rocks we put you in charge of.'

Without any preparation, it was prettily said—and the cheers that greeted the little speech echoed loud and long from many a lusty throat whose owner used the sea.

CHAPTER II

THE CONDEMNED CELL

Meanwhile, above them in the prison over which her father reigned supreme, a man sat in the condemned cell waiting for death. From far inland they had brought him, captured by the Black Police, after much hunting of that wild land where the Big Lignum Swamp runs up nearly to the spurs of the Basalt Ranges.

'Combo' Carter, so called because of his habit of at times associating with the blacks, and for long spells living as one of a tribe, was still quite a young man—not yet three-and-twenty. Born at one of the border townships of the hinterland, even as a boy he had begun his career by gaining the reputation of an expert horse-thief. Moving farther out, he and a gang of other rogues had 'lived on the game', as they termed it, *i.e.* stealing stock and taking them south for sale. But this business proving too tame for a born desperado like Carter, he one day made his appearance in his birthplace bent on bigger mischief. Quite alone, mounted on a splendid horse, and with a couple of revolvers stuck in his belt; cabbage-tree hat at the back of his head; blue shirt, riding breeches and boots, he rode down the dusty single street of the little township that lay roasting in the fierce western sun. Halting in front of the weather-board branch bank of Cooksland, he swaggered inside, and at once covering the manager with his pistol, ordered him to 'bail up'.

But the other, instead of doing so, made a dash for a drawer in which was a revolver. Even as he moved, Combo shot him dead. Just then the eldest son, a boy of fifteen, entering, and boldly rushing at the murderer, fell over his father with a bullet through his shoulder. But now some of the townspeople, aroused by the shooting, were making for the bank; and Combo, seizing a packet of notes from the open safe, ran out and, keeping the people at bay with his pistols, mounted, and rode away in safety.

The very next day he robbed and killed a travelling hawker, throwing his body into the tilted cart containing the latter's stock of goods, and setting the lot on fire. Then, driving the unfortunate man's horses before him, he had made back into the wild fastnesses of the Basalt Ranges, to live there a solitary outlaw, until, after months of weary tracking and trap-setting, at last the troopers, white and black, had made a surround and a capture.

Such was the man who sat in the condemned cell at Endeavour Gaol—a human tiger, whose face, with its long, straight, thin-lipped mouth, high cheek-bones, and slits of restless black eyes that seemed always trying to see each other over the flat, fleshy nose, formed a fit index to the cruel, brutal character of its owner. A fair type, 'Combo', of the back-blocks Bush-native, who fears neither God, man, devil, nor any living thing.

The condemned cell at Port Endeavour is merely a stone cage with the fourth side—the one that opens on to the broad corridor—formed of stout iron bars, in which is a wicket gate, just large enough to admit of one man passing through. And here, on the night after the christening of the 'Red Warder', sat Combo Carter, in the full glare of the electric light, watching with tigerish eyes the prison guard as he patrolled, rifle on shoulder, the length of the corridor, pausing each time he came opposite the bars to glance at the silent figure within.

The man, doomed to die three days hence, was not handcuffed. But a pair of strong though light irons, with a two-foot chain between them, confined his legs. Since his conviction the prisoner had altered nothing from the same sulky indifference that had characterized his manner throughout. Rejecting with scorn the ministration of the chaplain, he either lay in his hammock dozing, or sat, as now, on the little wooden shelf fixed to the wall, and with that evil-looking, hairless, pallid face resting on his hands, watched in a crouching attitude through half-closed eyes the ceaseless pacing of the warder.

The latter, a young Englishman not long joined the force,

had, when occasion offered, been able to do several little kindnesses to the convict, whose position, as one for whom life was getting so terribly short, appealed, in spite of his crimes, to a heart yet unhardened by much experience of prison sights and scenes. For the past few days he had suffered much from toothache, and even now his jaw was bound with a flannel bandage. Also, when he had relieved the last guard, he had casually mentioned to him the fact of his having procured leave to go into the town that night and have the tooth drawn. His watch was nearly over—only another half-hour or so more—when, passing the condemned cell, he saw something that drove all other thoughts out of his mind.

With a gurgling, choking sound, his legs apparently drawn up clear of the floor, Combo was hanging by a saddle-strap he used as a belt from one of the iron hooks of his hammock. An older hand might have paused a moment; for never, until now, had the prisoner shown the least inclination towards suicide, mouthing, indeed, with many oaths, his determination to 'die game'. But Ashton, laying aside his rifle, hurriedly pushed back the patent spring of the wicket, and in his eagerness almost tumbled into the cell. He had better have entered a tiger's. In a second the murderer was upon him with the whole weight of his long, lithe body bearing him down, and the sinewy hands gripping his neck like a vice, and throttling the life out of him even before they fell.

At last relaxing his fierce grasp, the prisoner rose and kicked heavily at the motionless thing that, with wide-open mouth and protruding eyes and tongue, stared blankly up at him. Then, giving a grunt of satisfaction as he saw that his work was complete, he searched the dead man's pockets, and soon finding what he sought, unlocked his leg-irons. Then, peering into the corridor, he listened intently. But not a sound broke the silence except the purring of a distant dynamo. He, long ago, had heard the report of the nine o'clock gun from the battery on Flagstaff Hill, and knew that he had therefore not much time to spare. Rapidly and thoroughly he went about his business, until once again a sentry with muffled face and shouldered rifle paced slowly up and down, pausing every now and then to glance into the cell where, over one side of the straining hammock, a glimpse could be gained of a manacled leg. Suddenly his eye was caught by a white, square object on the floor of the cell; and re-entering, he carelessly picked up a card and threw it into the hammock. If he had but known!

CHAPTER III

A HARBOUR OF REFUGE

'Och, be jabers, me poor man, an' is ut so bad agin, thin? Ay, shure, I see the brute's there all roight. Bedad, an' the suner his neck's stretched the suner we'll be at pace agin. Now aff wid ye, an' git the rotten thing out.'

Thus Relief-Constable Sullivan to the man with his swathed face in No. 4 corridor who, peaked cap drawn over his brows, and handkerchief to his mouth, seemed able to do nothing but shake his head and groan, whilst pointing to the cell in token that all was well with his charge.

Along the passage and down some stairs, and through another passage, all brilliantly lit, went the sham constable, one hand to his face, grasping his rifle with the other. At the end of the last passage was a covered yard, at the farther side of which he could see the great iron entrance gate of the gaol, through whose bars a big, round, white moon seemed to glare inquisitively, so close she looked. And now the road to freedom appeared clear; and, by instinct, depositing his rifle in the arm-rack on the left hand of the hall-way, he turned towards the little open gate to the right of the main entrance, always barred, this latter, except to admit the prison van—'Black Maria'.

But one does not get out of Port Endeavour Gaol so easily —bound or free. The Governor, an old Army colonel—martinet, and therefore in the regard of his men, faddist—saw to that. Thus, as the escaping felon stepped to the wicket, coolly exultant, and sniffing the fresh night air with all the eagerness of one long confined, a man issuing from the lighted guard-house said: 'Halloa, Ashton! Off to have it out? Well, it's the only cure. Give me your pass till I clock you,' and he extended his hand.

The cold sweat started in beads from the other's forehead as, to gain time, he mumbled indistinctly and groped with one hand in his pockets for the thing that now flashed into his mind with fatal certainty was not there. Idiot, ass that he was! The card, doubtless, that he had pulled out of the fellow's pocket with the key of the irons, and, neglecting to even glance at, had thrown into the hammock!

'Left it in your room, eh?' queried the other jokingly. 'Well, my son, you'll have to find it, tooth or no tooth. It's worth my jacket to let you out without it. Now, then, off you go and get your ticket.'

That, however, was more than even he dare do; although, for a moment, the thought occurred to him to return and kill Sullivan, and then possess himself of the pass lying on the dead body in the hammock. But he was now unarmed. Sullivan was a big, powerful man. No, plainly, there was nothing for it but a dash.

Where he stood was somewhat in shadow. Even now Sullivan might have taken it into his head to have a look at his prisoner. He could hear steps approaching. The constable on duty was, too, he thought, eyeing him suspiciously. In a second his resolution was taken. From the shadow of the porch he might still have made a dart, preserving his incognito, his escapade set down to pain, and the knowledge that he had lost his pass. All these alternatives flitted across his brain in a space of time measurable by a dozen heart-beats. Realizing that his case was desperate indeed, all the old murderous bravado rose up strong and fierce within him. He began to see red. Armed, he would have killed the man who stood there in his path, as he had so lately killed the other one. Suddenly, tearing off his bandages and pushing his cap away from his eyes, he thrust a distorted, furious face into the light. The guard stepped back appalled, and the next minute a crashing blow from the other's fist sent him reeling to the ground. Another minute, and the murderer was through the gate and speeding along to the town, ankle-deep in powdery dust that rose in white clouds into the white moonlight.

Zip, zip, ping, ping, came the bullets as the men on the watch-towers fired at the flying form, whilst the great bell rang out sharp and quick; and hurrying, half-dressed warders snatched up their Martinis and ran, firing as they went at the pillar of dust ahead.

Ping, ping, szz, szz! How the bullets hissed and whistled past him down the hill, kicking up little splotches of dust far in front! And how that infernal bell rang! He hated bells! Always had done so, since the old days at Arawatta homestead, when a boy, at the call of one, he rose at dawn to tramp through the wet grass after the station saddle-horses. If ever he owned a station, he'd take good care to have a night-horse kept in. Ah! that was a hit! He could feel the blood running down his leg into his boot. If he only had hold of the fellow that fired the shot!

He did not in the least know where he was making for, never having been at the port before, nor, indeed, anywhere except 'Out Back'; but still he kept going, and still the bullets sang past him and pecked at the dust in front. The way lay all down hill. In front of him he could see the harbour, and the masts of the shipping, clear in the moonlight. Behind him he could hear the muffled tramp of many steps. He felt weak, and staggered once or twice. All at once he became aware of shouts coming towards him. But by then he was at the foot of the steep descent on the brow of which was placed the gaol. To the right the road wound towards the heart of the town. To the left, close to the sea-beach, were some sheds and yards, stacks of timber, jetties, and a small coaster or two.

Dust was rising ahead, evidently from police or townspeople aroused by the firing and bell-ringing, and hastening towards the gaol. It was worse than useless to go on. The rifles were quiet now. Where he crouched, in the shadow of a paling fence, his pursuers could not see him. A storm, too, was coming up, and black clouds were already throwing their reflection on the white ground. Rising, he crept along the fence, till, finding a broken paling, he tore it out and squeezed through. He was in a yard; a long shed from which rose a chimney took up one side. There was a smell of hot iron and fresh paint in the air; his feet crunched cinders. Right against him loomed a big, curiously-shaped mass, whose possible use puzzled him as he limped into the shadow of it, and gave it a moment's vague speculation, whilst heavy raindrops splashed hollowly on its iron skin. At the height of his shoulder was an aperture big enough for him to get through, and so into the belly of the thing. He could hear his pursuers cursing the gloom at the other side of the fence. Just as well in there as anywhere else! And putting all his strength into the effort, he drew himself up by his wrists until he got his head in; and then, holding on by a cross-stay, he wriggled his whole body through.

He was a tall man; but swinging from the stay he could touch no bottom. Deciding to let go, he, however, only had to drop some three feet. And wherever he sat he sat on a slope, a matter that seemed so funny to him that he laughed aloud, whilst the lightning flashed and the thunder roared, and the tropical rain fell in streaming sheets over his refuge—kept dry by reason of the entrance being on the under side. The incessant lightning illumined his cavern continuously, enabling him to discover that his wound was not serious—a bullet had passed through the fleshy part of his thigh; and, tearing up a kerchief he found in the pocket of the constabulary tunic, he soon extemporized an efficient bandage. In another pocket he came across a plug of tobacco, of which taking a good chew, he lay back and stolidly awaited what fortune might have further in store for him.

CHAPTER IV

THE MOORING OF THE 'WARDER'

In spite of his wound, which smarted, Combo Carter slept until awakened by voices at the mouth of his shelter, where

Sam Johnson and a group of his men were conversing.

'It's the most extraordinary thing I ever heard of!' remarked Johnson. 'He's disappeared as if he was a ghost.'

'The storm did it,' said another. 'He got away under cover of that, with the traps close at his heels.'

'But where to?' asked a boyish voice. 'The police swear they were close to him when the storm broke—just near our fence here. I wouldn't have him escape for the worth of my right hand! I can't help fancying, yet, that he's planted somewhere about the waterside. If you don't mind, Mr Johnson, I'll just have one more look.'

'Look and welcome, Master Stratton,' replied the owner of the foundry. 'But every corner's been turned upside down, and no sign. I believe, myself, he's collared a boat, and is out at sea by this time.'

At the name of Stratton the hidden listener had pricked up his ears. Could this be the son of the bank manager that he had shot, after killing his father? It was funny if such should be the case. And he was not left long in doubt.

'Poor young chap!' remarked one of the men. 'I knew his father well, afore that brute Combo did for 'im. Plugged the kiddy, too, didn't he, boss?'

'Wounded him badly,' replied Johnson. 'His mother wanted him to take a billet in the bank, after he came out of the hospital. They offered him one at once, but he couldn't bear the notion. So they apprenticed him to me. Smart and handy he's turned out, too. Did most of the work on the "Red Warder" here, besides drawin' the plans for him. Now, lads, some of you go up to the Marine Storeyard and get the trolly to put the "Warder" on. They're going to take him out in the afternoon, as soon as poor Ashton's buried.'

'Yes, decidedly,' thought the murderer, hardly able to repress a chuckle, as he crouched away from the circular globe of light, 'it *was* funny that the son of the man he had shot because he wouldn't put up his hands when ordered should have been the one to have the biggest share in building this splendid hiding place. No one would ever dream of searching in there. That was evident. At nightfall he would come

out, and if he could but steal a horse, he might yet be able
to snap his fingers at them all. And they were, apparently,
going to take the thing he was in away somewhere. Up
country; perhaps on the railway. Likely enough it was a sort
of new-fangled tank for use on a station; maybe to dip sheep
in. If they'd only drop a bit of tucker in, he'd be fixed right
up to the knocker. But, failing that, the bacca'd have to stand
to him.' So ran the villain's thoughts, as already in his mind's
eye he saw himself once more free and back again in his old
haunts, or even farther out—right across to the Territory.

By-and-by he heard a voice close to the hole say: 'No
news?'

'None,' was the reply in the same youthful tones he recognized as young Stratton's. 'Port Endeavour's been searched
from top to bottom without success. Now a party has gone
inland, and another one down the harbour along each shore.
I came back because I thought the "Warder's" lid was a trifle
big for the slot, and I knew the Board people wouldn't care
about being kept waiting now they've got their moorings
ready at the reef.'

Then there was a sound of chipping as of a cold chisel
upon iron, and presently something was clapped into the
man-hole, fitting so closely as to show not the faintest gleam
of light. Suddenly the buoy was rolled over, shaking and
bruising its occupant considerably, and causing him to mut-
ter deep curses as he picked himself up and sought vainly for
something to hold on to. The darkness was intense, and the
heat, engendered by the sun beating on the iron plates all
the morning, grew almost unbearable now that the only opening was closed. In desperation, the wretch stripped off his
clothes and lay naked upon them, with the hot iron burning
his skin wherever it touched. All at once he felt that his
shelter had been lifted up bodily, and was moving. The heat
grew fiercer, and the sweat poured off him like rain. But he
set his teeth and suffered it. Presently he felt the thing he
was in moving with a new motion. Swinging through the air
this time, whilst a dim rattle came to his ears. This was when
the 'Warder' was being hoisted on to the Marine Board ten-

der *Thetis*, under the command of Captain Haynes; and the rattle was the noise of her steam winch.

It grew somewhat cooler now. But, presently, another and an altogether novel motion puzzled him. He had certainly never experienced anything like it before. It was not that of a railway. And what could be making him pant so distressfully, and draw his breath with such difficulty? Air! air, in Heaven's name! He fumbled vainly about in the inky blackness for the lid he had seen them put on, bruising his fingers and tearing his nails against clenched rivets. But he had lost all sense of locality, and kept groping upwards for the manhole when it was, in fact, under his feet. Nor would it have availed him any could he have found it—cunningly turned and slotted, and caulked with red lead and oakum, already as hard as adamant. Denser and denser grew the atmosphere; his breath came and went in wheezy pantings. There was a weight as of tons pressing on his chest, and his heart hit his ribs like a hammer.

For perhaps the first time in his life terror came upon him. Where was he? What was being done to him? And as he staggered here and there, bruised and bleeding, against the hot sides of his prison, gasping for breath, all at once his feet touched the murdered constable's handcuffs that, together with his belt, he had put on years ago—it seemed—in the gaol. Picking them up, he battered with all his feeble, sobbing might against the iron plates of the dreadful trap in which he had been snared.

Suddenly the thing changed its position to an upright one, and he fell headlong down to the bottom of it and lay there doubled up, the burning heat of his body turned in a moment to chilling cold; his chest felt as if it were bursting, and strange, flaming shapes rushed hither and thither before his staring eyes. The dismal tolling of a bell, too, in his ears! Ah, how he hated bells! ... Ding-dong-dong-ding! ... Now he knew.... They had hanged him at last.... That was the prison bell.... He wasn't quite dead yet, though.... Swinging at the end of the rope.... Curse them all!

'Didn't you fancy you heard something rattling and knocking when we lowered the "Warder" over the side, Haynes?' asked the President of the Marine Board as the *Thetis* steamed homewards from the Cat and Kittens.

'Rivet-heads and an odd bolt or two,' replied the old skipper shortly, casting a look back to where the great red buoy swung well out of the water, rocking and nodding to a westerly cross-swell, whilst to their ears came very distinctly the sullen booming of the bell.

Wolverden Tower

by

GRANT ALLEN

Novelist, philosopher and scientific writer Grant Allen (1848–1899) has been largely ignored by short story anthologists. He was born in Canada and educated in America, France and England, graduating from Oxford in classical moderations. He taught moral philosophy in Jamaica for three years. After many years of contributing scientific articles to magazines and newspapers, he wrote an article for Belgravia on man's improbability to recognize a ghost if he ever saw one and 'for the better development of my subject, threw the argument into the form of a narrative'. He was so successful with this story form that he was asked to contribute further stories, which he published under the pseudonym of J. Arbuthnot Wilson. When James Payn took over the Cornhill magazine, he determined to publish only short stories and Allen found himself in the unique position of one day receiving two letters from Payn, one addressed to himself refusing a scientific article and the other addressed to Wilson requesting some short stories. Allen published several books of his tales, including Strange Stories (1884) and The Beckoning Hand (1887). 'Wolverden Tower' first saw light in a Christmas number of the Illustrated London News and has remained out of print for three quarters of a century. It is a long tale, packed with convincing detail of folklore and the supernatural and is one of the best stories of the collection.

I

Maisie Llewelyn had never been asked to Wolverden before; therefore, she was not a little elated at Mrs West's invitation. For Wolverden Hall, one of the loveliest Elizabethan manor-houses in the Weald of Kent, had been bought and fitted up in appropriate style (the phrase is the upholsterer's) by Colonel West, the famous millionaire from South Australia. The Colonel had lavished upon it untold wealth, fleeced from the backs of ten thousand sheep and an equal number of his fellow-countrymen; and Wolverden was now, if not the most beautiful, at least the most opulent country-house within easy reach of London.

Mrs West was waiting at the station to meet Maisie. The house was full of Christmas guests already, it is true; but Mrs West was a model of stately, old-fashioned courtesy: she would not have omitted meeting one among the number on any less excuse than a royal command to appear at Windsor. She kissed Maisie on both cheeks—she had always been fond of Maisie—and, leaving two haughty young aristocrats (in powdered hair and blue-and-gold livery) to hunt up her luggage by the light of nature, sailed forth with her through the door to the obsequious carriage.

The drive up the avenue to Wolverden Hall Maisie found quite delicious. Even in their leafless winter condition the great limes looked so noble; and the ivy-covered hall at the end, with its mullioned windows, its Inigo Jones porch, and its creeper-clad gables, was as picturesque a building as the ideals one sees in Mr Abbey's sketches. If only Arthur Hume had been one of the party now, Maisie's joy would have been complete. But what was the use of thinking so much about Arthur Hume, when she didn't even know whether Arthur Hume cared for her?

A tall, slim girl, Maisie Llewelyn, with rich black hair, and ethereal features, as became a descendant of Llewelyn ap Iorwerth—the sort of girl we none of us would have called anything more than 'interesting' till Rossetti and Burne-Jones found eyes for us to see that the type is beautiful with a deeper beauty than that of your obvious pink-and-white prettiness. Her eyes, in particular, had a lustrous depth that was almost superhuman, and her fingers and nails were strangely transparent in their waxen softness.

'You won't mind my having put you in a ground-floor room in the new wing, my dear, will you?' Mrs West inquired, as she led Maisie personally to the quarters chosen for her. 'You see, we're so unusually full, because of these tableaux!'

Maisie gazed round the ground-floor room in the new wing with eyes of mute wonder. If *this* was the kind of lodging for which Mrs West thought it necessary to apologize, Maisie wondered of what sort were those better rooms which she gave to the guests she delighted to honour. It was a large and exquisitely decorated chamber, with the softest and deepest Oriental carpet Maisie's feet had ever felt, and the daintiest curtains her eyes had ever lighted upon. True, it opened by french windows on to what was nominally the ground in front; but as the Italian terrace, with its formal balustrade and its great stone balls, was raised several feet above the level of the sloping garden below, the room was really on the first floor for all practical purposes. Indeed, Maisie rather liked the unwonted sense of space and freedom which was given by this easy access to the world without; and, as the windows were secured by great shutters and fasteners, she had no counterbalancing fear lest a nightly burglar should attempt to carry off her little pearl necklet or her amethyst brooch, instead of directing his whole attention to Mrs West's famous diamond tiara.

She moved naturally to the window. She was fond of nature. The view it disclosed over the Weald at her feet was wide and varied. Misty range lay behind misty range, in a faint December haze, receding and receding, till away to the south, half hidden by vapour, the Sussex downs loomed vague in the distance. The village church, as happens so often in the case of old lordly manors, stood within the grounds of the Hall, and close by the house. It had been built, her hostess said, in the days of the Edwards, but had portions of an older Saxon edifice still enclosed in the chancel. The one eyesore in the view was its new white tower, recently restored (or rather, rebuilt), which contrasted most painfully with the mellow grey stone and mouldering corbels of the nave and transept.

'What a pity it's been so spoiled!' Maisie exclaimed, looking across at the tower. Coming straight as she did from a Merioneth rectory, she took an ancestral interest in all that concerned churches.

'Oh, my dear!' Mrs West cried, '*please* don't say that, I beg of you, to the Colonel. If you were to murmur "spoiled" to him you'd wreck his digestion. He's spent ever so much money over securing the foundations and reproducing the sculpture on the old tower we took down, and it breaks his dear heart when anybody disapproves of it. For *some* people, you know, are so absurdly opposed to reasonable restoration.'

'Oh, but this isn't even restoration, you know,' Maisie said, with the frankness of twenty, and the specialist interest of an antiquary's daughter. 'This is pure reconstruction.'

'Perhaps so,' Mrs West answered. 'But if you think so, my dear, don't breathe it at Wolverden.'

A fire, of ostentatiously wealthy dimensions, and of the best glowing coal, burned bright on the hearth; but the day was mild, and hardly more than autumnal. Maisie found the room quite unpleasantly hot. She opened the windows and stepped out on the terrace. Mrs West followed her. They paced up and down the broad gravelled platform for a while —Maisie had not yet taken off her travelling-cloak and hat —and then strolled half unconsciously towards the gate of the church. The churchyard, to hide the tombstones of which the parapet had been erected, was full of quaint old monuments, with broken-nosed cherubs, some of them dating from a comparatively early period. The porch, with its sculptured niches deprived of their saints by puritan hands, was still rich and beautiful in its carved detail. On the seat inside an old woman was sitting. She did not rise as the lady of the manor approached, but went on mumbling and muttering inarticulately to herself in a sulky undertone. Still, Maisie was aware, none the less, that the moment she came near a strange light gleamed suddenly in the old woman's eyes, and that her glance was fixed upon her. A faint thrill of recognition seemed to pass like a flash through her palsied body. Maisie knew not why, but she was dimly afraid of the old woman's gaze upon her.

'It's a lovely old church!' Maisie said, looking up at the trefoil finials on the porch—'all, except the tower.'

'We *had* to reconstruct it,' Mrs West answered apologetically—Mrs West's general attitude in life was apologetic, as though she felt she had no right to so much more money than her fellow-creatures. 'It would have fallen if we hadn't done something to buttress it up. It was really in a most dangerous and critical condition.'

'Lies! lies! lies!' the old woman burst out suddenly, though in a strange, low tone, as if speaking to herself. 'It would *not* have fallen—they knew it would not. It could not have fallen. It would never have fallen if they had not destroyed it. And even then—I was there when they pulled it down—each stone clung to each, with arms and legs and hands and claws, till they burst them asunder by main force with their new-fangled stuff—I don't know what they call it—dynamite, or something. It was all of it done for one man's vainglory!'

'Come away, dear,' Mrs West whispered. But Maisie loitered.

'Wolverden Tower was fasted thrice,' the old woman continued, in a sing-song quaver. 'It was fasted thrice with souls of maids against every assault of man or devil. It was fasted at the foundation against earthquake and ruin. It was fasted at the top against thunder and lightning. It was fasted in the middle against storm and battle. And there it would have stood for a thousand years if a wicked man had not raised a vainglorious hand against it. For that's what the rhyme says—

> 'Fasted thrice with souls of men,
> Stands the tower of Wolverden;
> Fasted thrice with maidens' blood,

> A thousand years of fire and flood
> Shall see it stand as erst it stood.'

She paused a moment, then, raising one skinny hand towards the brand-new stone, she went on in the same voice, but with malignant fervour—

> 'A thousand years the tower shall stand
> Till ill assailed by evil hand;
> By evil hand in evil hour,
> Fasted thrice with warlock's power,
> Shall fall the stanes of Wulfhere's tower.'

She tottered off as she ended, and took her seat on the edge of a depressed vault in the churchyard close by, still eyeing Maisie Llewelyn with a weird and curious glance, almost like the look which a famishing man casts upon the food in a shop-window.

'Who is she?' Maisie asked, shrinking away in undefined terror.

'Oh, old Bessie,' Mrs West answered, looking more apologetic (for the parish) than ever. 'She's always hanging about here. She has nothing else to do, and she's an outdoor pauper. You see, that's the worst of having the church in one's grounds, which is otherwise picturesque and romantic and baronial; the road to it is public; you must admit all the world; and old Bessie *will* come here. The servants are afraid of her. They say she's a witch. She has the evil eye, and she drives girls to suicide. But they cross her hand with silver all the same, and she tells them their fortunes—gives them each a butler. She's full of dreadful stories about Wolverden Church—stories to make your blood run cold, my dear, compact with old superstitions and murders, and so forth. And they're true, too, that's the worst of them. She's quite a character. Mr Blaydes, the antiquary, is really attached to her; he says she's now the sole living repository of the traditional folklore and history of the parish. But I don't care for it myself. It "gars one greet", as we say in Scotland. Too much burying alive in it, don't you know, my dear, to quite suit *my* fancy.'

They turned back as she spoke towards the carved wooden lych-gate, one of the oldest and most exquisite of its class in England. When they reached the vault by whose doors old Bessie was seated, Maisie turned once more to gaze at the pointed lancet windows of the Early English choir, and the still more ancient dog-tooth ornament of the ruined Norman Lady Chapel.

'How solidly it's built!' she exclaimed, looking up at the arches which alone survived the fury of the Puritan. 'It really looks as if it would last for ever.'

Old Bessie had bent her head, and seemed to be whispering something at the door of the vault. But at the sound she raised her eyes, and, turning her wizened face towards the lady of the manor, mumbled through her few remaining fang-like teeth an old local saying, 'Bradbury for length, Wolverden for strength, and Church Hatton for beauty!

> 'Three brothers builded churches three;
> And fasted thrice each church shall be:
> Fasted thrice with maidens' blood,
> To make them safe from fire and flood;
> Fasted thrice with souls of men,
> Hatton, Bradbury, Wolverden!'

'Come away,' Maisie said, shuddering. 'I'm afraid of that woman. Why was she whispering at the doors of the vault down there? I don't like the look of her.'

'My dear,' Mrs West answered, in no less terrified a tone, 'I will confess I don't like the look of her myself. I wish she'd leave the place. I've tried to make her. The Colonel offered her fifty pounds down and a nice cottage in Surrey if only she'd go—she frightens me so much; but she wouldn't hear of it. She said she must stop by the bodies of her dead—that's her style, don't you see: a sort of modern ghoul, a degenerate vampire—and from the bodies of her dead in Wolverden Church no living soul should ever move her.'

II

For dinner Maisie wore her white satin Empire dress, high-waisted, low-necked, and cut in the bodice with a certain baby-like simplicity of style which exactly suited her strange and uncanny type of beauty. She was very much admired.

After dinner, the tableaux. They had been designed and managed by a famous Royal Academician, and were mostly got up by the members of the house-party.

The first tableau, Maisie learned from the gorgeous programme, was 'Jephthah's Daughter'. The subject was represented at the pathetic moment when the doomed virgin goes forth from her father's house with her attendant maidens to bewail her virginity for two months upon the mountains, before the fulfilment of the awful vow which bound her father to offer her up for a burnt offering. Maisie thought it too solemn and tragic a scene for a festive occasion. But the famous R.A. had a taste for such themes, and his grouping was certainly most effectively dramatic.

'A perfect symphony in white and grey,' said Mr Wills, the art critic.

'How awfully affecting!' said most of the young girls.

'Reminds me a little too much, my dear, of old Bessie's stories,' Mrs West whispered low, leaning from her seat across two rows to Maisie.

A piano stood a little on one side of the platform, just in front of the curtain. The intervals between the pieces were filled up with songs, which, however, had been evidently arranged in keeping with the solemn and half-mystical tone of the tableaux. It is the habit of amateurs to take a long time in getting their scenes in order, so the interposition of the music was a happy thought as far as its prime intention went. But Maisie wondered they could not have chosen some livelier song for Christmas Eve than 'Oh, Mary, go and call the cattle home, and call the cattle home, and call the cattle home, across the sands of Dee.' Her own name was Mary when she

:igned it officially, and the sad lilt of the last line, 'But never
nome came she,' rang unpleasantly in her ear through the
:est of the evening.

The second tableau was the 'Sacrifice of Iphigenia'. It was
admirably rendered. The cold and dignified father, standing,
apparently unmoved, by the pyre; the cruel faces of the attendant priests; the shrinking form of the immolated princess;
the mere blank curiosity and inquiring interest of the hel-
meted heroes looking on, to whom this slaughter of a virgin
victim was but an ordinary incident of the Achaean religion
—all these had been arranged by the Academical director
with consummate skill and pictorial cleverness. But the group
that attracted Maisie most among the components of the scene
was that of the attendant maidens, more conspicuous here in
their flowing white chitons than even they had been when
posed as companions of the beautiful and ill-fated Hebrew
victim. Two in particular excited her close attention—two
very graceful and spiritual-looking girls, in long white robes
of no particular age or country, who stood at the very end
near the right edge of the picture. 'How lovely they are, the
two last on the right!' Maisie whispered to her neighbour—
an Oxford undergraduate with a budding moustache. 'I do
so admire them!'

'Do you?' he answered, fondling the moustache with one
dubious finger. 'Well, now, do you know, I don't think I do.
They're rather coarse-looking. And besides, I don't quite like
the way they've got their hair done up in bunches; too fashionable, isn't it?—too much of the present day? I don't care to
see a girl in a Greek costume, with her coiffure so evidently
turned out by Truefitt's!'

'Oh, I don't mean those two,' Maisie answered, a little
shocked he should think she had picked out such meretricious
faces; 'I mean the two beyond them again—the two with their
hair so simply and sweetly done—the ethereal-looking dark
girls.'

The undergraduate opened his mouth, and stared at her
in blank amazement for a moment. 'Well, I don't see—' he
began, and broke off suddenly. Something in Maisie's eye

seemed to give him pause. He fondled his moustache, hesitated, and was silent.

At the end of the tableau one or two of the characters who were not needed in succeeding pieces came down from the stage and joined the body of spectators, as they often do, in their character-dresses—a good opportunity, in point of fact, for retaining through the evening the advantages conferred by theatrical costume, rouge, and pearl-powder. Among them the two girls Maisie had admired so much glided quietly towards her and took the two vacant seats on either side, one of which had just been quitted by the awkward undergraduate. They were not only beautiful in face and figure, on a closer view, but Maisie found them from the first extremely sympathetic. They burst into talk with her, frankly and at once, with charming ease and grace of manner. They were ladies in the grain, in instinct and breeding. The taller of the two, whom the other addressed as Yolande, seemed particularly pleasing. The very name charmed Maisie. She was friends with them at once. They both possessed a certain nameless attraction that constitutes in itself the best possible introduction. Maisie hesitated to ask them whence they came, but it was clear from their talk they knew Wolverden intimately.

After a minute the piano struck up once more. As chance would have it, the vocalist began singing the song Maisie most of all hated. It was Scott's ballad of 'Proud Maisie', set to music by Carlo Ludovici—

> 'Proud Maisie is in the wood,
>   Walking so early;
> Sweet Robin sits on the bush,
>   Singing so rarely.
>
> "Tell me, thou bonny bird,
>   When shall I marry me?"
> "When six braw gentlemen
>   Kirkward shall carry ye."

"Who makes the bridal bed,
    Birdie, say truly?"
"The grey-headed sexton
    That delves the grave duly.

"The glow-worm o'er grave and stone
    Shall light thee steady;
The owl from the steeple sing,
    'Welcome, proud lady.'"'

Maisie listened to the song with grave discomfort. She had never liked it, and tonight it appalled her. She did not know that just at that moment Mrs West was whispering in a perfect fever of apology to a lady by her side, 'Oh dear! oh dear! what a dreadful thing of me ever to have permitted that song to be sung here tonight! It was horribly thoughtless! Why, now I remember, Miss Llewelyn's name, you know, is Maisie!—and there she is listening to it with a face like a sheet! I shall never forgive myself!'

The tall, dark girl by Maisie's side, whom the other called Yolande, leaned across to her sympathetically. 'You don't like that song?' she said, with just a tinge of reproach in her voice as she said it.

'I hate it!' Maisie answered, trying hard to compose herself.

'Why so?' the tall, dark girl asked, in a tone of calm and singular sweetness. 'It is sad, perhaps; but it's lovely—and natural!'

'My own name is Maisie,' her new friend replied, with an ill-repressed shudder. 'And somehow that song pursues me through life. I seem always to hear the horrid ring of the words, "When six braw gentlemen kirkward shall carry ye". I wish to Heaven my people had never called me Maisie!'

'And yet *why*?' the tall, dark girl asked again, with a sad, mysterious air. 'Why this clinging to life—this terror of death —this inexplicable attachment to a world of misery? And with such eyes as yours, too! Your eyes are like mine'— which was a compliment, certainly, for the dark girl's own pair were strangely deep and lustrous. 'People with eyes such as those, that can look into futurity, ought not surely to shrink from a mere gate like death! For death is but a gate—the gate of life in its fullest beauty. It is written over the door, "*Mors janua vitæ*".'

'What door?' Maisie asked—for she remembered having read those selfsame words, and tried in vain to translate them, that very day, though the meaning was now clear to her.

The answer electrified her: 'The gate of the vault in Wolverden churchyard.'

She said it very low, but with pregnant expression.

'Oh, how dreadful!' Maisie exclaimed, drawing back. The tall, dark girl half frightened her.

'Not at all,' the girl answered. 'This life is so short, so vain, so transitory! And beyond it is peace—eternal peace—the calm of rest—the joy of the spirit.'

'You come to anchor at last,' her companion added.

'But if—one has somebody one would not wish to leave behind?' Maisie suggested timidly.

'He will follow before long,' the dark girl replied with quiet decision, interpreting rightly the sex of the indefinite substantive. 'Time passes so quickly. And if time passes quickly in time, how much more, then, in eternity!'

'Hush, Yolande,' the other dark girl put in, with a warning glance; 'there's a new tableau coming. Let me see, is this "The Death of Ophelia"? No, that's number four; this is number three, "The Martyrdom of St Agnes".'

III

'My dear,' Mrs West said, positively oozing apology, when she met Maisie in the supper-room, 'I'm afraid you've been left in a corner by yourself almost all the evening!'

'Oh dear, no,' Maisie answered with a quiet smile. 'I had that Oxford undergraduate at my elbow at first; and afterwards those two nice girls, with the flowing white dresses and the beautiful eyes, came and sat beside me. What's their name, I wonder?'

'Which girls?' Mrs West asked, with a little surprise in her tone, for her impression was rather that Maisie had been sitting between two empty chairs for the greater part of the evening, muttering at times to herself in the most uncanny way, but not talking to anybody.

Maisie glanced round the room in search of her new friends, and for some time could not see them. At last, she observed them in a remote alcove, drinking red wine by themselves out of Venetian-glass beakers. 'Those two,' she said, pointing towards them. 'They're such charming girls! Can you tell me who they are? I've quite taken a fancy to them.'

Mrs West gazed at them for a second—or rather, at the recess towards which Maisie pointed—and then turned to Maisie with much the same oddly embarrassed look and manner as the undergraduate's. 'Oh, *those*!' she said slowly, peering through and through her, Maisie thought. 'Those—must be some of the professionals from London. At any rate—I'm not sure which you mean—over there by the curtain, in the Moorish nook, you say—well, I can't tell you their names! So they *must* be professionals.'

She went off with a singularly frightened manner. Maisie noticed it and wondered at it. But it made no great or lasting impression.

When the party broke up, about midnight or a little later, Maisie went along the corridor to her own bedroom. At the end, by the door, the two other girls happened to be standing, apparently gossiping.

'Oh, you've not gone home yet?' Maisie said, as she passed, to Yolande.

'No, we're stopping here,' the dark girl with the speaking eyes answered.

Maisie paused for a second. Then an impulse burst over her. 'Will you come and see my room?' she asked, a little timidly.

'Shall we go, Hedda?' Yolande said, with an inquiring glance at her companion.

Her friend nodded assent. Maisie opened the door, and ushered them into her bedroom.

The ostentatiously opulent fire was still burning brightly,

the electric light flooded the room with its brilliancy, the curtains were drawn, and the shutters fastened. For a while the three girls sat together by the hearth and gossiped quietly. Maisie liked her new friends—their voices were so gentle, soft, and sympathetic, while for face and figure they might have sat as models to Burne-Jones or Botticelli. Their dresses, too, took her delicate Welsh fancy; they were so dainty, yet so simple. The soft silk fell in natural folds and dimples. The only ornaments they wore were two curious brooches of very antique workmanship—as Maisie supposed—somewhat Celtic in design, and enamelled in blood-red on a gold background. Each carried a flower laid loosely in her bosom. Yolande's was an orchid with long, floating streamers, in colour and shape recalling some Southern lizard; dark purple spots dappled its lip and petals. Hedda's was a flower of a sort Maisie had never before seen—the stem spotted like a viper's skin, green flecked with russet-brown, and uncanny to look upon; on either side, great twisted spirals of red-and-blue blossoms, each curled after the fashion of a scorpion's tail, very strange and lurid. Something weird and witch-like about flowers and dresses rather attracted Maisie; they affected her with the half-repellent fascination of a snake for a bird; she felt such blossoms were fit for incantations and sorceries. But a lily-of-the-valley in Yolande's dark hair gave a sense of purity which assorted better with the girl's exquisitely calm and nun-like beauty.

After a while Hedda rose. 'This air is close,' she said. 'It ought to be warm outside tonight, if one may judge by the sunset. May I open the window?'

'Oh, certainly, if you like,' Maisie answered, a vague foreboding now struggling within her against innate politeness.

Hedda drew back the curtains and unfastened the shutters. It was a moonlit evening. The breeze hardly stirred the bare boughs of the silver birches. A sprinkling of soft snow on the terrace and the hills just whitened the ground. The moon lighted it up, falling full upon the Hall; the church and tower below stood silhouetted in dark against a cloudless expanse of starry sky in the background. Hedda opened the

window. Cool, fresh air blew in, very soft and genial, in spite
of the snow and the lateness of the season. 'What a glorious
night!' she said, looking up at Orion overhead. 'Shall we
stroll out for a while in it?'

If the suggestion had not thus been thrust upon her from
outside, it would never have occurred to Maisie to walk
abroad in a strange place, in evening dress, on a winter's
night, with snow whitening the ground; but Hedda's voice
sounded so sweetly persuasive, and the idea itself seemed so
natural now she had once proposed it, that Maisie followed
her two new friends on to the moonlit terrace without a
moment's hesitation.

They paced once or twice up and down the gravelled walks.
Strange to say, though a sprinkling of dry snow powdered
the ground under foot, the air itself was soft and balmy.
Stranger still, Maisie noticed, almost without noticing it, that
though they walked three abreast, only one pair of footprints
—her own—lay impressed on the snow in a long trail when
they turned at either end and re-paced the platform. Yolande
and Hedda must step lightly indeed; or perhaps her own
feet might be warmer or thinner shod, so as to melt the light
layer of snow more readily.

The girls slipped their arms through hers. A little thrill
coursed through her. Then, after three or four turns up and
down the terrace, Yolande led the way quietly down the broad
flight of steps in the direction of the church on the lower
level. In that bright, broad moonlight Maisie went with them
undeterred; the Hall was still alive with the glare of electric
lights in bedroom windows; and the presence of the other
girls, both wholly free from any signs of fear, took off all
sense of terror or loneliness. They strolled on into the churchyard. Maisie's eyes were now fixed on the new white tower,
which merged in the silhouette against the starry sky into
much the same grey and indefinite hue as the older parts of
the building. Before she quite knew where she was, she found
herself at the head of the worn stone steps which led into the
vault by whose doors she had seen old Bessie sitting. In the
pallid moonlight, with the aid of the greenish reflection from

the snow, she could just read the words inscribed over the portal, the words that Yolande had repeated in the drawing-room, '*Mors janua vitæ*'.

Yolande moved down one step. Maisie drew back for the first time, with a faint access of alarm. 'You're—you're not *going down* there!' she exclaimed, catching her breath for a second.

'Yes, I am,' her new friend answered in a calmly quiet voice. 'Why not? We live here.'

'You live here?' Maisie echoed, freeing her arms by a sudden movement and standing away from her mysterious friends with a tremulous shudder.

'Yes, we live here,' Hedda broke in, without the slightest emotion. She said it in a voice of perfect calm, as one might say it of any house in a street in London.

Maisie was far less terrified than she might have imagined beforehand would be the case under such unexpected conditions. The two girls were so simple, so natural, so strangely like herself, that she could not say she was really afraid of them. She shrank, it is true, from the nature of the door at which they stood, but she received the unearthly announcement that they lived there with scarcely more than a slight tremor of surprise and astonishment.

'You will come in with us?' Hedda said in a gently enticing tone. 'We went into your bedroom.'

Maisie hardly liked to say no. They seemed so anxious to show her their home. With trembling feet she moved down the first step, and then the second. Yolande kept ever one pace in front of her. As Maisie reached the third step, the two girls, as if moved by one design, took her wrists in their hands, not unkindly, but coaxingly. They reached the actual doors of the vault itself—two heavy bronze valves, meeting in the centre. Each bore a ring for a handle, pierced through a Gorgon's head embossed upon the surface. Yolande pushed them with her hand. They yielded instantly to her light touch, and opened *inward*. Yolande, still in front, passed from the glow of the moon to the gloom of the vault, which a ray of moonlight just descended obliquely. As she passed, for a second, a weird sight met Maisie's eyes. Her face and hands and dress became momentarily self-luminous; but through them, as they glowed, she could descry within every bone and joint of her living skeleton, dimly shadowed in dark through the luminous haze that marked her body.

Maisie drew back once more, terrified. Yet her terror was not quite what one could describe as fear: it was rather a vague sense of the profoundly mystical. 'I can't! I can't!' she cried, with an appealing glance. 'Hedda! Yolande! I cannot go with you.'

Hedda held her hand tight, and almost seemed to force her. But Yolande, in front, like a mother with her child, turned round with a grave smile. 'No, no,' she said reprovingly. 'Let her come if she will, Hedda, of her own accord, not otherwise. The tower demands a willing victim.'

Her hand on Maisie's wrist was strong but persuasive. It drew her without exercising the faintest compulsion. 'Will you come with us, dear?' she said, in that winning silvery tone which had captivated Maisie's fancy from the very first moment they spoke together. Maisie gazed into her eyes. They were deep and tender. A strange resolution seemed to nerve her for the effort. 'Yes, yes—I—will—come—with you,' she answered slowly.

Hedda on one side, Yolande on the other, now went before her, holding her wrists in their grasp, but rather enticing than drawing her. As each reached the gloom, the same luminous appearance which Maisie had noticed before spread over their bodies, and the same weird skeleton shape showed faintly through their limbs in darker shadow. Maisie crossed the threshold with a convulsive gasp. As she crossed it she looked down at her own dress and body. They were semi-transparent, like the others', though not quite so self-luminous; the framework of her limbs appeared within in less certain outline, yet quite dark and distinguishable.

The doors swung to of themselves behind her. Those three stood alone in the vault of Wolverden.

Alone, for a minute or two; and then, as her eyes grew accustomed to the grey dusk of the interior, Maisie began to perceive that the vault opened out into a large and beautiful hall or crypt, dimly lighted at first, but becoming each moment more vaguely clear and more dreamily definite. Gradually she could make out great rock-hewn pillars, Romanesque in their outline or dimly Oriental, like the sculptured columns in the caves of Ellora, supporting a roof of vague and uncertain dimensions, more or less strangely dome-shaped. The effect on the whole was like that of the second impression produced by some dim cathedral, such as Chartres or Milan, after the eyes have grown accustomed to the mellow light from the stained-glass windows, and have recovered from the blinding glare of the outer sunlight. But the architecture, if one may call it so, was more mosque-like and magical. She turned to her companions. Yolande and Hedda stood still by her side; their bodies were now self-luminous to a greater degree than even at the threshold; but the terrible transparency had disappeared altogether; they were once more but beautiful though strangely transfigured and more than mortal women.

Then Maisie understood in her own soul, dimly, the meaning of those mystic words written over the portal—'Mors janua vitæ'—Death is the gate of life; and also the interpretation of that awful vision of death dwelling within them as they crossed the threshold; for through that gate they had passed to this underground palace.

Her two guides still held her hands, one on either side. But they seemed rather to lead her on now, seductively and resistlessly, than to draw or compel her. As she moved in through the hall, with its endless vistas of shadowy pillars, seen now behind, now in dim perspective, she was gradually aware that many other people crowded its aisles and corridors. Slowly they took shape as forms more or less clad, mysterious, varied, and of many ages. Some of them wore flowing robes, half mediaeval in shape, like the two friends who had brought her there. They looked like the saints on a stained-glass window. Others were girt merely with a light and floating Coan sash; while some stood dimly nude in the darker recesses of the temple or palace. All leaned eagerly forward with one mind as she approached, and regarded her with deep and sympathetic interest. A few of them murmured words—mere cabalistic sounds which at first she could not understand; but as she moved further into the hall, and saw at each step more clearly into the gloom, they began to have a meaning for her. Before long, she was aware that she understood the mute tumult of voices at once by some internal instinct. The Shades addressed her; she answered them. She knew by intuition what tongue they spoke; it was the Language of the Dead; and, by passing that portal with her two companions, she had herself become enabled both to speak and understand it.

A soft and flowing tongue, this speech of the Nether World —all vowels it seemed, without distinguishable consonants; yet dimly recalling every other tongue, and compounded, as it were, of what was common to all of them. It flowed from those shadowy lips as clouds issue inchoate from a mountain valley; it was formless, uncertain, vague, but yet beautiful. She hardly knew, indeed, as it fell upon her senses, if it were sound or perfume.

Through this tenuous world Maisie moved as in a dream, her two companions still cheering and guiding her. When they reached an inner shrine or chantry of the temple she was dimly conscious of more terrible forms pervading the background than any of those that had yet appeared to her. This was a more austere and antique apartment than the rest; a shadowy cloister, prehistoric in its severity; it recalled to her mind something indefinitely intermediate between the huge unwrought trilithons of Stonehenge and the massive granite pillars of Philæ and Luxor. At the further end of the sanctuary a sort of Sphinx looked down on her, smiling mysteriously. At its base, on a rude megalithic throne, in solitary state, a High Priest was seated. He bore in his hand a wand or sceptre. All round, a strange court of half-unseen acolytes and shadowy hierophants stood attentive. They were girt, as she fancied, in what looked like leopards' skins, or in the fells of some earlier prehistoric lion. These wore sabre-shaped teeth suspended by a string round their dusky necks; others had ornaments of uncut amber, or hatchets of jade threaded as collars on a cord of sinew. A few, more barbaric than savage in type, flaunted torques of gold as armlets and necklets.

The High Priest rose slowly and held out his two hands, just level with his head, the palms turned outward. 'You have brought a willing victim as Guardian of the Tower?' he asked, in that mystic tongue, of Yolande and Hedda.

'We have brought a willing victim,' the two girls answered.

The High Priest gazed at her. His glance was piercing. Maisie trembled less with fear than with a sense of strangeness, such as a neophyte might feel on being first presented at some courtly pageant. 'You come of your own accord?' the Priest inquired of her in solemn accents.

'I come of my own accord,' Maisie answered, with an inner consciousness that she was bearing her part in some immemorial ritual. Ancestral memories seemed to stir within her.

'It is well,' the Priest murmured. Then he turned to her guides. 'She is of royal lineage?' he inquired, taking his wand in his hand again.

'She is a Llewelyn,' Yolande answered, 'of royal lineage, and of the race that, after your own, earliest bore sway in this land of Britain. She has in her veins the blood of Arthur, of Ambrosius, and of Vortigern.'

'It is well,' the Priest said again. 'I know these princes.' Then he turned to Maisie. 'This is the ritual of those who build,' he said, in a very deep voice. 'It has been the ritual of those who build from the days of the builders of Lokmariaker and Avebury. Every building man makes shall have its human soul, the soul of a virgin to guard and protect it. Three souls it requires as a living talisman against chance and change. One soul is the soul of the human victim slain beneath the foundation-stone; she is the guardian spirit against earthquake and ruin. One soul is the soul of the human victim slain when the building is half built up; she is the guardian spirit against battle and tempest. One soul is the soul of the human victim who flings herself of her own free will off tower or gable when the building is complete; she is the guardian spirit against thunder and lightning. Unless a building be duly fasted with these three, how can it hope to stand against the hostile powers of fire and flood and storm and earthquake?'

An assessor at his side, unnoticed till then, took up the parable. He had a stern Roman face, and bore a shadowy suit of Roman armour. 'In times of old,' he said, with iron austerity, 'all men knew well these rules of building. They built in solid stone to endure for ever: the works they erected have lasted to this day, in this land and others. So built we the amphitheatres of Rome and Verona; so built we the walls of Lincoln, York, and London. In the blood of a king's son laid we the foundation-stone: in the blood of a king's son laid we the coping-stone: in the blood of a maiden of royal line fasted we the bastions against fire and lightning. But in these latter days, since faith grows dim, men build with burnt brick and rubble of plaster; no foundation spirit or guardian soul do they give to their bridges, their walls, or their towers: so bridges break, and walls fall in, and towers crumble, and the art and mystery of building aright have perished from among you.'

He ceased. The High Priest held out his wand and spoke again. 'We are the Assembly of Dead Builders and Dead Victims,' he said, 'for this mark of Wolverden; all of whom have built or been built upon in this holy site of immemorial sanctity. We are the stones of a living fabric. Before this place was a Christian church, it was a temple of Woden. And before it was a temple of Woden, it was a shrine of Hercules. And before it was a shrine of Hercules, it was a grove of Nodens. And before it was a grove of Nodens, it was a Stone Circle of the Host of Heaven. And before it was a Stone Circle of the Host of Heaven, it was the grave and tumulus and underground palace of Me, who am the earliest builder of all in this place; and my name in my ancient tongue is Wolf, and I laid and hallowed it. And after me, Wolf, and my namesake Wulfhere, was this barrow called Ad Lupum and Wolverden. And all these that are here with me have built and been built upon in this holy site for all generations. And *you* are the last who come to join us.'

Maisie felt a cold thrill course down her spine as he spoke these words; but courage did not fail her. She was dimly aware that those who offer themselves as victims for service must offer themselves willingly; for the gods demand a voluntary victim; no beast can be slain unless it nod assent; and none can be made a guardian spirit who takes not the post upon him of his own free will. She turned meekly to Hedda. 'Who are you?' she asked, trembling.

'I am Hedda,' the girl answered, in the same soft sweet voice and winning tone as before; 'Hedda, the daughter of Gorm, the chief of the Northmen who settled in East Anglia. And I was a worshipper of Thor and Odin. And when my father, Gorm, fought against Alfred, King of Wessex, was I taken prisoner. And Wulfhere, the Kenting, was then building the first church and tower of Wolverden. And they baptized me, and shrived me, and I consented of my own free will to be built under the foundation-stone. And there my body lies built up to this day; and *I* am the guardian spirit against earthquake and ruin.'

'And who are you?' Maisie asked, turning again to Yolande.

'I am Yolande Fitz-Aylwin,' the tall dark girl answered; 'a royal maiden too, sprung from the blood of Henry Plantagenet. And when Roland Fitz-Stephen was building anew the choir and chancel of Wulfhere's minster, I chose to be immured in the fabric of the wall, for love of the Church and all holy saints; and there my body lies built up to this day; and *I* am the guardian against battle and tempest.'

Maisie held her friend's hand tight. Her voice hardly trembled. 'And I?' she asked once more. 'What fate for me? Tell me!'

'Your task is easier far,' Yolande answered gently. 'For *you* shall be the guardian of the new tower against thunder and lightning. Now, those who guard against earthquake and battle are buried alive under the foundation-stone or in the wall of the building; there they die a slow death of starvation and choking. But those who guard against thunder and lightning cast themselves alive of their own free will from the battlements of the tower, and die in the air before they reach the ground; so their fate is the easiest and the lightest of all who would serve mankind; and thenceforth they live with us here in our palace.'

Maisie clung to her hand still tighter. 'Must I do it?' she asked, pleading.

'It is not *must*,' Yolande replied in the same caressing tone, yet with a calmness as of one in whom earthly desires and earthly passions are quenched for ever. 'It is as you choose yourself. None but a willing victim may be a guardian spirit. This glorious privilege comes but to the purest and best amongst us. Yet what better end can you ask for your soul than to dwell here in our midst as our comrade for ever, where all is peace, and to preserve the tower whose guardian you are from evil assaults of lightning and thunderbolt?'

Maisie flung her arms round her friend's neck. 'But—I am afraid,' she murmured. Why she should even wish to consent she knew not, yet the strange serene peace in these strange girls' eyes made her mysteriously in love with them and with the fate they offered her. They seemed to move like the stars in their orbits. 'How shall I leap from the top?' she cried. 'How shall I have courage to mount the stairs alone, and fling myself off from the lonely battlement?'

Yolande unwound her arms with a gentle forbearance. She coaxed her as one coaxes an unwilling child. 'You will *not* be alone,' she said, with a tender pressure. 'We will all go with you. We will help you and encourage you. We will sing our sweet songs of life-in-death to you. Why should you draw back? All we have faced it in ten thousand ages, and we tell you with one voice, you need not fear it. 'Tis life you should fear—life, with its dangers, its toils, its heartbreakings. Here we dwell for ever in unbroken peace. Come, come, and join us!'

She held out her arms with an enticing gesture. Maisie sprang into them, sobbing. 'Yes, I will come,' she cried in an access of hysterical fervour. 'These are the arms of Death —I embrace them. These are the lips of Death—I kiss them. Yolande, Yolande, I will do as you ask me!'

The tall dark girl in the luminous white robe stooped

down and kissed her twice on the forehead in return. Then she looked at the High Priest. 'We are ready,' she murmured in a low, grave voice. 'The Victim consents. The Virgin will die. Lead on to the tower. We are ready! We are ready!'

IV

From the recesses of the temple—if temple it were—from the inmost shrines of the shrouded cavern, unearthly music began to sound of itself, with wild modulation, on strange reeds and tabors. It swept through the aisles like a rushing wind on an Æolian harp; at times it wailed with a voice like a woman's; at times it rose loud in an organ-note of triumph; at times it sank low into a pensive and melancholy flute-like symphony. It waxed and waned; it swelled and died away again; but no man saw how or whence it proceeded. Wizard echoes issued from the crannies and vents in the invisible walls; they sighed from the ghostly interspaces of the pillars; they keened and moaned from the vast overhanging dome of the palace. Gradually the song shaped itself by weird stages into a processional measure. At its sound the High Priest rose slowly from his immemorial seat on the mighty cromlech which formed his throne. The Shades in leopards' skins ranged themselves in bodiless rows on either hand; the ghostly wearers of the sabre-toothed lions' fangs followed like ministrants in the footsteps of their hierarch.

Hedda and Yolande took their places in the procession. Maisie stood between the two, with hair floating on the air; she looked like a novice who goes up to take the veil, accompanied and cheered by two elder sisters.

The ghostly pageant began to move. Unseen music followed it with fitful gusts of melody. They passed down the main corridor, between shadowy Doric or Ionic pillars which grew dimmer and ever dimmer again in the distance as they approached, with slow steps, the earthward portal.

At the gate, the High Priest pushed against the valves with his hand. They opened *outward*.

He passed into the moonlight. The attendants thronged

after him. As each wild figure crossed the threshold the same
strange sight as before met Maisie's eyes. For a second of time
each ghostly body became self-luminous, as with some curious
phosphorescence; and through each, at the moment of passing
the portal, the dim outline of a skeleton loomed briefly visible.
Next instant it had clothed itself as with earthly members.

Maisie reached the outer air. As she did so, she gasped.
For a second, its chilliness and freshness almost choked her.
She was conscious now that the atmosphere of the vault,
though pleasant in its way, and warm and dry, had been
loaded with fumes as of burning incense, and with somnolent
vapours of poppy and mandragora. Its drowsy ether had cast
her into a lethargy. But after the first minute in the outer
world, the keen night air revived her. Snow lay still on
the ground a little deeper than when she first came out, and
the moon rode lower; otherwise, all was as before, save that
only one or two lights still burned here and there in the great
house on the terrace. Among them she could recognize her
own room, on the ground floor in the new wing, by its open
window.

The procession made its way across the churchyard towards
the tower. As it wound among the graves an owl hooted. All
at once Maisie remembered the lines that had so chilled her
a few short hours before in the drawing-room—

> 'The glow-worm o'er grave and stone
>   Shall light thee steady;
> The owl from the steeple sing,
>   "Welcome, proud lady!" '

But, marvellous to relate, they no longer alarmed her. She
felt rather that a friend was welcoming her home; she clung
to Yolande's hand with a gentle pressure.

As they passed in front of the porch, with its ancient yew-
tree, a stealthy figure glided out like a ghost from the dark-
ling shadow. It was a woman, bent and bowed, with quivering
limbs that shook half palsied. Maisie recognized old Bessie.
'I knew she would come!' the old hag muttered between her

toothless jaws. 'I knew Wolverden Tower would yet be duly fasted!'

She put herself, as of right, at the head of the procession. They moved on to the tower, gliding rather than walking. Old Bessie drew a rusty key from her pocket, and fitted it with a twist into the brand-new lock. 'What turned the old will turn the new,' she murmured, looking round and grinning. Maisie shrank from her as she shrank from not one of the Dead; but she followed on still into the ringers' room at the base of the tower.

Thence a staircase in the corner led up to the summit. The High Priest mounted the stair, chanting a mystic refrain, whose runic sounds were no longer intelligible to Maisie. As she reached the outer air, the Tongue of the Dead seemed to have become a mere blank of mingled odours and murmurs to her. It was like a summer breeze, sighing through warm and resinous pinewoods. But Yolande and Hedda spoke to her yet, to cheer her, in the language of the living. She recognized that as *revenants* they were still in touch with the upper air and the world of the embodied.

They tempted her up the stair with encouraging fingers. Maisie followed them like a child, in implicit confidence. The steps wound round and round, spirally, and the staircase was dim; but a supernatural light seemed to fill the tower, diffused from the bodies or souls of its occupants. At the head of all, the High Priest still chanted as he went his unearthly litany; magic sounds of chimes seemed to swim in unison with his tune as they mounted. Were those floating notes material or spiritual? They passed the belfry; no tongue of metal wagged; but the rims of the great bells resounded and reverberated to the ghostly symphony with sympathetic music. Still they passed on and on, upward and upward. They reached the ladder that alone gave access to the final storey. Dust and cobwebs already clung to it. Once more Maisie drew back. It was dark overhead, and the luminous haze began to fail them. Her friends held her hands with the same kindly persuasive touch as ever. 'I cannot!' she cried, shrinking away from the tall, steep ladder. 'Oh, Yolande, I cannot!'

'Yes, dear,' Yolande whispered in a soothing voice. 'You can. It is but ten steps, and I will hold your hand tight. Be brave and mount them!'

The sweet voice encouraged her. It was like heavenly music. She knew not why she should submit, or, rather, consent; but none the less she consented. Some spell seemed cast over her. With tremulous feet, scarcely realizing what she did, she mounted the ladder and went up four steps of it.

Then she turned and looked down again. Old Bessie's wrinkled face met her frightened eyes. It was smiling horribly. She shrank back once more, terrified. 'I can't do it,' she cried, 'if that woman comes up! I'm not afraid of *you*, dear'—she pressed Yolande's hand—'but she, she is too terrible!'

Hedda looked back and raised a warning finger. 'Let the woman stop below,' she said; 'she savours too much of the evil world. We must do nothing to frighten the willing victim.'

The High Priest by this time, with his ghostly fingers, had opened the trap-door that gave access to the summit. A ray of moonlight slanted through the aperture. The breeze blew down with it. Once more Maisie felt the stimulating and reviving effect of the open air. Vivified by its freshness, she struggled up to the top, passed out through the trap, and found herself standing on the open platform at the summit of the tower.

The moon had not yet quite set. The light on the snow shone pale green and mysterious. For miles and miles around she could just make out, by its aid, the dim contour of the downs, with their thin white mantle, in the solemn silence. Range behind range rose faintly shimmering. The chant had now ceased; the High Priest and his acolytes were mingling strange herbs in a mazar-bowl or chalice. Stray perfumes of myrrh and of cardamoms were wafted towards her. The men in leopards' skins burnt smouldering sticks of spikenard. Then Yolande led the postulant forward again, and placed her close up to the new white parapet. Stone heads of virgins smiled on her from the angles. 'She must front the east,' Hedda said in a tone of authority: and Yolande turned her face towards the rising sun accordingly. Then she opened her lips and spoke in a very solemn voice. 'From this new-built tower you fling yourself,' she said, or rather intoned, 'that you may serve mankind, and all the powers that be, as its guardian spirit against thunder and lightning. Judged a virgin, pure and unsullied in deed and word and thought, of royal race and ancient lineage—a Cymry of the Cymry—you are found worthy to be intrusted with this charge and this honour. Take care that never shall dart or thunderbolt assault this tower, as She that is below you takes care to preserve it from earthquake and ruin, and She that is midway takes care to preserve it from battle and tempest. This is your charge. See well that you keep it.'·

She took her by both hands. 'Mary Llewelyn,' she said, 'you willing victim, step on to the battlement.'

Maisie knew not why, but with very little shrinking she stepped as she was told, by the aid of a wooden footstool, on to the eastward-looking parapet. There, in her loose white robe, with her arms spread abroad, and her hair flying free, she poised herself for a second, as if about to shake out some unseen wings and throw herself on the air like a swift or a swallow.

'Mary Llewelyn,' Yolande said once more, in a still deeper tone, with ineffable earnestness, 'cast yourself down, a willing sacrifice, for the service of man, and the security of this tower against thunderbolt and lightning.'

Maisie stretched her arms wider, and leaned forward in act to leap, from the edge of the parapet, on to the snow-clad churchyard.

V

One second more and the sacrifice would have been complete. But before she could launch herself from the tower, she felt suddenly a hand laid upon her shoulder from behind to restrain her. Even in her existing state of nervous exaltation she was aware at once that it was the hand of a living and solid mortal, not that of a soul or guardian spirit. It lay heavier upon her than Hedda's or Yolande's. It seemed to clog and burden her. With a violent effort she strove to shake herself free, and carry out her now fixed intention of self-immolation, for the safety of the tower. But the hand was too strong for her. She could not shake it off. It gripped and held her.

She yielded, and, reeling, fell back with a gasp on to the platform of the tower. At the selfsame moment a strange terror and commotion seemed to seize all at once on the assembled spirits. A weird cry rang voiceless through the shadowy company. Maisie heard it as in a dream, very dim and distant. It was thin as a bat's note; almost inaudible to the ear, yet perceived by the brain or at least by the spirit. It was a cry of alarm, of fright, of warning. With one accord, all the host of phantoms rushed hurriedly forward to the battlements and pinnacles. The ghostly High Priest went first, with his wand held downward; the men in leopards' skins and other assistants followed in confusion. Theirs was a reckless rout. They flung themselves from the top, like fugitives from a cliff, and floated fast through the air on invisible pinions. Hedda and Yolande, ambassadresses and intermediaries with the upper air, were the last to fly from the living presence. They clasped her hand silently, and looked deep into her eyes. There was something in that calm yet regretful look that seemed to say, 'Farewell! We have tried in vain to save you, sister, from the terrors of living.'

The horde of spirits floated away on the air, as in a witches' Sabbath, to the vault whence it issued. The doors swung on their rusty hinges, and closed behind them. Maisie stood alone with the hand that grasped her on the tower.

The shock of the grasp, and the sudden departure of the ghostly band in such wild dismay, threw Maisie for a while into a state of semi-unconsciousness. Her head reeled round; her brain swam faintly. She clutched for support at the parapet of the tower. But the hand that held her sustained her still. She felt herself gently drawn down with quiet mastery, and laid on the stone floor close by the trap-door that led to the ladder.

The next thing of which she could feel sure was the voice of the Oxford undergraduate. He was distinctly frightened and not a little tremulous. 'I think,' he said very softly, laying her head on his lap, 'you had better rest a while, Miss Llewelyn, before you try to get down again. I hope I didn't catch you and disturb you too hastily. But one step more, and you would have been over the edge. I really couldn't help it.'

'Let me go,' Maisie moaned, trying to raise herself again, but feeling too faint and ill to make the necessary effort to recover the power of motion. 'I *want* to go with them! I *want* to join them!'

'Some of the others will be up before long,' the undergraduate said, supporting her head in his hands; 'and they'll help me to get you down again. Mr Yates is in the belfry. Meanwhile, if I were you, I'd lie quite still, and take a drop or two of this brandy.'

He held it to her lips. Maisie drank a mouthful, hardly knowing what she did. Then she lay quiet where he placed her for some minutes. How they lifted her down and conveyed her to her bed she scarcely knew. She was dazed and terrified. She could only remember afterward that three or four gentlemen in roughly huddled clothes had carried or handed her down the ladder between them. The spiral stair and all the rest were a blank to her.

VI

When she next awoke she was lying in her bed in the same room at the Hall, with Mrs West by her side, leaning over her tenderly.

Maisie looked up through her closed eyes and just saw the motherly face and grey hair bending above her. Then voices came to her from the mist, vaguely: 'Yesterday was so hot for the time of year, you see!' 'Very unusual weather, of course, for Christmas.' 'But a thunderstorm! So strange! I put it down to that. The electrical disturbance must have affected the poor child's head.' Then it dawned upon her that the conversation she heard was passing between Mrs West and a doctor.

She raised herself suddenly and wildly on her arms. The bed faced the windows. She looked out and beheld—the tower of Wolverden church, split from top to bottom with a mighty rent, while half its height lay tossed in fragments on the ground in the churchyard.

'What is it?' she cried wildly, with a flush as of shame.

'Hush, hush!' the doctor said. 'Don't trouble! Don't look at it!'

'Was it—after I came down?' Maisie moaned in vague terror.

The doctor nodded. 'An hour after you were brought down,' he said, 'a thunderstorm broke over it. The lightning struck and shattered the tower. They had not yet put up the lightning-conductor. It was to have been done on Boxing Day.'

A weird remorse possessed Maisie's soul. 'My fault!' she cried, starting up. 'My fault, my fault! I have neglected my duty!'

'Don't talk,' the doctor answered, looking hard at her. 'It is always dangerous to be too suddenly aroused from these curious overwrought sleeps and trances.'

'And old Bessie?' Maisie exclaimed, trembling with an eerie presentiment.

The doctor glanced at Mrs West. 'How did she know?' he whispered. Then he turned to Maisie. 'You may as well be told the truth as suspect it,' he said slowly. 'Old Bessie must have been watching there. She was crushed and half buried beneath the falling tower.'

'One more question, Mrs West,' Maisie murmured, growing faint with an access of supernatural fear. 'Those two nice girls who sat on the chairs at each side of me through the tableaux—are they hurt? Were they in it?'

Mrs West soothed her hand. 'My dear child,' she said gravely, with quiet emphasis, 'there were *no* other girls. This is mere hallucination. You sat alone by yourself through the whole of the evening.'

Madam Crowl's Ghost

by

J. SHERIDAN LE FANU

*The man who influenced M. R. James can well lay claim
to being one of the finest ghost-story writers. This is the
case with J. Sheridan le Fanu (1814–1873) who was so
popular with M. R. James that he researched and edited
a volume of le Fanu's stories. An Irishman of Huguenot
descent, le Fanu was a great grand-nephew of Sheridan,
the famous 18th century playwright. He graduated from
Trinity College, Dublin, where he studied law, but soon
turned to journalism. In 1837 he wrote the ballad
'Shamus O'Brien' and continued writing from then on,
producing novels, short stories and articles. There are
many views of his finest work. Some say* The House by
the Churchyard *(1863), others* Uncle Silas *(1864). My
personal tastes lead me to quote* In A Glass Darkly
*(1872), containing as it does two of the finest horror tales
ever written, 'Carmilla' (the definitive vampire tale)
and 'The Watcher'. This particular story was not included
in that book but is still one of le Fanu's finest creations.
Readers may well have seen this before, for which I
apologize, but it is necessary reading for this anthology,
for it is a true Victorian tale of terror.*

I'm an old woman now; and I was but thirteen my last birthday, the night I came to Applewale House. My aunt was the
housekeeper there, and a sort o' one-horse carriage was down
at Lexhoe to take me and my box up to Applewale.

I was a bit frightened by the time I got to Lexhoe, and

when I saw the carriage and horse, I wished myself back again with my mother at Hazelden. I was crying when I got into the 'shay'—that's what we used to call it—and old John Mulbery that drove it, and was a good-natured fellow, bought me a handful of apples at the Golden Lion, to cheer me up a bit; and he told me that there was a currant-cake, and tea, and pork-chops, waiting for me, all hot, in my aunt's room at the great house. It was a fine moonlight night and I ate the apples, lookin' out o' the shay winda.

It is a shame for gentlemen to frighten a poor foolish child like I was. I sometimes think it might be tricks. There was two on 'em on the top o' the coach beside me. And they began to question me after nightfall, when the moon rose, where I was going to. Well, I told them it was to wait on Dame Arabella Crowl, of Applewale House, near by Lexhoe.

'Ho, then,' says one of them, 'you'll not be long there!'

And I looked at him as much as to say, 'Why not?' for I had spoke out when I told them where I was goin', as if 'twas something clever I had to say.

'Because,' says he—'and don't you for your life tell no one, only watch her and see—she's possessed by the devil, and more an half a ghost. Have you got a Bible?'

'Yes, sir,' says I. For my mother put my little Bible in my box, and I knew it was there: and by the same token, though the print's too small for my old eyes, I have it in my press to this hour.

As I looked up at him, saying 'Yes, sir,' I thought I saw him winkin' at his friend; but I could not be sure.

'Well,' says he, 'be sure you put it under your bolster every night, it will keep the old girl's claws aff ye.'

And I got such a fright when he said that, you wouldn't fancy! And I'd a liked to ask him a lot about the old lady, but I was too shy, and he and his friend began talkin' together about their own consarns, and dowly enough I got down, as I told ye, at Lexhoe. My heart sank as I drove into the dark avenue. The trees stands very thick and big, as old as the old house, almost, and four people, with their arms out and finger-tips touchin', barely girds round some of them.

Well, my neck was stretched out o' the winda, looking for the first view o' the great house; and, all at once we pulled up in front of it.

A great white-and-black house it is, wi' great black beams across and right up it, and gables lookin' out, as white as a sheet, to the moon, and the shadows o' the trees, two or three up and down upon the front, you could count the leaves on them, and all the little diamond-shaped winda-panes, glimmering on the great hall winda, and great shutters, in the old fashion, hinged on the wall outside, boulted across all the rest o' the windas in front, for there was but three or four servants, and the old lady in the house, and most o' t'rooms was locked up.

My heart was in my mouth when I saw the journey was over, and this, the great house afore me, and there was my aunt that I never saw till noo, and Dame Crowl, that I was come to wait upon, and was afeard on already.

My aunt kissed me in the hall, and brought me to her room. She was tall and thin, wi' a pale face and black eyes, and long thin hands wi' black mittins on. She was past fifty, and her word was short; but her word was law. I hev no complaints to make of her; but she was a hard woman, and I think she would hev been kinder to me if I had bin her sister's child in place of her brother's. But all that's o' no consequence noo.

The squire—his name was Mr Chevenix Crowl, he was Dame Crowl's grandson—came down there, by way of seeing that the old lady was well treated, about twice or thrice in the year. I saw him but twice all the time I was at Applewale House.

I can't say but she was well taken care of, notwithstandin', but that was because my aunt and Meg Wyvern, that was her maid, had a conscience, and did their duty by her.

Mrs Wyvern—Meg Wyvern my aunt called her to herself, and Mrs Wyvern to me—was a fat, jolly lass of fifty, a good height and a good breadth, always good-humoured, and walked slow. She had fine wages, but she was a bit stingy, and kept all her fine clothes under lock and key, and wore, mostly, a twilled chocolate cotton, wi' red, and yellow, and green sprigs and balls on it, and it lasted wonderful.

She never gave me nowt, not the vally o' a brass thimble, all the time I was there; but she was good-humoured, and always laughin', and she talked no end o' proas over her tea; and, seeing me so sackless and dowly, she roused me up wi' her laughin' and stories; and I think I liked her better than my aunt—children is so taken wi' a bit o' fun or a story—though my aunt was very good to me, but a hard woman about some things, and silent always.

My aunt took me into her bed-chamber, that I might rest myself a bit while she was settin' the tea in her room. But first she patted me on the shouther, and said I was a tall lass o' my years, and had spired up well, and asked me if I could do plain work and stitchin'; and she looked in my face, and said I was like my father, her brother, that was dead and gone, and she hoped I was a better Christian and would not do all that badly.

It was a hard sayin' the first time I set my foot in her room, I thought.

When I went into the next room, the housekeeper's room —very comfortable, oak wood all round—there was a fine fire blazin' away, wi' coal, and peat, and wood, all in a low together, and tea on the table, and hot cake, and smokin' meat; and there was Mrs Wyvern, fat, jolly, and talkin' away, more in an hour than my aunt would in a year.

While I was still at my tea my aunt went upstairs to see Madam Crowl.

'She's a-gone up to see that old Judith Squailes is awake,' says Mrs Wyvern. 'Judith sits with Madam Crowl when me and Mrs Shutters'—that was my aunt's name—'is away. She's a troublesome old lady. Ye'll hev to be sharp wi' her, or she'll be into the fire, or out o' t' winda. She goes on wires, she does, old though she be.'

'How old, ma'am?' says I.

'Ninety-three her last birthday, and that's eight months gone,' says she; and she laughed. 'And don't be askin' questions about her before your aunt—mind, I tell ye; just take her as you find her, and that's all.'

'And what's to be my business about her, please ma'am?' says I.

'About the old lady? Well,' says she, 'your aunt, Mrs Shutters, will tell you that; but I suppose you'll hev to sit in the room with your work, and see she's at no mischief, and let her amuse herself with her things on the table, and get her her food or drink as she calls for it, and keep her out o' mischief, and ring the bell hard if she's troublesome.'

'Is she deaf, ma'am?'

'No, nor blind,' says she; 'as sharp as a needle, but she's gone quite senile, and can't remember nowt rightly; and Jack the Giant Killer, or Goody Twoshoes will please her as well as the King's court, or the affairs of the nation.'

'And what did the little girl go away for, ma'am, that went on Friday last? My aunt wrote to my mother she was to go.'

'Yes; she's gone.'

'What for?' says I again.

'She didn't answer Mrs Shutters, I do suppose,' says she. 'I don't know. Don't be talkin'; your aunt can't abide a talkin' child.'

'And please, ma'am, is the old lady well in health?' says I.

'It ain't no harm to ask that,' says she. 'She's fadin' a bit lately, but better this week past, and I dare say she'll last out her hundred years yet. Hish! Here's your aunt coming down the passage.'

In comes my aunt, and begins talkin' to Mrs Wyvern, and I, beginnin' to feel more comfortable and at home like, was walkin' about the room lookin' at this thing and at that. There was pretty old china things on the cupboard, and pictures again the wall; and there was a door open in the wainscot, and I sees a queer old leathern jacket, wi' straps and buckles to it, and sleeves as long as the bed-post, hangin' up inside.

'What's that you're at, child?' says my aunt, sharp enough, turning about when I thought she least minded. 'What's that in your hand?'

'This, ma'am?' says I, turning about with the leathern

jacket. 'I don't know what it is, ma'am.'

Pale as she was, the red came up in her cheeks, and her eyes flashed wi' anger, and I think only she had half a dozen steps to take to get to me, I'd have got a wallop. But she did give me a shake by the shouther, and she plucked the thing out o' my hand, and says she, 'While ever you stay here, don't ye meddle wi' nowt that don't belong to ye,' and she hung it upon the pin that was there, and shut the door wi' a bang and locked it fast.

Mrs Wyvern was liftin' up her hands and laughin' all this time, quietly in her chair, rolling herself a bit in it, as she used when she was kinkin'.

The tears was in my eyes, and she winked at my aunt, and says she, dryin' her own eyes that was wet wi' the laughin', 'Tut, the child meant no harm—come here to me, child. It's only a pair o' crutches for lame ducks, and ask us no questions mind, and we'll tell ye no lies; and come here and sit down, and drink a mug o' beer before ye go to your bed.'

My room, mind ye, was upstairs, next to the old lady's, and Mrs Wyvern's bed was near hers in her room and I was to be ready at call, if need should be.

The old lady was in one of her tantrums that night and part of the day before. She used to take fits o' the sulks. Sometimes she would not let them dress her, and other times she would not let them take her clothes off. She was a great beauty, they said, in her day. But there was no one about Applewale that remembered her in her prime. And she was dreadful fond o' dress, and had thick silks, and stiff satins, and velvets, and laces, and all sorts, enough to set up seven shops at the least. All her dresses was old-fashioned and queer, but worth a fortune.

Well, I went to my bed. I lay for a while awake; for a' things was new to me; and I think the tea was in my nerves, too, for I wasn't used to it, except now and then on a holiday, or the like. And I heard Mrs Wyvern talkin', and I listened with my hand to my ear; but I could not hear Mrs Crowl, and I don't think she said a word.

There was great care took of her. The people at Applewale knew that when she died they would every one get the sack; and their situations was well paid and easy.

The doctor come twice a week to see the old lady, and you may be sure they all did as he bid them. One thing was the same every time; they were never to cross or frump her, any way, but to humour and please her in everything.

So she lay in her clothes all that night, and next day, not a word she said, and I was at my needlework all that day, in my own room, except when I went down to my dinner.

I would have liked to see the ald lady, and even to hear her speak. But she might as well have been in London all the time.

When I had my dinner my aunt sent me out for a walk for an hour. I was glad when I came back, the trees was so big, and the place so dark and lonesome, and 'twas a cloudy day, and I cried a deal, thinkin' of home, while I was walkin' alone there. That evening, the candles bein' alight, I was sittin' in my room, and the door was open into Madam Crowl's chamber, where my aunt was. It was, then, for the first time I heard what I suppose was the old lady talking.

It was a queer noise like, I couldn't well say which, a bird, or a beast, only it had a bleatin' sound in it, and was very small.

I pricked my ears to hear all I could. But I could not make out one word she said. And my aunt answered:

'The evil one can't hurt no one, ma'am, but the Lord permits.'

Then the same queer voice from the bed says something more that I couldn't make head nor tail on.

And my aunt answered again: 'Let them pull faces, ma'am, and say what they will; if the Lord be for us, who can be against us?'

I kept listenin' with my ear turned to the door, holdin' my breath, but not another word or sound came in from the room. In about twenty minutes, as I was sittin' by the table, lookin' at the pictures in the old *Æsop's Fables*, I was aware o' something moving at the door, and lookin' up I saw my aunt's face lookin' in at the door, and her hand raised.

'Hish!' says she, very soft, and comes over to me on tiptoe, and she says in a whisper: 'Thank God, she's asleep at last, and don't ye make no noise till I come back, for I'm goin' down to take my cup o' tea, and I'll be back i' noo—me and Mrs Wyvern, and she'll be sleepin' in the room, and you can run down when we come up, and Judith will gie ye your supper in my room.'

And with that away she goes.

I kep' looking at the picture-book, as before, listenin' every noo and then, but there was no sound, not a breath, that I could hear; an' I began whisperin' to the pictures and talkin' to myself to keep my heart up, for I was growin' feared in that big room.

And at last up I got, and began walkin' about the room, lookin' at this and peepin' at that, to amuse my mind, ye'll understand. And at last what did I do but peeps into Madame Crowl's bed-chamber.

A grand chamber it was, wi' a great four-poster, wi' flowered silk curtains as tall as the ceilin', and foldin' down on the floor, and drawn close all round. There was a lookin'-glass, the biggest I ever saw before, and the room was a blaze o' light. I counted twenty-two wax-candles, all alight. Such was her fancy, and no one dared say her nay.

I listened at the door, and gaped and wondered all round. When I heard there was not a breath, and did not see so much as a stir in the curtains, I took heart, and I walked into the room on tiptoe, and looked round again. Then I takes a peek at myself in the big glass; and at last it came in my head, 'Why couldn't I ha' a peek at the old lady herself in the bed?'

Ye'd think me a fule if ye knew half how I longed to see Dame Crowl, and I thought to myself if I didn't peep now I might wait many a day before I got so gude a chance again.

Well, my dear, I came to the side o' the bed, the curtains bein' close, and my heart a'most failed me. But I took courage, and I slips my finger in between the thick curtains, and then my hand. So I waits a bit, but all was still as death. So, softly, softly I draws the curtain, and there, sure enough, I saw before me, stretched out like the painted lady on the tomb-stone in

Lexhoe Church, the famous Dame Crowl, of Applewale House. There she was, dressed out. You never saw the like in they days. Satin and silk, and scarlet and green, and gold and pint lace; by Jen! 'twas a sight! A big powdered wig, half as high as herself, was a-top o' her head, and, wow!—was ever such wrinkles?—and her old baggy throat all powdered white, and her cheeks rouged, and mouse-skin eyebrows, that Mrs Wyvern used to stick on, and there she lay grand and stark, wi' a pair o' clocked silk hose on, and heels to her shoes as tall as nine-pins. Lawk! But her nose was crooked and thin, and half the whites o' her eyes was open. She used to stand, dressed as she was, gigglin' and dribblin' before the lookin'-glass, wi' a fan in her hand, and a big nosegay in her bodice. Her wrinkled little hands was stretched down by her sides, and such long nails, all cut into points, I never saw in my days. Could it ever a bin the fashion for grit fowk to wear their finger-nails so?

Well, I think ye'd a bin frightened yourself if ye'd seen such a sight. I couldn't let go the curtain, nor move an inch, nor take my eyes off her; my very heart stood still. And in an instant she opens her eyes, and up she sits, and spins herself round, and down wi' her, wi' a clack on her two tall heels on the floor, facin' me, staring at my face wi' her two great glassy eyes, and a wicked smile on her old wrinkled lips, and long false teeth.

Well, a corpse is a natural thing; but this was the dreadfullest sight I ever saw. She had her fingers straight out pointin' at me, and her back was crooked, round again wi' age. Says she:

'Ye little limb! what for did ye say I killed the boy? I'll tickle ye till ye're stiff!'

If I'd a thought an instant, I'd a turned about and run. But I couldn't take my eyes off her, and I backed from her as soon as I could; and she came clatterin' after, like a thing on wires, with her fingers pointing to my throat, and she makin' all the time a sound with her tongue like zizz-zizz-zizz.

I kept backin' and backin' as quick as I could, and her fingers was only a few inches away from my throat, and I felt

I'd lose my wits if she touched me.

I went back this way, right into the corner, and I gave a yell, ye'd think saul and body was partin', and that minute my aunt, from the door, calls out wi' a blare, and the old lady turns round on her, and I turns about, and ran through my room, and down the back stairs, as hard as my legs could carry me.

I cried hearty, I can tell you, when I got down to the housekeeper's room. Mrs Wyvern laughed a deal when I told her what happened. But she changed her key when she heard the old lady's words.

'Say them again,' says she.

So I told her.

'Ye little limb! What for did ye say I killed the boy? I'll tickle ye till ye're stiff.'

'And did ye say she killed a boy?' says she.

'Not I, ma'am,' says I.

Judith was always up with me, after that, when the two elder women was away from her. I would a jumped out at winda, rather than stay alone in the same room wi' her.

It was about a week after, as well as I can remember, Mrs Wyvern, one day when me and her was alone, told me a thing about Madam Crowl that I did not know before.

She being young, and a great beauty, full seventy years before, had married Squire Crowl of Applewale. But he was a widower, and had a son about nine year old.

There never was tale or tidings of this boy after one mornin'. No one could say where he went to. He was allowed too much liberty, and used to be off in the morning, one day, to the keeper's cottage, and breakfast wi' him, and away to the warren, and not home, mayhap, till evening, and another time down to the lake, and bathe there, and spend the day fishin' there, or paddlin' about in the boat. Well, no one could say what was gone wi' him; only this, that his hat was found by the lake, under a hawthorn that grows thar to this day, and 'twas thought he was drowned bathin'. And the squire's son, by his second marriage, by this Madam Crowl that lived so dreadful lang, came in for the estates. It was his son, the old lady's grandson, Squire Chevenix Crowl, that owned the estates at the time I came to Applewale.

There was a deal o' talk long before my aunt's time about it; and 'twas said the stepmother knew more than she was like to get out. And she managed her husband, the old squire, wi' her whiteheft and flatteries. And as the boy was never seen more, in course of time the thing died out of fowks' minds.

I'm goin' to tell you now about what I saw wi' my own eyes.

I was not there six months, and it was winter time, when the old lady took her last sickness.

The doctor was afeard she might a took a fit o' madness, as she did, fifteen years before, and was buckled up, many a time, in a strait-waistcoat, which was the very leathern jerkin I saw in the closet, off my aunt's room.

Well, she didn't. She pined, and wandered, and went off, fadin', fadin', quiet enough, till a day or two before she died, and then she took to ramblin', and sometimes skirlin' in the bed, ye'd think a robber had a knife to her throat, and she used to work out o' the bed, and not being strong enough, then, to walk or stand, she'd fall on the flure, wi' her old wizened hands stretched before her face, and skirlin' still for mercy.

Ye may guess I didn't go into the room, and I used to be shiverin' in my bed wi' fear, at her skirlin' and scrafflin' on the flure, and blarin' out words that id make your skin turn blue.

My aunt, and Mrs Wyvern, and Judith Squailes, and a woman from Lexhoe, was always about her. At last she took fits, and they wore her out.

T' sir (parson) was there, and prayed for her; but she was past prayin' with. I suppose it was right, but none could think there was much good in it, and so at long last she made her dyin', and a' was over, and old Dame Crowl was shrouded and coffined and Squire Chevenix was wrote for. But he was away in France, and the delay was so long, that t' sir and doctor both agreed it would not do to keep her longer out o' her place, and no one cared but just them two, and my aunt and the rest o' us, from Applewale to go to the buryin'. So the old lady of Applewale was laid in the vault under Lexhoe

Church; and we lived up at the great house till such time as the squire should come to tell his will about us, and pay off such as he chose to discharge.

I was put into another room, two doors away from what was Dame Crowl's chamber, after her death, and this thing happened the night before Squire Chevenix came to Applewale.

The room I was in now was a large square chamber, covered wi' oak panels, but unfurnished except for my bed, which had no curtains to it, and a chair and a table, or so, that looked nothing at all in such a big room. And the big looking-glass, that the old lady used to peek into and admire herself from head to heel, now that there was na mair o' that work, was put out of the way, and stood against the wall in my room, for there was shiftin' o' many things in her chambers, ye may suppose, when she came to be coffined.

The news had come that day that the squire was to be down next morning at Applewale; and not sorry was I, for I thought I was sure to be sent home again to my mother. And right glad was I, and I was thinkin' of a' at home, and my sister, Janet, and the kitten and the canary, and Trimmer the dog, and all the rest, and I got so fidgety, I couldn't sleep, and the clock struck twelve, and me wide awake, and the room as dark as pitch. My back was turned to the door, and my eyes towards the wall opposite.

Well, it could na be a full quarter past twelve, when I sees a lightin' on the wall before me, as if something took fire behind, and the shadows o' the bed, and the chair, and my gown, that was hangin' from the wall, was dancin' up and down, on the ceilin' beams and the oak panels; and I turns my head ower my shouther quick, thinkin' something must a gone a' fire.

And what did I see, by Jen! but the likeness o' the old beldame, bedizened out in her satins and velvets, on her dead body, grinnin', wi' her eyes as wide as saucers, and her face like the fiend himself. 'Twas a red light that rose about her with a spitting flame, as if her dress was blazin'. She was drivin' on right for me, wi' her old shrivelled hands crooked as if she was goin' to claw me. I could not stir, but she passed me straight by, wi' a blast o' cold air, and I saw her, at the wall, in the alcove as my aunt used to call it, which was a recess where the state bed used to stand in old times, wi' a door open wide, and her hands gropin' in at somethin' was there. I never saw that door before. And she turned round to me, like a thing on a pivot, flyrin' (grinning), and all at once the room was dark, and I standin' at the far side o' the bed; I don't know how I got there, and I found my tongue at last, and if I did na blare a yellock, runnin' down the gallery and almost pulled Mrs Wyvern's door, off t'hooks, and frightened her half out o' her wits.

Ye may guess I did na sleep that night; and wi' the first light, down wi' me to my aunt, as fast as my two legs cud carry me.

Well, my aunt did na frump or scold me, as I thought she would, but she held me by the hand, and looked hard in my face all the time. And she told me not to be feared; and says she:

'Had the appearance a key in its hand?'

'Yes,' says I, bringin' it to mind, 'a big key in a queer brass handle.'

'Stop a bit,' says she, lettin' go my hand, and openin' the cupboard-door. 'Was it like this?' says she, takin' one out in her fingers and showing it to me, with a dark look in my face.

'That was it,' says I, quick enough.

'Are ye sure?' she says, turnin' it round.

'Sart,' says I, and I felt like I was gain' to faint when I saw it.

'Well, that will do, child,' says she, softly thinkin', and she locked it up again.

'The squire himself will be here today, before twelve o'clock, and ye must tell him all about it,' says she, thinkin', 'and I suppose I'll be leavin' soon, and so the best thing for the present is, that ye should go home this afternoon, and I'll look out another place for you when I can.'

Fain was I, ye may guess, at that word.

My aunt packed up my things for me, and the three pounds

that was due to me, to bring home, and Squire Crowl himself came down to Applewale that day, a handsome man, about thirty years old. It was the second time I saw him. But this was the first time he spoke to me.

My aunt talked wi' him in the housekeeper's room, and I don't know what they said. I was a bit feared of the squire, he bein' a great gentleman down in Lexhoe, and I daren't go near till I was called. And says he, smilin':

'What's a' this ye a sen, child? it mun be a dream, for ye know there's na sic a thing as a ghost in a' the world. But whatever it was, ma little maid, sit ye down and tell us all about it from first to last.'

Well, so soon as I med an end, he thought a bit, and says he to my aunt:

'I mind the place well. In old Sir Oliver's time lame Wyndel told me there was a door in that recess, to the left, where the lassie dreamed she saw my grandmother open it. He was past eighty when he told me that, and I but a boy. It's twenty year sen. The plate and jewels used to be kept there, long ago, before the iron closet was made in the arras chamber, and he told me the key had a brass handle, and this ye say was found in the bottom o' the kist where she kept her old fans. Now, would not it be a queer thing if we found some spoons or diamonds forgot there? Ye mun come up wi' us, lassie, and point to the very spot.'

Loth was I, and my heart in my mouth, and fast I held by my aunt's hand as I stept into that awsome room, and showed them both how she came and passed me by, and the spot where she stood, and where the door seemed to open.

There was an old empty press against the wall then, and shoving it aside, sure enough there was the tracing of a door in the wainscot, and a keyhole stopped with wood, and planed across as smooth as the rest, and the joining of the door all stopped wi' putty the colour o' oak, and, but for the hinges that showed a bit when the press was shoved aside, ye would not consayt there was a door there at all.

'Ha!' says he, wi' a queer smile, 'this looks like it.'

It took some minutes wi' a small chisel and hammer to pick

the bit o' wood out o' the keyhole. The key fitted, sure enough, and, wi' a strong twist and a long skreeak, the bolt went back and he pulled the door open.

There was another door inside, stranger than the first, but the locks was gone, and it opened easy. Inside was a narrow floor and walls and vault o' brick; we could not see what was in it, for 'twas dark as night.

When my aunt had lighted the candle the squire held it up and stept in.

My aunt stood on tiptoe tryin' to look over his shouther, and I did na see nout.

'Ha! ha!' says the squire, steppin' backward. 'What's that? Gi'ma the poker—quick!' says he to my aunt. And as she went to the hearth I peeps beside his arm, and I saw squat down in the far corner a monkey or a flayin' on the chest, or else the maist shrivelled up, wizened old wife that ever was sen on earth.

'By Jen!' says my aunt, as, puttin' the poker in his hand, she peeked by his shouther, and saw the ill-favoured thing, 'hae a care, sir, what ye're doin'. Back wi' ye, and shut to the door!'

But in place o' that he steps in softly, wi' the poker pointed like a sword, and he gies it a poke, and down it a' tumbles together, head and a', in a heap o' bones and dust, little more than a hatful.

'Twas the bones o' a child; a' the rest went to dust at a touch. They said nowt for a while, but he turns round the skull as it lay on the floor.

Young as I was I consayted I knew well enough what they was thinkin' on.

'A dead cat!' says he, pushin' back and blowin' out the can'le, and shuttin' to the door. 'We'll come back, you and me, Mrs Shutters, and look on the shelves bye and bye. I've other matters first to speak to ye about; and this little girl's goin' hame, ye say. She has her wages, and I mun mak' her a present,' says he, pattin' my shoulder wi' his hand.

And he did gimma a goud pound, and I went off to Lexhoe about an hour after, and so home by the stagecoach, and fain was I to be at home again; and I never saw old Dame Crowl o' Applewale, God be thanked, either in appearance or in dream, again. But when I was grown to be a woman my aunt spent a day and night wi' me at Littleham, and she told me there was no doubt it was the poor little boy that was missing so long sen that was shut up to die thar in the dark by that wicked beldame, whar his skirls, or his prayers, or his thumpin' cud na be heard, and his hat was left by the water's edge, whoever did it, to mak' belief he was drowned. The clothes, at the first touch, a' ran into a snuff o' dust in the cell whar the bones was found. But there was a handful o' jet buttons, and a knife with a green handle, together wi' a couple o' pennies the poor little fella had in his pocket, I suppose, when he was decoyed in thar, and saw his last o' the light. And there was, among the squire's papers, a copy o' the notice that was printed after he was lost, when the old squire thought he might a' run away or bin took by gipsies, and it said he had a green hefted knife wi' him, and that his buttons were o' cut jet. Sa that is a' I hev to say consarnin' ald Dame Crowl, o' Applewale House.

The Cave of Blood

by

DICK DONOVAN

As with many Victorian fiction writers, Emerson J. Muddock was forced to adopt a pseudonym to enable him to issue his prodigious output (over 140 books). He had successfully published a book of ghost stories under his own name, Stories Weird and Wonderful *(1889). He used the alias of 'Dick Donovan' and published a string of detective stories, historical fiction and tales of the supernatural. His most memorable book was* Tales of Terror *(1899) one of the most surprisingly neglected items in the English macabre catalogue. If nothing else, this anthology will serve to bring Dick Donovan to the notice of the public again, for as 'The Cave of Blood' will show, Muddock had a talent for the supernatural story second to none.*

On the south-west coast of the Principality of Wales stands a romantic little village, inhabited chiefly by the poorer class of people, consisting of small farmers and oyster dredgers, whose estates are the wide ocean, and whose ploughs are the small craft in which they glide over its interminable fields in search of the treasures which they wring from its bosom. It is built on the very top of a hill, commanding on one side a view of an immense bay, and on the other of the peaceful green fields and valleys, cultivated by the greater number of its quiet inhabitants. At the period of this story distinctions were unknown in the village—every man was the equal of his neighbour.

But though rank and its unpolished distinctions were strange in the village, the superiority of talent was felt and acknowledged almost without a pause or a murmur. There was one who was as a king amongst them, by the mere force of a mightier spirit than those with whom he sojourned had been accustomed to feel among them. He was a dark and moody man—a stranger—evidently of a higher order than those around him, who had but a few months before, without any apparent object, settled among them. Where he came from no one knew. He was a mystery, and evidently knew how to keep his secrets to himself. He was not rich, but followed no occupation. He lived frugally, but quite alone, and his sole employments were to read during the day and wander out, unaccompanied, into the fields or by the beach during the night. He was a strange, silent, fearsome sort of man, with a certain uncanniness in his appearance that commanded respect no less than fear. It soon became a common belief that this man possessed miraculous powers, not only as a healer of human ailments, but as a prophet. It was, therefore, not to be wondered at that in that little community of simple fisherfolk he was looked up to as a superior being, who not only held the power of life and death in his hands, but was able to draw aside the veil that screened the future.

Sometimes he would relieve a suffering child or rheumatic old man by medicinal herbs, reprove idleness and drunkenness in the youth, and predict to all the good and evil consequences of their conduct. And in his success in some cases, his foresight in others, and his wisdom in all, won for him a high reputation among the cottagers, to which his taciturn habits contributed not a little, for, with the vulgar as with the educated, no talker was ever seriously taken for a magician, though a silent man is often decided to be a wise one.

There was but one person at all disposed to rebel against the despotic sovereignty which John Morgan—such was the name he chose to be known by—was silently establishing over the quiet village, and that was precisely the person most likely to effect a revolution. She was a beautiful young woman, the glory and boast of the village, who had been the favourite of, and to a certain degree educated by, the late lady of the manor; but the lady had died, and her *protégée*, with a full consciousness of her intellectual superiority, had returned to her native village, where she determined to have an empire of her own which no rival should dispute. She laughed at the girls and women folk who listened to the predictions of Morgan, and she refused her smiles to the young men who consulted him upon their affairs and their prospects; and as the beautiful Ruth was generally beloved, the silent Morgan was soon in danger of being abandoned by all save doting men and paralytic women, and feeling himself an outcast in the village.

But it was soon made clear that Morgan had no intention of allowing pretty Ruth to oust him from his position. He had essayed to rule the village, and he was resolved to retain his hold over the people. He knew, too, that from another point of view this ascendancy was necessary to his purposes, and as he had failed to establish it by wisdom and benevolence, he determined to try the effect of fear. The character of the people with whom he sojourned was admirably calculated to assist his projects. His predictions were now uttered more clearly, and his threats denounced in sterner tones and stronger and plainer words, and when he predicted that old William Williams, who had been stricken with the palsy, would die at the turn of the tide, three days from that on which he spoke, and that the light little boat of gay Griffy Morris, which sailed from the Bay on a bright winter's morning, would never again make the shore—the man died, and the storm arose, even as he said—men's hearts died within them, and they bowed down before his words, as if he had been their general fate and the individual destiny of each.

Ruth's beautiful face grew pale for a moment as she heard of these things; in the next her spirit returned, and she told some friend that she was going to Morgan to have her fortune told, and she would prove to every one that he was an impostor. She had no difficulty in getting up a party of young men and women to accompany her, and she set off for Morgan's house with the avowed intention of 'unmasking and humiliating him'. It was rather remarkable, seeing that the man had never done her any harm, that she should have taken such a prejudice against him. When they reached his residence they made it very evident that they intended to insult him. They made jests at his expense, and rudely and satirically alluded to his professed powers of prophecy. Had Ruth been more observant and less self-conscious, she could not have failed to note that Morgan was far removed above the common-place, and was possessed of mental powers far above anyone else in the village. He was greatly annoyed by her insulting manner and intentional rudeness, but he concealed his feelings, though he silently resolved to humble her pride. 'I will make him tell my fortune,' she said. His credit was at stake; he must daunt his enemy, or surrender to her power; he foretold sorrows and joys to the listening throng, and he made one of the young men present and Ruth herself feel exceedingly uncomfortable by revealing a secret which they themselves thought no human soul knew beside themselves. Then for the first time Ruth began to think she had made a mistake, and had underrated her opponent. Nevertheless, her self-possession did not desert her, and in an easy, flippant manner, in which there was a challenge as well as a sneer, she bade him read her future. Morgan remained silent for some moments, and steadily gazed at her. He had a large book before him, which he opened, shut, opened again, and again looked sadly and fearfully upon her; she tried to smile, but felt startled—she knew not why; the bright, inquiring glance of her dark eye could not change Morgan's manner. Her smile could not melt, nor even temper, the hardness of his deep-seated malice; he again looked sternly, and then coldly uttered these slow, soul-withering words, 'Woman, you are doomed to be a murderess!' At first she sneered at his prediction, and then laughed at him; but with greater solemnity, and speaking as if he were inspired, he exclaimed, 'I tell you, Ruth, you will become a murderess! I see blood upon your hands and blood upon your face, and the black stain of awful guilt upon your immortal soul.'

Her arrogance was subdued, her haughty spirit overcome, and with something like a groan she hurried away. But from that day she found that she was a marked woman. The superstitious villagers shunned her, and she became, as it were, an outcast.

Abhorring Morgan, she yet felt drawn towards him, and while she sat by his side felt as if he alone could avert the evil destiny which he himself had foretold. With him only was she seen to smile; elsewhere, sad, silent, stern; it seemed as if she were ever occupied in nerving her mind for that which she had to do, and she grew melancholy and morbid.

But there were moments when her naturally strong spirit, not yet wholly subdued, struggled against her conviction, and endeavoured to find modes of averting her fate; it was in one of these, perhaps, that she gave her hand to a wooer, from a distant part of the country, a mariner, who either had not heard or did not regard the prediction, upon condition that he should remove her far from her native village to the home of his family and friends, for she sometimes felt as if the decree which had gone forth against her could not be fulfilled except upon the spot where she had heard it, and that her heart would be lighter if men's eyes would again look upon her in kindliness and she no longer sat beneath the glare of those that knew so well the secret of her soul. Thus thinking, she quitted the village with her husband; and the tormentor, who had poisoned her repose, soon after her departure, left the village as secretly and as suddenly as he had entered it.

But, though Ruth could depart from his corporeal presence, and look upon his cruel visage no more, yet the eye of her soul was fixed upon his shadow, and his airy form, the creation of her sorrow, still sat by her side; the blight that he had breathed upon her peace had withered her heart, and it was in vain that she sought to forget or banish the recollection from her brain. Men and women smiled upon her as before in the days of her joy, the friends of her husband welcomed her to their bosoms, but they could give no peace to her heart; she shrunk from their friendship, she shivered equally at their neglect, she dreaded any cause that might lead to that which, it had been said, she must do; nightly she sat alone and thought, she dwelt upon the characters of those around her, and shuddered that in some she saw violence and selfishness enough to cause injury, which she might be supposed to resent to blood. Against the use of actual violence she had disabled herself; she had never struck a blow—her small hand would have suffered injury in the attempt; she did not understand the use of firearms, she was ignorant of what were poisons, and a knife she never allowed herself, even for the most necessary purposes. How, then, could she slay? At times she took comfort from thoughts like these, and at others she was plunged in the darkness of despair.

Her husband went forth to and returned from the voyages which made up the avocation and felicity of his life, without noticing the deep-rooted sorrow of his wife. He was a common man, and of a common mind; his eye had not seen the awful beauty of her whom he had chosen; his spirit had not felt her power; and, if he had marked, he would not have understood her grief; so she ministered to him as a duty. She was a silent and obedient wife, but she saw him come home without joy, and witnessed his departure without regret; he neither added to nor diminished her sorrow. But destiny had one solitary blessing in store for the victim of its decrees—a child was born to the hapless Ruth, a lovely little girl soon slept upon her bosom, and, coming as it did, the one lone and lovely rosebud in her desolate garden, she welcomed it with a kindlier hope.

A few years went by unsoiled by the wretchedness which had marked the preceding; the joy of the mother softened the anguish of the condemned, and sometimes when she looked upon her daughter she ceased to despair; but destiny had not forgotten its claim, and soon its hand pressed heavily upon its victim; the giant ocean rolled over the body of her husband, poverty visited the cottage of the widow, and famine's gaunt figure was visible in the distance. Oppression came with these, arrears of rent were demanded, and the landlord was brutal in his anger and harsh in his language to the sufferer.

Thus goaded, she saw but one thing that could save her—she fled from her persecutor to the home of her youth, and, leading her little Rachel by the hand, threw herself into the arms of her people. They received her with distant kindness, and assured her that she should not want. In this they kept their promise, but it was all they did for Ruth and her daughter. A miserable subsistence was given to them, and that was embittered by distrust, and the knowledge that it was yielded unwillingly.

Among the villagers, although she was no longer shunned as formerly, her story was not forgotten. If it had been, her strange beauty, her sorrow-stamped face, the flashing of her eyes, her majestic stature and solemn movements, would have recalled it to their recollections. She was a marked being, and all believed (though each would have pitied her, had they not been afraid) that her evil destiny was not to be averted. They declared that she looked like one fated to do some dreadful deed. They saw she was not one of them, and though they did not directly avoid her, yet they never threw themselves in her way, and thus the hapless Ruth had ample leisure to contemplate and grieve over her fate. One night she sat alone in her little hovel, and, with many bitter ruminations, was watching the happy sleep of her child, who slumbered tranquilly on their only bed. Midnight had long passed, yet Ruth was not disposed to rest. She trimmed her dull light, and said mentally, 'Were I not poor such a temptation might not assail me, riches would procure me deference; but poverty, or the wrongs it brings, may drive me to this evil. Were I above want it would be less likely to be. Oh, my child, for your sake would I avoid this doom more than for mine own, for if it should bring death to me, what will it not bring to you?—infamy, agony, scorn.'

She wept aloud as she spoke, and scarcely seemed to notice the singularity (at that late hour) of someone without attempting to open the door. She heard, but the circumstance made little impression. She knew that as yet her doom was unfulfilled, and that, therefore, no danger could reach her. She was no coward at any time, but now despair had made her brave. The door was flung open, a stranger entered, without either alarming or disturbing her, and it was not till he had stood face to face with Ruth, and disclosed his features to be those of John Morgan, that she sprung up from her seat and gazed wildly and earnestly upon him. He gave her no time to question.

'Ruth Tudor,' said he, 'behold I come to sue for your pity and mercy. I have embittered your existence, and doomed you to a terrible lot. What first was dictated by vengeance and malice became truth as I uttered it, for what I spoke I believed. Yet, take comfort, some of my predictions have failed, and why may not this one be false? In my own fate I have ever been deceived; perhaps I may be equally so in yours. In the meantime have pity upon him who was your enemy, but who, when his vengeance was uttered, instantly became your friend. I was poor, and your scorn might have robbed me of subsistence in danger, and your contempt might have given me up. Beggared by some disastrous events, hunted by creditors, I fled from my wife and son because I could no longer bear to contemplate their suffering. I have sought fortune in many ways since we parted, and always has she eluded my grasp till last night, when she rather tempted than smiled upon me. At an idle fair I met the steward of this estate drunk and stupid, but loaded with gold. He travelled towards home alone. I could not, did not, wrestle with the fiend that possessed me, but hastened to overtake him in his lonely ride. Start not! No hair of his head was harmed by me. Of his gold I robbed him, but not of his life, though, had I been the greater villain, I should now be in less danger, since he saw and marked my person. Three hundred pounds is the result of my deed, but I must keep it now or die. Ruth, you, too, are poor and forsaken, but you are faithful and kind, and will not betray me to justice. Save me, and I will not enjoy my riches alone. You know all the caves in the rocks, those hideous hiding places, where no foot, save yours, has dared

to tread. Conceal me in one of these till the pursuit be passed.
and I will give you one half my wealth, and return with the
other to gladden my wife and son.'

The hand of Ruth was already opened, and in imagination
she grasped the wealth he promised. Oppression and poverty
had somewhat clouded the nobleness, but not the fierceness
of her spirit. She saw that riches would save her from wrath,
perhaps from blood, and as the means to escape from so
mighty an evil she was not unscrupulous respecting a lesser.
Independently of this, she felt a great interest in the safety of
Morgan. Her own fate seemed to hang upon his. She hid the
ruffian in a cave which she had known from her youth, and
supplied him with light and food.

There was a happiness now in the heart of Ruth, a joy
in her thoughts as she sat all the long day upon the deserted
settle of her wretched fireside, to which they had, for many
years, been strangers. Many times during the past years of
her sorrow she had thought of Morgan, and longed to look
upon his face, and sit under his shadow, as one whose presence
could preserve her from the evil fate which he himself had
predicted. She had long since forgiven him his prophecy. She
believed he had spoken truth, and this gave her a wild confidence in his power—a confidence that sometimes thought,
'If he can foreknow, can he not also avert?'

And she thought she would deserve his confidence, and
support him in his suffering. She had concealed him in a
deep dark cave, hewn far in the rock, to which she alone
knew the entrance from the beach. There was another (if
a huge aperture in the top of the rock might be so called)
which, far from attempting to descend, the peasants and seek-
ers for the culprit had scarcely dared to look into, so per-
pendicular, dark, and uncertain was the hideous descent into
what justly appeared to them a bottomless abyss. They passed
over his head in their search through the fields above, and
before the mouth of his den upon the beach below, yet they
left him in safety, though incertitude and fear.

It was less wonderful, the suspicionless conduct of the villagers towards Ruth, than the calm prudence with which she

conducted all the details relating to her secret. Her poverty was well known, yet she daily procured a double portion of food, which was won by double labour. She toiled in the fields for the meed of oaken cake and potatoes, or she dashed out in a crazy boat on the wide ocean, to win with the dredgers the spoils of the oyster beds that lie on its bosom. The daintier fare was for the unhappy guest, and daily did she wander among the rocks, when the tides were retiring, for the shellfish which they had flung among the fissures in their retreat, which she bore, exhausted with fatigue, to her home, and which her lovely child, now rising into womanhood, prepared for the luxurious meal. It was wonderful, too, the settled prudence of the young girl, who made no comment about the food with which she was daily supplied. If she suspected the secret of her mother she respected it too much to allow others to discover that she did so.

Many sad hours did Ruth pass in that dark cave, where the man who had blighted her life lay in hiding; and many times, by conversing with him upon the subject of her destiny, did she seek to alleviate the pangs its recollection gave her. But the result of such discussions were by no means favourable to her hopes. Morgan had acknowledged that his threat had originated in malice, and that he intended to alarm and subdue, but not to the extent that he had effected. 'I know well,' said he, 'that disgrace alone would operate upon you as I wished, for I foresaw you would glory in the thought of nobly sustaining misfortune. I meant to degrade you with the lowest. I meant to attribute to you what I now painfully experience to be the vilest of vices. I intended to tell you you were destined to be a thief, but I could not utter the words I had intended, and I was struck with horror at those I heard involuntarily proceeding from my lips. I would have recalled them, but I could not. I would have said, "Ruth, I did but jest," but there was something which seemed to withhold my speech and press upon my soul, and a dumb voice whispered in my ears, "As thou hast said shall this thing be." But take comfort, Ruth. My own fortunes have ever deceived me, and doubtlessly ever will, for I feel as if I should one day return to this cave, and make it my final home.'

He spoke solemnly, and wept; but his companion was unmoved as she looked on in wonder and contempt at his grief. 'You know not how to endure,' said she to him, 'and as soon as night shall again fall upon our mountains I will lead you forth to freedom. The danger of pursuit is now past. At midnight be ready for the journey, leave the cave, and ascend the rocks by the path I showed you, to the field in which its mouth is situated. Wait me there a few moments, and I will bring you a fleet horse, ready saddled for the journey, for which you must pay, since I must declare to the owner that I have sold it at a distance, and for more than its rated value.'

Midnight came, and Morgan waited with trembling anxiety for the welcome step of Ruth. At length he saw her, and hastily speaking as she descended the rock :

'You must be speedy in your movements,' said she. 'When you leave me your horse waits on the other side of this field, and I would have you hasten, lest something should betray your purpose. But, before you depart, there is an account to be settled between us. I have dared danger and privation for you, that the temptations of the poor may not assail me. Give me my reward, and go.'

Morgan pressed his leather bag containing his gold to his bosom, but answered nothing. He seemed to be studying some evasion, for he looked upon the ground, and there was trouble in the working of his lip. At length he said cautiously, 'I have it not with me. I buried it, lest it should betray me, in a field some miles distant. When I leave here I will dig it up, for I know the exact spot, and send you your portion as soon as I reach a place of safety.'

Ruth gave him a glance of scorn. She had detected his meanness, and smiled at his incapacity to deceive. 'What do you press to your bosom so earnestly,' she demanded. 'Surely you are not the wise man I deemed you, thus to defraud me. Your friend alone you might cheat, and safely; but I have been made wretched by you, guilty by you, and your life is in my power. I could, as you know, easily raise the village, and win half your wealth by giving you up to justice. But I prefer reward. Give me my due, therefore, and be gone.'

But Morgan knew too well the value of the metal of sin to yield one half of it to Ruth. He tried many miserable shifts and lies, and at last, baffled by the calm penetration of his antagonist, boldly avowed his intention of keeping all the spoil he had won with so much hazard. Ruth looked at him with withering contempt. 'Keep your gold,' she said. 'If it can thus harden hearts, I covet not its possession; but there is one thing you must do, and that before you move a foot. I have supported you with hard-earned industry—that I give you; more proud, it would seem, in bestowing than I could be in receiving from such as you. But the horse that is to bear you hence tonight I borrowed for a distant journey. I must return with it, or its value. Open your bag, pay me for it, and go.'

But Morgan seemed afraid to open his bag in the presence of her he had wronged. Ruth understood his fears; but, scorning vindication of her principles, contented herself with entreating him to be honest. 'Be more just to yourself and me,' she persisted, 'the debt of gratitude I pardon; but, I beseech you, leave me not to encounter the consequence of having stolen from my friend the animal which is his only means of subsistence. I pray you not to condemn me to scorn.'

It was of no avail that Ruth humbled herself to entreaties. Morgan answered not, and while she was yet speaking cast side-long looks towards the spot where the horse was waiting, and seemed meditating whether he should not dart from Ruth and escape her entreaties and demands by dint of speed. Her stern eye detected this purpose, and, indignant at his baseness, and ashamed of her own degradation, she sprung suddenly towards him, made a desperate clutch at the leathern bag, and tore it from his grasp. He made an attempt to recover it, and a fierce struggle ensued, which drove them both back towards the yawning mouth of the cave from which he had just ascended to the world. On its very verge, on its very extreme edge, the demon who had so long ruled his spirit, now instigated him to mischief, and abandoned him

to his natural brutality. He struck the unhappy Ruth a re-
vengeful and tremendous blow. At that moment a horrible
thought glanced like lightning through her soul. He was to
her no longer what he had been. He was a robber, ruffian,
liar—one whom to destroy was justice, and perhaps it was
he—

'Villain!' she cried, 'you predicted that I was doomed to
be a murderess; are you destined to be my victim?' She flung
him from her with terrific force, as he stood close to the
abyss, and the next instant heard him dash against its sides,
as he was whirled headlong into the darkness.

It was an awful feeling, the next that passed over the soul
of Ruth Tudor, as she stood alone in the pale, sorrowful
moonlight, endeavouring to remember what had chanced.
She gazed on the purse, on the chasm, wiped the drops of
agony from her heated brow, and then, with a sudden pang
of recollection, rushed down to the cavern. The light was still
burning, as Morgan had left it, and served to show her the
wretch extended helpless beneath the chasm. Though his
body was crushed, the bones splintered, and his blood was
on the cavern's sides, he was yet living, and raised his head
to look upon her as she darkened the narrow entrance in her
passage. He glared upon her with the visage of a demon, and
spoke like a fiend in pain. 'You have murdered me!' he said,
'but I shall be avenged in all your life to come. Think not that
your doom is fulfilled, that the deed to which you are fated
is done. In my dying hour I know, I feel, what is to come upon
you. You are yet again to do a deed of blood!'

'Liar!' shrieked the infuriated victim.

'I tell you,' he gasped, 'your destiny is not yet fulfilled.
You will yet commit another deed of horror. You will slay
your own daughter. You are yet doomed to be a double murderess!'

She rushed to him, but he was dead.

Ruth Tudor stood for a moment by the corpse, blind,
stupefied, deaf, and dumb. In the next she laughed aloud,
till the cavern rang with her ghastly mirth, and many voices
mingled with and answered it. But the voices scared her, and

in an instant she became stolidly grave. She threw back her dark locks with an air of offended dignity, and walked forth majestically from the cave. She took the horse by his rein, and led him back to the stable. With the same unvarying calmness she entered her cottage, and listened to the quiet breathings of her sleeping daughter. She longed to approach her nearer, but some new and horrid fear restrained her, and held her in check. Suddenly, remembrance and reason returned, and she uttered a shriek so loud and shrill that her daughter sprung from her bed, and threw herself into her arms.

It was in vain that the gentle Rachel supplicated her mother to find rest in sleep.

'Not here,' she muttered, 'it must not be here; the deep cave and the hard rock, these shall be my resting place; and the bed-fellow, lo! now he awaits my coming.' Then she would cry aloud, clasp her Rachel to her beating heart, and as suddenly, in horror, thrust her from it.

The next midnight beheld Ruth Tudor in the cave, seated upon a point of rock, at the head of the corpse, her chin resting upon her hands, gazing earnestly upon the distorted face. Decay had already begun its work, and Ruth sat there watching the progress of mortality, as if she intended that her stern eye should quicken and facilitate its operation. The next night also beheld her there, but the current of her thoughts had changed, and the dismal interval which had passed appeared to be forgotten. She stood with a basket of food.

'Will you not eat!' she demanded; 'arise, strengthen yourself for the journey; eat, eat, sleeper; will you never awaken? Look, here is the meat you love'; and as she raised his head and put the food to his lips the frail remnant of mortality remained dumb and rigid, and again she knew that he was dead.

It was evident to all that a shadow and a change was over the senses of Ruth; till this period she had been only wretched, but now madness was mingled with her grief. It was in no instance more apparent than in her conduct towards

her beloved child; indulgent to all her wishes, ministering
to all her wants with a liberal hand, till men wondered from
whence she derived the means of indulgence, she yet seized
every opportunity to send her from her presence. The gentle-
hearted Rachel wept at her conduct, yet did not complain, for
she believed it the effect of the disease that had for so many
years been preying upon her soul. Ruth's nights were passed
in roaming abroad, her days in the solitude of her hut; and
even this became painful when the step of her child broke
upon it. At length she signified that a relative of her husband
had died and left her wealth, and that it would enable her
to dispose of herself as she had long wished; so, leaving
Rachel with her relatives, she retired to a hut upon a lonely
heath, where she was less wretched, because there were none
to observe her awful grief.

In many of her ravings she had frequently spoken darkly
of her crime, and her nightly visits to the cave; and more
frequently still she addressed some unseen thing, which she
asserted was for ever at her side. But few heard these horrors,
and those who did called to mind the early prophecy and
deemed them the workings of insanity in a fierce and imaginative mind. So thought also the beloved Rachel, who
hastened daily to visit her mother, but not now alone, as
formerly. A youth of the village was her companion and pro-
tector, one who had offered her worth and love, and whose
gentle offers were not rejected. Ruth, with a hurried gladness,
gave her consent, and a blessing to her child; and it was remarked that she received her daughter more kindly and detained her longer at the cottage when Evan was by her side
than when she went to the gloomy heath alone. Rachel herself soon made this observation, and as she could depend
upon the honesty and prudence of him she loved, she felt less
fear at his being a frequent witness of her mother's terrific
ravings. Thus all that human consolation was capable to afford
was offered to the sufferer by her sympathizing children.

But the delirium of Ruth Tudor appeared to increase with
every nightly visit to the secret cave of blood; some hideous
shadow seemed to follow her steps in the darkness and sit by

her side in the night. Sometimes she held strange parley with this creation of her frenzy, and at others smiled upon it in scornful silence; now her language was in the tones of entreaty, pity, and forgiveness; anon it was the burst of execration, curses, and scorn. To the gentle listeners her words were blasphemy; and, shuddering at her boldness, they deemed, in the simple holiness of their own hearts, that the Evil One was besetting her, and that religion alone could banish him. Possessed by this idea, Evan one day suddenly interrupted her tremendous denunciations upon her fate and him who, she said, stood over her to fulfil it, with imploring her to open the Bible which he held in his hand, and seek consolation from its words and its promises. She listened, and grew calm in a moment; with an awful smile she bade him open and read at the first place which should meet his eye : 'From that, the word of truth, as thou sayest, I shall know my fate; what is there written I will believe.' He opened the book and read :

' "Whither shall I go from Thy spirit, or whither shall I flee from Thy presence? If I go up into heaven, Thou art there; if I make my bed in hell, Thou art there; if I take the wings of the morning, and dwell in the uttermost parts of the sea, even there shall Thy hand lead me, and Thy right hand shall hold me." '

Ruth laid her hand upon the book. 'It is enough; its words are truth; it has said there is no hope, and I find comfort in my despair. I have already spoken thus in the secrecy of my heart, and I know that He will be obeyed; the unnamed sin must be—'

Evan knew not how to comfort, so he shut up his Bible and retired; and Rachel kissed the cheek of her mother as she bade her a tender good night. Another month, and she was to be the bride of Evan, and she passed over the heath with a light step, for the thought of her bridal seemed to give joy to her mother. 'We shall all be happy then,' said the smiling girl, as the youth of her heart parted from her hand for the night; 'and heaven kindly grant that happiness may last.'

The time appointed for the marriage of Rachel Tudor and Evan Edwards had long passed away, and winter had set in with unusual severity, even on that stormy coast, when, during a land tempest, on a dark November afternoon, a stranger to the country, journeying on foot, lost his way in endeavouring to find a short route to his destination, over stubble fields and meadow lands, by following the footmarks of those who had preceded him. The stranger was a young man, of a bright eye and a hardy look, and he went on, buffeting the elements and buffeted by them, without a thought of weariness or a single expression of impatience. Night descended upon him as he walked, and the snowstorm came down with unusual violence, as if to try the temper of his mind, a mind cultivated and enlightened, though cased in a frame accustomed to hardships, and veiled by a plain, almost rustic exterior. The storm roared loudly above him, the wind blowing tremendously, raising the new-fallen snow from the earth, which mingling with that which fell, raised a shroud about his head which bewildered and blinded the traveller, who, finding himself near some leafless brambles and a few clustered bushes of the mountain broom, took shelter under them to recover his senses and reconnoitre his position. 'This storm cannot last long,' he mused, 'and when it slackens I shall hope to find my way to shelter and comfort.' In this hope he was not mistaken. The tempest abated, and, starting once more on his journey, he saw some distance ahead what looked like a white-washed cottage, standing solitary and alone on the miserable heath which he was now traversing. Full of hope of a shelter from the storm, and lit onwards by a light that gleamed like a beacon from the cottage window, the stranger trod cheerily forwards, and in less than half an hour arrived at the white cottage, which, from the low wall of loose lime-stones by which it was surrounded, he judged to be, as he had already imagined, the humble residence of some poor tenant of the manor. He opened the little gate, and was proceeding to knock at the door, when his steps were arrested by a singular and unexpected sound. It was a choral burst of many voices, singing slowly and solemnly that magnificent dirge of the Church of England, the 104th Psalm. The stranger loved music, and the touching melody of that beautiful air had an instant effect upon his feelings. He lingered in solemn and silent admiration till the strains had ceased; he then knocked gently at the door, which was instantly and courteously opened to his inquiry.

On entering, he found himself in a cottage of a more respectable interior than from its outward appearance he had been led to expect; but he had little leisure or inclination for the survey of its effects, for his senses and imagination were immediately and entirely occupied by the scene which presented itself on his entrance. In the centre of the room into which he had been so readily admitted stood, on its trestles, an open coffin; lights were at its head and foot, and on each side sat many persons of both sexes, who appeared to be engaged in the customary ceremony of watching the corpse previous to its interment in the morning. There were many who appeared to the stranger to be watchers, but there were but two who, in his eye, bore the appearance of mourners, and they had faces of grief which spoke too plainly of the anguish that was reigning within. At the foot of the coffin was a pale youth just blooming into manhood, who covered his eyes with trembling fingers that ill-concealed the tears which trickled down his wan cheeks; the other—but why should we again describe that still unbowed and lofty form? The awful marble brow upon which the stranger gazed was that of Ruth Tudor.

There was much whispering and quiet talk among the people while refreshments were handed to them; and so little curiosity was excited by the appearance of the traveller that he naturally concluded that it must be no common loss that could deaden a feeling usually so intense in the bosoms of Welsh peasants. He was even checked from an attempt to question; but one man—he who had given him admittance, and seemed to possess authority in the circle—informed the traveller that he would answer his questions when the guests should depart, but till then he must keep silence. The traveller endeavoured to obey, and sat down in quiet contemplation of the figure who most interested his attention, and who sat at the coffin's head. Ruth Tudor spoke nothing, nor did she appear to heed aught of the business that was passing around her. Absorbed by reflection, her eyes were generally cast to the ground; but when they were raised, the traveller looked in vain for that expression of grief which had struck him so forcibly on his entrance; there was something wonderfully strange in the character of her perfect features. Could he have found words for his thoughts, and might have been permitted the expression, he would have called it triumphant despair, so deeply agonized, so proudly stern, looked the mourner who sat by the dead.

The interest which the traveller took in the scene became more intense the longer he gazed upon its action; unable to resist the anxiety which had begun to prey upon his spirit, he arose and walked towards the coffin, with the purpose of contemplating its occupant. A sad explanation was given, by its appearance, of the grief and the anguish he had witnessed. A beautiful girl was reposing in the narrow box, with a face as calm and lovely as if she was sleeping a deep and refreshing sleep, and the morning sun would again smile upon her awakening; salt, the emblem of an immortal soul, was placed upon her breast; and in her pale and perishing fingers a branch of living flowers were struggling for life in the grasp of death, and diffusing their sweet and gracious fragrance over the cold odour of mortality. These images, so opposite, yet so alike, affected the spirit of the gazer, and he almost wept as he continued looking upon them, till he was aroused from his trance by the strange conduct of Ruth Tudor, who had caught a glimpse of his face as he bent in sorrow over the coffin. She sprang up from her seat, and, darting at him a terrible glance of recognition, pointed down to the corpse, and then, with a hollow burst of frantic laughter, shouted:

'Behold, you double-dyed liar!'

The startled stranger was relieved from the necessity of speaking by some one taking his arm and gently leading him to the farther end of the cottage. The eyes of Ruth followed him, and it was not till he had done violence to himself in turning from her to his conductor that he could escape their singular fascination. When he did so, he beheld a venerable man, the pastor of a distant village, who had come that night to speak comfort to the mourners, and perform the last sad duty to the dead on the morrow.

'Be not alarmed at what you have witnessed, my young friend,' said he; 'these ravings are not uncommon. This unhappy woman, at an early period of her life, gave ear to the miserable superstitions of her country, and a wretched pretender to wisdom predicted that she should become a shedder of blood. Madness has been the inevitable consequence in an ardent spirit, and in its ravings she dreams she has committed one sin, and is still tempted to add to it another.'

'You may say what you please, parson,' said the old man who had given admittance to the stranger, and who now, after dismissing all the guests save for the youth, joined the talkers, and seated himself on the settle by their side. 'You may say what you please about madness and superstition, but I know Ruth Tudor was a fated woman, and the deed that was to be I believe she has done. Aye, aye, her madness is conscience; and if the deep sea and the jagged rocks could speak, they might tell us a tale of other things than that. But she is judged now; her only child is gone—her pretty Rachel. Poor Evan! he was her suitor. Ah! he little thought two months ago, when he was preparing for a gay bridal, that her slight sickness would end thus. He does not deserve it; but for her—God forgive me if I do her wrong, but I think it is the hand of God, and it lies heavy, as it should.' And the grey-haired old man hobbled away, satisfied that in thus thinking he was showing his zeal for virtue.

'Alas! that so white a head should acknowledge so hard a heart!' said the pastor. 'Ruth is condemned, according to his system, for committing that which a mightier hand compelled her to do. How harsh and misjudging is age! But we must not speak so loud,' continued he; 'for see, the youth Evan is retiring for the night, and the miserable mother has thrown herself on the floor to sleep. The sole domestic is rocking on her stool, and therefore I will do the honours of this poor cottage to you. There is a chamber above this containing the only bed in the hut; thither you may go and rest, for otherwise it will certainly be vacant tonight. I shall find a bed in the village, and Evan sleeps near you with some of the guests in the barn. But, before I go, if my question be not unwelcome and intrusive, tell me who you are, and whither you are bound.'

'I was ever somewhat of a subscriber to the old man's creed of fatalism,' said the stranger, smiling, 'and I believe I am more confirmed in it by the singular events of this day. My father was of a certain rank in society, but of selfish and disorderly habits. A course of extravagance and idleness was succeeded by difficulties and distress. Instead of exertion, he had recourse to flight, and left us to face the difficulties from which he shrunk. He was absent for years, while his family toiled and struggled with success. Suddenly we heard that he was concealed in this part of the coast. The cause which made that concealment necessary I forbear to mention; but he suddenly disappeared from the eyes of men, though we never could trace him beyond this part of the country. I have always believed that I should one day find my father, and have lately, though with difficulty, prevailed upon my mother to allow me to make my residence in this neighbourhood. But my search is at an end today. I believe that I have found my father. Roaming along the beach, I penetrated into several of those dark caverns. Through the fissures of one I discovered, in the interior, a light. Surprised, I penetrated to its concealment, and discovered a man sleeping on the ground. I advanced to awake him, and found but a fleshless skeleton, cased in tattered and decaying garments. He had probably met his death by accident, for exactly over the corpse I observed, at a great height, the daylight, as if streaming down from an aperture above. Thus the wretched man must have fallen, but how long since, or who had discovered his body, and left the light which I beheld, I knew not, though I cannot help cherishing a strong conviction that it was the body of John Morgan that I saw.'

'Who talks of John Morgan?' demanded a stern voice near the coffin, 'and of the cave where the outcast rots?' They turned quickly at the sound, and beheld Ruth Tudor standing up, as if she had been intently listening to the story.

'It was I who spoke,' said the stranger, gently, 'and I spoke of my father—of John Morgan. I am Owen, his son.'

'Son! Owen Morgan!' said the bewildered Ruth, passing her hand over her forehead, as if to enable her to recover the combination of these names. 'Why speak you of living things as pertaining to the dead? Father! He is father to nought save sin, and murder is his only begotten!'

She advanced to the traveller as she spoke, and again caught a view of his face. Again he saw the wild look of recognition, and an unearthly shriek followed the convulsive horror of her face. 'There! there!' she said, 'I knew it must be. Once before tonight have I beheld you. Yet what can your coming bode? Back with you, ruffian, for is not your dark work done!'

'Let us leave her,' said the good pastor, 'to the care of her attendant. Do not continue to meet her gaze. Your presence may increase, but cannot allay her malady. Go up to your bed and rest.'

He retired as he spoke, and Owen, in compliance with his wish, ascended the rickety stair which led to his chamber, after he had beheld Ruth Tudor quietly place herself in her seat at the open coffin's head. The room to which he mounted was not of the most cheering aspect, yet he felt he had often slept soundly in a worse. It was a gloomy, unfinished chamber, and the wind was whistling coldly and drearily through the uncovered rafters above his head. Like many of the cottages in that part of the country, it appeared to have grown old and ruinous before it had been finished, for the flooring was so crazy as scarcely to support the huge wooden bedstead, and in many instances the boards were entirely separated from each other; and in the centre, time, or the rot, had so completely devoured the larger half of one that through the gaping aperture Owen had an entire command of the room and the party below, looking down immediately above the coffin. Ruth was in the same attitude as when he left her. Owen threw himself upon his hard couch, and endeavoured to compose himself to rest for the night. His thoughts, however, still wandered to the events of the day, and he felt there

was some strange connection between the scene he had just
witnessed and the darker one of the secret cave. He grew
restless, and watched, and amidst the tossings of impatient
anxiety fatigue overpowered him, and he sunk into a per-
turbed and heated sleep. His slumber was broken by dreams
that might well be the shadows of his waking reveries. He
was alone—as in reality—upon his humble bed, when imagination brought to his ear the sound of many voices again
singing the slow and monotonous psalm. It was interrupted by
the outcries of some unseen things who attempted to enter his
chamber, and, amid yells of fear and execrations of anger,
bade him 'Arise, and come forth, and aid.' Then the coffined
form which slept so quietly below stood by his side, and, in
beseeching accents, bade him 'Arise and save her.' In his
sleep he attempted to spring up, but a horrid fear restrained
him, a fear that he should be too late. Then he crouched
like a coward beneath his coverings, to hide from the re-
proaches of the spectre, while shouts of laughter and shrieks
of agony were poured like a tempest around him. He sprung
from his bed, and awoke.

It was some moments before he could recover himself, or
shake off the horror which had seized upon his soul. He
listened, and with infinite satisfaction observed an unbroken
silence throughout the house. He smiled at his own terrors,
attributed them to the events of the day or the presence of
the corpse, and determined not to look down into the lower
room till he should be summoned thither in the morning.
He walked to the casement, and peered through at the night.
The clouds were many, black, and lowering, and the face of
the sky looked angry, while the wind moaned with a strange
and eerie sound. He turned from the window, with the intention of again trying to sleep, but the light from below
attracted his eye, and he could not pass the aperture without
taking one glance at the coffin and its lonely watcher.

Ruth was earnestly gazing at the lower end of the room
upon something without the sight of Owen. His attention
was next fixed upon the corpse, and he thought he had never
seen any living thing so lovely; and so calm was the aspect of

her repose that it more resembled a temporary suspension of the faculties than the eternal stupor of death. Her features were pale, but not distorted, and there was none of the livid hue of death in her beautiful mouth and lips; but the flowers in her hand gave stronger demonstration of the presence of the power before whose potency their little strength was fading—drooping with a mortal sickness, they bowed down their heads in submission, as one by one they dropped from her pale and perishing fingers. Owen gazed till he thought he saw the grasp of her hand relapse, and a convulsive smile pass over her cold and rigid features. He looked again. The eyelids shook and vibrated like the string of some fine-strung instrument; the hair rose, and the head cloth moved. He started up ashamed.

'Does the madness of this woman affect all who would sleep beneath her roof?' he thought. 'What is this that disturbs me, or am I yet in a dream? Hark!' he muttered aloud. 'What is that?'

It was the voice of Ruth. She had risen from her seat, and was standing near the coffin, apparently addressing someone who stood at the lower end of the room.

'To what purpose is your coming now?' she asked in a low and melancholy voice, 'and at what do you laugh and gibe? Lo! behold. She is here, and the sin you know of cannot be. How can I take the life which another has already withdrawn? Go, go, hence, to your cave of night, for this is no place of safety for you.' Her thoughts now took another turn. She seemed as if trying to hide someone from the pursuit of others. 'Lie still! Lie still!' she whispered. 'Put out your light! So, so, they pass by, and do not see you. You are safe; good night, good night. Now will I home to sleep,' and she seated herself in her chair, as if composing her senses to rest.

Owen was again bewildered in the chaos of thought, but for the time he determined to subdue his imagination, and, throwing himself upon his bed, again gave himself up to sleep. But the images of his former dreams still haunted him, and their hideous phantasms were more powerfully renewed. Again he heard the solemn psalm of death, but unsung by mortals. It was pealed through earth up to the high heaven by myriads of the viewless and the mighty. Again he heard the execrations of millions for some unremembered sin, and the wrath and hatred of a world was rushing upon him.

'Come forth! Come forth!' was the cry, and amid yells and howls they were darting upon him, when the pale form of the beautiful dead arose between them and shielded him from their malice. But he heard her say aloud:

'It is for this that thou wilt not save me. Arise, arise, and help!'

He sprang up as he was commanded. Sleeping or waking he never knew, but he started from his bed to look down into the chamber, as he heard the voice of Ruth loud in terrific denunciation. He looked. She was standing, uttering yells of madness and rage, and close to her was a well-known form of appalling recollection—his father, as he had seen him last. He darted to the door.

'I am mad!' said he. 'I am surely mad, or this is still a continuation of my dream.'

Some strange and unholy fascination drew him back again to the aperture, and he looked down once more. Ruth was still there, though alone.

But though no visible form stood by the maniac, some fiend had entered her soul and mastered her spirit. She had armed herself with an axe, and, shouting:

'Liar! liar! hence!' pursued an imaginary foe to the darker side of the cottage. Owen strove hard to trace her motions, but as she had retreated to the space occupied by his bed he could no longer see her, and his eyes involuntarily fastened themselves upon the coffin. There a new horror met them. The corpse had risen, and with wild and glaring eyes was watching the scene before her. Owen distrusted his senses till he heard the terrific voice of Ruth, as she marked the miracle he had witnessed.

'The fiend, the robber!' she yelled, 'it is he who hath entered the pure body of my child. Back to your cave of blood, you lost one! Back to your own dark hell!'

Owen flew to the door. It was too late. He heard the shriek, the blow. He rushed into the room, but only in time to hear the second blow, and see the cleft head of the hapless Rachel fall back upon its bloody pillow. His terrible cries brought in the sleepers from the barn, headed by the wretched Evan, and for a time the roar of the storm was drowned in the clamorous grief of those present. No one dared to approach the miserable Ruth, who now, in utter frenzy, strode round the room, brandishing, with diabolical laughter, the bloody axe. Then she broke into a wild song of triumph and fierce joy. All fell back, appalled with horror, and the wild screeching of the wind was like the exultant cry of the damned. Then an extraordinary thing happened—a blinding flash of lightning, as if the heavens themselves had burst into flame, illuminated every nook and cranny, and imparted an awful, ghastly, and weird effect to the dramatic scene. In a few seconds the lightning was followed by a terrific peal of thunder. The house seemed to rock to its foundations. The inmates were blinded and stunned, and, moved by some strange impulse, they all fell upon their knees and murmured a prayer. Presently, as their self-possession returned, they rose one by one, and then a feeling of unutterable horror held them spell bound. Ruth Tudor lay stretched upon the floor, half of her body under the coffin, her face distorted and horrible, while hanging half out of the coffin was the now dead body of her resuscitated daughter, a stream of hot blood flowing from an awful wound in the skull. Ruth Tudor was also stone dead, and in her hand she still grasped the axe with which she had battered out the life of her child, who had awakened from a trance to meet death at the hands of her maniac mother.

The predictions of John Morgan had been literally fulfilled.